Moms Love Boy Bands

Moms Love Boy Bands

Moms Love Boy Bands

Jenifer Goldin

Meet the Characters

KEY: Chapter Icons

Nicole

HUSBAND:
Garrett

CHILDREN:
*Hank, Mack,
and Chelsea*

Liliana

HUSBAND:
Josh

CHILDREN:
Evie and Esther

Angie

HUSBAND:
Patton

CHILDREN:
Ethan and Everett

Carly

HUSBAND:
Marco

CHILDREN:
Bianca

Contents

George

Now

Emerald Jewel All-Inclusive Resort
October 5th ♫ 4:00 a.m.

"WE NEED TO call the police." George, Emerald Jewel's newest security guard, lifts a hot pink dress over his head, as if it's evidence in a high-profile murder trial. The vibrant color glows against his brown skin. Although young, he's ready to prove himself. Someday he plans to be the boss of the island's prestigious resort.

He hands the dress to Mr. LaFleur, Emerald Jewel's general manager, hoping he's impressed.

Mr. LaFleur grabs the dress and runs his fingers over the silky fabric. His nose twitches from the dress's sharp smell, a potent mix of baby powder and floral perfume. He stuffs it under his arm like it's one of those day-old baguettes sold on the corner down the street.

George's confidence wavers. Mr. LaFleur seems irritated to be awake at four in the morning. *But a woman is missing!*

Three women, also wearing hot pink dresses, huddle together. One swipes her hand across her face, smearing her tears with runny mascara. "That's our friend's! We found it on the beach an hour ago!" She brushes away fine grains of sand clinging to her skin. "There has to be a logical explanation." She looks at George, her face pleading for information.

He wishes he knew the location of the missing woman. He'd love to be the hero.

"Haven't you seen those five-part Netflix documentaries about missing vacationers?" Another woman with big, messy hair stumbles forward, looking like she's had one too many mai tais.

George can't believe how wasted American tourists get on the weak drinks served at the resort. The other day, a bartender showed him his trick of intensifying the first sip by dipping straws in alcohol. George laughed as the bartender bragged about how the hotel guests always fall for it, saying the drinks are surprisingly strong for an all-inclusive.

"What will we tell her husband? You have to find her!" The third woman paces back and forth in front of Mr. LaFleur as if in a trance. Her torn dress strap slips down her shoulder.

George waits for Mr. LaFleur's response. *A woman is missing!*

Wiping a thin layer of sweat from his forehead, Mr. LaFleur looks at George. "Do a thorough search of the property." His deep voice remains steady despite the panicking women.

"Yes, sir," George says, noting how Mr. LaFleur's calm demeanor reminds him of the way his high school football coach never cracked under pressure. They even look alike, with pale skin, square heads, and cropped hair. George always loved the way his coach beamed at him after an amazing catch. Finding this missing woman would certainly make him Mr. LaFleur's MVP.

"Let's go to my office." Mr. LaFleur turns back to the crying women. "I'd like to get as many details as…"

But before he can finish, Jordan Knight from New Kids on the Block struts into the lobby. A throng of elated women rushes in behind the nineties heartthrob. Their ecstatic screams reverberate around the three women in hot pink dresses. They trail the boy band superstar, unaware that a resort guest attending Boy Bands at the Beach has vanished.

CHAPTER 2

Nicole

Hamilton Beach, California
October 1st ♫ Four Days Ago

"**B**END FORWARD AND push your breasts together. Let them spill out of your bra."

Leaning over, I press my arms against my sides. My boobs smash together, creating over-the-top cleavage. These boudoir photos are going to make me look as curvy as Kim Kardashian.

"Shake out your hair. Let it cascade around your shoulders. You're gorgeous!" Sheila, my photographer, winks.

I rake my fingers through my auburn waves to give them more volume. Recently, I cut bangs, hoping to draw attention to my green eyes and porcelain skin. I'm trying to freshen up my stale stay-at-home mom image. Side parts and beach waves are so basic.

"Perfect." Sheila snaps several more shots.

I lift myself off a bed covered in cheetah-print sheets and walk to the other side of the studio. Teetering across the floor on my gold stilettos, I strut across the room wearing nothing but hot pink lingerie and a matching garter belt. My kids have no clue how cool their mom was back in the day.

"Give me a sec to reapply some lipstick. Can you toss me my makeup bag?"

Sheila hands me a pouch stuffed with hundreds of beauty products I've bought from twenty-nothing-year-old TikTok influencers. I swipe a fuck-me-red shade over my lips, still tasting the fruity champagne I drank when I got here. Bubbly before noon may be the solution to all my problems. I swirl my hips as the nineties hip-hop music I chose for the photo shoot beats in the background.

"I love the hot pink lingerie." Sheila leans in, capturing a few images of me stretching on my back like a doodle basking in the afternoon sun. "Most of my clients choose red or black."

"I keep things fresh," I say. The day I snagged this set, I was shopping for the hot pink dress I need for my upcoming girls' trip. Excitement pumps through my body. I can't wait for this vacay! Boy bands, the beach, my besties. I'll crank up the fun like I always do. Peace out, *momlife*!

"Give me a sexy pout. Kick up the drama, Nicole!"

Ha! Drama. Three nights with my high school squad will definitely kick up some drama. I couldn't believe it when Carly and Liliana told me Angie was coming on the boy band trip. We haven't seen her in ten years, not since that hot mess of a trip we took to Miraval where Carly and Angie were at each other's throats. There's bound to be at least one blowup before we leave St. McAna Island.

"Can I throw around the hundred-dollar bills I brought for these next pictures?"

"Absolutely." Sheila brings over the stack of fake money. "Such a fun idea. How'd you come up with it?"

I take the bills and tuck a couple under my bra strap. "A Lil' Kim video." Growing up as a solid size twelve, I idolized the way she owned her curves when rail-thin heroin chic was in style.

Knock. Knock. We both turn our heads toward the sound.

"Excuse me for a moment." Sheila walks to her studio's door and cracks it open. I hear a man's voice. They chat for a second, then she shuts the door.

"Sorry about that. My husband watches the baby on Fridays, so I can keep doing my photo shoots. Teamwork makes the dream work."

She grins, unaware that the dynamic in my marriage is like a group project where Garrett gets an A, even though I'm doing all the work. He never pitches in, even when it's obvious I'm struggling. Just last night, I was cleaning the kitchen, folding laundry, helping Mack with his solar system diorama—when the dog started scratching to go out. Garrett didn't blink. He laid on the couch and continued to watch ESPN. I doubt he even noticed the way I slammed the door when I took Noodles to pee.

I can't lie to myself. Our relationship was better before kids. Instantly, I hear the *do, do, doop*, of Mariah Carey's "Always Be My Baby." It automatically plays in my mind when I think of us as twenty-somethings. It was our go-to duet for karaoke. Back in the day, Garrett and I were legends.

I throw fake money into the air to keep my thoughts from spiraling.

"Make it rain." Sheila circles around me. *Click click click.*

While Lil' Kim's voice pulses, I tap back into something that's eluded me since giving up my career, becoming a mom, and spending a couple months in a wheelchair. Sheila, the camera, the lighting—it all blurs and fades. In an instant, I'm connected to an earlier version of myself. A version that doesn't cater to everyone else's needs. *Slay, queen.* Isn't that what the cool kids say now? I feel fierce. This photo shoot proves the badass bitch I used to be hasn't completely disappeared.

But just as I'm losing myself in the power of it all, my phone pings. Trying to ignore it, I swing my legs off the couch, stomping my stilettos on the floor with boss energy. I toss the fake money over my head, but then my phone pings again. A second later, it's ringing. My head throbs. *What if something's wrong with the kids?* There's no school today, so they're at home with Harlow, my favorite babysitter.

"Shoot. Let me make sure everything's okay." I kick off my stilettos and rush toward my bag.

Pushing past a package of wipes and a handful of loose goldfish crackers, I find my phone. The missed call is from Harlow. The spell I was under a moment ago vanishes. I'm not a badass bitch. I'm a mom. And moms aren't sexy vixens. We're here to wipe snotty noses, change diapers, and plan bake sales. My face flushes, realizing how ridiculous

I look. I'm dressed like a seductress, throwing hundreds around, and popping champagne, *but I have to check in with the babysitter?*

"Everything good?" Sheila asks.

"I hope so." I call Harlow back, who confirms my kids are fine, but her grandmother is sick. She needs to go. *Ugh,* why is the universe hell-bent on making sure I'm a boring, suburban mom?

"What's wrong?"

"My babysitter has to leave."

Sheila's lips quirk. "Oh, no. Can your husband help?"

"Garrett?" I ask, surprised by her question. "No, he's at work. He never leaves the office early." *Except a few Fridays a month for golf with his buddies*, but I leave that infuriating detail out.

"We're only halfway through the shoot. Maybe call him and ask. I'm sure he wants these sexy photos of his wife." Sheila fiddles with her camera and waits for me to answer.

My stomach twists. She's assuming these photos are for my husband, which makes sense. I smile and play along. She doesn't need to know the truth.

THE BARELY OLD-ENOUGH-TO-GET-INTO-A-BAR waitress glides over to our table at O'Connell's Grill. I'm mad my boudoir photo session was cut short earlier. The one day I make time for myself, it's a total bust. Eyeing the waitress's wrinkle-free skin and obnoxiously shiny hair, I wish I could hit rewind and do things differently. At her age, I believed I'd be the edgy Anna Wintour of the advertising world, but instead of ruling *Vogue,* I would be the creative force behind the world's top brands. It was all right in front of me.

I should have pushed myself to go back to work after I recovered from the pelvic separation. But I was in a world of pain after the freak injury I experienced when Hank was born. It took me forever to get better, and when I could finally go back to work, I didn't. I never imagined I'd be one of life's boring side characters. There's no action, no suspense, no hero's journey. Just cooking, cleaning, and shuttling kids around.

"The dinner specials are on the board." The waitress drops a basket of busted crayons and a stack of paper on our table. Her bouncy hair cascades down her shoulders.

"You're the GOAT!" I consider asking what hair oil she uses, but then her lips twitch. Embarrassment knots my stomach. Is the use of slang off-limits just because I'm over forty? It's become a bad habit, ever since I figured out it's the only way to get my kids to listen. "And we need a kids' menu," I add, with a hint of annoyance.

I push the bangs of my edgy haircut away from my face, realizing I look ridiculous. She pulls a paper menu from her apron and dashes to her next table. It's a busy night at O'Connell's. Now I'm second-guessing coming here. I still have to pack, and the smell of fried food is making me nauseous. And I probably won't eat since the Ozempic injections are killing my appetite.

"Mommy, I'm hungee." Chelsea, my unplanned but very loved three-year-old, grabs a handful of crayons and drops them on the floor.

Mischievous, a rule breaker, always causing drama—Chelsea is a handful. And with that mess of auburn hair on her head, there's no denying that she's my mini-me. My six-year-old son, Mack, jumps out of his chair and picks up Chelsea's mess. As he dumps the crayons back into the bucket, I notice his hands are covered in restaurant floor grime.

"Hank, can you take Mack to the bathroom and help him clean his hands?" My ten-year-old son nods, and both my boys stand. They trot away in matching royal-blue LA Dodgers baseball caps and whale T-shirts. *Thank God for Hank.* He's the only one in my family who helps.

That's why my twenty-five-year-old niece, Natanya, is driving down from LA to stay with Garrett and the kids while I'm away. The *momlife* manifesto I spent this afternoon writing is for her. This document is like a graduate-level thesis, giving Garrett all the details he needs to handle his *own* kids. It provides granular details, such as which stuffed animals the kids sleep with—Hank claims he doesn't want his elephant but totally does; Mack's obsessed with his Build-A-Bear, Toby; and Chelsea sleeps with every single stuffed animal she can fit in her toddler bed. But I'm sure Garrett won't read one sentence of my manifesto.

Sometimes I daydream about what he would do if something happened to me. I imagine him hustling to keep up with the kids' well-checks, haircuts, and shoe sizes. I can almost see him searching for clean baseball pants, sorting through clothes that no longer fit, and keeping tabs on which friends are a bad influence. These are the countless tiny tasks that make up *momlife*. They seem mundane and manageable in isolation, but together, morph into an all-encompassing, never-ending set of responsibilities that refuse to release their grip when I try to sleep.

But, as I smile picturing Garrett arranging a tray of cookies for Treat Your Teacher Day, my lips turn down. Even if I disappear, Garrett will never know the challenges of motherhood. He'd hire a nanny, a cook, a house manager, and a driver, outsourcing all the tasks that rule my life. If reincarnation is a thing, I'd have kids again, but next time, I'm going for *dadlife*.

"Mommy, hungee." Chelsea pulls a chunk of my hair, wrapping the limp strands around her hand.

"Ouch." Pulling away, I take out my phone to send Garrett a text. Where is he? We've been waiting for twenty minutes. As I type, my phone pings with a message from the High School Besties Squad.

> **Carly:** Don't forget to bring a Yeti or a tumbler. TripAdvisor says the cups at the bar are tiny, but they'll fill up whatever you give them 😉

Oh, right, I forgot. Fingers crossed, I'll remember to snag my Stanley and toss it in my carry-on. As usual, I'm shoving aside the things I need to do for myself, like a toy my kids have outgrown. No wonder I resent Garrett. I'm disappearing while he remains crystal clear about who he is—the director of operations at a top consulting firm, who's got a killer backswing, and never misses a college football game. He never has to be selfless, the very definition of motherhood. Doesn't he get that it's my existence that allows him to remain so solidly himself?

I rumble in frustration, close the message from Carly, and start texting Garrett about his ETA. *Crap.* As I type, my battery dies.

"Where's Daddy?" Chelsea rubs her eyes with her chubby fists, squirming in her booster seat. She's over-tired and heading for a meltdown.

"Why's Daddy late?" Mack, who's returned to the table with Hank, picks up the saltshaker and starts sprinkling it over Chelsea's hands. She flips her chubby palms up as if the salt is falling snow.

I pull the saltshaker away. "Daddy will be here any minute," I say, recalling all those years ago, the way he flashed a sexy, irresistible grin when he admitted that he always runs twenty minutes behind. "But at least I'm consistent," he said. The joking way he fessed up seemed adorable, but listening to that same bit for fifteen years might land me in jail.

"Are you ready to order?" The young waitress bounces back over.

"We're still waiting for my husband."

Ten minutes later, Garrett appears dressed in a navy suit and red tie. I wish he'd embrace business casual like the rest of the world. It's kind of ironic that I loved how his buttoned-up vibe balanced out my glitter as we began dating after we met when I did a pitch at his company. He loved my hustle, and we'd spend hours discussing marketing strategies. My out-of-the-box ideas landed him several clients.

"Sorry, I was in the parking lot on a call." He gives me a sexy smile, oozing with charm. A rush of attraction makes my heart pump. Pulling out a chair, he pats Hank's head. "Hey, buddy, how was your day?"

Garrett's totally at ease. Clueless that the kids are about to implode because we've been waiting for him for thirty minutes. My attraction flips to irritation. I'm over it.

"We should order. I've got to pack, and Chelsea's tired." Swiveling my head around, I get the attention of our waitress. "We're kind of in a rush," I tell her once we order.

As she turns toward the kitchen, Chelsea tries to unsnap her booster seat. "Let me out." Her body rocks back and forth. "Out," she shrieks.

The people at the table next to us give me serious side-eye, while I try my best to ignore her. Eating with a squirmy toddler in your lap is its own kind of torture.

"Out, Mommy. Out." She continues thrashing around.

Garrett keeps talking with our boys, oblivious to what's going on. The chances of him offering to let Chelsea sit on his lap are about as likely as me agreeing to have sex with him tonight.

Sighing, I unsnap Chelsea. This situation is going from bad to worse. Doesn't Garrett notice?

"Mommy, go home now." The pitch of Chelsea's voice rises.

"Soon," I say in a light, singsong voice, but her eyes fill with tears. I grab my bag and dig through the clutter, searching for my phone. I know Chelsea won't make it through the rest of the night without watching *Bluey.*

"Shoot. I forgot my battery died." Holding up the phone, I show Garrett the black screen. "Can you give your phone to Chels? She's about to lose it."

He cocks his head like I've asked him to donate an internal organ. "She'll be fine," he says, and then changes the subject by asking Hank about his upcoming fall ball game.

Seriously??

Ten minutes later, as I try to soothe a wailing Chelsea in the parking lot, stabs of anger pummel my gut. Garrett couldn't give up his damn cell phone! I've given up everything. My career, my identity, my financial independence, my sleep, my sanity. I've given up my physical body, spending months in a wheelchair after giving birth to Hank. And Garrett can't give up his fucking cell phone?!

Suddenly, Josh's question plays on repeat in my mind. *Don't tell me you haven't thought about it. Let's make it official.*

The truth is, I have. But Josh is Liliana's husband. Am I brave enough to damage my relationship with my best friend?

I picture her face. How am I going to get through this trip without her finding out? Josh swore me to secrecy, even though I don't agree. I hate secrets. And this is a big one. But I understand his point of view. He's her husband. It's not my place to tell her. My heart thumps. Maybe I'm not a side character after all. Maybe my story is going to have a shocking plot twist.

CHAPTER 3

Liliana

Hamilton Beach, California
October 1st 🎵 Four Days Ago

"I'LL CALL YOU later if I need further clarification."

Later? But it's almost nine o'clock at night. My boss has no boundaries.

"Okay, but we've come up with a brilliant game plan." It's not the same as saying *don't call me again*, but hopefully, she gets the subtext.

I press the end call button and scream into the silence of my car. Despite telling Amanda I couldn't stay late, she barged into my office at six, demanding we draft a pleading for the Mitten lawsuit. Two hours later, when I told her I had to go, she insisted we continue our conversation during my forty-five-minute commute home.

I squeeze my phone with all my strength, hoping it shatters into a million pieces. My knuckles turn red, then white from the effort, and the pulsing pain replaces the tears welling in my eyes. Taking a deep breath, I throw my phone into my bag and ready myself for Josh's disappointment.

"You missed Shabbat again. Evie and Esther are about to go to bed." He frowns as I walk into the kitchen, then wraps the leftover chicken from dinner.

I put my work bag on the island and notice the Shabbat candles are close to flickering out. Guilt beats in my chest, as if it's a trapped bird trying to escape a cage. On top of missing dinner, I'm leaving for a trip with my girlfriends tomorrow to celebrate our forty-fifth birthdays. A trip I don't have time for. A trip I was going to skip until Angie said she'd be there. I'm shocked that she's coming. Carly still hasn't explained how she talked her into it.

Josh slams the refrigerator closed. "You're just like Garrett. I'm starting to resent it."

Right then, I know Josh is spending too much time with Nicole. As stay-at-home parents, they've grown close. Nicole may be one of my best friends, but I don't need her filling Josh's head with her issues. She's essentially a single parent with Garrett financing the operation.

"I am not Garrett," I say, defensive. "I pack lunches. I check the girls' homework. I take them to services on Saturdays and stay late at the kiddush to give you a break."

The corner of Josh's left lip pulls back. I miss the way he used to look at me with a casual, inviting smile—the perfect blend of intimidating good looks with approachable attractiveness. I close my eyes and let his sour expression dissolve into darkness. Ignoring his anger lets me pretend these moments aren't damaging our marriage. I wonder what strategy he's using to avoid our problems.

The thing is, though, I love Josh. He's one of those people who gives a friendly nod to every person he passes in the grocery store. He's the guy at the party everyone's clamoring to talk to. Unlike me. I've spent my life keeping my emotions in check, which people mistake for being aloof.

"Mommy, look, your pink dress!"

My eyes blink open, and Esther, my eight-year-old, appears, eating a brownie. She struts forward with one hand on her hip like a movie star walking the red carpet.

"Oh no, did you open my suitcase and take that out?" There's a smear of chocolate on her face.

Nodding, she twirls around, showing off my new dress. It drags on the floor behind her. Instead of yelling, I slide it over her head, careful to avoid the chocolate. With the Mitten case swirling, I haven't seen the girls much, so I don't get angry. Folding the dress, I place it on the counter as she skips away.

Josh continues to bang around the kitchen, making his anger obvious. I search for a string of words that will soften his frustration. But instead of a magic phrase, I say the words I say too often.

"I'm sorry."

He shakes his head, fixating on a mysterious point behind me, like he's searching for his ideal wife. "I told you it was important to be here tonight. Before you leave for your girls' trip." He emphasizes *girls* in a way that makes it sound like a bad word. He's clearly upset I've prioritized this vacation over family time. But ten years is a long time to go without seeing one of the friends that shaped my childhood.

"You know I'm only going to see Angie." I hope this reminds him how much I miss her. I miss Nicole and Carly, too, but missing people who you don't make time for feels more complex than the pure affection I feel for Angie, someone I've disappointed.

Unsurprisingly, instead of understanding, he looks at me like I've insulted him.

My guilt intensifies. It's disheartening knowing how different I feel about my job now than I did five years ago. Back then, when Amanda hired me to spearhead taking Click Com public, I felt completely satisfied. Even my mom seemed pleased when I secured Click Com's listing on the NASDAQ. Growing up, she's the one who told me it didn't matter that I was a girl. I could be anything I wanted. The sky's the limit. But she didn't mention that being *anything I wanted* was not the same as being *everything I wanted.* Where does being a mom factor in?

Josh runs a hand through his dark hair, and I'm desperate to give him hope that soon I won't be carrying the workload of both the vice president of operations and general counsel.

"Our new head of legal starts in a few weeks. This lawsuit will be off my plate."

He grins, but his lips come together unnaturally. There's so much unsaid in his tight smile. The way he feels worthless in a world that values a man for his job. The way his dad chastises him for being a stay-at-home dad rather than a doctor or a lawyer.

"You've made promises like this a million times. Nothing ever changes."

He's not wrong. But I refuse to admit it. Because if I admit he's right, I'm admitting I've put my job and career before my family. *Why is the cardinal sin of motherhood the noble pursuit of fatherhood?*

"I'm sorry." This time the words sound like a hiss. My remorse has morphed into anger. It's a protective mechanism I picked up from my mom. She taught me that women are better off expressing anger than vulnerability—a trait unacceptable in the boardroom. "We have so many expenses. I can't screw up." The combined stress of the lawsuit, Josh's disappointment, and the trip cause the words to jump from my throat.

"Seriously?" His shoulders curl inward like I've sucker-punched him.

My regret is immediate. I recall years ago wondering how Josh felt, knowing I made double his salary. When he decided to stay home, I agreed I would never use my position as the breadwinner for leverage.

But, damn it. I'm exhausted. It doesn't matter how many times Josh and I explain that he's the go-to parent for arranging Esther's piano lessons, organizing snacks for Evie's volleyball team, or dealing with friend drama, people find themselves incapable of embracing the revolutionary concept that they should call Josh.

"Sorry doesn't matter much when nothing changes."

I nod because I don't want to argue. But the truth is not so black and white. I'm the number two person at a company whose culture views beating deadlines, getting ahead, and achieving success as life's most treasured trophies. A perspective I've subscribed to my entire life thanks to my mother, who was the first female managing partner at her law firm. The DNA of ambition permeates every cell in my body.

"The kids are growing up, and you're missing it."

Josh's words send my stomach into a freefall. *Do my girls feel the same way he does?*

He peers at me. "Can you name Esther's and Evie's teachers?"

"I am not Garrett," I repeat, remembering how, last year, while

Nicole recovered from a hysterectomy, Garrett had to pick up their son Mack early from school. When asked the name of Mack's teacher, Garrett admitted he didn't know. A mom volunteering in the office disseminated that morsel of information to everyone living within a ten-mile radius. Nicole was furious. Apparently, marital struggles aren't unique to Josh and me.

"Esther's teacher is Mrs. Rosenstein and Evie's teacher is Mrs. Skatoff." Pushing my shoulders back, I take a defiant pose. But then, a burst of mom guilt almost knocks me over. *I'm proud of myself for knowing the names of my kids' teachers?*

"Missing Shabbat again, leaving for your girls' trip tomorrow…I'm done waiting around for you to find the balance."

My heart races, realizing Josh is at a breaking point. "What does that mean?" My voice wobbles, betraying me.

The words are barely out of my mouth when my phone rings, blaring the song "Manic Monday." It's the ringtone I use for my boss, Amanda. The timing's awful. My eyes search his, pleading for understanding.

"I need to answer it. I'll tell her I'm officially off the clock. I know I have to set a boundary right here, right now."

He narrows his eyes, as if I'm peddling broken trinkets at a garage sale. "There's leftover matzah ball soup." He gestures toward the pot on the stove. A faint smell of garlic hangs in the air. "Esther, it's time for you to take your shower," Josh calls toward the TV room.

She appears in front of me, taking a huge bite of her brownie. Another smear of thick fudge frosting clings to her lips. "Mommy, I want you to put me to bed tonight."

My phone rings again with "Manic Monday."

Josh marches over, wiping the frosting from Esther's face. "Mommy can't."

I feel tears welling and pull my eyes taut to keep them from falling.

Esther's smile disappears. "Here." She hands me a bracelet with a string of black and white Hebrew letters. "I made this at school." Her golden curls bounce when she removes the elastic bracelet.

Taking it from her, I slip it around my wrist, noticing the way her blue eyes and loose curls mimic my own. *What kind of mother am I if I can't participate in bedtime?*

My phone lets out a barrage of pings. Amanda switched from calling to texting. I know she's fuming. Feeling defeated, I walk toward my bag to respond. "Mommy's going to make a quick call, then we can do bedtime." But when I look back at Esther, she's already turning toward Josh.

"Come on, Esther. Time to go upstairs." Josh scoops her into his arms and buries his face in her neck.

"Daddy, you're silly." Esther giggles, unfazed that I can't help her.

"I'm searching for brownie crumbs," Josh laughs.

They continue along, and it strikes me I am an insignificant part of my child's routine, like a meaningless cog in a wheel.

SINKING INTO THE chair in my home office, I hit send and hear the swish of my outgoing email. Regret tugs at my heart. I'm disappointed I didn't push back when Amanda called earlier. I should've told her I'd create the spreadsheet of potential defenses after I returned from vacation. But old habits die hard. A lifetime of acquiescing to my mom's unreasonable expectations has trained me to be Amanda's lackey. Whether it was being valedictorian of my high school, becoming the chief of the *Yale Law Journal*, or interning at the most prestigious law firm in the country, I did everything to hit a mark. While I understand that I've swapped my mom's unreasonable demands for Amanda's, I feel powerless to change it.

I glance at the clock, and my shoulders tighten. It's almost one in the morning. I missed the chance to spend time with the girls before I leave tomorrow, and I'm sure Josh is asleep. I shift my eyes back to my computer, hating everything it represents. My thoughts scramble back to the statement Josh made earlier tonight—*I'm done waiting around for you to find the balance.* It's cryptic and unsettling.

Slamming my laptop closed, I grab it off my desk and shove it into my carry-on bag. I'll end up working half of this vacation. Yet, I have to see Angie. In my heart, I know I failed. I wasn't there for her the way she needed when her mom died. I should have let her cry on my shoulder. But it was too uncomfortable, too emotional, and too difficult to face. A pattern of avoidance I'm repeating with Josh.

All of a sudden, I'm sprinting toward my bedroom. It's been months since Josh and I had sex. Stepping into the darkness, I drop my phone on my bedside table and undress. I slide under the covers, curling my body around his back. His body shifts, but he remains asleep.

Determined to wake him, I plant soft kisses on his neck. I expect him to turn toward me, but he tenses, like he's uncomfortable. Before I can figure out what's going on, his body relaxes again. I'm certain he's awake. My thoughts swirl. *Is he pretending to be asleep?*

I shake his shoulder until he responds.

"What?" he whispers, without facing me.

"Sorry about tonight." Gathering courage, I continue. "I miss you. I want to be with you." I kiss his shoulder, hoping he rolls over and enfolds me in a loving embrace, but he doesn't react. "I know I need to make changes. I don't want to lose you." My whispered words hang in the air. The thought of his rejecting me makes my eyes water. But before he does anything, my phone interrupts the awkward silence, blaring, "Manic Monday."

"You'd better get that." Josh's words drip with contempt. He scoots his body further to the edge of the bed.

I can tell he's furious, even though, a moment ago, it felt like he was going to turn me down. *Was he going to turn me down?* I'm too afraid to ask. I'm not ready to find out that anger outweighs every other feeling he has for me. Instead, I reach for Amanda's call like it's a life vest.

"I have a question about the spreadsheet." Her voice fills my ear.

Looking down, I stare at the two inches of high thread count sheets separating Josh and me. It might as well be an ocean.

Angie

St. Louis, MO
October 1st 🎵 Four Days Ago

'M DREADING THIS VACATION. The thought churns in my brain, making my head pound. Why would I want to go away with my childhood friends? It reminds me of the mistakes I've made. Mistakes I always promise I'll confess but then never do. That's why it's been a decade since I've attended the milestone birthday trip we've been taking every five years since we turned twenty. I hesitate before placing black leggings and a few tankinis into my suitcase. *Can I get out of this?* Heat floods my neck knowing Carly's airtight plan makes skipping it impossible.

"You got me what?" I tried to hide the shocked look on my face when Patton and the boys gave me my Mother's Day present last May.

My sons held up a collage filled with images of Lance Bass, Nick Carter, Donnie Wahlberg, and all the heartthrobs I dreamed about in the nineties.

Patton smiled with a satisfied grin. "You're going on a boy band vacation with your friends! Carly and I arranged the whole thing." His excitement was palpable. It makes sense that Carly reached out to Patton, suggesting he surprise me with the trip. As the mother hen of our friend group, she always took charge. Whether it was making sure we never got stuck with smelly Joe Childer while playing seven minutes in heaven or helping Nicole clean her locker after someone spray-painted it with the words *fat cow* in middle school, Carly always ran the show, protected us, and aimed to make everything perfect. I understand why Patton fell for her trap, and I wasn't going to tell him the truth about why I didn't want to go. He doesn't know the pain I put my friends through during senior year of high school.

Grabbing a pair of sensible shoes and my favorite St. Louis Cardinals baseball hat, I suddenly remember the dress. What color did they decide on? I pick up my phone and find the group text, High School Besties Squad. I cringe. People who regularly get Botox and color their gray hair should not use the word *besties*.

Scrolling down, I find the text about the dress color.

> **Liliana:** How about hot pink for this year's dress?

> **Carly:** Yes! I've got that pink sequin dress I bought for Taylor's Eras Tour.

> **Nicole:** Winning! After all the drama. 😌

> **Liliana:** Still can't believe you spent all that money on counterfeit tickets. 😡

> **Carly:** I may need a therapist to work through it. 😭 😌

A hot pink dress. How did I forget this important detail? Carly always insists we wear the same color dress on the last night of these trips. A tradition of matching that began with those awful yellow dresses she made us wear to prom. But hot pink? I'm a practical person with a brown bob and a two-step beauty routine. I have a capsule wardrobe consisting of essentials suitable for any occasion, except, apparently, this trip. I've never been one for trends. Not even in high school when Nicole, Liliana, and Carly wore pastel plaid blazers and skirts circa the movie *Clueless*. With my preference for band T-shirts, I didn't exactly fit in with them. But our differences never mattered. We built a solid foundation as kids, dressing up as Disney princesses, crimping each other's hair, and spending countless hours circling the blocks between the playground, the neighborhood pizza restaurant, and Blockbuster video—where Nicole always got into trouble for sneaking into the over-eighteen section.

My mind drifts to an image of the clay tile roof and arching windows of my childhood home. The Spanish colonial was ground zero for my friends and me, since my mom was the linchpin that brought us together. She'd noticed Liliana's mom was always working, and Carly's mom was consumed with tennis and bunco, and Nicole's mom was always late and never able to fulfill her PTA responsibilities, so she started helping, eventually moving four random girls into a perfect square. In my geometry class, I always picture Nicole, Liliana, Carly, and me when I explain to my students that a square represents balance, symmetry, and genius. But the pleasing analogy quickly gives way to heartache, knowing everything changed senior year when my mom died.

I push the pain into that deep place I keep hidden and shift my attention back to the pink dress. *What am I going to do?* I'd bring a simple black dress, but I can already hear Carly whining about how my achromatic dress color is ruining her Instagram post. Not that I'm on social media. Being a private person, it's impossible to understand its appeal. But she's obsessed with life's fake highlight reel.

Opening my phone's browser, I type *hot pink comfortable dress* into the Amazon search bar. As usual, I click on the *Amazon overall pick*. It's a flowing maxi. I ship it directly to the resort on St. McAna Island. The customs fees are outrageous. Here's hoping it gets there on time.

"How's the packing going?" Patton enters our room. He smiles widely.

"Are you sure you don't want me to stay home and help with the boys? It's a busy weekend with homecoming tomorrow night and the college fair on Sunday."

He squints at me like a bright light has suddenly turned on in a dark room, and I blurt something to avoid causing suspicion. "The boys are growing up fast. They'll be leaving for college in a blink."

He sits on the bed next to me. "If you don't go on this trip, you'll regret it." His green eyes meet mine with sincerity.

I shake my head. "But I want to see Ethan and Everett in their tuxedos."

Patton scoots closer, putting his hand on my shoulder. His familiar fresh scent calms my agitation. "The boys are only sophomores. There will be other homecomings." Patton pulls me closer. His body is warm and comforting. It reminds me he's my rock. "Your friends are the last connection you have to where you grew up. It's been ten years since you've seen them."

His insistence that I stay tied to my place of origin is irritating, but not surprising. Patton's a hometown boy. Born in St. Louis, bred on midwestern values, and thrilled to be raising our boys in the same community where he grew up.

He tangles our fingers together, holding my hand, and continues. "Don't you think it's crazy you haven't been back to Hamilton Beach since you left for college?"

I pull away from him. "But my dad moved to Florida, so there was no reason to go back."

Patton doesn't understand what it was like having to live in a world that kept spinning after cancer invaded my mom's body like a violent tornado touching down with no warning. Everyone around me was enjoying senior year, "*the best time of our lives,*" but all I felt was a huge hole in my heart. And even though I've told Patton how my dad laid on the couch crying for months, and I've explained that my dad and I avoid each other because being together forces us to relive the pain of the three months between my mom's diagnosis and death, I haven't told him everything about my past.

"There wasn't any reason to go back to Hamilton Beach."

My reaction doesn't surprise him, and I can tell he's thinking carefully about what to say next. He's always been good at pausing instead of responding with a knee-jerk reaction. It's one of the many reasons I love him.

"I know this trip stirs up memories of your mom, but there's something important about staying connected with childhood friends."

I shrug off his comment.

He continues anyway. "Your friends are excited to see you." Standing, he grasps my other hand and gently tugs me off the bed, then wraps his arms around me. "You can do this," he whispers in my ear. "I bet your friends have lots of great memories of your mom. Ask them to share one or two? Maybe it would be good for you?"

I lay my head on his shoulder, savoring the scent of his hair. He's a good man, trying his best to help me based on limited information. What would he say if he knew I traumatized the people I love?

Releasing me, he looks at the suitcase expectantly.

I think about backing out of the trip again. But I know I owe it to Nicole, Liliana, and Carly to show up. It's the best I can do since I'm unwilling to tell them the truth. My body pulses the way it did that first night after my mom died. Sleepless hours left me feeling like I was falling off a cliff. Desperate for relief, I jumped out of bed and ran outside. I remember walking into the pitch-black darkness and feeling defenseless against the world's evils. Instantly, my grief transformed into a tightening in my chest. That's when I understood how fear could overpower my sadness.

"Zip up your suitcase. I'll bring it downstairs."

I nod, cursing Carly for her clever plan. I slide the zipper around my luggage, then place my flip-flops and sun hat in my carry-on.

Patton picks up the suitcase and smiles. "You'll have a great time."

As he wheels it down the hall, blood rushes through me with enough force to launch a rocket into outer space. He doesn't know I ran away senior year of high school. He doesn't know how the situation escalated, forcing me to keep secrets from Nicole, Liliana, and Carly. Just like my friends, Patton doesn't know everything about my past.

MY EYES FIXATE on the suitcase Patton brought down earlier, wishing it would spontaneously combust. What other fantasies can I concoct to get out of this reunion trip?

"You look pretty." Patton gives me a flirtatious smile from across the kitchen. I'm amazed his eyes still sparkle when he sees me, day after day, in simple neutral-colored clothing. I hate standing out in a crowd. "We know you're anxious about this reunion trip. The boys bought you something to get you in the right frame of mind."

"A gift for me?" I play it cool.

Ethan and Everett hand me a bright-yellow bag overflowing with tissue paper.

"It's an early birthday present." Everett grins, showing off his left dimple. The one he gets from Patton.

Ethan chimes in. "It was all Dad's idea."

"Aww, that's sweet. Thanks." I pull apart the bag and take out a neatly rolled white T-shirt. Holding it up, I let it unfold. "Ha, very cute." I glance at the cartoon image of Justin Timberlake with the words *Raised on '90s boy bands*. This trip is happening. I need to mentally prepare myself for Carly. Postcard images of each birthday trip we've taken in the past appear in my mind—Key West for our twentieth, a Caribbean cruise for our twenty-fifth, skiing in Colorado for our thirtieth, and the spa trip to Miraval for our thirty-fifth.

That trip to Miraval was my breaking point. Carly spent the vacation intent on stirring up confrontation. What was the point of arguing over whether we should take part in spiritual drumming or meditation? With all the tension, I realized Carly would never get over her anger that I left Hamilton Beach, and I would never have the courage to admit why. Plus, with Patton and my boys, I was building a world where friendship wasn't necessary.

"You have to wear it on your trip." Everett points to my new shirt.

"Yeah, we want photographic evidence." Ethan pushes a bushy clump of chestnut-colored hair out of his eyes.

My heart skips, missing the defined, clean-cut hair style my boys had when they were younger. It's hard to believe they'll be seventeen next year, the age I was when I started stealing five- and ten-dollar bills out of my dad's wallet. Enough to get me started when I disappeared, but not enough for him to notice. Although, given my dad's state of mind, I could have emptied his bank account without him realizing. As I look at Ethan's and Everett's innocent, trusting smiles, I know how crazy I was for throwing myself into the madness of the real world at their age.

"Mom sandwich," Ethan calls out.

Everett moves in front of me, while Ethan moves behind. They reach their arms out and hug each other, squeezing me between their muscular bodies. The pungent smell of spicy deodorant makes my eyes water.

"Boys, your mother's five inches shorter than you. She can't breathe." I hear Patton's voice.

The boys step back, allowing my face to peek out from between them.

"Thanks for the gift." Walking to my suitcase, I place the shirt on top.

"Dope." Ethan brushes away another clump of messy hair hanging over his eyes. "See you in the a.m. We gotta bounce."

Everett grabs car keys off the counter. "Later."

"Make good decisions at homecoming. Good luck at the college fair. I can't wait to hear all about it." I wave goodbye, and my boys walk out the door.

As I hear their car pull away, my insides flutter thinking about them leaving for college. But the soft feeling changes to anger, remembering how I had to handle my dorm paperwork and financial aid forms after my mom died. By mid-senior year, I knew I'd have to defer Washington University to take care of my dad. And no one—not even my friends—noticed my world was unraveling.

"We need to leave for R-Dog's birthday dinner." Patton cuffs the sleeves of his blue plaid button-down shirt. "Rolled or buttoned?"

"Either way." I try to keep my voice steady while my stomach knots. I wish he knew that being with his tight-knit group of childhood friends is difficult for me. But how could he know something I've never told him?

Fifteen minutes later, when Patton and I walk into Charlie Gitto's on the Hill, we're greeted with loud hoots and hollers, followed by the shout, "General Patton!" When will we reach the expiration date of these stupid teenage nicknames? I try to imagine Patton as *General Patton*, but instead I see an image of myself at seventeen. The swatch of freckles that spread across my nose, and the way I hid behind the face-framing chunks of my Rachel haircut to conceal my teary eyes. Unable to function after losing my mom, I just smiled and went along with whatever meaningless distraction Carly suggested—meeting at the mall food court for an Orange Julius, taking Glamour Shots, even going to the arcade, which we had outgrown years earlier. The pretending created a disconnect within me, like an actor playing a role. A role that led me down a path that would hurt the people I love most.

Ignoring my thoughts, I walk beside Patton toward his friends. The first round of buddy backslapping begins. A waiter walks by with a tray of toasted ravioli, and my nose bristles from the smell of Italian spices.

"Happy Birthday, Rowan." I use his full name, unable to bring myself to utter the phrase R-Dog.

"Thanks!" Rowan smiles and then lifts his arms in a muscle man pose.

I won't even try to understand the psychology behind why men do this. I give him an awkward thumbs-up and take a seat with the wives. We fall into a conversation about our husbands, our kids, and life's trivial happenings. These women are always pleasant, but I can't help feeling like an outsider.

I think about what Patton said earlier. *It's crazy you haven't been back to Hamilton Beach since you left for college.* I should have told him about the monstrous eighteen-wheeler and the big rig driver who flashed his lights when he saw me walking near the main road before dawn, and how I made the horrible mistake of leaving the safety of Hamilton Beach and jumping inside.

The hostess appears, and my mind clears. Our group follows her past tables set with stiff white tablecloths and candles to offset the restaurant's low lighting.

"Enjoy your evening." She escorts us into a private room, then leaves.

We take seats around a table under an elaborate chandelier, while Rowan continues with a story about high school. I'm sure it will end like all the others. Someone passed out drunk or half-naked in an unfortunate location.

When Rowan finishes, the table erupts with laughter. He stands, raising his glass of bourbon. "Man, those were the days! Cheers to high school."

Everyone raises their glasses.

"Speaking of high school." Patton places his glass down on the table. "Angie's leaving for St. McAna Island tomorrow. Meeting up with her high school friends."

"Oh, fun." Rowan's wife catches my eye, then takes a sip of wine. "St. McAna was my first international trip. I went there when I was in college in Florida. It was easy to get to since it's just north of Cuba."

"Tell them about your trip!" Patton puts a hand on my shoulder, encouraging me to speak.

Sweat prickles my back. Tomorrow I'll be with the people I still haven't been fully honest with. My breath quickens. I part my lips to speak but remain silent.

Patton jumps in. "She's going to see a bunch of nineties boy bands. It's a whole thing."

"Like New Kids?" The women at the table bounce around in their seats like toddlers about to have ice-cream for dinner. Everyone's staring at me, waiting for me to say more, but my mind spins, picturing weathered hands turning an enormous steering wheel and the way the big rig driver's eyes creepily slid from the road to me when he said he felt a duty to get young girls where they wanted to go safely.

I rush away before Patton can ask what's wrong. Hiding inside a bathroom stall, I lean against the cold tile wall. My mind rushes with images—the woods surrounding the highway leading out of Hamilton Beach where I would take my predawn walks, my entire town gathered searching for me, people wearing navy jackets with *FBI* written in large yellow letters on the back.

If I hadn't made the reckless decision to run away, none of it would have happened. But how could I know running away was going to spark the demented mind of a drifter?

CHAPTER 5

Carly

Hamilton Beach, California
October 1st 🎵 Four Days Ago

PRESS RECORD, AND my Insta feed goes live. I sing the chorus of NSYNC's "Bye Bye Bye" into one of those neon-colored plastic microphones. *Eye-catching content = more views!* This song is the obvious choice given that I'm leaving for a boy band vacation tomorrow.

"Hi, Moms. It's finally here!" I jump with excitement. My screen floods with heart emojis. I glance at my live follower count. Five hundred and eleven people have stopped what they're doing at this exact moment to tune in. *Not bad!* The forty-five minutes I spent perfecting my messy ponytail look was worth it.

I playfully turn my head, highlighting the loose blond wave near my ear. It took five tries to get it right. I might as well show it off.

Staring into my phone's camera, I continue. "My trip to St. McAna is tomorrow! Don't miss my outfit of the day posts to see my top picks for a girls' beach trip. I've got a ton to do before I leave, so I'm keeping this short."

I watch as my live follower count climbs to six hundred and twenty-nine. My goal is at least eight hundred. *I'm close!*

"Let's talk about my outfit of the day. Hashtag OOTD." I step back from the extendable selfie stick I'm holding, allowing my phone's camera to capture my full image. "Lounge wear is the perfect choice for packing, so I'm wearing this comfy, cozy, tan, cashmere sweatsuit. It's soft like butter." I say the word *butter* like I grew up in one of the five boroughs of New York.

My screen blows up with laugh emojis, and my live follower count has climbed to seven hundred and fifty-three.

"And wait until you see my shoes." I tilt my selfie stick down and click my heels together like I'm Dorothy in the *Wizard of Oz*. "These white leather, low-top trainers are going to be all the rage. The rhinestone details are gorgeous."

I pause for a beat, then tilt the camera back to my face, showing off my earrings. "And of course, a few understated gold accessories are the key to making this outfit pop."

A couple of hearts cross my screen, but there should be more. *Damn it.* I know my live follower count is dropping. Glancing at the number, I see it's at six hundred and seven. With video rolling, I battle the downturn of my lips, force a smile, and continue.

"Links to all these products and more are in my bio. Keep checking in to see the fabulous fashions I'm wearing while away. Bye, bye, bye, for now, and remember, *master your fashion, master your life*."

Live follower count three hundred and seventeen. *That stings.*

I press the red button and end my live stream. I turn my attention to the designer resort wear on my bed, checking that each outfit contains the coordinating underwear, bra, and jewelry. Growing up observing my father, a senator with coiffed hair and custom suits, taught me the importance of a shatterproof public image. *Perfect is a way of life.* And perfect is what my sponsors expect. Several of whom are paying me to spotlight their products while on vacation.

To be honest, I never planned to become a fashion influencer with over 300,000 people subscribing to my Insta. It happened organically eight years ago with my *@masterofmomfashion* account. *Master your fashion, master your life.* My account went viral after a series I did on how to coordinate outfits for family photos. It may be a first-world problem, but nothing stresses moms out more than having to choose their family's clothing for professional photos. Especially when those pictures will be the centerpiece of the holiday card.

The posts I created included guidelines on color palettes, pattern choices, and background settings. Each post featured a picture of my husband Marco, my daughter Bianca, and me, showcasing my suggestions. Momstagram went crazy. I'm used to being the center of attention, but this was a whole new level. The posts got over 500,000 likes, and the comments were endless. The thread became a hilarious accounting of all the things that can go wrong during a family photo shoot.

> *- My six month old refused to wear the plaid bow tie and almost choked himself with it. Yes, we got that on film.*
>
> *- Our dog is pooping in the one picture where everyone is smiling.*
>
> *- Can you say wrinkles- linen was not a great choice.*
>
> *- Should I be concerned that my photographer emailed me the name of her divorce attorney after watching my husband and me bicker?*

Media outlets like *BuzzFeed, Huffington Post,* and *Scary Mommy* shared it, blowing it up more. I was even the focus of a short segment on the *Today Show* where Jenna and Hoda told moms to forget Pinterest and instead follow my account.

It wasn't all that surprising. Even in high school, I set the trends—like wearing a baby-doll dress with a T-shirt underneath. By graduation, every girl wore that outfit like it was our school's uniform. Now, with social media, I'm able to influence the masses. However, creating content, posting daily, and meeting the goals of paying sponsors, all while maintaining my perfect image, keep me incredibly busy. Thank goodness I love a to-do list. *Anything to fill the time.* Marco's the same way. He stays busy, always swamped at work and traveling to put out fires for his clients. For a long time, I've wondered if I feel lonely in our marriage because we're each busy, or if I stay busy to escape feeling lonely.

But that was before I discovered the text messages between him and his colleague, Lilly, last week. I remember meeting her at Marco's company's holiday party last year and thinking she was flirty. Seriously, how dumb is Marco to save her as "Lilly from Accounting" in his phone? If you're going to send questionable texts to your colleague, consider changing their contact name so it's not so obvious. My father warned me not to marry the gorgeous Italian exchange student I met at UCLA.

As I finish putting my things in the suitcase I recently featured as my go-to roller bag, I wonder if Angie's going to cancel at the last minute. We haven't seen each other since the trip we took to Miraval. I'll admit I ruined our getaway with pointless arguments about things like whether we should grab a smoothie or sit-down lunch after getting facials. Every meaningless decision on that trip became a side door to expel the pain I've felt since Angie moved away, further complicating our already difficult relationship.

Ouch! I feel the rough weave of my designer straw beach tote digging into my arms. It takes me a second to realize I'm hugging it to comfort myself. I drop it on my bed, unable to understand how Angie turned her back on everything we'd shared. Maybe I should feel bad for tricking her husband into gifting her with this boy band trip. But I don't! I deserve a chance to make things right.

Walking to my dresser, I flip through an album of childhood pictures. Lifting the clear adhesive, I retrieve the photo from our senior prom that is sure to kick-start a fun conversation. *How in the world did I convince everyone to wear canary-yellow ball gowns?* Nicole smirks, surrounded by a cascade of red waves. Liliana's hand wraps around Nicole's shoulder, covered in a lace fingerless glove. I'm teasingly scowling at the glove, although I was angry that she added the accessory without checking with me first. And then there's Angie. She's staring straight ahead, smiling, but it's the same smile I make for my Insta posts—soulless and hollow. I run my finger over the fading picture of us, each holding a yellow silk parasol trimmed in white lace. A photo that proves I was a master at creating eye-catching content before Instagram even existed. Looking at it, I remember how each mother pulled her daughter aside for a separate mother-daughter photo after we put our parasols down.

At the time, I didn't pay much attention to the way Angie rushed over to the group of boys taking us to prom. But now, with the luxury of knowing how things unfolded, it's clear she hurried to her date's side to avoid the painful reminder that her mom was missing.

How did I fail to notice?

I slide the photo into the pocket of my beach bag, wishing Angie understood that there's an outline of our relationship in my heart, but the space inside is empty.

Setting aside my distress, I enter my walk-in closet, turning toward the section dedicated to dresses. My eyes travel to the pink section, landing on the sequined stunner I bought for the Taylor concert. Perfect for her Lover Era.

Unzipping the garment bag, I trace my fingers over the delicate puff sleeve and see an image of my sixteen-year-old daughter Bianca's crumpled face when we learned our tickets were fake.

"I have a daughter," the concert venue's security officer told us. "I know how devastating this is."

I never considered that the Insta follower who sold me tickets was a scam artist. Losing four thousand dollars to a con was humiliating. The experience left me ashamed and embarrassed. Why wouldn't it? My father was in the image management business, i.e., politics. Mistakes were unacceptable errors that lost elections and had to be covered up.

As I take the pink, sparkly dress out of my closet, I remember the tears that streamed down Bianca's cheeks when she told Marco what had happened. He spent the next hour irate about the thousands I spent on fake tickets.

"*Ma dai!* How you can be so gullible! Of course, some scammer promises the perfect deal for the tickets. Social media *is all fake!* But that's what you like, no? Always pretending life is *perfect.* It's your damn *specialità!*" His words stung, especially knowing that his use of Italian was a clear signal of his intense rage.

Zipping up the garment bag, I carefully fold my dress in half. If Marco only knew it cost as much as the Taylor tickets, he'd have a fit. I revel in my feelings of spite for a few moments, but when I put the dress into my suitcase, the suspicious texts with his colleague burst through my mind.

Lilly from Accounting: What are your plans tonight

Marco: I've got that dinner

Lilly from Accounting: Can I go as your date

Marco: I'd love to bring you as my date

Dizzy, I drop onto my bed, reminding myself that I will not say a word to Marco until I come up with a plan. Growing up, I watched my father shake hands and smile at people who betrayed him countless times. He'd do anything to protect his image, and so will I.

"LET'S SET UP the ring light over there." I point to the California black oak in the center of Hamilton Beach Gardens. Purple clouds shimmer in the twilight sky. This backdrop is the ideal setting for the photo shoot I'm doing to promote Arctic Coolers and will distract me from those texts between Marco and his colleague. Their flirty tone. The playful innuendo of the word *date*. Perfect time to get away. Sure, I'll have to face the tension with Angie, but right now, I'd prefer that over the exhaustion of pretending with Marco.

Maybe this explains why my father has spent the last ten years at home doing puzzles and bird watching. Years of playing perfect have left him with a fatigue that's infiltrated every single cell of his body.

Bianca pulls a large wagon filled with all the items needed to create the perfect Insta post. "Did you get everything on here?" She smirks, making fun of my long to-do list in her hand. "When's Dad coming?" she asks as her eyes dart from the walking path to the yellow rose bushes, back to the path, and then further down toward the park's entrance. I know she's feeling uneasy, and I can understand why. There's been more tension than usual between Marco and me, which makes sense now, knowing about the texts.

My mind travels backward, trying to pinpoint when our relationship shifted. I'm almost relieved when I don't come up with one significant, monumental moment that led us to where we are now—married, yet profoundly lonely. It was a slow chipping away, rather than a sudden fracture. We haven't done simple things like watch TV or cook home-made pasta together in years. We don't know each other anymore.

"Has he texted?" Bianca wraps and unwraps a piece of her long brown hair around one of her fingers. She's restless.

"He should be here any minute." I force my voice to sound light-hearted, although I'm simmering inside.

Marco's fifteen minutes late, even though I made it clear he needed to be on time. He barely lifted his eyes from his phone this morning when I told him to meet us here at six. Each time he tapped his screen, he grinned wider, and I wondered if he was texting *her*. I wanted to snatch his phone and see the reason for his smile, but instead, I explained that Arctic Coolers moved up their new product launch, and I promised them I'd post the first series of pictures tonight.

"Yes, yes, I'll be there," he said, annoyed. Not bothering to look at me.

"And make sure you wear the blue shirt I left on the island in our closet. Arctic Blast expects us to wear its brand colors. It's in my contract."

Marco nodded, but he might as well have been in a spacesuit drifting over Mars. His attention was a million miles away.

Did I make a mistake involving Marco in the campaign? But Arctic Blast specifically asked that I include him. The request was almost a deal-breaker. I've been phasing Marco out of my content since last year when he told me he was tired of the perfect couple we portray on Instagram.

"It's all fake. We've lost our connection," he said. "We need to figure out how to get it back." His words bounced rhythmically, punctuated by his Italian accent.

However, instead of addressing his concerns, I ignored them. And after seeing the ridiculous amount of money Arctic Coolers was going to pay me to promote a product that somehow links masculinity, dominance, and power to a 25" x 16" x 15" plastic tub, I included him, despite his annoyance with how we come across on Instagram.

Bianca takes the ring light and picnic blanket out of the wagon, then waves to a figure in the distance. "Dad's here!"

Turning, I see Marco walking in our direction. My head throbs. He's not wearing the shirt I left for him. *He makes everything so hard!*

My anger increases as he takes slow, casual steps. There's no sense of urgency. He doesn't care that I have a million things to do before I leave for my trip. But most notably, his phone has his undivided attention. I watch as his eyes suddenly light up, as if they've tapped into the universe's energy source. It reminds me of the way he looked at me when we had our very own meet-cute in college, where, during a tennis match, I lobbed a ball that flew over the fence and almost hit him on the head. He retrieved said ball, and we chatted. He was gorgeous with a sexy Italian accent!

Later that night, a tennis ball appeared at my sorority house, on which was written, *I think it's "LOVE."*

But now, as I watch him send a message back to whoever he's texting, I wish a tennis ball would wallop him in the face. Right away, my mind fills with more of the text messages I read between him and his colleague.

I scrunch my eyes closed, trying to clear it from my mind. But it's no use. The words explode in my head, refusing to be ignored.

Marco: I need to get my bag out of your room.

Lilly from Accounting: Sure. I'll grab it after this session is over.

CHAPTER 6

Mr. LaFleur

Now

Emerald Jewel All-Inclusive Resort

October 5th ♫ 5:00 a.m.

T HE HOUR IS ungodly. Three hysterical women in dresses the same color as bubble gum sit in Mr. LaFleur's office at the Emerald Jewel Resort. The bare beige walls and cheap furniture contrast with the resort's luxury finishes. He wonders if they know how lucky they are to live so comfortably.

"Call the police! We found our friend's dress on the beach, and she's M.I.A." The woman with the ripped dress glares at Mr. LaFleur. Her eyes are wild with fear. "Haven't you seen all those Lifetime movies about women in peril?!"

Haven't you seen all those Apple TV shows about rich people behaving badly? Tapping his pen against the desk, he tries his best to look concerned. He knew the guests coming for Boy Bands at the Beach would be high maintenance. He's looking forward to next week's Sail Away with Yacht Rock. That crowd is easygoing and a bit older.

"And you've tried calling your friend's cell phone?"

"Yes," the three women blurt in unison.

"We've called and texted a million times." The woman with wild hair pulls out her phone and shoves it in front of Mr. LaFleur's face, as if he needs proof.

With so little sleep, he struggles to keep his temper from boiling over. But he knows he'd be stupid to unravel now. He's in line for a promotion at the corporate office in Florida, which would mean no more dealing with guests.

"And when was the last time you saw her?" He continues tapping his pen nonchalantly, as if the women are complaining about not being able to find empty lounge chairs at the pool.

"I was the last one with her. It was about one in the morning. Please call the police. What are you waiting for?" The woman with streaks of black makeup running down her face pushes her hands together and stares at the ceiling. "Why? Why did I let her walk away alone in the darkness?"

Her voice swells with emotion, but the drama doesn't affect Mr. LaFleur. He's heard hundreds of guests yell, scream, and cry over things like weak shower pressure and unsupportive pillows. He's become desensitized.

Laying his pen on the desk, he wonders the best way to tell these women why he's not contacting the police. "In my experience, these situations are usually delicate." He hopes these words offer enough of an explanation without him having to get into more detail.

"Delicate?" The woman with wild hair tilts her head. "What do you mean? We found our friend's dress on the beach. We can't get in touch with her. Call the damn police." Her hands flail angrily.

"Delicate." The woman with streaks of black makeup repeats the word. "I think he means she's getting physical."

The mouth of the woman with the ripped dress hangs open. "No way, there's absolutely no way she'd cheat on her husband."

Mr. LaFleur nods his head slowly, feigning sympathy. "Unfortunately, I've seen this situation many times, and each time the missing person was involved with another guest." He enunciates the word *involved,* making his thoughts on their missing friend crystal clear.

"That's insane!" The voice of the woman with streaks of black makeup bangs through the small room like a gunshot. "You need to take this seriously. She's missing!"

Taking a deep breath, Mr. LaFleur ignores the annoyance stirring in his chest. It was only a few months ago that a husband was in his office, terrified about his missing wife. An hour later, the staff discovered her and another guest half-naked and passed out in the lobby's supply closet. He reminds himself to confirm that the closet door now locks automatically.

"I understand your opinion. But, like I said, usually these situations work themselves out quickly."

The woman with wild hair jumps out of her chair. Her body shakes. "But you haven't heard everything. We know a guest at this resort has something to do with her disappearance!"

"What do you mean?" Mr. LaFleur restrains himself from pointing out this is what he meant. Guests meet someone interesting and then take it too far.

"I mean foul play." The woman with streaks of black makeup slumps back as if she hasn't slept in weeks. She rubs her puffy eyes.

"Yes," the woman with wild hair agrees. "There's something sketchy going on."

Mr. LaFleur's stomach clenches, wondering how much more of this manufactured drama he can take. These music-themed events may kill him.

Shifting in his cheap rolling chair, he pictures the home his wife's been eyeing in Florida. It's in a wonderful neighborhood with a highly rated school district. Perfect for his daughter. "You mean criminal activity?"

"Yes," the woman with the ripped dress nods. "We were just saying, we think—"

Suddenly, the door to the office opens, and George, the resort's newest security guard, rushes in. "I found something! I need to know if it belongs to your friend." He towers over the group with a prideful look on his face.

Mr. LaFleur stifles a sigh, irritated by the kid's eagerness. But then again, George is huge, easily six foot five, two hundred and twenty pounds, and built like a Mack truck. Perfect for appeasing rich American guests who demand security after flying on private jets to get to the Emerald Jewel. Unfortunately, St. McAna made headlines last year when a criminal network got away with stealing high-end watches and diamond jewelry from several of the island's resorts. Luckily, a few key reporters were more than happy to take a small bribe to keep the Emerald Jewel out of the headlines. Mr. LaFleur's ability to contain the story impressed the corporate office.

"No!" The woman with the wild hair leaps out of her chair. "Whatever you found, I hope it's not hers!"

"Come with me." George and the women exit the office before Mr. LaFleur can get a word in.

Frustrated, he follows them through the lobby, around the enormous pool, and down to the beach. Sand fills his dress shoes, and he chastises himself for not removing them. After fifteen years of working here, he knows better than to wear his oxfords while walking on the beach.

Turning right, the group moves past a small boathouse until they reach the boardwalk of a gazebo nestled next to the water. The moon sits near the horizon, as jagged streaks of early morning light push through the sky. They walk down the wooden planks leading to the gazebo in a single-file line, like they're participating in some type of sunrise parade.

"I left it where I found it. In case it's evidence."

The woman with the ripped dress gasps. "It's hers!"

Blood rushes to Mr. LaFleur's heart. George is taking his position too seriously. The word *evidence* makes it seem like there's been a crime. This is not an idea he wants to reinforce.

"This belongs to your friend?" He points to the item, and all three women nod their heads, circling their arms around each other for comfort.

The woman with wild hair sniffles. Her lips quiver in the shadowy light. All three women move to the gazebo's edge and peer into the water.

"Is it possible…do you think…?" The woman with streaky black makeup stammers. Her eyes swoop over the water, searching.

"No!" The woman with the ripped dress breaks free from her friends and runs toward the beach, crying.

The unpleasant sensation of grainy sand in Mr. LaFleur's shoes spreads through his entire body. He knows he must find this woman before the other guests find out someone's missing. Soon he'll have to call the police.

"Let's sweep the property one more time." He directs his statement to George, who walks closer to the missing woman's travel companions.

"Send me a picture of your friend so I can question guests. Maybe someone knows something."

Mr. LaFleur lunges in front of George's large body. "That won't be necessary." He'd rather set fire to the resort than have a bunch of people posting reviews on Tripadvisor about a missing resort guest.

"Do one more sweep. I'm sure there's a simple explanation." He speaks in a calm tone as the image of a lifeless body drifting past sunbathers consumes him.

CHAPTER 7

Angie

St. McAna Island
October 2nd ♫ Three Days Ago

"**W**E HOPE YOU enjoyed your flight from St. Louis to St. McAna Island." The overhead speaker crackles, and the captain's voice fades.

I picture Patton waving goodbye to me this morning at the airport. Did he notice how tightly I hugged him?

The flight attendant walks past me, collecting empty cups and wrappers. "Bring your forms with you. You'll turn them in when you go through customs. Have a great vacation!" He doesn't know how anxious I am with my past lurking.

I exit the plane, seeing others who must be here for Boy Bands at the Beach. Groups flutter all around, decked out in nineties retro clothing. A couple of women wearing vintage *90210* T-shirts get behind me in line. Brandon Walsh beams at me, with that smile that always made my heart speed up. It reminds me of Thursday nights spent with Carly, Liliana, and Nicole, watching episodes showcasing frenemies Brenda, Kelly, and Donna as my mom popped in with snacks and Jolt Colas.

As I snake up and down the metal rails leading to a customs officer, I notice several more groups here for the shows. Nothing brings women of my generation together like boy bands. Carly probably picked this vacation knowing my weakness for male singers with highlighted hair and an incredible ability to harmonize. My fingers twitch with muscle memory, recalling how difficult it was to get the thin plastic covering off a brand-new CD. After finally opening the case, my friends and I would huddle around a stereo system the size of a small foreign car. As we listened to heartfelt songs about first loves and heartbreak, we'd imagine we were being serenaded by our future husbands. My mom even let us use her wedding veil as we took turns pretending to marry the heartthrobs in the posters plastering my bedroom walls.

"Next." The customs official waves me over.

I pull my passport from my bag. Surely, I can ignore my past for three nights with Jordan Knight crooning "I'll Be Loving You Forever." But as I hand it over, my mind rewinds to the news segment of my dad, pale and trembling, pleading for my safe return. Instantly, my seventeen-year-old self hijacks my body.

"You okay?" The agent, a large man with smooth dark skin, smiles before glancing at my passport.

I soften my tense expression, trying to ignore my anxiety and guilt.

"Relax and have a good time. You're on vacation." He lights up like a brightness filter turned on maximum, and hands me back the passport wallet I recently purchased on Amazon.

I force a tight smile.

"Have fun and enjoy the sunshine."

I EXIT THE resort's shuttle, and a bellman in an orange hibiscus-patterned shirt takes my suitcase. Following him to the lobby, my eyes sweep the space. My jaw drops. Bright-white leather couches and oversized, emerald-green, velvet wingback chairs sit between columns covered in sparkling glass tile. Large, plush pillows with a modern banana leaf print lay on the furniture, adding a cozy touch. Temperate air flows from outside through the open-air space.

I take a deep breath, and the scent of coconut and vanilla wraps around me like a hug. Gazing beyond the lobby, my eyes land on the huge infinity pool and then bounce further down to a heart-stopping view of the ocean. I'm whisked back to the incredible honeymoon Patton and I took in Hawaii. I already miss the lightness of being around him, free from regret.

"Miss?" A woman's voice calls to me from the check-in desk.

Unable to tear my eyes away from the breathtaking scenery, I walk toward her without looking. A moment later, I'm colliding with another person. Shifting my eyes, I watch as the young guy I've crashed into falls to the floor.

"Oh, my gosh. I'm so sorry." I reach out to help him stand.

He pops up from the ground. Given his young age, I'm not surprised by how fast he's back on his feet. He can't be over twenty-five.

He slings his backpack over his shoulder. "All good."

"I'm sorry. I was caught up in the view. I wasn't paying attention." As I apologize, my face flushes. This guy is gorgeous in a way that reminds me I'm just a mere mortal. His facial features mirror a painstakingly crafted Greek sculpture.

"Ready to check in?" The woman behind the desk waves me over.

"I hope you're okay," I say to the guy before I turn and walk toward her.

"Everything's chill." He smiles, and my eyes burn like I'm staring directly at the sun. His thick dark hair frames his perfect face, and his green eyes sparkle like crown jewels. He continues, "I'll follow you over. I need to get checked in too."

We walk to the desk side by side. I place my bag on the counter. He puts his backpack next to it, and we wait for instructions from the employees at the front desk.

A woman with creamy skin and long blond braids smiles at us. "Welcome to the Emerald Jewel Resort. Can I get your last name?"

"Novello." I hand her my passport, and she types my information into the computer.

"There's only one person on this reservation." Her forehead scrunches in confusion. "Since our resort is all-inclusive, there's a per-person charge."

I stare for a moment, unsure what she means, until I realize the young guy is standing next to me. A jolt of current pulses through my core. "Oh, we're not together."

"Oh." She smiles nervously. "Sorry about the mix-up."

"Us? No, we just met." The young guy reiterates our separateness but is remarkably cool about the situation. I'm sure he's outraged that anyone would put us together—a midlife mom with a bob and an Adonis.

The woman smiles, but I can tell she's embarrassed. She gets the attention of another employee a few feet away. "Can you help me get these guests checked in?"

The employee nods and waves me over as the bellman returns with two glasses of champagne.

"By the way, I'm Luca. Nice meeting you." The young guy gives me his million-dollar smile.

My insides buzz like I've been shocked with a live electrical wire.

"I'm Angie." I feel my cheeks flush again. I grab a tall, fluted glass of bubbly and hold it in my sweaty palms, embarrassed I'm acting like a schoolgirl with a crush.

After taking several large sips, I put the empty glass on the edge of the counter, but it wobbles and crashes onto the hard tile floor. Humiliation causes the heat on my cheeks to spread across my entire face.

"Oh, no." Luca stares at the ground as the bellman rushes forward.

Another hotel worker runs over with a mop and garbage can.

"I'm such a klutz." Embarrassed, I grab my things and quickly slide to the other end of the desk to finish checking in.

"Have a great vacation." Luca shifts his attention to the woman with the braids at the check-in desk.

"You too," I say, hoping I don't run into him again.

Ten minutes later, I exit the lobby and walk to my room. Palm tree leaves rustle high above against the backdrop of a brilliant blue sky.

Yellow, two-story buildings line the pathway. "I can do this," I whisper, like it's some pathetic self-affirming mantra. "It's just three nights."

I haul my suitcase onto the elevator. When the doors open, I roll it down the open-air hallway and insert my key card into the door. A king-sized bed sits in the center of modern tropical décor. Moving aside the bright coral and navy throw pillows, I sink into the mattress, drained from traveling and anxious about seeing my friends.

For a second, I promise myself I'll find time during this trip to tell them why the way they welcomed me back after running away made me feel like a fraud. But then I picture their faces and know it's not possible. They would never forgive me.

Ping. My eyes flutter open at the noise. I'm confused at first but then remember I'm in St. McAna. I must have fallen asleep. Carly, Liliana, and Nicole are en route from California. They have a layover in Charlotte and won't be here until the afternoon. It's a momentary relief. Once they arrive, I'll have to endure their never-ending chatter. And even worse, the usual tension with Carly. I wonder what she'll find to fight with me about on this trip. Whether we should go to trivia night or the nineties fashion show the hotel is encouraging guests to participate in? Luckily, the Backstreet Boys show starts right after they get here, leaving just enough time for excited squeals about how fantastic everyone looks and nothing else.

My phone pings again.

> **Carly:** OMG our connecting flight from Charlotte is CX. 😠 No flights until tomorrow. We're in crisis mode

My stomach churns. Are they going to make it? Shooting up from the bed, I hit Carly's number. It rings several times before going to voicemail.

A moment later, my phone pings with another text.

> **Carly:** Can't talk now. Working with ticket agent. Call soon

My heart thumps. What if they can't reschedule their flights? Although being with them is stressful, being by myself in a sea of cliquey women trying to relive their youth is more terrifying. I'm not the type to make friends on vacation.

I dial Patton and relay the details. "Should I call the airlines and find a flight home?"

"I'm sure they'll make it tomorrow." Patton is always an optimist. "But if they don't, stay. You love these bands, and it will still be fun."

"Yeah, Mom," I hear Ethan and Everett say in the background. "YOLO!" they yell enthusiastically.

"I guess I'll stay in my room tonight. I'm not going to the show by myself." I slump further into the bed.

"Listen, Ang, go have some fun. I know you'll technically be alone, but that doesn't mean you should hide in your room. Everyone at that resort is there specifically to listen to that music. They're your people. Throw on your *raised on '90s boy bands* T-shirt and go."

After hanging up, I open my carry-on and pull out the T-shirt. Maybe being here by myself is what I need. If I'm alone, there won't be any tension with Carly. If I'm alone, I won't feel guilty for hiding the truth about what happened after I got into the big rig. Tonight is my last chance to be around strangers before my past catches up with me.

Right then, I decide I'm going to embrace spontaneity, living as if guided by chaos theory—the subject of my applied mathematics thesis. For tonight, I'm going to live as if I don't have regrets. For tonight, I'm going to live like I'm not the girl from Hamilton Beach who was kidnapped.

CHAPTER 8

Carly

Charlotte, North Carolina
October 2nd ♫ Three Days Ago

#OOTD: Four-way stretch water repellent black joggers. Easy-fit cropped white tank with cinch tie back. Gray brushed cotton boyfriend hoodie. Retro-inspired gray and pink sneakers with lace-up closure. Sterling silver huggie earrings. Apple Watch with ceramic pink link band. Black canvas Gucci belt bag with large initial motif.

"THE FIRST FLIGHT to St. McAna is tomorrow at one twenty in the afternoon. This gets you in at four thirty." The ticket agent continues pecking at her keyboard.

Frustration makes my head pound. The moment brings me back to my honeymoon flight's cancellation. My emotions were already high because Angie, stuck on bed rest before having her twins, missed my wedding. I burst out crying as the agent explained she'd rebook Marco and me on the next flight to Italy, eight hours later.

Marco spent the rest of the day stroking my hair while I cried into his chest about Angie. "It will be okay, amore mio," he cooed, then cheered me up by describing every detail of the incredible three-week honeymoon he'd planned.

I miss the loving way he used to call me *my love* in Italian.

Looking at the ticket agent in front of me, anger swells. *This wasn't the plan!* "Unacceptable. We'll miss two days of our trip. Not to mention the Backstreet Boys show."

The agent's face freezes, and I can tell she's judging my response to what she considers a stupid problem.

"I'll have you know I have a huge following on Instagram and will trash talk this airline every day if we can't get to St. McAna today."

Threats aren't my usual style, but I'm desperate to fix this. *Our trip can't go off the rails!* I picked this vacation knowing Angie's fondness for boy bands, confident she wouldn't turn down her husband's surprise gift. She wants to let our friendship go, but I can't. I still ache remembering how I spent every second until her safe return begging God to bring my best friend home.

"Ma'am, I'm doing the best I can. Your flight had an equipment malfunction. Safety is our priority." She lets out a frustrated breath and continues to type.

"Check a different airline," I bark. The people nearby stare. I feel my face flush, knowing my angry outburst would disappoint my dad. *Over-the-top emotional reactions in public are a no-no.*

The agent sighs. "Give me a minute." She focuses on her computer screen. "Blue Flight Airlines has a seven a.m. tomorrow."

"That would work." Nicole beams while the agent's artificial nails continue to clack against her keyboard.

I'm surprised Nicole's not being pushier. She used to be such a go-getter. Full-time motherhood has worn her down. Her words, not mine. But I see what she means.

The agent shifts her gaze back to me. "But there are only two seats in coach on that flight. You need three."

The spark in Nicole's green eyes fades.

"What about first class?" Liliana squeezes between Nicole and me, leaning her body against the counter. "I'm a diamond flyer on Blue Flight Airlines."

Normally, Liliana's habit of flaunting her *female executive taking over the world* status would annoy me. But in this instance, I hope that her high rank will solve our travel chaos.

The agent's eyes bounce from left to right, reading something on her screen. Shaking her head, she frowns. "I'm sorry, but there isn't anything available but the two coach seats."

"Great. Just great." My words stretch tight like a rubber band about to snap. Anger winds through me, turning me into a Hamilton Beach Karen. Opening my Gucci belt bag, I take out my phone and wave it around. "I bet my three hundred thousand followers will be interested in hearing about how my travel day is unfolding. In fact, I think I'll hop on right now and do a live video."

Is threatening people my new thing? It's possible that stress about my marriage is pushing me to the brink.

Liliana, always the levelheaded one, apologizes to the agent about my rude behavior as Nicole pulls me away. We sit down in a row of empty chairs.

"I know you're upset. But it's not the agent's fault. We can figure this out without throwing shade."

I nod in agreement, biting back my annoyance at Nicole's constant use of teen slang.

She digs through her bag. When she can't find what she's searching for, she stands and fishes around in her pocket. I can't help but notice how thin she's become in the last few months. She's frail.

"Found it." She holds up an individually wrapped peppermint Lifesaver. Her newly cut bangs hang over her eyebrows. Her haircut's a bit much. Something about it seems desperate.

When she unwraps the mint and pops it into her mouth, I can't help myself from calling her out about her weight.

"So, is that your lunch?"

Shrugging off my comment, she sits back down, focusing on her phone. She's lost at least twenty pounds. It's obvious she's using one of those new weight-loss drugs, but she's staying tight-lipped about it. Why won't she tell us? We're her closest friends. But then again, I haven't told a soul that I suspect Marco's cheating. *My father always said, "Keep private matters to yourself."*

As I take another glance at Nicole's shrinking frame, my insecurity surges. I felt the same way on back-to-school night, seeing so many people who had taken similar medicine over the summer. It's not that I'm against people using it for weight loss. It's that Nicole's thinness is making me anxious about my body. I kill myself on the Pilates Reformer and Peloton and stick to a strict macro-based diet to maintain my weight. But now that everyone around me is skinny, my primary source of self-esteem is fading away.

"I can't believe Angie's in St. McAna without her squad." Nicole pulls me out of my spiraling insecurities.

"At least she made it."

Liliana approaches, her shoulders hunched in defeat. "That was a bust."

Ugh, the one time we need her professional status to save us, and she doesn't come through. What's the point of working so hard if you get nothing out of it?

"What's our next move?" Nicole asks.

"We need to find a hotel." I pull out my phone and Google *Charlotte airport hotels*. As I scroll through a list of options, my phone pings with a text.

> **Marco:** I'm heading to Atlanta. Something came up with my new client. Your mom has everything under control with Bianca.

> **Me:** What? I just left this morning. That happened fast.

My body tingles with fear. Lately, Marco's had a lot of last-minute business trips. I can't help but wonder if it involves his colleague.

> **Marco:** New client. Need to get on their good side after another website security breach. Great opportunity.

Peering at his text, snippets from that text exchange I found when he was in Chicago burst in my mind.

Marco: My flight delayed 4 hours

Lilly from Accounting: What concourse are you on? I'm not leaving for another few hours.

Marco: I'm at B

Lilly from Accounting: I'm at C. I'll jump on the train and meet you at B. We can hang out

I tried to rationalize why a colleague would meet up at a completely different concourse just to kill time.

"Carly, what's up? You seem rattled." Liliana takes the seat next to me, placing her hand on my shoulder.

Glancing at my phone, I wonder if I could share my suspicions about Marco. I'm terrified he's having an affair, and that the entire world will have a front-row seat as my perfect life comes crashing down. I can see the clickbait headline—*Popular mom influencer's marriage bombshell!* I need support from my best friends.

But everyone has secrets, so instead of admitting the truth, I tell them exactly what he texted. "Marco's leaving for Atlanta. Something came up with a new client."

"Atlanta!" Liliana practically falls out of her chair. Her topknot of curls falls around her shoulders. "He's going to Atlanta. That's it!"

She stands abruptly, and my entire body freezes. *Does she know something awful about Marco?*

She continues. "Let's book a flight early tomorrow morning from Atlanta. It's the world's biggest airport and has a million options. We can leave from there and get to St. McAna much earlier."

Nicole's eyes cross in confusion. "But how are we going to get from here to Atlanta?"

Liliana motions for Nicole and me to get out of our chairs. "Let's rent a car. It's only a four-hour drive. Carly, make one of your to-do lists—call the airline, find a hotel in Atlanta, reschedule the shuttle pickup in St. McAna. I'll book a rental car."

I do as she says. But all I can think about is how I can spy on Marco while we're both in Atlanta.

CHAPTER 9

Liliana

Somewhere between Charlotte and Atlanta
October 2nd ♫ Three Days Ago

"GREAT TALKING. I look forward to working with you." Pulling AirPods out of my ears, I press the end call button on my phone.

I send a quick text to Josh.

> **Me:** Just spoke to new head of legal. She's great. I won't have to work so much. Everything will be better. Have girls FaceTime me later.

After hitting send, I reread the message. My voice mocks me inside my head. *You're counting on this new hire to fix your marriage?* That's when it occurs to me I should attack the problems in my marriage the same way I attack a new case. I need to be proactive and take initiative. I need to devise a plan to win him back.

I stare at a smear of green trees gliding through my window as Nicole drives to Atlanta. "Glad I got on that call. We hired a new attorney, and she's moving her entire family to Hamilton Beach to take the job."

"Slay, queen. You and Click Com will achieve world domination."

Why does she sound like my teenage daughter? But then again, Nicole's always been over-the-top. I haven't seen her for more than a few minutes here and there for months. I wonder how long she's been talking like this.

She glances in the rearview mirror at Carly curled against the window, sleeping. "Do you think something's off with her?" she asks in a hushed voice. "Threatening the ticket agent, checking her phone every second. She seems kinda jumpy."

"Carly? No. Her recent Instagram post probably didn't get enough likes." As usual, I don't jump to conclusions. Though, the truth is, I'd have no idea if she was acting off. I haven't seen her since the summer.

"Did you see the post?" Nicole glances in my direction and then moves her eyes back to the road.

Opening my Instagram, I stare at the image of Carly in stylish joggers and trendy sneakers in front of the rental car. She's like a Barbie doll, with her long blond hair, bright-blue eyes, and slim figure. The caption reads *perfect outfit for a last-minute road trip*. It's hard to recall even one day in high school when she wasn't flawlessly styled, straight out of *Seventeen* magazine. Just once, it would be great to see her in an old T-shirt with disheveled hair and no makeup. When will she realize imperfections don't make you defective? They make you human.

Nicole smirks. "Are you offended she didn't use the picture she took of us with her selfie stick?"

"No. I don't want to be part of her Instagram feed. And by the way, what forty-five-year-old woman has a selfie stick?"

"Her selfie stick is required as an iconic Instagram influencer. I'm into it," Nicole laughs.

"Of course you are." Suddenly the car fills with the sound of "Manic Monday." "Shoot, it's Amanda. Let me grab this." I bring the phone to my ear.

But instead of my boss, it's her secretary. "Amanda stepped away. She needs to set up a Zoom to talk about the Mitten case. She has a new strategy idea and wants your input. The only opening she has is tomorrow at six. I'll send you the link."

My head pounds. Tomorrow is Sunday! It was only two weeks ago that she demanded I come into the office on Yom Kippur.

My fingers mindlessly move to the bracelet Esther gave me last night. I snap the elastic back and forth against my wrist. Something about the way it stings my skin soothes my anger. "Fine, send the link. But can you remind her I'm on vacation?" Hanging up, I slump into my seat, remembering all the spring breaks, boyfriends, and carefree moments I gave up to land a job like this. *Isn't this what I've always wanted?*

Or is it what my mother always told me I wanted?

"Hey, don't let your boss bring down the vibe."

"Right," I agree, not wanting to explain to Nicole how Amanda expects me to be at her beck and call twenty-four-seven. Answering her calls at dinner, Zooming from my bedroom, and even Zooming from vacation, seem normal, especially when I recall my mom having a fax machine in our dining room and making calls whenever her beeper went off.

"Hey, do me a solid and connect this?" Nicole gestures to her phone lying on the console. "I need to DJ this ride."

"Not if you plan to listen to that nineties rap you're obsessed with." I chuckle, relieved to move on from thoughts about my job.

Nicole lets out a playful growl. "Don't be hatin' my Salt-N-Pepa." Her voice beats like the music she loves. "You know I was a boss female rapper in another life." She shakes her body suggestively while she sings the lyrics to "Push It."

"I'm flashing back to the infamous karaoke night," I say, almost smelling the stale beer and body odor of the bar where Nicole's work happy hour had stretched into a late Tuesday night. When I walked in, she was center stage singing Sir Mix-a-Lot's "Baby Got Back."

Everyone in the bar stood mesmerized by her suggestive portrayal of the dancers from the video. It was typical Nicole, stealing the show before anyone realized there was a show to steal. I marched close to the stage, furious she'd called wasted, begging me to get her back to our apartment in Santa Monica. She knew I was working grueling hours as a first-year associate at a top law firm.

As soon as she noticed me, she gave me a devious smile, getting me to join her on stage by choosing the song "End of the Road" by Boyz II Men. A song she knew I had a soft spot for since Brian Fineman and I danced to it at my bat mitzvah. Before I knew it, I was a few drinks in and butchering song lyrics without a care in the world.

"My peak era!" she says. "Those work happy hours were fire. I loved that job. The buzz of creating an advertising pitch. Coming up with award-winning concepts." Her voice trails off. Her buoyant energy vanishes.

I rush to fill the void, circling back to a fun fact. "Isn't it crazy to think that Evie and Esther wouldn't exist if Josh and I hadn't met that night?" I disregard my uneasy feelings about the state of my marriage and picture Josh in his cargo shorts and flannel shirt, singing Nirvana all those years ago. "Thank God you two had such a miserable date before I met him."

I smile, thinking about the way Josh always describes his one date with Nicole as a case study of incompatibility. Knowing them, I couldn't agree more. Josh's dry, subtle disposition and Nicole's boisterous personality would never have worked. Their close friendship is quite surprising.

I wait, expecting Nicole to laugh about her awful date with Josh, but her body stiffens. *Did I say something wrong?* I should change the topic of conversation to something other than her old job. She's always telling Josh that she regrets giving up her career. I'm glad they've become close as stay-at-home parents, but then I remember Josh's accusation the other night that I'm turning into Garrett. *Are they spending too much time together?*

A strange feeling travels through my body. There's something unsettling about my best friend and my husband being each other's confidants.

"Anyway, can you put the address of the airport hotel into my Google Maps? Carly texted it to me earlier, but I was already driving."

It's obvious Nicole doesn't want to spend any more time reminiscing about her *peak era*.

Taking her cue, I drop further discussion about the past and tap in the hotel's address.

"How long until we get there?" Carly pipes up from the backseat.

"About two hours," Nicole says. "We should be there around six or seven." Nicole repeats her words in that annoying singsong voice kids use for six-seven, while briefly juggling her hands off the steering wheel.

Carly leans her head toward the front seat. "Oh, my God, Nicole. Cut it out with the teen slang. It's annoying. Liliana, back me up here."

"I'm going to have to agree with Carly on this one. You're a forty-five-year-old mother of three."

"You guys are a total buzzkill!" Nicole's eyes bounce from Carly to me and then back to the road.

"Ahh, that's more like it—buzzkill. That's some nineties slang I can relate to." I'm amused by my joke.

"Yeah, Nicole," Carly continues. "It's like how you wear mini Uggs, Aviator Nation, and carry a Stanley everywhere. That stuff's for teenagers. Stay in your lane, as a teen would say," Carly quips.

"FYI, my hot pink dress is from Abercrombie. And get ready because, this entire trip, I'll be glowing up, using teen slang, and carrying my Stanley everywhere."

Carly snorts. "You're not even using the term *glow-up* correctly. You might want to check your Urban Dictionary."

"Guys, look, another sign for Buc-ee's," I interrupt and point to the bright-yellow billboard with a cartoon drawing of a beaver that reads *My overbite is sexy*. "It's like the tenth sign I've seen."

Carly gets on her phone. "Google can tell us what it is." She spends a moment reading. "Wow, this place has a cult following. It's a mega super-sized gas station and convenience store."

"Who cares?" Nicole shrugs her shoulders. "You can get chips and soda anywhere."

"Um, no, this goes way beyond that. Fudge, tacos, brisket sandwiches, a soda fountain with hundreds of options, an entire wall of gummy candy."

"An entire wall of gummy candy." I picture rows and rows of bags filled with neon-colored sugary treats. "I'm definitely in. We should stop. I need to pee anyway."

"Says here they have the world's cleanest bathrooms too." Carly throws her hands up in the air and silently cheers.

Nicole exits the highway laughing. "That soda fountain sounds like the perfect place to fill up my Stanley."

"We should get the biggest bag of Swedish Fish we can find for Angie. It's her favorite," Carly says.

I nod. "Great idea. Speaking of Angie. Has anyone heard from her?"

Everyone shakes their heads.

"I'll check in with a text."

A moment after sending it, all our phones ping with a photo of Angie wrapped around a tall, gorgeous, younger man. Her eyes are half closed, and her body slouches into him, making it seem like he's the only thing keeping her from falling over.

I'm not one to overreact, but why is Angie drunk and hanging all over a twenty-year-old?

Carly describes the image to Nicole as she pulls into the parking lot of Buc-ee's.

Confusion overtakes Nicole's face, listening to Carly's description. "Wow. That's off the hook. Should we be worried?"

CHAPTER 10

Nicole

Atlanta, Georgia
October 2nd ♫ Three Days Ago

WE LOADED UP on snacks at Buc-ee's and made it to Atlanta thanks to my alpha driving skills. Stuck in traffic, I check out the city skyline. Tall office buildings shoot up on my left, and Georgia Tech's red brick campus is on my right. I shake my head, trying to get a chunk of bangs out of my eyes. My impulsive haircut's a major fail.

Liliana rolls her eyes as we pass under a bridge. "Another street called Peachtree. I'm super confused." She points to a green highway sign that lists exits for Peachtree Road, Peachtree Boulevard, and Peachtree Street.

Taking a quick look in the rearview mirror, I wait for Carly to hit us with some insight she's gleaned about Atlanta from Insta, but she's not paying attention. Her eyes dart around like she's searching for a lost dog. Something's definitely up.

"Looking for something?" I shift my gaze between the road and the back seat.

Carly's body jerks, like she's coming out of a trance. She digs through her Gucci belt bag, looking for something. I was right. She's acting nervous. I wonder if I should push her to spill the tea but know it's not worth the effort. She never shares her problems. I was shocked when she told us about the fake Taylor tickets, but I guess there wasn't any way to hide it. She made a bigger deal out of it than it is. But it may be the first time she's been publicly humiliated. I, on the other hand, have had plenty of practice, starting with when my bikini top flew off as I jumped in the water during a fifth-grade pool party. As I held my breath underwater to hide my half-naked body, Carly, Angie, and Liliana swam around me for cover. I'll admit it was mortifying, but hundreds of embarrassing moments later, I'm pretty immune to humiliation.

"What are you looking for? You're acting sus, or would you prefer me to say the proper term, *suspicious*?" I'm low-key annoyed at the way she and Liliana made fun of me earlier for using slang.

She lets out a breath. "I'm fine." Popping gum in her mouth, she chews it aggressively.

When will Carly get that it's unexpected and embarrassing moments that make life interesting? They're not always fun, but you should see the look people give me when I say the words *pelvic separation*! I'd take that big mess over her perfect little cage any day.

Liliana interrupts, having spotted the restaurant we're eating at. "There, I can see it off the highway."

Glancing out the window, I see a huge red V with the word *varsity* written over a silver backdrop. I take the next exit, following directions to Atlanta's iconic restaurant, The Varsity.

Liliana groans. "Fast food? Hot Dogs? This is where we're eating?" She frowns.

As I park between two insanely large pickup trucks, I hope I can find something to eat that won't upset my stomach. One of the awful side effects of the weight-loss injections is queasiness.

When we exit the car, Carly leads us toward the restaurant's entrance. "According to my Insta research, The Varsity is a must when in Atlanta. It will make a great post. And anyway, we need something fast. Our flight leaves at five in the morning. Everyone huddle together for a quick picture."

Liliana and I reluctantly agree. I don't want to be on Carly's Intsa feed either. Especially with these bangs. It looks like I'm trying to be cool, which makes me *so* uncool. Maybe this was the point my friends were trying to make earlier.

"Let's go grub." I shrug off my insecurities about using slang. "I love a good hot dog."

When we walk inside, I'm shocked by the massive line. Rows of hungry people cram together in front of the cashiers taking orders. This place has a fifties diner vibe, with a black-and-white checkered floor, red countertops, and chrome finishes. The entire restaurant buzzes with the sound of meat sizzling on the grill.

Liliana reads the overhead menu out loud. "Chili cheese slaw dogs, onion rings, fried apple pie, double bacon cheeseburgers—my Jewish grandmother would roll over in her grave."

Laughing, I read through all the choices. "Girls, we're definitely not in Southern California anymore. This menu would be straight-up illegal in Hamilton Beach."

"It smells like a county fair. Fried everything." Carly waves her hand around, trying to clear the air. "I thought they'd at least have one salad option. I miss my Trendy Greens."

"I hate Trendy Greens," I say. The cookie-cutter tennis moms, always lunching there, are lame. I never wanted to become one of those Hamilton Beach Stepford Wives. I avoid the mom cliques. They're like street gangs, but instead of identifying themselves with tattoos and graffiti tags, they use designer purses and SUVs. *No thanks.*

It's all so disappointing. I was destined to become advertising royalty. But then my career got off track while I was recovering from the pelvic separation. My boss gave someone else my role as the assistant director for the brilliant Target campaign I came up with, and I knew I wouldn't get promoted to account executive.

"What'll ya have?" A young kid with a mullet drawls his question.

Reading through the menu, I pick something that won't give me a major stomachache. It's weird. I never cared about my curvy body until now. I wonder if Carly and Liliana suspect I'm using the latest craze in weight loss. I don't think they would care, but people are quick to pass judgment, thinking it's the easy way out. But since my hysterectomy, the pounds keep accumulating, no matter what I do. And for the last few months, when I look in the mirror, all I see are thick thighs and a round stomach, not the curvy badass bitch I used to be. Picking up my tray of greasy food, I wonder why I'm suddenly focusing on dropping pounds.

We find an empty booth and sit down.

"Any new texts from Angie?"

Earlier, at Buc-ee's, while we debated adding Hot Tamales or Sour Patch Kids to our Swedish Fish, we agreed that it's strange she sent that pic with some young, hot stud. Especially when Patton seems like a great guy.

We all shake our heads, confirming no one's heard more from Angie, but then again, she never communicates much on our group chat. She's had a wall up ever since her mom died. She was so destroyed, she ran away, and none of us saw it coming. We were supposed to have her back.

"I've always worried that what happened in high school would catch up with her. All the stories about her kidnapping. All the TV coverage." Carly forcefully pushes a napkin into her onion rings, trying to remove the grease. She's fighting a losing battle, but as usual, she'll do anything she can to keep her calorie count low.

I wonder if she's thought about trying Ozempic. It wouldn't surprise me, although she'd have to go to some quack online doctor to get a prescription.

"Do you think Angie would do something irrational?" she asks.

That summer before college pops right into my head. Angie was home safe. We were relieved and excited to have several weeks together before we headed off as freshmen. But Angie went into a hole. She didn't want to swim in the lake. She said she was tired when we made plans to go to the mall. She never wanted to get her nails done or watch reruns of *Full House*. She seemed ready to get rid of us. We weren't old enough to know that, sometimes, people don't ask for help because they're scared of being let down. Instead, they wait for you to read between the lines. The same way I wait for Garrett to read between the lines, because I'm worried he won't help with the kids, even if I ask. *And then what?* So, I wait, and wait, and wait, but he just coasts in the blank space between the lines, blind. The same way we did with Angie.

"Let's call her." After dialing the number, I hear it ring a few times before it goes to voicemail. "She's not picking up."

"I'll text her." Liliana taps her phone. A moment later, it pings.

"What does it say?" My body tingles with nerves. Angie's solo in another country, drunk, and getting cozy with a guy who's young enough to be her son. Are we ignoring another bright-red flag?

Liliana reads the text out loud. "*Sitting across the bar from Nick Carter and Howie Dorough. Made a new best friend, Luca. We're doing shots.* Then she punctuates the text with an obscene number of emojis."

"The Backstreet Boys! I can't believe we're missing the show." Carly's voice rises about ten octaves.

Liliana's phone pings again.

"What else?" Carly asks.

"It's another picture." Liliana shows us her phone. The photo shows Angie's right eye and cheek smashed up against someone else's forehead. "I'm assuming that's Luca."

"I can't believe this. I hope she's okay." Carly says, concerned.

Liliana slides her tray of uneaten food away. "Let's remember, Angie's forty-five. She's not the seventeen-year-old kid she was when she got out of that police car all those years ago."

"But she was never the same." Carly looks down at the table.

Out of nowhere, a toddler with white-hot blond curls, wearing a smocked plaid jumper, teeters to our booth, bawling. He reaches up, grasping the side of our table, and then collapses to the ground, crying. A woman I assume to be his mom hurries behind him.

"Sorry, ya'll. He's madder than a wet hen." She glances at us apologetically, scoops up her child, and carries him away.

"This place feels like the Twilight Zone." Liliana shifts her eyes back and forth.

"Or at least a *Dukes of Hazzard* episode." I joke.

"Ya'll are being so judgmental." Carly drags out the word, *ya'll* playfully. "Atlanta is quite cosmopolitan, with a great food scene and cutting-edge style."

"Incoming Insta post," I say.

Carly's lips round into a snarky pout.

I shrug. "It's hard not to joke about your side hustle." It figures Carly's Instagram blew up. She took her flawless high school persona digital.

Staring at her pile of uneaten onion rings, Carly picks up the biggest one and chucks it at my face. It lands on the table, leaving a slick of oil.

"Missed," I tease, then take a bite of my slaw dog. It's crazy good. Despite the meds killing my appetite, I manage a few fries before nibbling the rest.

Thirty minutes later, we're back in the car.

"Can you connect my phone?" I glance at Liliana.

She taps Google Maps, and we're off to the hotel. As I drive out of The Varsity's parking lot, my phone pings.

"I bet that's Garrett looking for Hank's uniform for practice, even though I printed and emailed him all the information he needs to get through the next few days." How does he handle being a managing partner when he can't even get his kid ready for baseball?

"No, it's from Jessica." Liliana reads the text out loud. "*Don't forget what we talked about. Stick to the plan.* That sounds ominous. Who's Jessica?" She waits for me to answer.

"Oh, Jessica. She's a new friend." My entire body ignites with heat. If Liliana only knew Jessica was her husband, Josh.

Detective Ellis

Now

Emerald Jewel All-Inclusive Resort
October 5th ♫ 5:30 a.m.

DETECTIVE ELLIS WATCHES a woman with splotchy black patches under her eyes pace the small meeting room that's become his command post at the Emerald Jewel. Despite the cheery wallpaper featuring tropical birds, the atmosphere is bleak. Two other women in pink dresses sit on the floor with their backs pressed against the image of a turquoise and yellow macaw. Their eyes are bloodshot from crying.

"Did you find Luca?" The pacing woman glances at Mr. LaFleur and Detective Ellis hopefully.

"We've been by his hotel room, but he's not answering the door." Mr. LaFleur gestures toward the detective, cueing the woman to direct her question to him.

While Detective Ellis is prepared to talk with the missing woman's friends, he wants to get an update from Officer Claasen, his senior investigating officer, first. This case is already ten steps behind. LaFleur should have called him an hour ago.

"Do we have the timeline of events?" Detective Ellis leans toward his stocky, uniformed officer with bushy red hair and an unruly mustache. "And who was the last person to see the missing individual?" Detective Ellis tries to ignore the woman hovering near him.

"Here's what I've put together so far." Officer Claasen hands him a clipboard.

Detective Ellis examines the officer's meager notes. He's not surprised at the lack of information. This isn't his first time working a case at the Emerald Jewel. After the jewelry heist, he knows LaFleur prioritizes the hotel's image over police matters, but that will not stop him from conducting a proper investigation. "We need more details. Interview guests without causing alarm."

"Is that really necessary?" Mr. LaFleur interjects as if on cue.

Detective Ellis's palms round into fists. He wouldn't punch LaFleur, although it's tempting. Instead, he wonders how the hotel's manager doesn't understand the disastrous implications of a missing American woman on an island whose economy depends on tourism.

But before he can set LaFleur straight, the pacing woman is next to him.

"It's Luca! I'm telling you. Find him and you'll find our friend!"

Detective Ellis relaxes his palms and places a hand on the woman's shoulder. "This is a difficult situation. I understand your concern. We're reviewing information about the man in question." He studies her reaction, searching for any sign that she may be involved with her friend's disappearance. He knows that most crimes, especially violent ones, are committed by people who know each other.

"But have you found him?" One of the women slouching on the floor suddenly sits upright. A jagged piece of fabric hangs over her left shoulder.

He wonders if this is a clue. Was her dress torn during an altercation? He watches as she stands and stomps toward him.

Opening her mouth, words rush out, as if they're tumbling down a mountain. "Have the US Embassy do a background check on him!"

Detective Ellis's muscles forcefully contract as the irate woman questions his professional capabilities. He takes a shallow, calming breath. "We've informed the embassy. I cannot share further information because of privacy laws." He keeps his tone neutral as his attention shifts to the woman still sitting on the floor. Knots of hair clump around her face. He's learned not to underestimate the quiet ones.

"Not good enough!" The quiet woman jumps up and joins her friends. Her hands shake.

Here we go. Detective Ellis knows the missing woman's friends want answers. But they need to be patient. In addition to their unreasonable ice requirements, Americans are incredibly demanding.

"The embassy sent a communication to our local hospitals and law enforcement agencies," he explains. "I will update you if I hear anything."

"Hospitals? This is scary. Do you think she's hurt? Are you holding back?" The woman with knotty hair inhales deeply. She places her hand on her heart. "I can't catch my breath." She gasps for air.

"She's going to pass out! Quick, get a chair!" The woman with black patches under her eyes lunges toward her friend, stabilizing her body as the woman with knotty hair faints.

Pressure fills Detective Ellis's chest. He knows the chief of police will be breathing down his neck. Another rich, foolish tourist has disappeared into the temperate, tropical air, leaving the weight of St. McAna's gross domestic product squarely on his shoulders. But what did he expect? It's just another day for the island's tourism crime division chief.

CHAPTER 12

Angie

Emerald Jewel Resort
October 2nd ♫ Three Days Ago

"**Y**OU'RE MY BESTIE. I love you!" I wrap my arms around Luca and hug him tightly.

He takes my phone, studying the picture I sent to Carly, Liliana, and Nicole. He collapses onto my shoulder, chortling with a belly laugh. "You sent a picture of your eyeball against my forehead." He bursts out howling.

"Blah ha ha." My body buzzes as alcohol swishes through my veins. It's possible I'm taking this *chaos theory–live like I have no regrets* thing too far, but I'm anxious about the upcoming reunion with my friends. Here's hoping the drinks calm my nerves.

Looking around, I see groups of people happily chatting. Bartenders dressed in tropical print shirts shake, blend, and pour island-themed cocktails from behind a large wood bar. It all bends and sways.

Nick Carter and Howie Dorough push their stools out.

"I better see you two in the front for the show. It starts in an hour." Howie steps next to Nick, and they walk toward the beach with their entourage.

The sky shimmers with streaks of pastel colors as the sun dips toward the horizon.

"Did the Backstreet Boys legit talk to us?" Luca tugs at the sleeve of my shirt. "Booyah!"

Glancing at him, I'm puzzled. He's like a frat boy in his navy-blue polo, khakis, and backward sun visor. "How are you a fan of nineties boy bands? You're like twenty-five years old." I run my eyes over his face, mesmerized by his chiseled jaw and luminous green eyes. "And you're here by yourself?"

He shrugs. "The girl I'm dating wasn't feeling it." Running his hand through his thick jet-black hair, he winks. "Nineties music has a vibe. I'm here for it. And my mom, she was a superfan." His face collapses. "Anyway." Turning in the other direction, he waves the bartender down for another round of drinks.

It clicks right away, and my stomach clenches. The sadness on his face is familiar. It's the same expression I made in the bridal gown store all those years ago when I tried on the perfect wedding dress and turned to see my mom's smile before remembering she wasn't there.

"My mom died when I was seventeen." The words fly out of my mouth, seeing Luca's devastated face. My heart jumps in my chest. I never share this with anyone, but I don't want him to grieve alone, the way I always do. I don't recall my friends crying a single tear after my mom's funeral.

Luca turns his face back toward mine. His shoulders round down. "Cancer," he whispers. "Eight years ago. She'd blast these tunes, belting out every word while she drove me to school, baseball…everywhere." He stares at his empty hands, clutching them together.

"Here are your drinks." The bartender interrupts the moment and puts two large, brown tumblers in front of us. He moves to a group of women who hand him matching purple Yetis that say, *Can't. Boy Bands. Bye.*

"I still can't believe we brought the same shit-brown cups." I laugh, giving Luca an out if he doesn't want to talk about his mom.

"Right!" Luca agrees. "It's like a mind meld."

"A mind what?" I continue, repeating his words under my breath, "Mind meld, mind meld."

"You know, like we share a brain. We both always order Amazon's overall pick. We think alike."

"Ohhhh! Yes, totally." It was just an hour ago that I ran into him here at the pool bar with my shit-brown-colored cup and we discovered our shared habit of ordering Amazon's overall pick. "We have a mind meld," I repeat. I turn to the woman sitting next to me. "Can you believe this guy and I have a mind meld?"

Her lips turn downward.

"This open-bar all-inclusive is fire!" Picking up a shot, Luca gulps the alcohol down. "Drink yours. Let's bounce. We need to be in the front of the pit for the show." He grabs our matching cups.

I stare at my shot. I should skip it. But then again, I'm embracing the chaos theory, hoping my uncharacteristic behavior will help me survive this trip with my friends. I swallow it down and then follow him to the stage.

A WARM BREEZE tickles my skin as the Backstreet Boys perform on a large stage set up in the sand next to the ocean. Every detail is perfect. Crashing waves, warm sand, the moon hanging in the background like a prop.

Nick Carter motions for Luca and me to join him on stage. I'm still tipsy from the tequila shot we did and wonder if I'm imagining it.

"Nick recognizes us from the bar!" Luca leads me through the crowded pit to where Nick's pointing, confirming it isn't alcohol playing tricks on me.

My feet kick the sand leading to the stage. A bouncer moves aside and lets us join where one of my favorite boy bands is performing "As Long as You Love Me." I feel like I'm floating above, watching an alternative version of myself. *Is this really happening?*

Nick puts his hand on my shoulder and then drops to one knee, as he and Howie serenade me with the song's sappy lyrics. My heart is beating so loudly I wonder if the entire audience can hear it. I focus on Nick's lips and let his voice transport me back to middle school. Beside me, Carly, Liliana, and Nicole pretend to slow dance with their crushes while the show *The Baby-Sitters Club* plays in the background. My mom's in the kitchen making Totino's Pizza Rolls. My heart is full. My heart is bouncing.

"Kiss her!"

I hear someone scream and turn my head away from Nick toward the electrified crowd. Every single person is staring at me. My entire body vibrates. I hate being the center of attention. I've preferred being background noise since experiencing the swirl of media coverage all those years ago. Kidnapping stories always captivate the public. Mine was no different, even though, in some ways, it was. People craved every detail, devouring it as if it were a fancy steak dinner.

Nick kisses me on the cheek. He waves goodbye, and the bouncer directs Luca and me off stage. The fans explode with applause, and the show ends. Adrenaline courses through me like I've just dodged a car accident.

"Mind completely blown!" Luca opens and closes his palms, mimicking an explosion.

"That was wild," I agree, as my anxiety and excitement settle.

"I know my mom made that happen." Luca glances at the sky and takes a deep breath. He closes his eyes. A few tears glisten in the corners.

My heart constricts. I know this pain.

He remains quiet for a moment. His thick, dark hair hangs slightly over his eyes. "Both of us lost our moms. It can't be a coincidence that we met."

I nod, uneasy about opening up. "Yeah, it is a weird connection."

His expression suddenly morphs into that of a young boy gripped by loss. Immediately, I picture Ethan and Everett, and my maternal instincts kick in. I make myself ask if he wants to talk about the very thing I refuse to discuss with anyone.

"I'd love to hear about your mom if you want to tell me."

Wiping his hand over his eyes, he smiles. But it's less a smile and more a half attempt to raise the corner of his lips. "Let's grab a bottle of tequila."

Relief washes over me. Maybe, like me, he'd rather skip a conversation about his mom. Maybe, like me, his friends moved on quickly instead of letting him sob in the dark while holding his hand.

Ten minutes later, we're sitting on the beach in a quiet area by the boathouse. Most of the crowd is eating from a large midnight breakfast buffet by the stage. The air is still. The silvery water laps gently in the moonlight.

"That show was epic." He takes a swig from the tequila bottle he convinced a bartender to give us. "We have to find someone who got us on video. I want to send it to my girlfriend." He stares at the ocean and passes me the bottle.

I take a small sip. I've had more alcohol tonight than I planned to have the entire trip. Being onstage, making a vacation friend, doing shots—all of it would shock Patton and my sons. I should rein it in before things get out of hand. The way they did after I ran away.

"So, who's the lucky girl?" I ask, circling back to Luca's comment. I'm glad we're not talking about our moms. I'm going to follow Luca's lead.

"Oh, girlfriend is too strong a word. It's a situationship. Keeping my options open." He winks in the shine of twinkling stars.

"I bet you've broken hundreds of hearts." Someone as gorgeous as Luca must be constantly fighting off the advances of others.

"Eh." He breathes out a sigh. "I'm more emotionally tuned in than most guys because of everything that happened with my mom. I'm sure you get what I mean."

My insides flutter as the topic of conversation turns.

"My mom was my ride or die." He picks up a handful of sand and lets it fall between his fingers. "And then I lost her at fourteen. Man, I wish she'd been around when I was a teenager. I got into a lot of trouble at first." He takes the tequila back, lifts it to his mouth, and gulps. "Woot woot! I can feel that hit my insides." His shoulders bounce up and down like he's trying to shake off the burn.

Watching him, I wonder about the trouble he got into. Is it possible that he would understand why I took my predawn walks, glad to replace my grief with fear? Is it possible he would understand why I jumped into that big rig? I want to ask more about his past, but I'm not brave enough to admit mine. And how could I tell a perfect stranger the mistakes I haven't admitted to my friends, and confess something I've never told my husband?

"But I'll tell you what," he continues. "My dad saved me."

I picture my dad after my mom's death, listlessly orbiting a life that lost its sun.

I grab the bottle again and take a large sip to dull the memory. "Your dad, he saved you." The rise in my inflection makes it clear my statement is a question.

"Yeah, my dad. He's the reason I kept going. He was the reason I had to be strong."

"What did your dad do?" Given my dad's breakdown, I'm eager to know how his dad helped him.

"What did he do?" His words have a sarcastic edge. "It's more like what he didn't do. He couldn't deal with anything for like five years after my mom died. I had to step up and take care of my younger siblings. I had to be strong for them."

Pausing, I try to wrap my head around his words. Having to step up and take care of his siblings makes sense when I think about it through the lens of motherhood. Over the years, I've had to rise above physical exhaustion and mental turmoil to care for my boys. The demands of raising children leave little time to feel or process overwhelming emotions.

But more than this understanding, I'm overcome with emotion, knowing Luca and I have had a similar experience. We both lost the support of our dads after our moms passed away. I feel deeply known and understood.

Then it hits me. It's a bond I've denied my marriage because I've never told Patton the whole truth.

"My dad shut down after my mom died too. Maybe I wouldn't have hurt all the people I love if I had siblings?" I'm surprised to hear myself say these words out loud. The buzzy warmth of the tequila must be setting in, dulling my inhibitions.

"I'm sorry," Luca says. "I have a lot of resentment toward my dad. He was supposed to take care of me. But I took care of everyone."

I think about Christmas and Memorial Day, the two times we see my dad each year. I've approached the visits as an opportunity for my dad and boys to spend time together. Not as a chance for us to reconcile.

Luca squints his eyes, and I wonder if he's holding back tears. "We should switch it up and talk about something else. Didn't mean to be a downer."

"Oh." I'm surprisingly disappointed he doesn't want to discuss the dark places we went. But then my simmering buzz opens my mind, and I understand I can talk about it if I want to. Luca would understand. I'm the one holding myself back. I'm the one who's kept the pain buried, allowing it to fester for over two decades.

At this very moment, I'm desperate to unload my past. It feels strangely safe to tell Luca the intimate details while we sit on the beach sharing a bottle of tequila in St. McAna. The slow beating in my heart turns to a rumble, and then a roar.

"I really messed up my life after my mom died." And then, I'm sobbing.

Luca embraces me in a firm hug. I lean my body against his solid frame. Tears spill from my eyes. I inhale, tasting the salty ocean air.

A second later, two women taking a midnight stroll appear. One stares at me with a mix of curiosity and disapproval. I'm sure she thinks Luca and I are hooking up. She doesn't understand I feel a kinship with Luca.

I pull out of his arms, and we watch as the women continue down the beach to the gazebo by the water.

"You okay?" he asks. "Let's talk about something else."

"Actually." I take another gulp of tequila. "I need to unload this weight I've been carrying. It's about the trouble I got into after my mom died. I was seventeen and a senior in high school." Oddly, this feels right. I'm not ashamed to open up.

"Hit it," Luca says. "Whatever happened, I'm here for it. I can handle it."

Squeezing my eyes shut, my body trembles like I'm standing on a cliff, trying to gather the courage to jump into the water below. I picture my toes dangling over the edge, and then I'm flying.

"Here's how my picture ended up on the front page of every newspaper in Southern California."

CHAPTER 13

Carly

Atlanta, GA
October 2nd ♫ Three Days Ago

"I HAVE TO FIND a drugstore," I lie, walking out of our hotel room's bathroom, determined to spy on Marco while we're in Atlanta. I doubt Nicole and Liliana will suspect anything anyway. Tomorrow's flight to St. McAna is at the crack of dawn. They're focused on getting a few hours of sleep. At our age, we need at least seven. *Under-eye gel patches aren't magic!*

"Oh no, what happened?" Liliana opens her suitcase and pulls out her pajamas.

"The joys of perimenopause." I know Liliana won't question me. We've both entered the alternate universe of hot flashes, night sweats, and irregular cycles.

"The upsides of having a hysterectomy." Nicole taps her abdomen and grins.

"You're lucky. I swear I never know when my period's coming." I lean into my storyline about needing to go to the drugstore. "Can I get the keys to our rental car?"

Nicole grabs her bag, searching. "Here." She tosses them to me.

Liliana's phone rings. "It's the girls." She opens the sliding door to the balcony and goes outside to take the call.

Perfect! I can get out of here without either of them asking more questions. Stuffing my Gucci belt bag into my tote, I swing it over my shoulder. "Text me if you think of anything you need me to get while I'm out."

Taking the elevator down to the lobby, I find the bathroom and pull out the black mini dress I stuffed in my tote. I change into the form-fitting dress and put enormous hoop earrings in my ears. I don't have a fleshed-out plan but start by sending Marco a text.

> **Me:** Funny we're both in Atlanta. Where r u staying

I wait a few minutes, hoping he'll divulge his location. I'm not sure what I'm going to do with the information, but I feel desperate to have it. I ponder what tasks should go on a to-do list for spying on your husband.

> **Marco:** Somewhere in midtown. I'll try to call later. In the middle of dinner at an awful Italian restaurant.

If there's one thing Marco's consistent about, it's his hatred of Americanized Italian food. "Spaghetti and meatballs aren't even a thing in Italy," he'd always say on the many nights we spent cooking homemade cavatelli, drinking wine, and snuggling together on the couch. But now, here I am trying to track him down to find out if he's cheating.

I do a quick Google search of the Hutchin Hotels in Midtown and see I'm only ten minutes away. Marco is a loyal Hutchin Hotel customer. He's been amassing points for years. I'm assuming this is where he's staying.

A plan takes shape in my mind. *Am I really going to sit at the hotel bar and spy on him?* But then again, we're both in Atlanta.

I send a text to Liliana and Nicole, so they don't wonder why my fake trip to the drugstore is taking longer than expected. They're probably half asleep by now anyway.

> **Me:** In a cool area of town. Going to take some photos I can use for @masterofmomfashion. I'll check in when I'm done.

Driving to the hotel, I make myself focus on the post I planned for today instead of the possibility that I may be about to catch Marco cheating. Today's #OOTD was supposed to showcase my top mom bikini pick in front of St. McAna's sparkling ocean. I tap the steering wheel, stressed that my posts are already off schedule. I can't lose any followers.

A little while later, I pull up to the hotel's valet and send another text to Marco. I need more information.

> **Me:** Oh nice. Where are you having dinner

Maybe the restaurant is close by and I can walk there. I take a large, gauzy, black scarf out of my tote and wrap it around my hair, letting the extra fabric drape over my shoulders. I find the bright pink lipstick I never wear and put a heavy coat on my lips. My attempt to disguise myself is ridiculous. *What am I doing?*

"Checking in?" The valet opens my car door.

"No, just getting a drink at the bar."

The valet nods with a weird expression. "Should I tell your friend to meet you there?"

I'm confused, but then I hear my phone ping. *Is it Marco?* Nervous energy ripples inside my chest.

"Sure." I rush off, anxious to read Marco's text.

Stepping inside, I pull out my phone. My heart sinks. The text is from Nicole.

> **Nicole:** You're sourcing Insta pics? Obvi 😬

Disappointed, I throw my phone back in my bag and walk by the check-in desk. The lobby is quiet and forgettable with its gray neutral décor. I picture myself grabbing one of the huge, silver, ceramic vases placed on the center table and hurling it at Marco and his colleague as they walk in. *Imagine their shock at getting caught!*

As I look around, I find a seat at the hotel bar that gives me a view of the hotel's entrance but is out of sight. I settle onto a stool, trying to look casual.

"What can I get you?" A hipster bartender hands me a drink menu, and I move on from my revenge fantasy.

"I'll have a club soda with lime." I keep my eyes fixed on the hotel's entrance, ignoring the way my heart keeps skipping a beat.

"Coming right up." He moves to a stack of clean glasses.

I inhale but feel short of breath. *This is insane.* And what will I do if Marco walks in with a woman by his side? I'm certainly not going to throw mass-produced cheap décor at their heads.

"One club soda with lime." The bartender places the drink down, but I keep my focus on the door. He turns his head toward the lobby, trying to figure out what's got my attention.

"Waiting for a friend?" he asks.

A crawling sensation climbs up my neck. "Yes, a friend." I glance at him. He's got one of those twisty, attention-getting mustaches that are popular with men in their twenties.

"Visiting from out of town?" he continues.

"Yes," I say, not wanting to chitchat.

I'm here to spy on my husband, and I'm in no mood for idle conversation. This guy's too young to comprehend the complexities of marriage. After twenty years together, Marco and I have learned to replace our lack of connection with the comfort of daily routines. As long as we stay on the hamster wheel of life, attending Bianca's soccer games, focusing on our clients, and shopping at Costco, our loneliness stays contained safely under the surface. But any blowup to our monotonous, expected routine, and boom, our mutual frustration and contempt explodes. I'm still reeling from the things Marco said after the Taylor Swift ticket fiasco. He made me feel stupid and then took it one step farther by calling me out for pretending our life is perfect.

A portly older man walks into the bar area and takes a seat on the other side. He nods and gives me a sly smile. There's something creepy about his slicked-back hair and macho energy. My shoulders stiffen as his eyes take me in.

The bartender approaches his new customer, taking the man's focus off me.

A few more minutes tick by. So far, I've only seen a family and an older lady enter the hotel. Checking my phone, I realize I've been gone for over an hour. I'll need to leave soon, or Liliana and Nicole could get suspicious. I'm equally relieved and disappointed I haven't spotted Marco.

Should I text him again? I'm unsure what to say and toss around some ideas. *What client are you meeting with? Are you flying home tomorrow? Are you here with any colleagues? Are you fucking someone else?*

As I imagine Marco's stunned face after reading my imaginary texts, the bartender interrupts me. "I think the friend you've been waiting for is here." He eyes the cheesy man across the bar.

The man winks at me.

"What?" I'm confused. Then I remember the weird way the valet also mentioned something about me meeting a friend. *What's going on?*

But before I can ask, the cheesy man walks over and sits on the stool next to me. He leans so close that I can see several coarse, black nose hairs sticking out from his left nostril. "You're prettier than the picture. And much prettier than the girl they sent last time."

"What are you talking about?" I snap.

The man must have noticed the bewildered expression on my face. He stares at the bartender like he's given away the nuclear codes.

"My apologies, sir. I must be mistaken."

The cheesy man's face morphs into an expression of fury as a woman in lacy black stockings and a tiny red bandage dress appears. Her outfit makes it easy to make assumptions about why she's here. I could be wrong, but given the circumstances, I'm confident she's a high-end call girl, here to see the grotesque man seated next to me.

I swivel my head between her, the cheesy man, and the bartender. *This is fucking unreal. They think I'm a hooker out on a job!*

My hand reflexively moves to my mouth, wiping off my bright pink lipstick. Jumping up from the stool, I pull down my tight dress and flee the hotel.

CHAPTER 14

Angie

Emerald Jewel All-Inclusive Resort
October 3rd ♫ Two Days Ago

O BNOXIOUSLY LOUD VOICES bounce down the hallway leading to my hotel room. I recognize the sound. My head throbs against my skull. I just puked for the second time this morning. There's no way I can play nice with the high school gang, particularly because Carly tricked me into coming. I've contemplated confronting her, but that would unleash a lot of drama I'd rather avoid.

Vague memories of last night flash through my mind. Nick pulled Luca and me up on stage, and then Nick serenaded me. After that, things get fuzzy.

For a moment, my heart rocks in my chest. Did I do something stupid with gorgeous young Luca? I'd never cheat on Patton, and Luca feels like a son, not a romantic interest. But then it all comes flooding back. The show ended, but we continued drinking and had our heart-to-heart on the beach. Afterward, I could barely walk straight. Luca brought me to my room. As he turned to leave, I jolted out of bed and threw up in the toilet. I could hear him pacing outside the bathroom door.

"You alright?" he asked.

"Let yourself out," I mumbled. "I feel dumb. I drank too much."

But the truth was not that I felt dumb. The truth was that I felt immense guilt for telling Luca what I'd never shared with my husband. Motionless on the bathroom floor, I recalled Patton's quizzical look after Rowan's dinner. He knew I had fled to the bathroom because I was triggered. But he didn't understand why. Then I puked again.

"Are you sure I should go?" Luca asked. "You're in bad shape."

"Yes, I'll be okay," I said, pressing my cheek against the cold tile. "Cool."

A few minutes later, I heard the door to my room scrape as Luca left.

"Angieee!!" High-pitched squeals from the hallway leap forward, bringing my focus back to this morning's hangover. *There's no getting out of this.*

"Angie! Open up!" Carly bangs her fist against the door like a cop busting a drug ring.

My body sinks further into the mattress. Getting out of bed seems as impossible as solving the Riemann Hypothesis, a math problem with a one-million-dollar prize.

"Angie, we made it. Let us in." Liliana's commanding voice makes my eardrums pulse.

I take a deep breath, struggling to get up. Standing, I steady myself for the ambush of faces that are about to surround me. I drag myself to the door and open it. Three smiling faces I haven't seen in ten years stand before me. My heart fills with affection, but it quickly dissolves, remembering the way I hurt them. I force myself to half-smile.

"Ang," they sing out my name like a one-hit wonder.

I scrunch my eyes closed. Arms encircle my shoulders, and freshly glossed lips kiss my cheeks.

Carly speaks in a shrill voice right by my ears. "The three of us talked about it, and we want to get the elephant out of the room. Yes, we haven't seen you in ten years, and we're happy you're here. But we're not getting sappy on you because we know you'd hate that." Carly pulls back and examines my face. "Oh, you look hungover."

My body tenses as my eyes sweep over her thick blond hair and trendy clothes. *Not everyone can be perfect like you.*

"Yeah," Liliana chimes in before I can say anything. "We were worried about you…hammered and hanging out with some random guy."

"Who was that smoke show?" Nicole winks. "Get it, girl!" She bumps her hip against mine and then plops herself on my bed. A curtain of copper-colored bangs hangs around her eyes. But something else is different about her. It takes me a minute to realize she's half the size she used to be.

"I've got to pee. I swear, since I've turned forty, the only time I don't have to pee is when I'm peeing." Liliana goes into the bathroom while Carly walks out of my hotel room's door.

"Our rooms aren't ready." She rolls in an enormous, shiny pink suitcase. "We'll keep our bags in here. I'm putting on my bathing suit. Let's get changed and go to the beach."

"Whoa, tough night last night." Liliana exits the bathroom holding her nose. "How do you feel?" She walks over to the thick, coral-colored blackout curtains covering the sliding door to my balcony and pulls them open.

My eyes water from the bright light. I want to scream. These women have been in my room for over five minutes, and I haven't spoken one word.

"Glad we made it," Liliana continues. "What an ordeal. A canceled flight, a rental car, chili dogs. I need a drink immediately." She pulls her golden curls out of a hair tie, and they fall around her face.

"Go off, homie." Nicole eyes Liliana as she rolls her suitcase inside next to Carly's.

"Oh, ignore her," Carly laughs. "She talks like she's a sixteen-year-old. We told her she's ridiculous."

Nicole playfully sticks her tongue out at Carly, who claps her hands like she's a kindergarten teacher trying to get her students to come inside after recess.

"Get moving, ladies. I need to make my outfit of the day post, and I want to do it in front of the ocean."

Why does she always take charge? Less than ten minutes into our vacation, and I already sense tension. I shuffle into the walk-in closet to get some space. Looking around, I can feel my eyes bulging. It's like a toddler's ransacked the space. My shoes are scattered in unmatched pairs. The black palazzo pants I wore last night are rolled into a ball in the corner. And most of my clean clothes are on the ground. *Strange.*

I pick up my black tankini from the floor and pull on my bathing suit, trying to remember why my closet is as messy as Ethan and Everett's room.

Carly pops her head in before I come up with anything.

"Boundaries," I snip. It's the first word I've said.

"Oh, please. I've seen you naked at least five hundred times. Remember all those sleepovers where we would dress up like Cinderella?"

Sadness mixes with elation remembering the day my mom gave my friends and me a treasure chest filled with crystal-encrusted crowns, plastic high-heeled dress-up shoes, and jewel-colored Disney princess dresses. An image of my mom's wide smile crashes through my mind, almost knocking me over. For a moment I feel justified, leaving Hamilton Beach and its painful memories, but then Patton's words echo in my mind. *Your friends are the last connection you have to where you grew up.* I need to lighten up if I'm going to get through the next few days.

Carly stares at me, waiting for me to corroborate her memory. But then she tilts her head, distracted by my bathing suit. "Nothing says middle-aged mom like a black tankini."

Seriously, she's a pain. But she's right about this. I can't help but laugh. Perhaps we will get along on this trip. Perhaps we can move forward without rehashing the past.

"You should wear one of my bikinis. I have a mint-green one that would look great with your olive complexion and brown hair. Have I ever explained how to use a color wheel to determine the best colors to wear for your skin tone?"

"Um, black is my best color. I'm still suffering from PTSD from those yellow dresses you made us wear to prom."

We both giggle, and for a split second the broken part of our relationship disappears. She reaches out like she's about to grab my hand but then stops herself as if the hurt between us is a strong gust of wind pushing her palm away.

She steps back, putting space between us. "Fine, stick with your granny bathing suit." She shrugs, looking around the messy closet. "What happened in here? You should hang your clothes and keep your outfits organized." She points to various items on the floor, reminding me I still haven't figured out what happened.

"Save it for one of your Insta posts." Liliana peeks her head of curls inside the closet. "Where's your safe? I want to put my wallet and passport inside."

"Oh, good idea," Carly agrees. She zips open a large Gucci belt bag and takes out her wallet.

"And me too." Nicole walks into the already crowded closet.

I move aside the clothes still hanging in the closet to open the safe built into the wall. "What in the hell?" Jumping back, I clasp my hand over my mouth.

"What's wrong?" Carly moves beside me, looking at the safe.

"Why is it open?" Panic makes my stomach flip. Glancing into the safe, I see my wallet unzipped, and the cash I brought to tip the resort staff strewn about.

"What's wrong?" Carly asks, unsure why I'm freaking out.

"Why is the safe open? Why is all my stuff spilled out? This is not how I left it." My heart pounds.

"Huh?" Carly asks, confused.

I pick up my passport wallet and open it. "And oh my God. Where's my passport?"

CHAPTER 15

Carly

Emerald Jewel All-Inclusive Resort
October 3rd ♫ Two Days Ago

#OOTD: Iconic leopard print triangle top bikini. Lightweight silk cream cover-up with chain-link print and slide sandals. Black oversized chunky rectangular sunglasses. Raffia-effect tote bag. Large-brimmed straw hat with embroidered black and white band. Black canvas Gucci belt bag with large initial motif.

"WHAT DO YOU mean? Where's your passport?" My mind flashes with an image of Bianca's face after we learned our Taylor tickets were fake. Angie has the same shocked expression.

"Someone ransacked my closet. And opened my safe. Why is my stuff everywhere?" She frantically searches through the dollar bills and credit cards. "I don't see my passport. I put it in here yesterday, knowing I wouldn't need it until I flew home."

She holds up a cheap, light-blue leather passport case with a white airplane embossed on the cover. But the place where her passport should be is empty. A queasy feeling churns in my gut remembering I couldn't hide how I was scammed.

Liliana and Nicole huddle around us.

"Do you think someone broke into your room? Or maybe it was the resort staff?" Nicole rummages through the safe. Her distressed face triggers vivid memories of the police questioning us after the first kidnapping note arrived.

> *Angie did not vanish. I have her. I'm taking good care of your beautiful little girl.*

Suddenly I'm in the woods outside Hamilton Beach watching search and rescue dogs track Angie's scent. I failed to protect her back then. I will not let that happen again.

"Let's not jump the gun." Liliana stays composed. "You were drunk and out of your mind last night. It's possible you moved things around and don't remember. Let's search every inch of this room."

As always, Liliana downplays the concerning situation.

"This can't be happening." Angie throws her arms up into the air. Her words sound emphatic, but her eyes dart back and forth, making it seem like she's unsure. Like she's trying to put the pieces together. I bet she's combing through every detail she can remember, the same way I did when trying to figure out how I trusted a stranger enough to Venmo their account a ridiculous amount of cash. An account that disappeared after I was conned.

"Tell us more about last night. What did you do after the show ended?" I lead everyone out of the closet. I need to figure this out for Angie. I won't let her down.

She sits on the corner of her bed. Her body sags inward. Burying her face in her hands, she covers her eyes. "It can't be."

"Did you remember something?" Liliana asks.

Angie drops her hands from her eyes. "There's absolutely no chance."

"No chance, what?" I ask.

"Luca. He walked me back to my room. Came inside for a few minutes. I was throwing up in the bathroom. I told him to leave."

"The kid you were hanging out with last night? He was in this room? While you were drunk?" Liliana's using her high-power lawyer voice.

"Lay off, Liliana," Angie says. "There's no way he has anything to do with this. He's here because his mom died, and she loved nineties boy bands."

Liliana, Nicole, and I give each other a look, recognizing the strange coincidence that this guy Luca claims to have lost his mom, like Angie. Are they thinking what I'm thinking?

"Hmph." I can't help but express my disbelief. "He sounds like a scammer. A young, good-looking, twenty-ish-year-old shows up at a weekend meant for women old enough to need hormone replacement therapy. I think he's working an angle." It occurs to me that Angie's just like her mom was, always believing the best about people.

Angie's eyebrows furrow together, exacerbating the fine lines on her forehead. "Just because you fell for that Taylor ticket scam doesn't mean that's what's happening here."

Embarrassment makes my face heat. "We should go find him." I redirect everyone's attention away from the ticket scam. *Always keep the focus on other people's problems!* "We need to confront Luca."

"No, we are not doing that. It has nothing to do with him." Angie crosses her arms.

Really? It's been less than thirty minutes, and Angie and I are already disagreeing. My heart sinks, knowing we are right back where we left off after the Miraval trip.

"It's all in the way you approach him," Nicole says. "Be mindful. Be demure. Ask casually what happened and don't accuse him of anything." She places her hand on Angie's shoulder.

"What does *be demure* even mean?" I snap, annoyed that Nicole's trying to be funny to defuse a serious situation. Some things never change.

Angie shakes her head. "There's no way I'm doing that."

"Fine then. I'll handle it." Here I am, breaking my promise to myself and getting into it with Angie on day one, hour one. It's frustrating. But I'm determined to right past wrongs. I will not let her be a victim. Angie needs to seize this chance. I'd love to confront the deviant who stole my money and broke Bianca's heart. "Nicole, come with me."

Instead of listening, Nicole takes a seat next to Angie on the bed. "I'm going to stay here and keep searching. Maybe Angie's passport is under one of her orthopedic shoes or something."

My pulse skyrockets hearing her make another untimely joke.

She gently leads Angie back to the closet.

"Well," I look at Liliana like she's left her ringer on during the school play. "Are you coming? Someone needs to back me up."

Liliana nods. "I've perfected a combo of chutzpah and humility that will be just right in this situation." She pulls off her Spanx AirEssentials hoodie, a product I've posted about several times, and ties it around her waist. "Let's go."

We take hurried steps, making our way to the lobby. It's empty. Rounding the pathway that leads outside, we glance at people on lounge chairs. I scan a group sitting at the swim-up bar but don't see Luca.

"Over there?" Liliana points to an area of tall palm trees lined with luxurious, dark wood cabanas. The space is a perfect tropical oasis.

Walking by, we still don't see Luca.

"He shouldn't be hard to find." I pull up one of the pictures Angie sent us. "He's the youngest person here and practically the only man."

As I say the words out loud, I'm even more convinced Luca's a con artist. *Why is a kid born a decade after boy bands here?* My suspicions heighten as my eyes bounce around, searching.

"I don't see him." Liliana shrugs.

"Me either. Let's try the beach."

We pass a group of women doing water aerobics led by one of the resort's male entertainment staff. The song "No Diggity" blares.

"Squeeze your booty and jump," the instructor orders as the women in the pool fawn over the leader's hard, muscular body.

"Let's go down there." I point to a crowded area of lounge chairs on the beach, next to a small boathouse. The warm sand coats my feet as we get closer.

"There he is." Liliana points to Luca, who's sitting on the edge of a chair with a girl who looks around twenty.

"That's weird." We walk closer. "Angie said he was here by himself. Do you think he was lying and came here with this girl to scam older women?"

"What?" Liliana's eyebrows rise. "I'm not into conspiracy theories."

Unbelievable! Nothing ever fazes her. All she did after Angie's mom died was explain the stages of grief, as if Angie's mom's death was a challenging test Angie had to study for. But why does her comment about conspiracy theories feel like a dig? This has nothing to do with spending four thousand dollars on fake Taylor tickets. Something about this Luca situation isn't sitting right.

"Can you wait for me to go to the bathroom?" Liliana asks, walking toward the boathouse. "I can't hold it."

"But you just went." I'm annoyed.

"And I'll have to go again in twenty minutes."

"Fine. It will give me a chance to observe Luca and this girl for a few minutes."

I slip on my sunglasses so they can't tell I'm staring. They continue talking and laughing in a flirtatious way. It's hard to tell if they're familiar with each other or just getting acquainted.

The minutes tick by. What's taking Liliana so long? I'm hot and sweaty, possibly from the tropical sun, but more likely a hot flash. I watch as a waiter approaches, handing Luca and the girl frozen drinks.

Another few minutes pass, and my impatience overwhelms me. This trip is starting off on the wrong foot. I wanted everything to be perfect, but it's already a dumpster fire. I don't need to wait for Liliana.

Tightening the sash on my cover-up, I stomp through the sand and walk directly up to Luca and the girl. "Hey, it's Luca, right?" I dig my feet into the soft ground beneath me.

"Facts." He flashes a gorgeous smile in my direction.

"So, I'm a friend of Angie's. You were hanging out with her last night."

He beams back at me, and for a moment I'm lost in his jade-green eyes. "Angie's the GOAT."

Ugh, this stupid slang. Where's Nicole when I need her?

"Angie, yeah, she's cool." He rephrases his statement, clearly aware I have no clue what GOAT means.

"Anyway. Can we find a place to chat?" I watch his facial expression to see if he seems rattled.

He doesn't seem shaken, just curious. "What's up?"

"Everything's fine." I lie. "Can we talk?"

The young girl sits up. Her white string bikini barely covers her sun-kissed body and leaves nothing to the imagination. I want to lecture her on the importance of sunscreen to avoid wrinkles and sunspots later in life, but I have more important things on my mind.

"Go ahead." She gives him a coy smile.

"Okay." He winks at her and stands.

We walk a few feet away, toward the boathouse. I'm kind of wishing Liliana were here now that I'm about to confront Luca. She'd be better at taking the right approach. This is the exact situation where her levelheaded demeanor is an asset.

"Angie told us you helped her get back to her room last night." We stop in the shade provided by the boathouse's decaying roof.

He nods but doesn't say anything.

"What happened when you got back?" I continue.

"Um, what happened?" he repeats my question. "Nothing. She puked, and I left."

I read his body language, trying to determine if he's telling the truth. My spy instincts resurface, reminding me of last night when I tried to catch Marco cheating. *That was a disaster.*

"I think there may be more to the story." My tone is thick with accusation.

"Huh?" He sounds agitated. "Nothing happened. We did not hook up, if that's what you're implying."

"That's not what I'm implying." Now I'm wishing I'd waited for Liliana. *How long does it take to pee?*

"Well, what are you asking me?" His eyes shift away from my face, focusing on the small forklift parked in the sand next to some construction materials.

"I'm going to be blunt. Her passport is missing. Someone dumped out her wallet."

His eyes jerk back and lock with mine. "What the hell? Are you accusing me? I had nothing to do with it."

"Yeah, maybe I'm accusing you. You're the only one who's been in her room. And honestly, I'm curious why someone your age is on a boy band trip. Seems like the perfect chance to pull a scam on older women." Con artists like him need to be held accountable for their crimes.

"Lady, you're crazy. I'm out." He steps around me, walking past the boathouse.

"Don't walk away! I'll speak to resort security if I have to." I pause, searching for words that let him know I'm not backing down. "Just so you know, my husband's a detective. I can have him make some calls." I leave out that Marco investigates cybercrimes for maximum impact.

"Your husband." He gapes at me. "Man, do I feel sorry for him being married to a mental case like you." He turns back toward the beach and leaves me standing there.

A mental case. I'm immediately overtaken by an image of myself sitting at the bar last night and being mistaken for a hooker. All to spy on Marco, who hasn't bothered to call or text since I asked him where he was having dinner last night.

It's hard to believe that, only six months ago, he sent me the app *couplehood* asking me to join. *It will be a fun way to reignite our romance,* he texted with a heart-eyes emoji, but I ignored the message. There was no way I was going to download some stupid app with daily quizzes and questions that claimed it could help us gain a deeper understanding of each other.

I can feel my eyes roll at the memory before I let it evaporate into thin air. I'm not going to think about my marriage. Instead, I'm going to focus on finding out what happened to Angie's passport.

CHAPTER 16

Liliana

Emerald Jewel All-Inclusive Resort
October 3rd 🎵 Two Days Ago

USING ALL MY weight, I press my shoulder against the decaying bathroom door. It doesn't budge. It's been over fifteen minutes since I left Carly on the beach. Isn't she wondering what happened to me? I should've found a different bathroom after reading the sign on the boathouse. *Do not enter, construction workers only.* But I was about to pee in my pants. When I walked inside, I found my way to this grimy toilet and closed the door behind me. As I peed, I couldn't help but wonder if there's such a thing as Botox for your bladder.

Banging on the door now, I scream out Carly's name, hoping she'll hear me. I've texted several times. For a moment, I consider calling my secretary in California so he can contact the front desk. Charlie is forever coming to my rescue. Usually, to warn me that Amanda's stomping down the hall in a rage.

Josh never misses a chance to point out that Charlie's my "work husband." It always seemed playful, but maybe it's not.

My mind slides back to his strained face the other night when he told me *I'm done waiting around for you to find the balance.* What did he mean? I would have asked if Amanda hadn't called and interrupted. I would have asked if he had been home yesterday when I spoke to the girls. But now that I'm approaching our marriage with the detached seriousness of a significant legal case, I'm developing a strategy. First, I need to tell him I spoke with our new hire, and she's ready to jump in and alleviate my workload. Next, I need to dive into the self-help book I bought at the Atlanta airport. From there, I will make a list of key facts supporting the narrative that our marriage can overcome this impasse and move forward. It's clear the only way I am going to get through this is to keep my emotions out of it.

I shove away my sadness, thinking of all the empty promises I've made, saying I'll find work-life balance after the next project, promotion, or work crisis. But each time I'm about to tell Amanda I need to scale back, I see my mom's face and am hit by my lifelong fear of disappointing her.

Suddenly, my phone rings. Relief courses through my body.

"Liliana, where are you?" Angie asks.

"I'm stuck in the bathroom in the boathouse."

A moment later, I hear feet shuffling inside.

"We're here." Carly's voice travels through the warped bathroom door. She jiggles the handle, but the door doesn't open.

"Shoot." Angie lets out a frustrated breath. "The door's stuck."

I can't help but laugh. "No kidding."

"Let me find something to help push it open. Stand back."

"Oy vey."

I'm unsure what Angie's doing, so I move back, standing next to a rusted-out sink. I snap at the bracelet Esther gave me. *Snap. Snap. Snap.* I should be home with her and Evie, not trapped in a dingy bathroom thousands of miles away. My regret pounds in sync with the heavy object striking the door. I watch the center swell with each blow, before it finally creaks open. Angie tosses a paddle to the side.

"We found you!" Carly and Angie grasp my arms and pull me into the center of the boathouse near an old rowboat.

"Didn't you read the *do not enter* sign?" Clearly, Carly's annoyed.

"Who cares?" Angie stares at Carly like she's a cat about to pounce on its prey. "I can't believe you accused Luca of stealing my passport. What happened to taking a soft approach, like Nicole suggested?"

Uh-oh, these two always find something to argue about on these trips. Now I understand why I haven't seen Angie in ten years. Carly keeps punishing her for cutting us out of her life.

"Yes, I accused him. You didn't find your passport. He took it." Carly's eyes roll like Esther's do when I tell her she doesn't need another Lululemon top.

"He didn't take it," Angie says through gritted teeth. "I need to find him." She storms out of the boathouse.

Carly and I follow. Angie glances at the people on beach chairs a few feet away until she spots him sitting alone. I wonder where the girl in the white bikini went.

"I'm going to talk to Luca. Don't even think about coming with me." She frowns at Carly and turns toward the beach.

"Angie." Carly reaches for her arm but then hesitates. "Don't engage with him. I'm sure he stole your passport. You should report him to security."

Angie's eyes pop wide open. They look like they're going to fall out of their sockets. "Are you crazy? He's here mourning his mother, and you're accusing him of stealing. You should be ashamed of yourself." She plods toward Luca.

Carly shifts her gaze to the ground. It seems like she's avoiding eye contact while getting over the sting of Angie's reaction. Or maybe she's connecting the dots between Luca and Angie's stories. It's a strange coincidence that they both lost their moms at a young age. If this isn't a scam, it's hitting close to home.

When Carly looks at me again, she pleads for support. "I'm trying to fix this."

"You're known for that," I say.

"Helping friends isn't a crime." Carly's voice vibrates with anger. "Don't you think he took it?"

"You and Angie need to have a heart-to-heart."

"That's not what this is about! Luca stole Angie's passport. We have to help her. We have a chance to help her."

When she says the last bit, I get it. Right away, I think about how we didn't realize Angie was putting on a smile, pretending, all those years ago. An uncomfortable sensation bubbles inside me. Cupping my hand over my eyes, I peer down the beach at Luca and Angie. She has her hand on his shoulder, and he's nodding along while she speaks.

"I don't know. I guess it's possible that he took it. But it could be a misunderstanding."

"Fine," Carly grumbles. "Why does everyone treat me like I'm a QAnon conspiracy theorist since the Taylor ticket mess? Scammers exist. People steal and take advantage."

Why's Carly unhinged? Maybe Nicole's right. Something's off.

"Ugh! Nothing gets to you, Liliana. It's not normal."

Not normal? I always thought of my ability to stay levelheaded and squelch my emotions as a superpower. Her anger's excessive, but I will not let it get under my skin. See! She's benefiting from the very levelheadedness she's angry about.

"The world's not overrun with cheaters." I try to comfort her. But instead of it bringing things down a notch, her eyes prick with tears. "Are you okay?" I ask. "Why are you upset?"

Carly wipes her eyes. "Forget it. Where's Nicole?" she asks, changing the subject.

I don't push her to say more, knowing she's too focused on upholding her perfect image. She'd never tell me if her life was going sideways. It's surprising she told us about the Taylor concert.

"Nicole's talking to Laura. She said she had to take the call."

"Laura?" Carly asks, her voice rising. "Laura only calls if she's trying to sell you property."

"I know. We used to be good friends, but now she gets on my nerves. She's either pitching me on a new house or talking about that Facebook page she started for the Hamilton Beach Moms. She's always had an agenda. Even back in high school."

"So true." Carly laughs, and I'm glad to see her relax. "Do you think Nicole and Garrett want to move? Why else would she be talking to Laura?"

I shrug and feel my face tense. Josh has mentioned that Nicole's unhappy enough times that, for a split second, I wonder if she and Garrett are putting their house up for sale and divorcing. But the thought is illogical, so I dismiss it.

Carly's eyes cloud with worry. "Is something going on with Nicole and Garrett? I mean statistically, two of us will end up divorced." Her voice wobbles.

"Divorce?" My expression obviously gave away my strange thought.

Now Carly's anxious, and I am too. While I know Josh and Nicole confide in each other as they coordinate playdates and carpool duty, I can't imagine Nicole would tell Josh that her marriage is ending before she told me. *Or would she?* My heart beats erratically.

"Is Garrett cheating on her?"

I suck in a breath, startled by Carly's question. "Cheating? Why did your brain go there?"

Her face freezes like she's forcing her features to appear neutral. But before she can tell me why she jumped to cheating, "Manic Monday" is playing on my phone.

Carly peers at my beach bag as if the song is a magnet pulling her eyes forward. "Your boss again. She knows you're on vacation, right?"

I nod, humiliated, pulling out my phone.

"Don't answer it." Carly places her hand on my phone and waits to see if I resist. When I don't, she takes it and drops it in her belt bag.

The phone continues to ring, then hangs up and rings again. I move forward, defeated that I'm not willing to ignore it. Amanda's always pushing, pushing, pushing, the same way my mom did.

Carly lifts her palm with the universal sign for stop. The ringing subsides, but then my phone pings with several text alerts.

"You're on vacation." Carly moves back, and I let her.

Right now, Carly's putting up a boundary my mom never allowed. Sure, when I'm working on a case, I can be as cutthroat as the next person. But because of my mom, I lose my edge with Amanda. History repeats itself.

Carly takes another step back with my phone in her bag, and I let her do what I can't. I picture Amanda's face, furious with anger that she can't reach me.

And then a strange thought enters my mind. Maybe the only way to change this toxic situation is to get fired. Would I let it go that far?

CHAPTER 17

Nicole

Emerald Jewel All-Inclusive Resort
October 3rd 🎵 Two Days Ago

"**T**HANKS, LAURA. SOUNDS dope."

"Yes, it's the perfect idea for this next chapter!" Laura's voice beats with excitement. "But we'll talk more when you're back in Hamilton Beach."

After hanging up, I stash my phone in the pocket of my Free People flirty athletic shorts and take a deep breath. Things with Josh are happening fast. Maybe too fast. Although we have a plan and have run through different scenarios, our lives could blow up. And now that things are picking up speed, it's getting harder to be around Liliana. Every time I see her, my stomach flips.

Shoving my hands in my pockets, I ignore my anxiety, and walk through the open-air lobby to the pool, looking for my friends. This is a problem for after St. McAna.

A woman limps by me while her friend lectures her. "We're too old for high heels. You should've at least worn platforms last night."

I swallow a laugh thinking about how different things are now compared to when we first started these trips in our twenties. Back then, we brought thongs and body glitter. Now we pack hundred-dollar retinol serums and gray hair cover spray.

When I reach the beach, I head toward a small bar nestled in the sand. Guests sway back and forth on wood swings, in the place where there would normally be stools. My face breaks into a smile. This beach bar understood the assignment. But as I walk closer, I don't see my friends. Peering down the shoreline, I find Carly and Liliana standing by a broken-down boathouse. Why are they over there, and where's Angie?

Sand creeps over my toes as I walk over. "What's up?"

Carly and Liliana give me death stares. "It's been crazy since we got here," Liliana says. "First with Angie's missing passport, and then I got locked…"

Before Liliana can finish, Angie's standing next to us, with Luca by her side. I have to smother a gasp when I see him up close. He's tall, with golden skin and broad shoulders. His turquoise swim trunks sit low on his waist, showing off each chiseled row of his perfect abs. He's got serious rizz.

"We're going to the karaoke party by the pool." He puts his hand into a fist and pretends it's a microphone.

A tingly feeling spreads through my body. This guy's a total thirst trap.

"Yes, can't wait." Angie claps her hands together. "And I told Luca no one thinks he stole my passport." The face Angie gives Carly screams: *Don't you dare say a word.*

Whoa, what did I miss? Cue the drama.

"Go ahead to karaoke." Carly's words sound like ice. "I'm going to talk with the front desk about your missing passport." She emphasizes the word *missing*, making sure we know she doesn't agree.

I'm spot-on. The heat between them is turning up full blast. I'm not surprised, remembering the way the staff at Miraval's Life in Balance Spa couldn't get those two to stop throwing shade so others could relax. It's wild knowing that, back in the day, they used to spend every minute together, braiding each other's hair, baking Angie's mom's chocolate chip cookies, and watching endless hours of *Clarissa Explains It All* and *My So-Called Life*.

Luca's eyes narrow, listening to Carly's insinuation that he stole Angie's passport, and an awkward silence hangs in the air. He's fuming, but I would be too if someone accused me of stealing.

"Give this a try." A waiter approaches with a tray of frozen cocktails, cutting the tension.

"Slay." I'm ready to throw back my first beverage.

"What is it?" Carly asks, eyeing the pink, green, and yellow layered frozen drink.

"It's the St. McAna Mai Tai." The waiter's voice bounces like a song. "Delicious." He pushes the tray toward us.

"Oh, yes," Angie giggles. "We had this last night!" She smiles at Luca, who takes two drinks from the tray, handing her one. They stare at each other like naughty toddlers plotting to spill a massive tub of LEGO pieces.

"Boss!" I grab one. "But this is the smallest cup I've ever seen."

"Yes, you need your tumbler." Luca grins at Angie. "Preferably a shit-brown one."

They crack up.

"Hmm, seems like an inside joke," I say.

But instead of explaining, Luca pulls Angie forward. "Let's go. We need to pick our songs. I'm doing 'The Hardest Thing' by 98 Degrees!"

"Tsk tsk." Carly shakes her head after they walk away. "How's Angie going to get home without a passport? I'm going to the front desk." She stares at us as if we're supposed to respond. "Is anyone coming with me?"

Classic Carly. She always puts herself in charge. Like when she gave Liliana and me a color-coded activities schedule to keep Angie busy twenty-four seven after her mom's funeral. As if shopping at Claire's for new earrings and then eating dinner at the Pizza Hut buffet would somehow make Angie forget her mom died. No thanks. I'm not boarding that train again.

"I need to relax," I say.

Liliana remains quiet.

Carly's eyes bulge, annoyed that neither Liliana or I will go with her. But a nap on the beach is the best move for calming down after my conversation with Laura. Are Josh and I going to continue what we started at the playground a few months ago?

"Unbelievable," Carly huffs. "Why am I the only one concerned about Angie's missing passport?"

Carly's pouty face reminds me of Chelsea's when I pull away the candy she's grabbed in the grocery store checkout line. Placing chocolate bars within a toddler's reach is a brilliant marketing strategy. I see you, Hershey's.

"Let's let things play out until this afternoon," Liliana says, always chill. "Maybe her passport will show up."

"I'm going to find someone to report this to." Carly stomps toward the lobby.

I make no move to join her. I'll let her do her thing and stay on the sidelines. Fun over drama any day! Especially while on vacay away from my kids. Although I'd be lying if I didn't admit to missing them. I make a mental note to FaceTime them later.

"Wait, my phone." Walking toward Carly, Liliana points to the Gucci belt bag lying against Carly's waist but then stops mid-step. "Actually, do you mind bringing it upstairs to your room? I'm on vacation. I'm not taking any more calls from my boss."

Wow, Liliana's going to ignore her boss? Josh warned me she'd be getting calls every second. I get why he's had it. It's crazy how much we've opened up to each other. It started when he asked me if Liliana ever complained about Amanda.

"Not really," I admitted, unable to remember the last time I spent time with Liliana solo.

From there, it felt easy to talk to Josh about my marriage and how I have to give Garrett a play-by-play of the kids' needs, and when he completes one little task, he looks at me like he should receive the best dad of the year award. What Garrett doesn't understand is that I need him to think about the larger context. The reasons behind all the little tasks. That's the ten-ton weight pressing on my shoulders every day. But my tongue gets twisted every time I try to explain this.

Carly gives Liliana a firm nod. "Sure, I'll bring it to my room. I'm glad Amanda won't be able to reach you." She walks away.

Oh, shoot. Now I'm solo with Liliana. I messed up. I'm afraid of getting into a conversation and letting something slip.

"Come on, let's go find beach chairs." Liliana gently pulls me forward before I can come up with an excuse to go with Carly.

My heart drops. But I don't want her to think I'm avoiding her. "Sure." I follow behind her.

"Two chairs in the shade, please." Liliana smiles when we reach the resort's waterfront staff.

An older teen with short cornrows leads us to a large, bright-blue umbrella attached to a permanent wood base. He unfurls thick blue-and-white striped towels and tucks them into our lounge chairs.

"Press this button if you need anything." He points to what looks like a doorbell built into the wooden base of the umbrella. "It's like the flight attendant call button on a plane."

"Cool!" Liliana slides her hand over the button, then slips him a five-dollar bill.

Lying down on my lounge chair, I sink into the cushy towel and try to push today's drama out of my mind. I take the last sip of my tiny mai tai. When the icy liquid hits my stomach, I feel like I want to puke. RIP frozen drinks. You don't mix with my weight-loss injections. I put my tiny cup in the sand, and a gentle tropical breeze warms my skin.

"This is heaven." Liliana opens her beach bag and pulls out the self-help book that's blowing up the internet.

I stare at the lime-green cover, wondering if the book will help her get through what's coming, but then quickly shift my focus, trying to dodge the guilt building in my gut. I'm too late. She noticed that the cover got my attention.

She holds up the book so I can get a better look. "Self-help, I know." She sounds doubtful. "It's a struggle lately. I'm trapped in a cycle I can't get out of. And Josh isn't happy. But I'm sure he's told you."

I try to play it cool. But I'm a hundred percent not comfortable with where this conversation is going. She holds my gaze, waiting for me to talk, but I just nod again. She doesn't want to hear what I know. My hands tremble.

Sitting up, she swings her legs off her lounge chair and puts her feet on the sand. "Listen, Nicole, we've been friends all our lives. And I want to make sure, if something is going on with Josh…something I needed to know about…something crucial, that you would tell me." She exhales a long breath.

My heart pounds. I hate secrets. I'm a terrible friend.

"Because something's off with him. He made a weird statement the other night about making a change. But we got interrupted before he could say more. And to be honest, I felt like he didn't want to say more."

Suddenly, it feels like ants are crawling all over me. I shift in my chair, hoping the creepy sensation goes away. I know I have to say something. Liliana expects me to say something.

My head scrambles searching for words. "Hmm…" I drag out the sound, giving my brain time to come up with something. "We mostly talk about kid stuff and school. I don't know anything else."

I feel awful lying to her. Especially when she's being honest and open. Words spin in my head. Is there a way I can be there for her without admitting that Josh and I have big plans? My mind goes blank as the water crashes against the shore.

Then Liliana's talking again. "All I know is that something needs to change."

I shiver despite the red-hot sun. I wonder if Liliana will remember saying these words to me, on this beach, in St. McAna Island as the waves rolled in and out, whispering their secrets.

CHAPTER 18

Officer Claasen

Now
Emerald Jewel All-Inclusive Resort
October 5th ♫ 6:00 a.m.

OFFICER CLAASEN TWIRLS his mustache trying to smooth the red swath of hair covering his lip. He puts a stack of papers on a small table and pulls up a couple of chairs, thinking about the ending of *A Study in Scarlet*. Last night he finished reading his favorite Sherlock Holmes book for at least the twentieth time. The unflappable and eccentric character has been his favorite since he was a child. It's the reason he became a police officer.

Drinking a few sips of strong coffee, he wonders how his idol would go about interviewing absurd American tourists—a task he loathes. He finds them to be almost a satirical take on human beings.

He glances at the door. "Please let the first person in."

Mr. LaFleur, the resort's manager, glares at him before letting the first guest into the meeting room. Officer Claasen knows St. McAna's luxury hotel industry never wants the police to get involved in anything until there's a body, but by then it's too late. For now, Detective Ellis has agreed to say they're investigating a disturbance, but Officer Claasen knows it's only a matter of time before everyone learns a woman is missing.

As the door swings open, he notices a small crowd of people waiting to share information. This surprises him. It's early. He figured most guests would be sleeping. Two women wearing sunglasses and matching neon-orange trucker hats that say *Vacay Mode* walk in. They pause as Mr. LaFleur greets them with a welcoming smile. When they see Officer Claasen, they look at each other with disappointment.

"Damn, I was hoping he'd look like Ryan Gosling, but he looks more like Yosemite Sam." The taller one speaks under her breath, thinking Officer Claasen can't hear her.

He doesn't have time to react to her comment before they place enormous beach bags on the floor and sit down.

"I apologize, but police protocol requires each person to be interviewed separately." He scowls at the tall woman who just compared him to the redheaded cartoon character known for throwing temper tantrums. An insulting comparison he's been subjected to for years. For a second he considers shaving his mustache but then decides against it—it's modeled after Sir Arthur Conan Doyle, the author of the books that have shaped his life.

"I'll leave." The tall woman stands and rushes out of the room.

"Good morning," he says to the rude woman's friend.

She pushes her sunglasses onto her hat and smiles, almost blinding him with her bright-white teeth. Her unusual features distract him. Surely, she wasn't born with these monstrous eyelashes. And why do her lips look like swollen balloons? He ignores these thoughts and begins.

"We are investigating a slight disturbance last night."

"Yes, I heard. And that it involved those women wearing pink."

The officer nods, and she continues. "We were told to speak with you if we saw anything noteworthy. Is everything okay?"

"Yes," he speaks quickly, not wanting to give her any reason for concern. At least not until it's absolutely necessary.

"I'll start by saying that a woman in that group was aggressive and rude to my friends. So, if there's trouble, focus on her."

Although the missing woman's friends appear concerned, it's possible one of them could be involved in her disappearance. Officer Claasen pulls out his phone, showing a selfie the women in pink took the previous night.

"Which one acted aggressively?"

The woman focuses on the picture. Her thick eyelashes remind him of spider legs. "She accused us of cheating after they lost trivia night." She points to one woman in the picture. "This one, right here, with the ridiculous bangs."

"Trivia night?" the officer asks, confused.

"Yes, they lost by five points, and she was pissed." A cocky smile crosses the woman's puffy lips. "We won. What a poor loser. She cursed us out."

Officer Claasen tenses, wondering if this woman is here to brag about winning trivia. It always amazes him how fast adults on vacation revert to immature children. He realizes he's going to need to ask more specific questions if he wants useful information. "Do you know if any of these women have been spending time with other guests?"

"Actually, that's the main reason I came to talk with you. On the first night, I saw one of those women with that hot young guy."

Officer Claasen refocuses his attention. The missing woman's friends keep insisting that a young guest named Luca has something to do with this. "What did you see?"

"They got called up onstage together by Nick Carter. He serenaded her. I still don't understand why he picked her. She's very plain Jane."

The officer makes a note in his case file, ignoring the woman's rude comment.

She continues. "After the show ended, my friend and I were walking down the beach. They were together. They seemed really cozy."

Officer Claasen flips through his notepad. Angie was the only one here the first night. "Was it this one?" He points to Angie in his photo.

"Yeah, that's her."

"Can you tell me more about what you saw?"

"She was crying. He was consoling her. But I also think they were getting to know each other better, if you know what I mean." She winks with her gigantic spider lashes.

"Getting cozy," he repeats. "You mean being romantic?" Adrenaline pumps through his body as he wonders if there's something here worth pursuing. "Did you see anything else?"

The woman leans back in her chair. "No, that was it. That's all the information I have. I don't know if it helps. Maybe she's in her cougar era?"

"Her cougar era?"

"Yes, like Anne Hathaway in *The Idea of You*. Or Nicole Kidman in *A Family Affair*."

He gives her a blank stare but is unable to ask for further explanation before Detective Ellis walks through the door.

"I need to speak with you." Detective Ellis points at Mr. LaFleur.

Officer Claasen notices the woman's face flush. Detective Ellis is popular with the ladies. People say he looks like Denzel Washington.

A heated, though quiet, conversation begins between the detective and Mr. LaFleur. The exchange ends with Mr. LaFleur reluctantly handing Detective Ellis a key. The detective walks to the table where Officer Claasen is conducting his interview.

"We have another matter that needs attention."

The woman being interviewed gives Detective Ellis a flirty smile with her balloon-like lips.

"Sure, I was just finishing up." He reaches out to hand the woman a form, but her eyes lock on Detective Ellis's muscular biceps, and she doesn't notice. Officer Claasen can't help but feel like a dorky high schooler being compared to the star athlete.

"Fill this out with your name and contact information. Leave it on the table. Come back later if you think of anything else."

Taking the paper, the woman nods, fills in her information, and stands to leave.

Detective Ellis sits in the chair across from Officer Claassen as Mr. LaFleur escorts the woman out of the meeting room.

"I convinced LaFleur to let us search Luca's room."

Relief makes him smile. Maybe today will be more than boring interview after boring interview. "I take it Luca's still missing."

"Yes." Detective Ellis taps his fingers on the table several times. It's a tell that he's fired up. "Let's go. I'll brief you on the details as we walk over."

As he and the detective stand, the women in pink walk through the door. The one with a rat's nest of hair runs toward them.

"Any news? We need good news." She presses her hands together in a prayer-like gesture.

Officer Claasen shakes his head back and forth.

The woman with the torn dress inhales a gulp of air. "But it's been hours. The sun's out. It's morning, and she's still missing." Her voice wobbles, then trails off.

The woman with remnants of last night's makeup peers at Detective Ellis. "Tell us where you're going. We're coming!" She grabs the hands of her friends, and they form a chain in front of the detective.

"I'm sorry, but this is a police matter. You need to stay here. Your safety comes first."

The women look at Officer Claasen as if he may give them a different answer, but he knows going into Luca's room could be dangerous. What if he's in there, holed up with a weapon? Or what if something happened and he's dead? He hates how his mind spins with the worst-case scenario. But his job is a compilation of worst-case scenarios.

"Our safety?" The woman with the torn dress goes pale. "Do you think he's armed and dangerous?"

Detective Ellis exhales in frustration like he's a parent trying to teach his child how to tie their shoe. "This is a precautionary measure. Now please excuse us." He gently moves past the women in pink, and Officer Claasen follows. They exit the lobby and head down the path toward Luca's room.

"I'll knock. If he doesn't answer, I'll enter. You'll cover. The other officers have cleared bystanders from the area and are ready to assist as necessary."

They climb the stairs leading to Luca's room. Both men pull their weapons. Detective Ellis beats his fist against the door. Sweat drips from his forehead.

"Luca, are you in there? I need you to open the door!" His voice booms.

The moment passes in silence. With a nod from Detective Ellis, Officer Claasen moves next to the door and pushes his back flat against the wall, ready to cover. He imagines he's a character in the novels that captivate him.

Detective Ellis slides his key card into the door. "Luca, I'm coming in. If you have a weapon, drop it now and put your hands in the air."

Everything happens fast. Detective Ellis charges through the door. Officer Claasen rushes in behind him. They move through the room with their weapons, turning from side to side, checking the bathroom, the closet, and behind the curtains.

Detective Ellis shakes his head. "No one's here."

As he runs his gaze over every inch of the room, Officer Claasen's mouth goes dry. It's completely empty. No clothes, no shoes, no toothbrush, no suitcase. Luca has vanished, and it's not even seven in the morning. He methodically analyzes every surface for the kind of insignificant clues Sherlock uses to solve mysteries.

His eyes focus on the bed. It's perfectly made, with tucked corners and a neatly folded blanket. The small chocolates the maids put out in the evening lie untouched on top of fluffy pillows. "Looks like he didn't sleep here last night." Officer Claasen pats down his bushy mustache. "And his stuff is gone."

"Right," Detective Ellis agrees. "So, where did he sleep? And who was he with last night?"

CHAPTER 19

Angie

MY VOICE CRACKS through the last lyric of Britney Spears's "Hit Me Baby One More Time." I've never been able to sing. For a moment, I'm transfixed by a twenty-something-year-old girl in a white string bikini. Where did she come from? We lock eyes before she darts from the stack of pool towels she's hiding behind. Am I hallucinating? Taking that gummy Luca offered after the dust-up with Carly might have been a mistake.

As the song ends, I bop my head around like I don't have a care in the world. It's strange. Karaoke's not my thing. It's Nicole's. Dull, boring, lackluster…these are the adjectives I would use to describe myself. Ever since running away, I've committed to following the rules. I never make waves, and I avoid attention. This is the only way I know how to escape the feelings that remind me of my past.

"Please, please, let Angie come home." I still remember the way Carly's whole body shook as she pleaded with the kidnapper on live TV until her father pulled her away.

Yet, last night, I ended up onstage, and today I'm doing karaoke. And twenty minutes ago, I took the gummy Luca offered. It appears I'm experiencing the full effect of chaos theory. I wave my arms around, trying to convince myself they're still attached to my body.

"Yass! Give it up for Angie." The DJ claps, but it's hard to hear over the deafening scream coming from Luca.

"Britney would freaking love that!"

Walking toward him, I plop my body onto the edge of his lounge chair. He leans into me and gives me a lopsided smile. "Time to fill up our shit-brown tumblers." He picks up our matching cups and waves over a server.

I can't believe I made a vacation friend! This is not like me, but it's fun! I feel lighter than air. It goes beyond my high. Is it possible that the heart-to-heart I had with Luca last night was what I needed to release my guilt? Telling him the details about my past felt like opening the lid of a jar that contained my shame. It spilled out of me, freeing my regrets to scatter.

But the comforting thought quickly dissolves. I know I'll never be free from guilt if I don't tell the people I love what happened those weeks I was gone.

"Next up, Luca singing 'The Right Stuff.'" The DJ glances at us, the only two people who've been participating in poolside karaoke.

I refocus on Luca.

"Drinks later. It's go time!" He stands, reaching his arms toward the sky, and then alternates between leaning his body left and right.

"You look like you're stretching for the New York Marathon." I snort with laughter.

"Bruh, I gotta loosen up. It's all about the choreo." He jumps and spreads his feet apart, pointing his left arm forward. It's a classic nineties boy band move. The only thing missing is a crew of bandmates doing the same thing.

Jogging up to the stage, he gives me a wink and begins. His baseball cap sits backward on his head, pulling his silky dark hair away from his mesmerizing eyes. The women in floppy sun hats and designer sunglasses around me quiet. All eyes settle on the gorgeous man onstage.

I lean back in the lounge chair, grinning like a schoolgirl. The women in the pool's crystal-clear water dance while Luca sings New Kids on the Block's hit song. When the crowd of women erupts, singing the chorus, I can't help but jump up and shake my body to the catchy beat. I'm present, but I'm also far away. Everything around me is fuzzy.

A woman standing by the edge of the pool grabs my hand. We swing each other around, singing like we're ten-year-olds using hairbrushes as microphones. Combined with my high, it's almost as if the unbearable events of my past never happened.

"Ang, there you are."

Hearing Carly's voice, I turn around. She's striding toward me with purpose. My joy instantly falls away like the music I'm dancing to is playing on a scratched record.

"I spoke with the front desk. You need to file a police report." She stares at me, waiting for a response, but I say nothing. My head's too wobbly to deal with Carly's intense personality.

"Ang, did you hear me? You need to file a police report."

Ignoring her, I move closer to the pool and face the woman I've been dancing with. "Let's keep this party going!"

"Ang! You need to file a police report so you can contact the US Embassy and get an emergency passport."

Ugh, Carly's ruining all the fun. Glaring, I face her, hoping my severe expression will make her go away. Why do we always end up in a standoff?

"Oh, wow. Are you high?" Carly steps in between me and my dancing partner.

But I continue to jump around until the song ends. The crowd bounces up and down, applauding, and then quiets with the hum of conversation.

"What's gotten into you?" Carly's forehead half scrunches in confusion. Clearly, she's overdone the Botox. "You need to stop acting like a drunk teenager or you're going to be stuck in St. McAna." Her face is beet red. She's not used to people ignoring her advice. But this isn't Instagram.

"Damn it!" She bellows in frustration.

I half expect steam to shoot out of her ears as she tries to convince me to listen. Her brain can't handle this imperfect, nonchalant reaction I'm having to my lost passport. Why can't she let me deal with it tomorrow? Of course, I need to file a police report. I'm not an idiot.

She flails her arms and screams over the din of conversation. "Fine, stay on this island. Vanish like you did in high school. I don't give a fuck."

The women close by watch us like we're a reality show. My head pulses. She's crossed a line, and she knows it. The word *vanish* blasts through my mind, a word used repeatedly in the letters sent to my dad.

> *Angie did not vanish. I have her. I'm taking good care of your beautiful little girl.*

> *Angie has chosen a new life with me. People do not vanish into thin air.*

Carly's word choice is a trigger. Her word choice is a taunt. Before I know what's happening, I charge forward.

"I can't believe you said that!" I bolt for the beach, accidentally colliding with her thin frame.

She gasps as our bodies smash together. Staggering backward, she loses her balance. Suddenly, a burst of pool water rises into the air, splashing around my feet. My nostrils flare from the pungent smell of chlorine.

When I look over my shoulder, Carly's in the pool.

CHAPTER 20

Carly

Emerald Jewel All-Inclusive Resort
October 3rd ♫ Two Days Ago

COLD WATER SWALLOWS me, causing me to shiver. Lifting my head up, I gulp for air, blinking my eyes open. My body trembles, and it takes a moment to realize Angie pushed me into the pool.

"Oh, no, Carly! I'm sorry." She leans over the edge to help me. She's wasted.

"I don't want your help," I snap. "And you're high, anyway. You need to sober up." My brand-new Gucci belt bag floats by, along with my beach tote. *Fabulous.*

As I collect my soaked things, I hope no one's recording me. My father's lucky his days as a public servant ended before the invention of the iPhone. My cheeks heat, realizing every woman here is my target audience. This had better not end up as a meme.

"Here's your phone." A member of the resort's staff hands me my wet phone with a sheepish look on his face. "It hit the side of the pool and then bounced into the water."

"Thank you. I appreciate your help, but this isn't your fault. It's hers." I scowl at Angie. Inspecting my phone, I see there's a crack, and the screen is black. I press down on every button, but it doesn't come to life. *Are you kidding me!* How will I post my Insta content without my phone? My hands shake with anger.

Holding my dripping Gucci bag and phone above my head, I sling my beach tote over my shoulder and climb up the pool stairs.

Angie rushes over. "I'm sorry. I didn't mean to push you." Her facial features twist like she's in physical pain.

I step past her, refusing to acknowledge her apology. Walking toward a table and chairs near the pool bar, I take the soaking items out of my bag. The same resort staff member who gave me my phone hands me a couple of towels.

"Thanks."

He nods and leaves me to dry off.

My La Mer sunscreen wipes off easily enough, but my Apple Watch displays a water drop icon. I pull out my soaking sun hat, wondering how long it will take to dry. The luxury brand sent me the four-hundred-dollar hat in exchange for a post about its packability and UPF 50+ protection.

"Fuck!" I whisper under my breath. Today's planned Insta post is wrecked. My perfect girls' trip won't look so perfect if I post a photo of myself dripping wet after being pushed into the pool.

"Carly. There you are. We're going to get lunch." Liliana appears with Nicole. They pull out chairs and sit down. "You went for a swim with your cover-up on?" Liliana looks at me in surprise before she notices that every single item of mine is wet.

Nicole picks up my copy of Jennifer Weiner's latest and shakes it. Water droplets spray around her. "What's the tea?"

"Damn it! Just talk like a forty-five-year-old." Grabbing my book from her hands, I slump into my chair.

Nicole and Liliana exchange glances that silently accuse me of acting like a bitch. And they're right. I made Nicole the target of my anger at Angie.

"Sorry, Nicole, I shouldn't have snapped at you. I'm mad."

She puts her hand on my shoulder. "What happened?"

"It was Angie." My voice is tight with a mix of irritation and sadness. *We were like sisters, and then she disappeared from my life.*

"What was Angie?" Liliana asks, confused.

I skip my feelings about the past and focus on what just happened. "She was by the pool dancing, drunk and high as a kite. I told her she needs to file a police report. She wouldn't listen." My voice drops off at the end as I consider if I want to confess what set Angie off.

"And then?" Nicole scoots her chair closer to mine.

"Well, I was mad. No one else cares about Angie's stolen passport. Not even Angie. I'm the one trying to fix it." Pausing, I wait for Liliana or Nicole to apologize, but neither one does. And they wonder why I always put myself in charge. Don't they understand Angie's not getting home without a passport?

"Then…and then…" I stammer, not wanting to admit how low I sank.

"And then what?" Liliana asks impatiently.

"And then I screamed something about the way she vanished in high school and maybe she was trying to do the same thing now."

When I say the word *vanished,* I understand Angie's reaction. The word is a chilling reminder of those terrifying letters. As I listen to myself, my anger turns to guilt, and my guilt is overwhelming. How could I?

"Oh no." Nicole's lips turn down. "I can't believe you brought that up and said that word."

"Not the best thing to say," Liliana agrees.

"But why are you all wet?"

"Angie was furious and started to take off, but banged into me, and that's when I fell into the pool."

"O.M.G." Nicole shakes her head. "Are you okay?"

"Yes, I'm just all wet. And all my stuff is wet. And my phone may never work again." Picking it up, I show them the black screen. "I feel awful for bringing up the letters." Remorse overwhelms me. I don't want to hurt Angie. I want her back in my life. My eyes well. I swipe my palm over my face, wiping away a few stray tears.

"Wow, we've only been here for three hours, and the drama on this trip is next-level." Nicole giggles, lightening the mood. At this moment, I appreciate her humor.

"Agreed." Liliana laughs. "We should have a Bravo reality show—*Real Housewives of Hamilton Beach—Perimenopause Edition*."

"We definitely have enough material." I picture Angie and I arguing by the pool. "Let's find her. I think I saw her walk toward the beach."

The three of us get up from our chairs. I stuff my wet items in my beach bag and wrap a towel around myself.

Liliana speaks. "Do you want us to text Marco and let him know your phone isn't working?"

My temples throb hearing Marco's name. His potential infidelity hasn't crossed my mind since I've been busy figuring out how to get Angie a new passport. The magic of focusing on other people's problems is real. *But then again, Angie's missing passport kept me from thinking about something that would change my life forever!* The realization is mind-blowing.

"In case he needs to get in touch with you," she continues, as if I need an explanation.

"Sure. And text Bianca. Tell her I'll call her later, either from my phone or one of yours." I push out the words, still reeling from how easy it is for me to bury my own issues when I help others.

Liliana leans toward Nicole. "Actually, can you text them? Carly took my phone to her room because my boss won't stop calling."

Nicole shakes her head. "Shoot, my phone's dead. I've been listening to the ultimate boy band mix on Spotify."

Liliana glances at me. "Give me your key. I'll run upstairs and get my phone from your room."

"Are you sure?" I ask, knowing that she's trying to avoid her boss.

"Yeah, it's fine. I should make sure I'm not fired." She laughs but seems concerned.

I give her my key, and she leaves to get her phone.

Once she rounds the corner, I lean toward Nicole and lower my voice. "Getting fired is what she needs. Her boss is the worst. Her job runs her life." *Wow, I didn't realize that focusing on other people's problems is my main coping mechanism.*

Nicole remains silent, then turns toward the pool, like she doesn't want to talk about it.

"She's all work and no play, as always," I continue. "Remember how she skipped our tenth-grade DC trip to study for the AP US Government exam? She didn't understand the irony." I laugh, but Nicole continues ignoring me, watching a woman do a cannonball into the water.

Why is she acting weird?

But before I can ask, Liliana returns.

"Got it. I sent Bianca and Marco a text."

"Thanks." My heart rattles. I ignore it and suggest we walk to the beach and find Angie. Passing the pool area, I glimpse the brilliant blue ocean. Small boats with sails the color of pineapples glide across the water.

I point to a crowded area of lounge chairs with blue-and-white striped umbrellas. "Let's walk over there."

We wind our way through several rows of women relaxing in the sun with beach reads in one hand and drinks with umbrellas in the other.

"I don't see Angie." Liliana scans the beach again. "Let's try calling." She pulls her phone from her beach bag. "Oh, there's a text from Marco." She reads it out loud. "*Hi Liliana. Thanks for letting me know.* Wait, he's typing more." She continues. "*I don't think I can get away again. Carly's getting back from that trip. I'll see what I can do.*"

"Huh?" Nicole asks, confused.

My body bursts with heat. Something about that text is off.

"Oh wait," Liliana says. "There's more." She pauses, reading the words as they appear on her phone. "*That second text was for someone else. A work thing.*" Liliana sighs. "Work. Work. Work. At least it sounds like he's better at setting boundaries than I am. Anyway, let's see if Angie picks up."

It takes only a second to connect the dots. My stomach drops. I start to sweat. Liliana just texted Marco about my broken phone, and her message is at the top of his chats. He meant for the next text to go to Lilly. "Lilly from Accounting", his colleague from work.

The one he might be having an affair with.

I repeat the words Marco texted silently in my head. *I don't think I can get away again. Carly's getting back from that trip. I'll see what I can do.*

Liliana and Lilly, close enough to make a texting mistake if you're not paying careful attention.

CHAPTER 21

Liliana

Emerald Jewel All-Inclusive Resort
October 3rd 🎵 Two Days Ago

HANG UP THE unanswered call to Angie and notice several missed calls from my boss. Amanda's relentless. I'll call her back later. Right now, we need to find Angie. I know the past makes Carly and Nicole nervous, but it shouldn't. Angie's proven herself to be a steady, reliable adult, regardless of her choice to separate herself from us.

"She's not answering. What's our next move?"

"We should split up and search," Nicole says. "I'll look in the lobby."

"I'll comb the beach. Carly, can you go to Angie's room? Maybe she went to lie down."

Carly stares at me, blank-faced.

"Earth to Carly." I wave my hands around, trying to snap her back into the moment.

"Oh, sorry, I didn't hear what you said."

"Angie's not picking up my call," I repeat, wondering why Carly's distracted. Maybe it's the sun. Or that she can't make an Instagram post from her broken phone. Or that she looks like a rain-soaked, disheveled, wet dog. Is it bad that I'm glad she's a total mess for once?

"Wait, is that her?" Nicole points to a woman slumped over the beach bar, passed out.

Carly nods. "That explains why she wasn't answering her phone."

"She's lit." Nicole walks toward the bar.

Carly and I follow. "Manic Monday" starts playing from my phone. Sweat drips down my back.

Carly's eyes widen. "Your boss, again?"

I snap the bracelet Esther gave me against my skin. The sting of the elastic is easier to focus on than my stress about work.

"Doesn't she understand the meaning of vacation?" Nicole sounds agitated.

"I know." I agree with them. "But there's this lawsuit, and I'm the point person. And no one else is up to speed. And…and…" I stumble over my words, which is unusual for me. Time to rein in my emotions. "Just forget it." My voice rises as anger replaces my insecurities. "I need to call her. It will only take a minute. I'll meet you by the bar." Don't they realize all the sacrifices I've made would be pointless if I jeopardize my successful career?

Nicole and Carly give each other conspiratorial nods, and I wonder if they've been gossiping about how I'm on call for Amanda. The thought of them talking behind my back makes me squirm. But, then again, side gossip on a girls' trip is as certain as death and taxes.

Taking a few steps, I feel like the ground is swaying under my feet. I don't know why I thought getting fired was a good idea earlier. Why did I work so hard my whole life, only to quit now? Plus, there's the mortgage, the bills, day school tuition, and sleep-away camp costs. Evie's bat mitzvah is coming up. All of it needs to be paid for.

I stop walking and plant my flip-flops in the sand. Scorching hot, minuscule shells and rocks fall on my feet, burning my skin. My phone continues to ring with Amanda's special ringtone. There's a sinking sensation in my body. It's almost like I'm standing in quicksand. *Snap, snap, snap.* My skin swells under my bracelet as I answer Amanda's call. Apparently, my work stress packed a suitcase and crashed this girls' trip.

"Liliana, I need to know if you submitted those financial records for the Mitten case." My boss over-enunciates her words, giving them sharp edges. She doesn't apologize for interrupting my vacation. She doesn't even say hello.

"The financial records," I repeat. I scroll through the endless data in my mind, searching for the last thing I can remember.

"Liliana, are you there? Things are blowing up." I can hear her team of advisors barking questions in the background.

My mind goes blank under pressure. "Um, let me think for a moment."

Her exasperated sigh hisses through my phone. "I don't have time for this."

My free hand forms a tight fist. I want to yell at her for interrupting my vacation without an apology. I want to scream about the overwhelming load of carrying the responsibilities of two jobs. But then the information she needs pops into my mind. "Yes, I emailed the second set of documents to our outside counsel. I'll resend the email I sent to you before I left."

"Great. I'll call you if I need anything else." She hangs up without saying goodbye.

My head pounds. But then I remember our new hire, Julie, will take over all business contract disputes. Relief is on the horizon. It's time to execute step one of my plan for repairing my relationship with Josh. I'll call him later to explain that I only need to put up with my boss's unreasonable expectations for a couple more weeks. As soon as Julie's in place, I'll have more time for our family. We both just need to hold on a little longer.

Walking over to the bar, I shake out my arms to relieve the last remnants of stress caused by the call. The bracelet Esther made rolls down my wrist, revealing a red angry blotch from my snapping.

Nicole waves me over to where Angie is squished between her and Carly. "We're bringing her up to her room." They wrap their arms around her and take a step forward. Angie's head bobs around in a slow, awkward motion.

"I'm out of it. Luca gave me a gummy." With a wobble, she moves forward.

Carly wraps her left arm tighter around Angie's shoulder. "Can I say one thing about your missing passport without you getting angry?"

When will Carly learn to read the room? Doesn't she see that Angie's too out of it to process anything? She doesn't need to fix this right now.

Angie clumsily points one finger up into the air and waves it around. "One thing. You're only gonna say one thing? You never say only one thing," she slurs.

I stifle a laugh. Although Angie's wasted, she's right.

Carly makes a serious face. "After falling into the pool, I think I deserve the chance to say one thing to you."

"Oh yeah, you fell into the pool. I'm so so so so sorry. I didn't mean to shove you. Say your one thing. But Luca is innocent. He's my best friend."

I could be wrong, but her emphasis on *best friend* seems intentional. It stings hearing Angie call Luca that, even though she's out of her mind right now.

"This isn't about Luca. I know that's a sore subject. It's about your passport. You need to file a police report to get the paperwork from the embassy to get home. That's it. That's the one thing I wanted to say."

"Yes! Yes! I need to get home to Patton and my boys and toasted ravioli. Mmm. Fried cheese."

"Toasted what?" I ask, confused.

"Toasted ravioli. A St. Louis specialty." Angie makes a smacking sound with her lips.

Although I want to say, *We'd know that if you ever invited us to St. Louis*, unlike Carly, I know now isn't the right time.

Suddenly, Angie exhales a discordant sound. "Oh no, the hiccups. I think I need to lie down."

"Genius!" Nicole blurts. "Naptime. We'll call the police later once Angie sobers up."

"Try to walk." Carly tugs Angie along, but Angie's feet drag through the sandy floor as if wading through deep muddy sludge.

"Uh-oh." Angie speaks between several more hiccups.

"What's wrong?" I ask, moving closer to the tangle of Carly, Angie, and Nicole's intertwined bodies.

Angie smiles at me with a sloppy grin. "I need to pee. I'm going to pee in my pants."

The three of them stare at the ground, confirming there's no pee, and then snap their heads up in unison.

I laugh. "You look like a three-headed monster."

"No, no. No laughing," Angie drawls. "Take me to pee."

"I also need to pee," Nicole says.

"I just peed. But I have to go again." Carly laughs.

"Peeing around the clock. A sure sign you were born before nineteen eighty-five," I giggle.

We all burst into laughter. For a brief moment, it's like we're fifteen again.

CHAPTER 22

Nicole

"**C**RAZY HOW A quick nap can turn things around."

My squad wades through the crisp pool water. That nap was next-level. With three kids to chase after, I'm lucky if I get one minute to scroll Facebook. Napping? That's a hard no. Meanwhile, Garrett spends every Sunday sleeping on the couch, watching football. At least in the fall. Once baseball season starts, he spends most of his free time coaching one of our boy's baseball teams. I'll admit all the parents love Garrett's approach. He's patient, fun, and isn't one of those over-the-top baseball dads who can't handle losing because their self-worth depends on the final score of a Little League game.

"And we still have a few hours to enjoy the sunshine before we need to get showered for dinner." Liliana glides forward on a neon-blue pool noodle.

"Time for some day drinking!" Swimming past Angie, I sit on a concrete stool under the thatched roof of the swim-up bar. Although it was nice to FaceTime with my kids after the beach, right now Garrett and my children—it's almost like they don't exist. No one needs a cheese stick, a ride to baseball, or their dry cleaning dropped off. I'm basically a sorority girl on spring break. Freedom, hell yes!

"Grab the rest of those." Carly points to three empty seats. With her oversized sunglasses, she resembles a movie star. Textbook Carly.

"I'll pass on drinks." Angie winks. "I hit my limit for the day. Plus, the police are coming any minute about my passport."

My body relaxes hearing that the passport drama's over. Here's hoping Carly calms down. She's never bounced back from losing Angie's friendship. But it seems like this vacay is finally on the right track. I'll keep turning up the fun until it feels like the good old days.

"I'm in for a drink." Liliana sits on a stool close by. "Let's toast to our do-over."

Carly waves her hand, getting the attention of the bartender. "I'll have a vodka tonic with a lime."

"That's so mid," I say, positive she's placed her order based on some macro calculation. "Get a piña colada or something that screams vacation."

"No, thank you." She flips her hand in the air, like I've suggested she buy her fall wardrobe at Old Navy instead of Bloomingdale's. "I don't need an eight-hundred-calorie drink."

Bingo. I fight the urge to roll my eyes. The crazy thing is, she's naturally skinny. It's sad that she bases her self-worth on her clothing size.

Smiling, the bartender places Carly's drink down and glances my way. "What can I shake or pour for you?"

"I'll have a piña…" I stop, remembering my stomach can't handle frozen drinks on the weight-loss meds. Wow, I'm a total hypocrite. I should cut Carly some slack. Or maybe I should figure out why I suddenly care about being thin. "Actually, I'll have the same." I slide my eyes to Carly's drink.

"What happened to having something that screams vacation?" Carly smirks, but I ignore her, watching as the bartender grabs vodka from a line of bottles filled with alcohol in every color of the rainbow.

Liliana orders an Aperol spritz, and Angie gets water. We settle around the bar, half submerged in the pool's cool water, while the Bob Marley song "Three Little Birds" plays in the background.

"To ditching the rocky beginning of this trip and vibing together from here on out."

We tap our tiny cups together. Drips of water slide down our arms.

"Cheers! Wish we had our tumblers to supersize these drinks." Liliana takes a long sip. "And what exactly does vibing together mean?"

Surrounded by the smiling faces of my friends, I realize how badly I needed to get away from the demands of *momlife* and how great it is to be with my besties. Carly, Liliana, and I never make time for each other. And Angie. Well, she's here! Yes, there's been some drama, but that's all behind us now.

"Vibing. You know. Hanging out, connecting, spending quality time."

"I have to ask." Angie catches my eye. "Why do you talk like my sixteen-year-old sons?"

Carly giggles. "Yeah, why do you talk like a Hamilton Beach High School student?"

"Oh, I don't know." Shrugging, I feel my face flush. I hate talking about stay-at-home mom life. "I'm with my kids all day, every day. One time, I said *bruh*, and my kids couldn't stop laughing. I started using slang to get them to listen."

"Wow!" Carly teases. "You've completely evolved from a party girl into a full-on suburban mom."

Her words hit me with the force of a gut punch. She doesn't get it. It's more like a wilting than an evolution.

"Yeah, you used to be the one introducing us to cool, edgy rap, and now it's all Kidz Bop." Liliana leans into me, grinning. "And you were vegan forever, and now you love dinosaur nuggets."

"Prehistoric-shaped poultry is epic." I fake a laugh, but inside, I feel a stabbing discomfort.

They're spot-on. I've lost my identity since I gave up my career to be a mom. In fact, last week, I fell down an Amazon rabbit hole debating lunch box options. It's hard not to question my life choices when I waste entire days researching pointless products I'm going to return or let sit in my car for months before finally going to the UPS store. But I made the choice to end my career. That's on me.

Needing to redirect this chat, I'm hit with an idea. I pull my phone out of its waterproof case and click open my photos. "There's more to me than *momlife*." I force my words to sound confident, pretending I'm the CEO of a Fortune 500 company talking to stockholders. "Look at these."

While I never planned to show my boudoir pictures to my friends, I'm desperate to win back my cool-girl status. There's nothing scarier than being perceived as a person whose entire life revolves around being first in the carpool line. Even if, deep down, I know being first is the only way to avoid getting stuck behind kindergartners climbing into minivans.

"Oh. My. God!" Carly squeals, grabbing my phone.

"Let me see." Angie swims over, and Liliana peers over her shoulder.

"Boudoir photos! You took sexy, slutty, boudoir photos?" Carly stares at me like I'm an alien.

"I'm still a badass edgy bitch. Don't let my mom uniform of athleisure wear fool you." Scooting closer to Carly, I look at the picture of me lying on my side, cupping my lacy bra. A hot pink, feathery garter belt surrounds my right thigh.

"Holy shit. I wish I had the confidence to do this."

Carly's comment causes an intense surge of emotion to spread through my body. I think it's pride. A feeling that's hard to experience when my kids wear dirty uniforms to school because I can't keep up with the never-ending laundry. And don't get me started on getting it folded and put away.

Moving her sunglasses onto her head, Carly swipes to the next photo. I'm sitting on a concrete floor, my legs spread in a V, leaning toward my stilettos. My breasts spill out of my bra, and hundred-dollar bills are scattered around me. When taking this picture, I felt like I was invincible. Like I could still be whoever I wanted to be.

But the feeling didn't last. I couldn't finish my boudoir session because my babysitter needed to leave early. I'm still searching for a way to connect with the old me. The cool, self-confident ad executive who had a thriving career, a great salary, and won the prized karaoke cup at my favorite bar three years running. I'm unbeatable singing "Baby Got Back."

I need to get my mojo back. The urge to do something extreme overwhelms me. Josh's offer jumps to the front of my mind.

Don't tell me you haven't thought about it.

Maybe he's right. I should jump feet first. The future might be bright.

"Garrett hit the wife jackpot! Josh would go crazy if I did this." Liliana bounces excitedly. Her voice echoes in the pool bar's enclosure.

My face tenses, but I quickly smooth out my expression. Garrett hasn't seen these pictures, and he never will.

CHAPTER 23

Liliana

Emerald Jewel All-Inclusive Resort
October 3rd 🎵 Two Days Ago

MY COMPUTER BAG bumps my leg as I power walk to keep up with Nicole. Our afternoon at the swim-up bar, followed by a hot shower and a delicious dinner, fooled me into thinking my work stress was melting away. But my anxiety is back now that my Zoom with Amanda is an hour away. While I get why Nicole struggles with being a stay-at-home mom, I would love to have endless days to focus on Josh and my girls instead of my job.

"Amaze! They're playing the movie *She's All That*! I always loved me some Freddie Prinze Jr.!" Nicole makes a heart shape with her hands and beats it against her chest. Images of her boudoir photo shoot flash through my mind.

I wish I had her chutzpah. She'd never agree to a Zoom meeting while on vacation. She's not someone who lets others push her around.

"Over here." Angie grabs us a table beside the lobby's bar. Groups of women sit in clusters, excited for nineties trivia night.

"We're counting on your big brain." Carly gives me a nod.

"I'll play as long as I can." I explained about the Zoom at dinner. I felt awful interrupting a hilarious conversation about our ugly yellow prom dresses to tell them.

Instead of getting angry, Carly changed the subject back to the dresses, admitting she had brought the picture. "I'm going to get it!" She jumped out of her chair and was back ten minutes later.

All of us broke into hysterical tears seeing ourselves in those Civil War-era-style dresses with matching parasols. When we showed the picture to our waiter, he brought us a round of bright-yellow lemon shots to commemorate our fashion faux pas.

Tapping my watch, I set the alarm so I don't miss my meeting. Without thinking, my fingers slide onto the bracelet Esther gave me, snapping it against my wrist. I texted her and Evie, but a FaceTime call would be better. I want to see their faces and have an actual conversation with Josh. We've texted, but only about the girls. I still need to complete step one of my plan and tell him that, once this new attorney starts, I will not work all day and night.

Angie takes a deep breath. "How do they make this lobby smell so good?"

"You can buy a diffuser in the gift shop that has the same scent. But it costs a hundred dollars."

All of us inhale, delighted by the fragrance. A mix of coconut and vanilla. The pleasing aroma provides a brief moment of zen.

Exhaling, I take it all in. Sun-kissed faces, gorgeous tropical flowers, and the enormous crystal chandeliers hanging overhead. Maybe I can disconnect from my work stress after all.

As I place my computer bag under the table, a resort staff member built like a professional wrestler appears.

He gives Angie a trivia answer sheet. "Hi, ladies, I'm Adio."

"Hi, Adio!" the four of us say in unison.

He puts a shoebox in the center of our table. "Turn off your phones and watches and put them in here. If we hear any ringing or dinging, your team loses ten points."

"Wow, you guys take trivia night seriously, but my phone's broken, anyway." Carly's face lights up with a playful grin.

Seems like she's over the pool incident. I hope nothing else flares up between her and Angie, although I understand why Carly's still wounded. It was awful, those weeks Angie was missing. The police grilled Carly, Nicole, and me, asking question after question about Angie's life, trying to find any clue. Then a tip came in about her being in LA, but then the strange letters started coming, and the FBI took over. I've never been so scared in my life. But Nicole and I have healed better than Carly.

I hold my phone in my hand and try my best not to care about what's going on at the office—on a Sunday!

Adio adjusts his man bun and looks at us apologetically. "I get it. No one wants to shut off their phones. We'll take a break halfway through so everyone can catch up on texts and emails." He smiles, showing off his strong, well-defined jawline. "But, ladies, don't forget you're on vacation. Who cares what's going on at home!" He winks, and Angie and Nicole throw their phones in the box without thinking twice.

"Come on, Liliana. You're on vacay, as Nicole would say. Turn it off." Angie gestures toward the box.

Carly, Angie, and Nicole start to chant "turn it off" like it's a battle cry. I take a deep breath, power my phone down, and add it to the box.

"Nailed it!" Nicole laughs.

I can feel my cheeks flush. It's humiliating that everyone knows my boss controls my life, even if Nicole's joking.

"What about your watch?" Adio gestures to my wrist.

Shoot, I need the alarm. I can't miss my meeting. "How about I put it in my work bag? I have an alarm set."

"Okay, but no cheating. Good luck, ladies!"

I slip my watch into the pocket of my computer bag as Adio moves to the women seated at the next table.

"Welcome to trivia!" A peppy member of the resort staff lowers the volume of the movie. "I'm Marina, and I'll be tonight's MC. I'm super excited to tell you that the winning table gets an autographed Boyz II Men poster and a complimentary poolside cabana tomorrow." Her red corkscrew curls bounce around her face.

"Whoo-hoo!" Nicole jumps out of her seat and fist pumps the air. "Guys, we have to win!"

Forty-five minutes later, our table's in the lead. Round one consisted of twenty softball questions such as, *Name the best friend in love with Dawson Leery on Dawson's Creek?* And *What 1992 reality TV show followed seven strangers who stopped being polite and started getting real?*

"Don't you guys remember how much my mom loved *The Real World*!" Angie's face lit up after hearing the question.

Carly and Nicole froze mid-laugh after hearing Angie's comment. She never talks about her mom. I wondered if they also sensed that Angie's letting down her guard and that our friendships may finally heal.

As Marina is about to close out round one with the final question, my head spins with the past—making mix CDs, watching *Saved by the Bell*, and eating raw cookie dough late into the night with these same faces smiling back at me. The number of times we've cackled in laughter in the last thirty minutes almost makes up for the stress of taking a few days off work. Almost.

"Alright, this is the last question. But I have a huge surprise before we move to round two. We have a special guest MC." Marina claps her hands together like she's a mom about to tell her kids they're going to Disney World.

Nicole jumps out of her seat.

"And here's our special guest right now." Marina's eyes fly to a man walking toward the bar wearing an Austin Powers mask. The quirky instrumental sixties music from the movie plays.

"This is exciting! Who is it?" Angie grabs Nicole's hand, overflowing with anticipation.

The masked man takes his place next to Marina. He exudes confidence, wearing fitted black jeans and a tight white V-neck that shows off his biceps.

"Adio, play us a tune. Let's have some fun before we reveal who our celebrity guest is."

The song switches to "You Sexy Thing." The masked man gyrates his hips, and the trivia crowd goes wild. He spins around a couple of times and then pulls off his mask.

"Holy shit! It's Joey Fatone from NSYNC!" Carly gasps as the entire lobby fills with the sound of high-pitched screams.

"O.M.G., my younger self is straight-up losing it!" Nicole wipes a couple of excited tears from her eyes.

"Not surprising! Remember how you used to practice kissing Joey using the poster on my wall?" Angie laughs.

"Yes!" Carly joins in with Angie. "Should we tell him to get a restraining order?"

Angie and Carly fall into each other, gasping for air, laughing. My heart smiles, seeing them like that. They are relaxed and having a great time together.

"Hi, ladies." Joey winks.

"This is amazing!" I beam.

"Alright, everyone, settle down, so I can read this last question for round one."

"Let's go!" Nicole screams. "You're coming to our cabana tomorrow, after we win this thing."

"That sounds fun." Joey's voice is as sexy as ever. "Here's the last question, and it's worth double points."

Everyone focuses their attention on him like it's 1996 and they're trying to get the high score in *Super Mario Bros.* "What was the name of Hillary and Bill Clinton's cat?"

My friends' eyes land on me. "Oh, oh. I swear I know this." My head scrambles for the answer. The question has everyone stumped.

"Hold up." Nicole eyes the table next to us. "They're cheating."

Looking over, we see a woman discreetly talking into a watch she's trying to hide in her hand. A second later, she shouts. "Socks, the cat's name was Socks!"

Nicole springs to her feet, pointing an accusatory finger. "They cheated. She has a watch. Open your hands. Let everyone see!"

The woman makes a face at Nicole like she's been caught paying an admissions specialist to get her kid into college. She opens her palms, her expression softening as she shows everyone they're empty.

"You just had a watch!" Nicole yells.

"I don't know what you're talking about," the woman says coolly.

Nicole stomps over to the table. "Where's the watch?"

Carly, Angie, and I jump up, ready to hold Nicole back from doing something stupid. She always goes overboard.

"You'd better get out of my face." The woman crosses her arms, locking eyes with Nicole.

The entire lobby goes quiet.

"You're a cheater. Where did you put the watch?"

There's a loud squeak as the woman Nicole's accusing pushes back her chair and stands. "What did you say?"

Joey runs over. "Ladies. Let's move on. We've still got round two. And I'll swing by the winners' cabana. But only if we get back to trivia." He puts his arm around Nicole and sings a lyric from "This I Promise You."

"Sure, I guess that works." Nicole's suddenly under the spell of a boy band superstar.

The four of us sit back down. Nicole gives the woman the finger. Once again, she won't take anyone's bullshit.

The alarm for my meeting goes off as the tense situation defuses. I pull my watch out of my bag.

"Sorry, guys, I've got to jump on this Zoom." I try to make my voice sound nonchalant, even though I'm angry at myself for agreeing to meet with Amanda.

"You can't leave now. We have to take those losers down." Nicole gives the table next to us another dirty look.

"You'll beat them. Keep it up for round two." I eke out my words, heartbroken for leaving right when it seems like we've recaptured something we've lacked since our senior year. Getting out my chair, I pick up my watch and grab my computer bag.

Carly rolls her eyes. "I can't believe you're doing a Zoom with your boss at nine p.m. on a Sunday, on vacation. Are you going to miss the Boyz II Men concert too?"

"But it's only six p.m. in California." Immediately, I realize how pointless my response is. "Be back soon." My shoulders tense. Why am I choosing Amanda over my friends? Why am I always putting Amanda first? Suddenly, I realize that standing my ground, right here, right now, will prove I'm ready to make the changes my family needs.

This is my chance to set boundaries. "You know what, I'm skipping the Zoom!" I sit back down in my chair.

"Really? I'm proud of you!" Angie nods her approval. For a moment, she looks like her mom.

Instantly, I'm reminded of the gentle way Angie's mom always encouraged me to slow down and enjoy life. But just as I'm processing this, my watch alarm buzzes for the second time.

"Turn it off." Annoyed, Carly glances at my watch on the table.

A moment later, my secretary Charlie is calling. When I don't answer, he hangs up and calls again.

Carly reaches out to grab my watch, but I shove her hand away. It feels like a powerful magnetic force is pulling me down, and I have no way to fight it. I have to answer Charlie's call, or my anxiety will consume me. Maybe I need to take a baby step before I push back. I try to rationalize, although I'm crushed with disappointment in myself.

"I'm sorry, but I really can't miss this meeting." I grab my things and rush off to find a quiet spot before anyone else can comment. I don't need my friends to make me feel worse.

As I walk through the lobby, I justify joining the Zoom by reminding myself of my lifelong, compulsive drive for achievement. *Or my mom's lifelong compulsive drive for achievement?* How do I just stop? Isn't realizing that I *want* to stop a positive step forward? I convince myself that's enough of a win for now.

"Hey, Liliana!" Luca waves at me from a couch in the lobby.

I notice that young girl sitting on the couch a few feet away. It doesn't seem like they're together.

"Hi." I'm glad to have the distraction.

I doubt he took Angie's passport. I bet Angie misplaced it. She was drunk the night she lost it. Really drunk. Too drunk. *Hmm.* It makes me wonder if Carly and Nicole may be right. Is it possible that the emotional consequences of the FBI's involvement in bringing her home are lurking under her do-over life? I picture the pushy reporters who swarmed around her as she hurried inside her house and how it felt to hug her after being afraid she was dead. Am I too consumed with work to notice the ripple effects on Angie's life?

Outside, there's a courtyard next to a row of plants with exotic yellow leaves. I take a seat at a wooden table next to a wall covered in vines. Pulling out my computer, I log onto the meeting link. When the window pops open, Amanda's on my screen in a blood-red suit, flanked by her secretary and mine. Our new hire, Julie, smiles from a video frame. I'm surprised she's on the call, but the earlier we loop her in on this case, the sooner it will be off my plate.

Charlie smiles. "How's St. McAna? Looks lush."

Amanda cuts in before I can answer. "This is the worst possible time for you to be away."

Charlie stares straight into the camera, his eyes bulging at Amanda's angry comment. My body stiffens like she's about to throw a punch through my computer screen. We spend the next hour going back and forth about details that could have waited until I got back to California. I'm sure I've missed the rest of trivia night, and for what? So, Amanda could try to control the uncontrollable?

I snap the bracelet around my wrist, reminding myself I'm on the cusp of change.

Just as we end the meeting, my computer rings with a FaceTime call from Esther. I click the button, eager to answer it. I miss my girls, and this is a great opportunity to connect with Josh.

"Hi, sweetie," I say, but all I see is her face from the nose down. She's smiling, and her line of crooked teeth fills my screen. The image wobbles and then she reappears. This time I see her entire face. My heart swells.

"Where were you?" She twirls an unruly blond curl through her fingers.

"What do you mean?"

"Daddy's been calling you. But you didn't pick up."

Shoot, my phone's in the box on the table. "I'm sorry. I don't have my phone with me."

"But you have your computer?" I hear Josh but don't see him. I assume he's standing beside Esther.

My head throbs, hearing his irritation. "It's a long story. I had a Zoom with Amanda." *Why did I say that?*

"A Zoom with Amanda?" Josh's face replaces Esther's. "But you're on vacation." He shakes his head. "I wish you could unwind. You need a break."

Disappointment flickers in my heart. This call is already going downhill. I debate telling him more about the new hire and saying some things I've learned in that self-help book, but maybe I should wait to do it when he's not upset with me.

I disregard his comment. "Is everything okay?" I ask. "Esther said you've been trying to reach me."

"I don't understand why you're Zooming with Amanda while you're away." Josh ignores my question.

Snap, snap, snap. The bracelet Esther gave me stings my wrist. I push myself to say the things I've been wanting to tell him. My body freezes as soon as I open my mouth. I'm afraid if I let an ounce of emotion creep in, I won't be able to.

Taking a deep breath, I aim for a professional approach and *cry on the inside* the way my mom taught me to do. "You're right. I shouldn't have agreed to the Zoom, but on a positive note, it afforded me the opportunity to talk further with our new head of legal. She'll be taking over a portion of my responsibilities. This will improve our circumstances."

Listening to myself, I know it sounds like I'm speaking to opposing counsel, not my husband. Years of controlling my emotions have a chokehold on my ability to interact naturally in such a stressful situation. When was the last time Josh saw me cry?

A strange look crosses Josh's face. "You sound weird. But honestly, I've heard all this before."

Sadness descends. My composure begins to crumble but quickly turns to anger. "Aren't you excited? I'm telling you what you've been waiting for. I'm going to set firmer boundaries. I'll be home more. I'll have less work to do." I shift my head toward the table and take a breath, reminding myself I'm trying to keep my emotions out of this.

"Okay," he says, responding in the same dismissive tone he uses with Esther when she says something fantastical, like that she's going to get a unicorn and ride it to the moon.

"Okay?" I ask. "Okay," I say again, irritated. "Aren't you excited? This is great news."

"I guess," he says again dismissively, then Esther's face takes over the screen.

She smiles while my heart shatters. Josh is neither excited nor angry about my news. He is completely indifferent. Entirely uninterested. I'd prefer *any* reaction over his apathy, even him accusing me of false promises.

"Mommy, I got to hold the Torah at Simchat Torah." Esther beams with pride.

I soak in her smile and let the warm sensation in my heart replace the sadness I feel.

"Yes, Rabbi Dalia picked her to dance with the Torah at school tonight," Evie shouts in the background.

"Wow, Esther! That's amazing," I manage to say, despite feeling overwhelmed by despair. I'm disappointed I've missed another special moment. I'm disappointed I got on the Zoom call. I'm disappointed my kids don't need me. I'm disappointed I made time to go on vacation with my friends although I never make time for my family. I'm disappointed I thought it would be easy to repair my marriage. I'm disappointed about so many things.

I squelch my distress and focus back on Esther. "I bet holding the Torah was fun."

"Until she almost dropped it," Evie shouts from beyond my view, never missing an opportunity to tease her little sister.

"Did not," Esther singsongs back.

"Did too. Daddy, tell her."

"Evie's right. It was dicey for a moment." Josh rushes through his words off camera. Is he too frustrated to talk to me?

The image wobbles again, and then Evie's on my screen, standing close to Esther. "But Rabbi Dalia saved the day like a boss hero."

Esther giggles. "The Torah is really heavy."

I force myself to smile even though my heart is sinking toward the floor.

"Girls, time to get ready for bed." I hear Josh's voice again, but this time it sounds far away. He must be calling them from another room. He didn't even say goodbye. *He didn't even say goodbye.* The words repeat in my head over and over.

"Bye, Mommy." Esther waves and then my screen goes dark.

Closing my eyes, I picture her twirling with the Torah as everyone celebrates finishing and restarting the sacred text. The holiday is a joyous occasion about the opportunity to start over. *Was Esther's FaceTime a sign that it's time for me to do the same?* After this disastrous call, I'm ready to hit the reset button no matter what it takes. I'm ready to let Josh see me break down and beg him for another chance.

I FaceTime him from my computer, but he doesn't pick up. I try again as desperation closes in. How foolish of me to think I could approach our problems with the levelheaded, non-emotional demeanor I use in my career. I don't care if Josh sees me sobbing from thousands of miles away. I'm ready to make changes. But is it too late?

CHAPTER 24

Nicole

Emerald Jewel All-Inclusive Resort
October 2nd 🎵 Two Days Ago

SNOOP DOGG LEANS into me, and we both rap the lyrics for "Gin and Juice." The crowd around the pool sways to the beat in perfect rhythm. This is lit! Snoop showed up at this nineties boy band weekend. And we're onstage, vibing to one of his greatest hits!

Reaching out his hand, he tries to give me the microphone. But then I hear a strange buzzing sound. I ignore it. It's like my entire life has been leading to this moment. My badass bitch self is about to burst through my suburban mom exterior.

I grab the mic, but then the strange noise booms again and again. I glance at the DJ, trying to figure out where it's coming from. My body jolts up, and I realize I'm in bed at the Emerald Jewel Resort. I was dreaming. I hear the sound again. It's my phone. It's vibrating against the glass top of the nightstand.

The shots I did after we lost trivia are messing with my head. But the cheaters who won were so smug, making fun of me for giving the wrong answer to the tie-breaking question. *What stuffed animal fad debuted in 1993?* I thought the answer was the Furby, remembering the weird hamster-owl creature I was nuts about. But the correct answer was Beanie Babies. Of course, it was Beanie Babies. Epic fail!

My phone rings again, and I grab it. Garrett's name flashes across the screen. But it's the middle of the night. Why is he calling? The kids. Are the kids okay?!

I push the button on my phone, answering his call. "What's wrong?" My heart beats so fast and hard, it's like a time bomb is about to explode in my chest.

"The kids are throwing up. All of them are sick."

"Oh, shit." My poor kids!

"And that too," he says, dead serious.

"Huh?" I ask, confused.

"They can't stop going to the bathroom. They've got it coming out of both ends."

I picture my kids sprawled across the bathroom floor crying. I feel awful that I'm not there to help them. My poor, poor babies.

Garrett lets out a forceful breath. "I'm in over my head. You need to come home."

"But Natanya's there. It sucks that the kids are sick, but she's there to hold it down. And since she's a nursing major, she's got this." My mom guilt nearly chokes me as I speak. I should be there with them.

"That's exactly the problem. She caught the norovirus at her internship. She went home a few hours ago. Now the kids have it."

"Crap."

"Literally and figuratively," Garrett replies.

In any other situation, I'd laugh at his sarcasm. He's always had the best deadpan humor. But I'm worried. Garrett has no clue how to care for our sick kids. I've always handled everything—crushing pills and putting them in applesauce, running a bath for high fevers, setting up the humidifier. It's always been easier for me to do it myself. Taking the time to explain what had to be done was an extra step.

Pulling my phone away from my ear, I toss my head back and stare at the ceiling, completely over it. I haven't spent a night away from my kids in over a year. Can't a girl catch a break? I prepped for every scenario ahead of time, leaving extra baseball pants in Natanya's room, in case Garrett couldn't find any clean ones. Making playdates for Chelsea so Garrett wouldn't have to listen to episodes of *Bluey* on repeat. Giving my kids vitamin C and elderberry for the last few days to keep them from getting sick.

As I spiral, I hear Garrett's voice and push the phone back up against my ear.

"So, there's a flight that leaves in the morning. It flies through Raleigh. I'm going to book a ticket so you can get home." He sounds really panicked.

I stare at the sliver of moonlight streaming through my curtains. Yes, I'm worried about my kids. They're sick, and Garrett doesn't have a clue how to deal with this. Does he even know the name of our pediatrician? But I shouldn't have to fly home because my kids are puking. And what would my friends think? I've convinced them I'm not lame with the boudoir photos. I can't ditch this vacation because Garrett needs me to take care of the kids. Plus, last night, partying with them at the resort's disco after Boyz II Men was a ten out of ten. I got Angie, Carly, and Liliana to do the Macarena. Line dancing! All of us together! Angie even mentioned that her mom taught us the dance. She was talking about a fun time with her mom. Twice in one night! It was shocking in the same way it's shocking when I put the kids to bed and not one of them comes out needing something the entire night. Shockingly awesome!

"I'm sorry, Garrett. I'm not heading back. Besides, I'm only here for one more night. You got this." Telling him I can't be his crutch isn't stressing me like I thought it would.

"Are you kidding me? I have work tomorrow. What am I supposed to do? Cancel my appointments, reschedule my calls?"

Every muscle in my body clenches. But it's not because I'm nervous. It's my body's way of solidifying into something hard and indestructible. This *dadlife* Garrett's living is out of hand. "Yes, Garrett. That's exactly what you're supposed to do. Cancel your day, stay home, and take care of your kids."

"You're on vacation for fun. You're not doing anything essential.

Please, I need you to come home. I don't know what to do. You always take care of the kids when they're sick."

That's when it hits me. I'm part of the problem. The pelvic separation is part of the problem. Garrett bathing baby Hank as I watched, stuck in a wheelchair, is part of the problem. The way he gently washed Hank's wispy hair, then wrapped him in a red towel, playfully making him fly like he was a superhero, made me feel pointless. For almost a year, I had to depend on Garrett, my mother, and a nanny to take care of Hank. When I could finally carry him, feed him, change his diaper, and give him a bath, I refused to let anyone else, even Garrett, help. And when I finally got the go-ahead to go back to work, I still felt the same way. There was no way I was going to let someone else take care of my baby. If only I'd thought more about the big picture before leaving my job. How it would affect my self-worth. How it would force Garrett and me into traditional parenting roles. But, at that moment, all I cared about was making up for the months I missed with my baby. I overcompensated after recovering by not letting Garrett help at all.

But, right now, I don't want to think about how my pelvic separation has had a domino effect on my life.

Who does Garrett think he is to say what I'm doing isn't essential? I'm so angry, I start to sweat. Why are stay-at-home moms expected to be mothering every hour of every day? People see anything else as indulgent. God forbid a mom hires a babysitter to play tennis, get a manicure, read a book, or *take a vacation*. The world judges us for daring to be multifaceted.

I scream into the phone. "I'm sick of being one-dimensional. I'm not a Flat Stanley!"

"What are you talking about?" Garrett's confused. He has no idea what a Flat Stanley is. Of course, he doesn't know what it is. I've never asked him to help with the project done by every preschool in America, even though I've been through three rounds of it.

I'm kicking myself for contributing to this situation by not asking more of Garrett. But even if that's true, I'm furious he thinks I should come home. What the actual fuck!

"I'm allowed to be on vacation and to stay on vacation. Even if the kids are sick!" The words fly out of my mouth. Closing my eyes, I try to catch my breath. I'm on the verge of a panic attack.

"Why are you so mad? It's just that…"

I drop the phone on the bed. Garrett continues to talk. I inhale to the count of four and blow out to the count of eight. I can't wait to tell Josh how insane Garrett is. Josh gets how hard it is to be the default parent. But, as soon as I think this, I realize how crazy it is that my first instinct is to tell Josh. My *best friend's* husband! Guilt beats in my body.

Patting down drips of sweat on my face, I tell myself *it is essential* that I get this break from *momlife*. Developing beyond the constraints of motherhood is vital to my existence. Plus, my childhood besties and I are one step away from version 2.0. I can't leave now.

I put my phone back to my ear. Garrett's still discussing flight options.

"And I can use miles, so it won't cost us anything to change your flight."

"Listen, Garrett, I'm not coming home. You'll figure it out with the kids. I'm going back to bed." I hang up before he can say anything.

Climbing under the covers, my head pounds. Should I go home and take care of my sick kids? Should I stay here and spend quality time with my friends?

Five minutes later, I receive a text from Garrett.

Garrett: Got you this one-way flight.

I stare at the link that follows his text. Am I getting on that plane?

CHAPTER 25

Resort Guest Melissa Henson

Now
Emerald Jewel All-Inclusive Resort
October 5th ♪ 6:30 a.m.

"I SAW ONE OF those women push another one into the pool." Melissa adjusts the knot in her kaftan, aware the police officer she's talking to doesn't recognize the latest in fashionable resort wear. "They were fighting. It was during karaoke." She takes a sip from her enormous water bottle and reads the name on the officer's badge, *Claasen*.

The officer sighs, twirling the edge of his orange mustache. "Yes, I've heard about the pool fight. Can you remember which women were fighting? He flips his phone, showing the guest an image of the four women in pink.

She shifts her body forward to get a better look. As she bends toward him, water from the straw of her ridiculously large jug drips onto the officer's phone.

"Oh, I'm sorry," she says, sick of consuming one hundred and fifty ounces of water every day. She wonders which of the health gurus she follows came up with this number. It's beyond unreasonable.

Pulling his phone away, the officer wipes the drips with his sleeve. "You're the fourth guest today with a monstrous steel cup," he complains.

"American women take their hydration seriously." Melissa laughs, hoping her joke will quell his irritation, but Officer Claasen ignores her and flips his phone back in her direction. She refocuses on the image, realizing he's all business.

"I can't remember which two were involved. I was wearing dark sunglasses."

Wait. Were the blinding black polarized lenses with UV ray protection also recommended by the health guru who insists she drink one hundred and fifty ounces of water a day? Now she's concerned she's getting all her health advice from fifteen-second TikToks.

"So, you couldn't really see who was fighting," Officer Claasen continues.

"No, but it seemed more like one of those asinine incidents that occur when people drink before noon on a weekday. I think someone took a video. It could be a meme by now."

The officer rolls his eyes. "A meme? Those short videos that go viral often showcasing cats?"

Melissa nods, sensing the officer's frustration. It's annoying. She could be lounging by the pool, but she's here trying to help him sort out a disturbance from last night. She heard that a woman had her passport stolen. The small number of guests who are up this early don't seem to care. Everyone wants to get more time in the sun before the buses come to take them to the airport later.

"Did you witness anything else I should know about?" Officer Claasen's leg bounces up and down.

"Show me that picture again." She feels the knot of her kaftan slipping for the second time. *Fashionable but not practical.* She tightens her garment, then points at the picture. "This one in the sparkly dress fell by the bar last night while some of her friends were dancing. She got mad and started yelling at someone. Maybe you've seen him? He's the only young, good-looking man here." Suddenly, she's fantasizing about what the hot kid looks like naked. Warmth inflames her thighs as she wonders just how big—

"Why was she yelling at him?"

The officer's question startles her, pulling her mind away from the pleasing image. "I'm not sure why. I think he may have tripped her."

"They were arguing?" Officer Claasen's bushy eyebrows rise.

"I wouldn't call it arguing. He was angry. He stormed off."

"On a scale from one to ten, how angry was he?"

"Oh, I don't know. I saw him not too long after at the bar in the lobby. He sat next to me." She remembers she considered spilling a drink on his lap as an opener and a way to judge if he was worth her time. But then, that young girl showed up.

"You saw him at the bar?" the officer confirms.

"Yes, he was with that beautiful young girl who's been traipsing around the resort in a white bikini. I mean, why bother wearing a bikini if it's white? Just walk around naked." She tightens her lips, showing her disapproval.

"Wait, with who? No one's mentioned this young girl. Do you know anything about her? Did they come here together?"

"I'm sorry, I don't know. All I can say is that I've seen them sneaking around together. It's like they don't want to get caught. But she's all over him. I mean, who can blame her? He's gorgeous." She brushes a hand over the laugh lines around her mouth, wondering if she should schedule that mini facelift she's been considering—then she'd have a chance with a young stud.

"What were they talking about?" Officer Claasen leans forward.

She stares off to the side for a moment, thinking. "I'm not sure. But the girl was trying to calm him down."

"Think hard. Can you remember anything he said?"

"Hmm." She closes her eyes. "They didn't stay at the bar for long. Like I said, they were trying to keep a low profile."

"Take a second. Put yourself back in that moment. See if any of their conversation comes to mind."

She closes her eyes again, then pops them open. "Yes! I remember a weird thing he said. It was something like, 'We're not going to do that.'"

"So, the young man said, '*We're not doing that*'?" the officer confirms.

"Yes." She nods, momentarily distracted by her streaky fake tan.

"What was his tone? Or his body language? Did either give you an idea of what he was feeling when he said that? Did he seem excited, happy, scared, angry?"

She watches the police officer, feeling sorry that he has to go through life with hair the color of a tangerine. "I'm not sure what it was about, but whatever she was asking him to do, he definitely didn't want to."

CHAPTER 26

Carly

Emerald Jewel All-Inclusive Resort
October 4th 🎵 Yesterday

#OOTD: Five-pocket, four-way stretch 25-inch fuchsia tights. Slim fit, waist-length, dry-fit, lemon-colored tank. Yellow breathable mesh platform running shoes with bright pink laces. Lightweight gray baseball cap with moisture wicking. Apple Watch with breathable sports band.

PULL ON MY Fast and Free Lululemon bottoms and coordinating tank. I'll admit, I love the way these clothes highlight my firm muscles and lack of body fat. Yes, I notice when jealous moms check me out. While some women parade around in spandex for show, I make sweating a priority. Daily Pilates and Peloton workouts are part of my routine. Not too hard when you're staring at the adorable face of a hot instructor like Bradley Rose.

As I walk toward the resort's main building, I slip in my AirPods and put on my watch. It's almost recovered from the pool. It plays music, but I still can't use it to send texts or make calls. Walking into the lobby, I recall the crowd of people last night. I picture Nicole unleashing a string of curse words at the trivia winners. She's never been able to control herself. But that's what makes her fun. That vintage

TV footage of her gyrating in a yellow bikini onstage at MTV's Spring Break in Panama City Beach is iconic. Looking back, I can't believe Angie's mom volunteered to take us to Florida as juniors in high school. Unfortunately, she didn't know the hotel she booked was a short beach walk from MTV's party on the sand. Nicole seized her chance, and Angie's mom handled it well, letting us stay for a couple of songs while she hid behind a fifteen-foot MTV sign in front of the ocean.

As I exit toward the pool, I drop towels, bags, and flip-flops on several lounge chairs. Since I'm an early riser, I save chairs for everyone. *Who cares if it's against the rules!*

Walking past the pool, I step onto the beach. The calm turquoise water stretches out, meeting the horizon. There's not a single person out here. Looks like I'm the only one up for a morning beach run.

I take a few minutes to stretch, pulling my ankle to my rear end. Skipping this crucial step always results in knee pain or a back spasm. I resent reaching the age where I wake up with aches and pains from routine exercise. But what I resent more is waking up with aches and pains for no reason at all. Those stupid reels are true. I can pull a muscle by breathing wrong.

For a moment, I think about where I want to position myself for my #OOTD post, but then remember, my phone's still not working. It's sitting in a container of rice I got from the concierge. Hopefully, it's drying out. I need to post soon, or my follower count is going to plummet. But even worse, my sponsors are going to drop me.

Ignoring my stress, I open the Peloton app on my watch, choose an outside run, and start moving. As I pick up speed, I try not to think about Marco and instead concentrate on helping Angie with her lost (*stolen*) passport at the embassy later. But thoughts of Marco interrupt every thought of Angie. I move my legs faster, hoping the burn helps me concentrate on Angie's problem instead of my marriage.

But then something strange happens. I contemplate letting myself go there. Perhaps it's the salty air and the calming ocean, and the knowledge that, right at this moment, my relationship with Marco is a far-off construct, like perfect abs or Pinterest-perfect holiday decorating. *Even after ten trips to HomeGoods, I couldn't achieve the elevated Christmas aesthetic I was going for.*

My mind flips through my fears about Marco, sorting, analyzing, and imagining how different scenarios may play out.

What if I had caught him having an affair at the hotel?

I can't believe I was mistaken for a hooker while I was spying on him.

Maybe he's not having an affair.

When did we become strangers?

I should have agreed to try the couplehood app.

Does he want to leave me?

Do I want to leave him?

Are we using my broken phone as an excuse to ignore each other?

Was I fooling myself thinking our marriage was fine just because we don't fight?

Do other people's marriages lack emotional intimacy?

How is it possible to be with someone all the time but still feel alone?

Can we save our marriage?

What would Bianca do if we split up?

What would I do if we split up?

What would people think if they knew I wasn't perfect?

By the time I've considered every situation imaginable, forty-five minutes pass and my workout is over. *There! I DID IT!* I thought about my problems and I'm still standing, breathing, in fact—although my breathing feels labored.

Looking around, I don't know where I am. I turn back to the hotel. It's a bright-yellow dot in the distance.

Suddenly, I'm fighting for air like it's the last designer dress at a sample sale. My watch shows my heart rate's sky high. The scorching sun beats down on my head. I have to find shade. I scan the land behind me. There's a large, salmon-colored house a few yards away. I walk to it, trying to keep my breath steady. As I get closer, I see a cabana inside a low fence nestled next to a patch of palm trees. A "For Sale" sign's stuck in the sand. I hop over the fence, hoping the house is vacant.

Opening my Spotify, I click on my high school hits playlist, lay down in the cabana, and take several deep breaths. The mix of Hootie & the Blowfish, Alanis Morissette, Wilson Phillips, and other sentimental tunes does the trick. My heart rate eases.

Minutes later, I notice a couple walking down the beach holding hands. As they move closer, I realize it's Luca and the young girl. *Why are they this far from the hotel?* It's suspicious. I crouch down, trying to stay out of sight.

I'm startled when he points to this house, and they walk in my direction. Luckily, they're still far enough away that they don't see me. In fact, Luca and the girl are so caught up in kissing each other, they don't realize I'm watching them. *Now's my chance to find out what he's up to.*

I crawl through the sand and hide behind the trunk of a large palm tree, trying to eavesdrop. Here I am again, in investigation mode, like I was at the hotel the other night. I'm turning into some type of perimenopausal spy.

But what if Luca says something about Angie's passport?

This afternoon, I'm going with her to the embassy. Maybe I'll hear something that will prove I have her best interests at heart. She finally seemed to relax last night at trivia and the disco club. I swear I could feel the abyss between us narrowing as we stood side by side doing the Macarena.

I hear the girl's voice as they approach. "I keep telling you, it's no big deal. Just chill."

Luca stops and faces her. "We don't need to take it that far. I don't want this to blow up."

My mind spins. *Take what too far?*

"We're in a good spot," he continues. "That's it. It goes no further."

I don't want this to blow up. It goes no further.

His words beat through my brain, making my temples throb. I knew I *was right* about Luca! Fortunately, he seems satisfied that he has Angie's passport. But wouldn't it be great if I could record some of their conversation? To prove I'm not crazy!

My hands shake as I tap my watch. I'm sweating but unsure if it's from fear or a hot flash.

All of a sudden, my watch blares the song "Ironic." *Oh no, I hit the wrong button!*

My insides twist when Luca and the girl stop short. What should I do? Come out from behind the tree or let them find me hidden here? I decide to take control of the situation.

"Oh, hey." I walk toward them. *Act casual!*

Luca's face contorts into a strange expression. "What are you doing here?"

Fidgeting with my hat, I answer his question with the truth. "I was out running, took a break in that cabana, and now here we are."

The girl glares at me, and I can't tell if it's the angsty expression of someone her age annoyed by the interruption of her tryst, or if she's worried I overheard something. Which I *did*!

Luca's eyes slide to the tree and back to my face. His nostrils flare. "Well, why didn't you say hi? Why are you hiding behind a tree?"

"I…um. I was… It was just… I was trying to give you privacy." *Stop stammering!*

The girl faces Luca, and I can't help but stare at the way her white thong bikini bottom shows off her perfectly sculpted ass.

"I think she was spying on us."

"Spying on you," I repeat the girl's words. "But I was here first. That doesn't make sense." I act shocked the girl would suggest such a thing while my heart hammers against my ribs.

Luca's face has a quizzical expression. "Are you spying on us?"

Why are they both concerned I'm spying? They must be hiding something! "Like I said, I was here first."

"Maybe that's true, but you were eavesdropping." The girl faces me, this time showing off her round, pert breasts. *Oh, to be twenty again!*

Luca inches closer. "I know you think I have something to do with Angie's passport, but I don't. Ease up. You're crossing a line." His eyes narrow with anger.

The girl leans into Luca and whispers in his ear. He nods. "And if you're smart, you won't tell anyone you saw us."

"I was not spying on you." I repeat. This time, my voice is more convincing.

They both give me disapproving stares and walk to the cabana. They sit down, uninterested in questioning me further. There's a slow pulsing in my ears. Although it seems like Luca's done with Angie, I should tell her what I overheard, even though I know she'll be angry I'm still accusing him of stealing her passport.

Then again, I could create a to-do list for the embassy and skip right over it. She'll need proof of her address, the security guard's report, and any photo identification in her wallet. *Even a Costco card.*

But as I let my mind race with ways I can distract myself from talking with Angie about Luca, I realize covering up problems with a stupid to-do list doesn't work. Why did I think rollerblading and getting French manicures would comfort Angie after her mom died? I wish I had asked her what she needed instead of swooping in with quick fixes. It's possible my dad got it wrong. Maybe I shouldn't immediately solve problems with superficial solutions. Maybe I should let problems fester so I can learn from them.

"One more thing before you go," the girl calls out, meeting my eyes with a cold, hard stare. "If you don't stay out of our business, you'll regret it."

CHAPTER 27

Angie

"I'M GONNA BE sick." Carly leans out the window, gagging. Her long blond ponytail whips in the wind as our cab bumps and swerves on our way back from the US Embassy.

I'm convinced I've misplaced my passport. Maybe it got pushed behind the tray in the safe or something? There's no way Luca took it.

Carly pulls her head back inside the car and takes a deep breath. I have to admit it was great having her help today. She knew which forms I needed to fill out and told me to bring proof of my travel itinerary. Most importantly, she's the one who insisted we take pictures of our passports before we left for St. McAna. That photo expedited the entire process. My replacement passport will be ready tomorrow.

Watching Carly take charge made me realize I should have been honest and admitted I just wanted to cry and cry and cry after my mom died. All those meaningless things she planned to keep me busy made me feel like she didn't know me at all and just added to the stress I felt about my dad. Didn't she notice he was a shell? I was certain she'd realize after he sat despondent while we took prom pictures. But she didn't.

"I'm going to puke." Carly cups her hand over her mouth.

"Sir, pull over!" I point to the side of the road, and our driver parks his cab.

Carly jumps out and vomits into an abandoned grassy field. I rush out after her. When she looks up, her eyes are glassy.

"You still get carsick."

"I'm better now." Her words sound thick and slow.

The cab driver sits in his silver Suzuki, unconcerned.

"His driving's pretty awful," I agree. "I kept my eyes closed."

Carly leans over again, dry heaving. When she recovers, I lead her to the sidewalk, and we both sit down.

"I didn't puke last night, but I'm puking now from a cab ride." Her voice rises as she speaks, making her statement sound like a question.

"You feeling better now?"

"Yeah, I'm tired. We were out late. It was worth it, though. Last night's 'In da Club,' theme brought back lots of memories."

A smile spreads across my face. Nothing tops nineties dance music like "Tootsee Roll" and "Groove Is in the Heart." The only strange thing is that I didn't see Luca the entire night. I tried texting him, but he never responded.

"Can you get back in the cab? I think we're close to the hotel."

"I need a few more minutes. This guy drives as badly as Nicole did when she first got her license."

We both laugh.

Carly continues. "Three fender benders before she was seventeen. You'd think she'd have learned the first time not to *Cabbage Patch* while driving." Carly clenches her fists and moves them around in front of her body, doing the hip-hop dance move.

I do the same. A moment later, our cab driver joins in.

"Bust a move!" I shout.

Carly and I lean into each other, giggling—just like last night at trivia. There's a feeling of hope about our relationship that almost brings me to tears.

"Last night was a good time," I say, happy Carly and I have not only pushed past the Luca drama but are tapping into something we'd lost. It's stupid that we always fight on these trips. I know part of it's because Carly's hurt I left Hamilton Beach. But it's also because I keep a wall up when we're together. A wall that protects me from my guilt. But a wall that's also prevented me from doing things like dancing the *Cabbage Patch* with her on the side of a road in St. McAna Island.

I clasp my hands together, aware I'm acting differently than I did in Miraval. Is it possible these little chaos theory tweaks are having an impact? I'm letting my guard down and enjoying this time with my friends—and genuinely connecting with them. I even brought up my mom last night. *What's changed?*

Then I remember how good it felt to tell Luca about my past that first night on the beach. Maybe the best way to knock down the barrier that's been keeping me from connecting with my friends is to talk about what happened. Maybe my shame's power comes from the secret place I've buried it inside of me.

Carly picks up a blade of grass and smooths it through her fingers. "Seeing Boyz II Men last night was a bucket list item. And then a surprise appearance by Cody from Peloton!"

I grin, thinking more about last night. After losing trivia and licking our wounds, Liliana returned from her work call. I feel bad that her boss is unreasonable. On past trips, I got the impression that she loved her job and the climb to the top. But it's obvious she's miserable.

Carly pulls a piece of gum from her belt bag. I'm relieved to see it's dry after her unplanned dip in the pool.

"This vomit taste is disgusting." Unwrapping the gum, she pops it into her mouth. "I wonder if Nicole got sick? How does she handle all those shots?"

"Nicole's always been a party girl."

"I probably shouldn't say anything." Carly shifts uncomfortably. "But I got a feeling from Liliana that things aren't going well for Nicole and Garrett."

My mind wanders to Patton for a moment, thankful for our solid partnership. "Oh no. Hopefully, it's one of those low points and the upswing is around the corner. You know how marriage is."

Carly's face goes pale.

"Shoot, are you going to be sick again?"

She nods weakly and stares into the distance. "I'm fine," she says, but her lower lip trembles. I wonder if she's on the verge of tears.

"Wait, is everything okay?"

She shrugs a couple of times, like she's trying to ease an uncomfortable sensation. "I'm fine. Just not feeling a hundred percent."

I pause, sensing there's something else going on. But she stays quiet, twisting another blade of grass in her hand. Sadly, if she needed support, I'm the last person she'd turn to. We haven't been close for decades. But I take a chance and dig in.

"Are you sure there's nothing you want to talk about? I'm great at listening, and our cab driver seems happy to keep the roadside dance party going." I add a bit of humor, knowing she's unlikely to open up. Especially to me, the best friend that abandoned her.

"It's just the nausea."

I try again. "You can tell me anything, Carly. I know our relationship has been difficult. And Miraval…well, it wasn't great." I pause, unsure of what I'm trying to say. The rawness of the moment is overwhelming.

"Yeah, Miraval was an epic fail, as Nicole would say." She laughs, skipping the fact that I said she could tell me anything. Obviously, she doesn't feel comfortable confiding in me.

It's clear I can't tell her the full truth about the weeks I was missing. Telling her will reopen old wounds and may ruin this chance to rebuild our friendship.

"Well, somehow you still look amazing, despite puking on the side of the road." I fill the silence. "Do you think you can make it back to the resort?"

"I'll make it." She stands and adjusts her belt bag.

We climb back inside the cab.

"Thanks again for coming to the embassy."

"You're lucky you'll get the paperwork in time to leave tomorrow night as planned."

My heart pangs, wondering if this trip will end like all the others. With no forward movement in our relationship. The sadness catches me off guard. I don't remember feeling this way on other trips.

The cab swerves right. Our bodies slide toward the driver's side.

"Sir, you need to slow down, or my friend is going to puke in your cab."

The driver's eyes catch mine in the rearview. He smiles, not understanding that I'm mad. "Yeah, no problem."

Back at the resort, we stumble into the lobby as if we just got off a booze cruise and collapse on two enormous, cushy chairs covered in a leafy print.

"There you are!" Luca appears, almost like he's been waiting for me.

I wave hello, and he sits on the couch. "Where were you last night?"

He glances away for a moment. There's a long pause. "I got high before dinner. I couldn't move. It sucks that I missed the concert."

Should I be suspicious? No, I will not feed Carly's distrust. Getting too high is a legitimate excuse for a twenty-something-year-old.

He scoots closer to me. "Word on the street is that you called the cops about your passport."

Carly gives me an aggressive stare, unable to control herself. I tried again to explain about his mom while we were at the embassy, but she told me she didn't want to talk about it.

Shifting back to Luca, I continue. "Yes, my temporary paperwork will be ready in time to catch my flight home."

"St. Louis, right?" He nods to confirm his statement is correct.

"Yeah, but did we talk about that? I can't remember."

Carly jumps out of her chair. "Are you asking if she's from St. Louis? Why do you care?"

Luca's face turns red. "For the millionth time. I did not take your friend's passport," he snarls.

Carly takes a step back. "Come on, Ang. Let's go find our friends."

In a blink, Luca's standing in front of her. Nervous energy runs down my spine. He leans close to her face.

"I'm here because my mom loved boy bands, and she's dead!" He storms away.

My eyes trail him to the lobby's gift shop. Why does Carly keep provoking him? Losing a parent at a young age is a deeply painful wound that never heals. To this day, I can't see a black dress without remembering the one I wore to my mom's funeral. It hung in my closet for months after, a cheap polyester symbol of my grief. I wonder if Luca's closet had a dark suit that embodied his pain. Carly's wrong on this. She's just wrong. She needs to let it go.

I leap up and follow him to the gift shop, wanting to smooth everything over. Peeking through the window, I watch him walk inside. The young girl that I saw during karaoke hurries over to him by a display of cheap souvenirs. So, I wasn't hallucinating when I saw her the other day.

Luca waves his hands around, almost knocking over a shelf full of St. McAna snow globes. The young girl pats his shoulder, trying to soothe him.

My insides flip over. Am I wrong about Luca? He said he came here solo, but who's this girl? She's the only other person close to his age at the boy band weekend. It's like they're a pair.

"Be careful what you tell him." Carly moves beside me. "How did he know you're from St. Louis if you didn't mention it?"

I think about the deep conversation Luca and I had on the beach that first night. You can't fake those emotions.

Shaking off my suspicions, I face her. "Oh, I bet I told him. I've been drunk this entire trip. I can't remember half the things we talked about."

Her eyes meet mine but flicker with uncertainty. "I wanted to tell you something but was waiting for the right time. We were having fun today—besides the puking part—and I didn't want to ruin it with Luca drama."

"What?" Sweat trickles down my back.

We were having fun. So much so that the loneliness that's frozen over my heart like a solid block of ice is finally cracking.

"I saw him and that girl this morning when I was running. I overheard them talking. Something's up. Or something *was* up and now they're moving on. You need to ask him what he meant so we can find out if he took your passport."

"Carly, I'm telling you to drop it," I huff, annoyed she's trying to fix everything as usual.

"But don't you want to know what they were talking about?"

"No!" Just when things were softening between us, we're back to square one. All my hurt feelings from the past come rushing back. *You can't get over a death by making a to-do list!*

Carly's gaze shifts to the ground. "Fine," she mumbles. "But only because, based on what I heard today, he seems to have gotten what he wanted. But I'm going to keep an eye on him."

"I'm going to take a nap," I say, changing the subject.

"Good idea." Carly moves her hand toward mine but then pulls it back. "You know, I just want to protect you."

My head spins. I don't need her protection! I don't need her to fix my problems! She tried to do that after my mom died but was so focused on keeping me busy she didn't even notice I couldn't leave for college because of my dad!

Wow, am I really still this angry at Carly? It hardly seems fair. I'm the one who ruined everything by running away.

I force myself to take a calming breath. "Thank you," I say, hoping that will be the end of it. But she continues.

"I wish I had known you were planning to run away back then. I would have done anything and everything to help you."

I nod again, while my eyes dart around, searching for an excuse to break away. Yet, part of me wants to tell her everything so we can find our way back to each other. The seventeen-year-old version of myself shudders remembering the woman with all the piercings who looked the other way. The kidnapping headlines. The broken-down motel.

"But you went along with whatever dumb activity I suggested. You laughed at Nicole's jokes. You asked Liliana questions about the stages of grief. You made us believe you were alright. We didn't know what you were planning. We didn't know you were pretending."

Carly stops walking and faces me. Her lips turn downward. I can sense the pain she feels at not having been there in the way I needed all those years ago. I can sense the pain she feels about the loss of our friendship. Guilt descends as I remember waking up in that dilapidated motel, lying stiff and straight on the old bed's thin mattress. I focused on a large yellow stain in the cracked ceiling. I wasn't even afraid. I was a shell devoid of life.

Carly steps in closer. "And we were afraid to show how sad we were about losing your mom because we didn't want to upset you more. But oh, how we cried. Your mom was the linchpin. Your mom was the force that brought us together. We loved her. She gave us all the most amazing gift—each other."

My body vibrates. *They cried?* They were in pain?

"Are you okay?" Carly asks.

My expression must convey the avalanche of feelings I'm having now that I know they were grieving back then too. But then anger. Anger at myself. Why didn't I tell them all I wanted to do back then was sit in my room and cry? Carly's words are a bomb—*your mom was the linchpin.* Was I afraid of losing my best friends after my mom passed away because she was the person who held us all together? Was I afraid I'd lose them by making the situation more difficult, by collapsing into tears, by telling them about my dad?

This fear feels familiar, even though I know it's irrational now. But it's true. *I was afraid of losing them.* The realization takes my breath away.

"Are you okay?" Carly asks again, looking concerned.

I nod. "I'm just exhausted," I say, then take a step forward.

Carly falls in line next to me as we walk to our hotel rooms. Because of what she just said, I finally understand why I didn't tell my friends I was falling apart. And why, when I finally came home, I didn't say more about the fake kidnapping letters.

CHAPTER 28

Carly

Emerald Jewel All-Inclusive Resort
October 4th ♫ Yesterday

ANGIE AND I take the stairs up to our rooms. I shouldn't have brought up the past. But laughing together while dancing the *Cabbage Patch* felt magical. Right then, I decided I needed to apologize for failing her. But I went one step too far, talking about her mom. The thing is, I really, really loved Angie's mom. We always had her full attention, and it was easy to tell she loved spending time with us. Unlike *my* mom and dad, who could barely fit me in between galas and fundraisers.

She slides her key card into her door. "I'm getting into bed." Her face is blank, and I can sense that wall. It's firmly back in place.

Why am I surprised? Instead of apologizing and saying the word *sorry*, I said I didn't know you were pretending? *Really! How stupid!* That's not an apology. That's an accusation.

"I'm tired too." I ignore the whirl in my head.

"Don't forget, we're meeting in Liliana's room at five to get ready together." Her voice is deadpan. She pushes her door open. "I'd text you to remind you, but your phone."

"I'll remember."

I watch as she goes into her room, and the door shuts behind her. *That's clearly a metaphor.* My heart sinks. I blew it.

Entering my room, I walk to my phone. I punch the power button, but the screen stays black. I pick it up, and rice scatters onto the floor. Shaking it around, I will it to come back to life. I'm in danger of losing my sponsors. The twenty-four-hour posting cycle moves fast, and if I don't keep up, my audience will forget I exist. *But would I care?* Does it even matter when I've ruined things with Angie and my marriage is in trouble? Does Marco even care he can't reach me? He hasn't texted Liliana since the suspicious message he sent yesterday.

Breathing in and out, I try not to think about whether he's cheating. *Keep it a secret!* Saying it out loud will make it real. Look at the way I almost lost it in front of Angie before we got back inside the cab. I'm an idiot for mentioning Nicole and Garrett's problems. She sensed I was upset. *What was I thinking?!*

Fortunately, I deflected Angie's concerns about my life by steering the conversation back to *Nicole's* marriage. But the painful truth is sinking in. Decoys are my version of Angie's emotional wall. We will never rebuild our friendship if we don't drop our defenses. But could I really tell her about Marco? Could I tell anyone?

My heart skips envisioning how my followers would react if I shared my suspicions on my feed. I'd, of course, make the post Insta-worthy, using a cool graphic created on Canva with a cliffhanger hook written in the trendiest font—*POV: Why I'm writing a thank you note to the woman my husband cheated with. More in the comments.* My mind takes over with a B-movie reel of Marco and me telling Bianca our marriage is over. She falls into my arms.

"Please work it out," she begs.

"I tried. I really tried," Marco says.

Bianca's imaginary sobs echo in my head. My entire body shakes. I think of all the times Marco made himself vulnerable over the years, asking me to work on our marriage—most recently with that app. Why do I treat my marriage like everything else, dipping it in veneer so it looks polished on the outside? *I have to stop these thoughts right now!*

I take a few quick breaths, forcing myself to replace this vision of Bianca with anything else. I close and open my eyes several times, feeling like I'm on the verge of a breakdown. Getting into bed, I cover my face with a pillow and unleash a scream.

When my voice quiets, I hear my phone ping. *Finally!*

I jump out of bed and grab it. Bianca's texted several times to see if my phone's up and running, but nothing from Marco. Is it because he's with *her* in Atlanta, or is it because he thinks my phone's dead? Either way, I can't reach out. I'm afraid I'll confront him. And if I find out anything that confirms he's having an affair, I'll never make it through tonight.

I exit my text messages and call Bianca. Her voice will ease my nerves.

I HEAR POUNDING on my door, and my eyes pop open. I must have fallen asleep while scrolling Insta after talking to Bianca. She confirmed Marco's home, but he still hasn't tried to reach me.

I hate that I was trying to get information from her. She's old enough to know something's going on. I don't want her to feel like she has to take sides. I don't want her to feel caught between us. But more than that, I don't want her to feel like she has to be perfect. That's partly why Marco and I are struggling. *What example have I set?* The thought sends a shiver down my spine.

"Carly, open up. It's Liliana."

I glance at the clock. *Shoot.* I should already be in her room. Stumbling out of bed, I open the door. "Sorry, I fell asleep. But the good news is my phone came back to life."

"Fabulous. Meet us in my room as soon as you can. We've got champagne."

When she leaves, I take a quick shower, then pull on the resort's fluffy bathrobe. I pack up my makeup, pink dress, and shoes. When I approach her door, I hear Nicole singing the NSYNC song "Tearin'

Up My Heart." My body buzzes with anticipation. I'm more than happy to push aside the impending collapse of my life and have fun. Tonight's going to be unforgettable.

"Let me in!" I shout, knocking on the door.

It swings open. Nicole stands before me in a sexy shorts romper. Her silky auburn hair pops against the hot pink. Her bangs sweep to the side. They're growing on me.

"You look fantastic!"

"I've never worn a romper before." She puts a hand on her hip and struts around like she's Bianca, showing off her new clothes for the first day of school.

I opt not to tell her that rompers are fantastic until the moment you have to pee.

She pulls my arm, leads me inside, and gently pushes me onto Liliana's bed.

"Show her your stash!" Liliana walks over with two enormous glasses of bubbly.

"I'm about to." Nicole looks around, searching for something.

"Do you want some?" Liliana places a glass in my hand before I answer.

"Where's Angie?" I ask, glancing around the room. I'm hoping we can push through the awkward moment we had after the embassy and keep moving forward.

"She went to meet Luca. He called and said he needed to talk."

My jaw clenches. I open and close it a few times, reminding myself I can't control the situation with Luca. He told the young girl *it goes no further.* I've helped Angie get a new passport. That's all I can do.

"Don't worry. She just texted. She's on her way back." Nicole unzips a pink tote bag with large fuzzy letters in pastel colors that say *GLAM.*

"What's in your bag? A bunch of stuff teenagers love?" Laughing, I peek inside.

"No cheating!" She pulls the bag away playfully. "It's the exact opposite of today's trendy gear. Welcome back to the nineties!" She dumps the bag over and starts organizing the items in a neat row.

"Are you kidding me!" I pick up a bottle of Love's Baby Soft and inhale the nostalgic perfume. "And wow, Bonne Bell Lip Smackers." I put one in my Gucci bag.

"Yup." Nicole puffs out her chest proudly. She runs her fingers over a package of butterfly-shaped Goody hair clips.

Opening the Baby Soft, I spray myself with the powdery floral scent. Nicole grabs it and gives herself and Liliana a quick spritz. The strong smell fills the entire room. A mix of joy and longing hits me seeing the trinkets that were popular in my youth. *Where has all the time gone?* I can easily picture the four of us walking down the halls of Hamilton High, gushing about the Oasis song "Wonderwall," even though we were all secretly still obsessed with boy bands. My eyes well with tears, but I know it's not from the incredibly potent perfume.

"Someone has to wear these tonight." Nicole holds up the package of brightly colored butterfly clips.

"I will." Liliana brings them to the mirror. She opens the clips and spills them onto the dresser. As she divides her curly hair into neat sections, her phone pings. Butterfly clips fall around her when she hurries to grab it.

"Work again?" Why won't her boss let her have a moment of peace?

"What the fuck!" Liliana screams.

Nicole and I exchange a look. It's strange to see Liliana having a big emotional reaction.

Her phone rings with the song "Manic Monday."

Liliana glances at it, then looks back at us. "I can't set a boundary with her. I blame my mom."

The ringing stops for a moment, then starts again.

"Do you guys even know I wanted to be a *teacher*? And why did I let my mom force me to spend summers rotating between summer programs at places like Duke and Yale, when what I really wanted was to go back to sleep-away camp?" Liliana's voice cracks.

I sit, speechless, surprised by Liliana's display of anger and sadness.

"I always thought you loved those summer leadership symposiums," Nicole says.

Liliana's phone pings several times with text notifications.

"Amanda is not your mom," I say. "It's just a job, Liliana. You're brilliant. Maybe it's time to move on."

Before Liliana can respond, her phone rings again.

"Enough is enough!" Liliana picks up the phone. "Amanda, I'm on vacation. Your incessant calls have ruined my trip." It's impossible not to notice the fury in Liliana's normally even-keeled demeanor. She puts the call on speaker.

"What?" Amanda says.

There's a pause, and I assume Amanda's recovering from Liliana's unexpected comment.

"I'm going to disregard your impolite tone." Amanda's voice slithers through the phone like a snake in the grass. "I need you to get on Zoom right now. I'll have Charlie send you a link."

Liliana's face turns red. "No, Amanda. I'm not joining the Zoom. You have all my notes and the rest of our legal team."

Amanda sighs heavily. "Liliana, you can't be serious! Look at what we've built. You're going to watch it collapse?"

"Amanda. I am not getting on a Zoom right now." Liliana's voice is a growl.

Amanda sighs again. "You've let me down."

The color in Liliana's cheeks deepens. Her gaze drops to the floor. I wonder if she's about to break down in sobs. I jump up off the bed and stand in front of her. When she looks up, I mouth the words *you can do this*.

Her eyes suddenly light up like there's a blazing fire roaring behind her pupils.

"I've had it, Amanda! Unless you can respect the boundaries I need for my personal life, I can no longer work for Click Com."

The three of us wait for Amanda to respond. Nicole hops off the bed and grabs my hand, shocked Liliana's standing her ground.

Then the phone goes dead.

"Oh, my God. Did I just lose my job?" Liliana's fingers travel to the bracelet on her wrist. She pulls the elastic and reads the string of Hebrew words. "*Ve'im lo achshav, em'matai?* If not now, when?" She sits on the corner of the bed. "How strange. I've been wearing this bracelet for days but haven't read the words.

"If not now, when?" I repeat. "Maybe it's a sign about your job?"

She repeats the words again like she's in a trance. "It feels like a cog in my brain that's been teetering between two points just fell solidly into place." She inhales deeply and lets out a long breath.

"Are you okay?" Nicole asks.

"Honestly. I'm angry. Angry that Amanda, my mom, and many others have held me to such unreasonable expectations, and angry that I've run myself ragged trying to live up to other people's standards."

"You have every right to be angry," I say.

Liliana jumps off the bed. "You know what? I don't want to waste another second talking about Amanda. What do you think of my dress?" Facing me, she drops further conversation about her job.

I run my eyes over the hot pink, leopard-print pattern and decide to follow her lead. "The fit is perfect, and it's very on trend. I love dresses with pockets!"

Nicole glances at me and gives a subtle nod, like she's silently agreeing that we should drop what just happened. I nod back.

"I absolutely adore the pockets." A smile lights up Liliana's face as she slips her hands inside them. "Thank God, I got the seal of approval from Instagram's famed master of mom fashion."

"Oh, that stupid account. I think I may retire from Insta." The words surprise me when they leave my mouth.

They stop and stare. Nick Lachey's voice croons in the background.

"It's not fun anymore," I admit, realizing how nice it is not having to respond to each and every comment made on my posts. *Screw visibility!* Right now, I couldn't care less about *viewing my insights* and if my follower count is going up or down.

And most significantly, I feel complete and total relief that I don't have to pretend my outfits, this trip, and my life are perfect. Maybe thinking about the example I've set for Bianca is making me see things differently.

"I'm back." Angie walks in and saves me from having to explain anything more.

"What did Luca say?" I ask, trying to keep my voice neutral.

"He apologized for getting angry with you. He wants to have a good time tonight." She sits next to me on the bed. "Can you trust me on this? He's a good kid."

"Totally, he's harmless. Hot as hell, but harmless." Nicole winks.

"Fine," I reply, accepting that I could be wrong. Who knows what Luca and that girl were talking about? It could have been anything. No one suspects he took Angie's passport but me.

"Thank you."

As Angie speaks, I notice the color of her dress. "Um, why are you wearing black?" I frown at her simple black cotton dress like she's worn mom jeans to the Golden Globes.

The features on her face fall. "I know. I ordered a hot pink dress from Amazon. It didn't come in time."

"You have to wear hot pink." I shake my head, disappointed.

"Yes, you have to, Angie," Liliana says. "This is our thing. This is what we do. It started with those hideous yellow prom dresses. One night, we all dress in the same color. And this year the color is hot pink."

Angie shrugs her shoulders. "I'm sorry, guys. I am. I don't have a pink dress. To be honest, I wish it had come in time. I hate to mess up our long-standing tradition."

My heart bounces when she says this.

"I got you!" Nicole's green eyes twinkle. She jumps off the bed, runs to the door and lets it slam behind her. A second later, she's back with two hot pink dresses. "You guys know I'm a chronic over-packer. Angie, pick one."

Angie runs her hands over the two choices. Her nose scrunches. "Hmm, I don't think I'll be comfortable in either of these."

"Wait." Nicole unfolds one option. "This one is cozy with a flowy cut. It's got serious drip."

Ignoring Nicole's slang, Liliana gestures to the dress, encouraging Angie to take it. "Come on, Angie. It's fun when we wear the same color. Remember, in Key West when we all wore green?"

"Ha!" I laugh. "How could anyone forget that weird guy in the green suit following us around all night? And the drag queen with the green wig who bought us a round of drinks. The magic only happens if we're all wearing the same color."

Angie smiles but doesn't reach for a dress.

"Listen." Nicole plops dramatically onto the bed. "I didn't want to get into it, but Garrett called me last night and asked me to come home. Everyone has a stomach virus."

"Ugh, stomach virus. The worst." Liliana sits next to Nicole.

"Yes, and he booked a plane ticket. The flight left this morning." She looks back at us, and I wonder if she'll tell us more about what's going on with Garrett.

"Why is marriage so hard?" Nicole's face takes on a serious expression.

Finally! Someone has admitted this truth. My muscles loosen, making me realize that tightly coiled is my default setting. We all look at Nicole.

"You know Garrett, he's like a parenting apprentice. Not fully qualified and working under my expert supervision." She laughs it off, but I can tell she's frustrated.

I'm hoping she'll say more, so I feel less alone with my problems.

But instead of continuing, Nicole leaps off the bed. "There was no way I was getting on that plane. Hell no, bitches! I texted him this morning and told him he'd figure it out. He responded with a million poop emojis. Whatever, I don't care!"

Evidently, she's not saying more. A sad realization hits me. It's impossible to know what's going on in someone else's mind. The only time I can recall having this superpower was when Bianca was young. It was easy to understand her thoughts and motivations, as if her mind was made of glass that I could see through. But as she grew into adolescence, I'd be left wondering what private turmoil consumed her. Her mind suddenly closed off to me, as if made of solid, indestructible steel. *Is this adulthood? Locking our most tender selves behind an impenetrable blockade?*

Nicole pushes one of the pink dresses back to Angie. "Garrett is going to throw this in my face forever, but being with you guys is worth it. So put on this dress and let's turn it up full volume."

Grabbing the dress, Angie grins. "Oh fine! I'll wear it. Let's get this party started!"

CHAPTER 29

Liliana

Emerald Jewel All-Inclusive Resort
October 4th 🎵 Last Night

"HOW DO I look?" Angie comes out of the bathroom in Nicole's pink dress.

"Fire!" Nicole squeals.

"Confidence, femininity…I'm almost speechless seeing you in a bright color. I'm sending you a link for a Veronica Beard top that you absolutely must purchase!" Carly taps on her phone.

"You look…you look…" I tilt my head to the side, and then it comes to me. "You look happy!"

Angie twirls around like Cinderella arriving at the king's palace for the royal ball. There's a look on her face I haven't seen since before her mom passed away. It's amazing.

"Okay, enough gushing." She winks playfully. "Are we ready to go?"

"Let me call Josh really quickly," I say. "I'm not bringing my phone tonight in case Amanda calls me. I'm so done."

"Good for you!" Angie glances at me affectionately. "My mom always said you chased gold stars like they were the force behind your beating heart. She always looked for ways to help you take it easy."

Her words pulse around me like an inescapable force, confirming that my mom had unreasonable expectations. Her words are an unbiased validation of my past.

"You probably don't know this," she continues, "but my mom got into a big fight with your mom over that spring break trip to Florida. My mom said she wasn't going without you. It's a miracle your mom gave in."

"What?" I can feel my eyes open wide in shock.

"Yeah, my mom knew you needed a break and to have some fun."

I remain quiet for a moment, my head swirling with thoughts. "You know I always believed Ivy schools and top-tier jobs were what I wanted. But I unconsciously adopted my mom's ambition, drive, and need to overachieve, swallowing her values as if they were a magic bean. But it turns out her magic bean isn't mine."

Carly grabs my hand. "But you don't have to stay on this path just because it's the path you've always been on."

"That's a mind-blowing insight," I say, feeling grateful.

"Mantra material," Nicole says quickly before looking away.

"Every so often I say something that actually matters!" Carly pushes her shoulders back proudly.

Angie claps her hands together. "Yay! I'm proud of you for standing up to Amanda. Call Josh. We have big plans tonight!"

I pick my phone up off the dresser, determined to apologize to Josh and tell him what just happened with Amanda, even though I know we need to have a deeper conversation in person. A hot sensation spreads through my body, recalling Josh's indifference last night when Esther called about Simchat Torah. I've called a few times since then, but he only texts back saying he'll call soon. I know talking about this with Josh will cause my emotions to spill over, but the amount of crying I do doesn't matter to me anymore.

My heart beats heavily while I dial. It rings several times. Right when I'm about to hang up, he answers. I'm equally relieved and panicked. I walk into the bathroom to get some privacy.

"Hi." I can hear Esther giggling in the background as I speak. Adrenaline floods my system.

A second later, I hear Evie's voice. "Hi, Mom!"

"Hi, baby. I miss you."

"Nah. I bet you're having the best time listening to those vintage jams."

"Hi, Mommyyyyyyyyyy!" Esther screams in the background.

"You're annoying!" Evie shouts.

"Girls, Mom didn't call to hear you fight. Let me have the phone."

My neurons fire aggressive hits of neurotransmitters hearing his voice. I hear a muffled sound as the phone passes from Evie to Josh.

"Hey."

My body shakes. What happens when I cry? What if he hangs up on me? What if it's too late? My lizard brain is relentless. I start with something easy.

"I wanted to say hi to the girls before we leave for the concert tonight. I'm not bringing my phone."

"Why?"

The heat in my chest turns to fire. I'm scared to keep going after the way he responded on FaceTime. "Because I'm done with Amanda. This trip has proven that my relationship with her is toxic." I brace myself for his apathy, terrified of what it means. Tears stream down my face, although I know he doesn't know I'm crying.

The phone remains silent for a beat too long.

"Josh, are you there?"

"Yes, I'm here." He lets out an intense exhale, causing my phone to tickle my ear. It sounds like relief. Or at least I hope it does.

Encouraged, I swallow hard and share what's in my heart, knowing my fear of not meeting expectations has been like a time bomb ticking inside of me my entire life, but the clock has stopped. The fear is suddenly meaningless.

"I just told Amanda I can't keep working for her unless she respects my boundaries. I'm not sure I still have a job, and I'm okay with that." An immense wave of gratitude glides through my body. I feel liberated from self-imposed constraints.

He clears his throat. I'm anxious to hear what he's going to say.

"Wow. I wasn't expecting that. Glad you see that dynamic is unhealthy."

I detect a tenderness in his voice. It's a tone I haven't heard him use with me in a very long time, but I need to confirm that I'm interpreting his reaction right. I need to say more.

"I am so incredibly sorry for having my priorities wrong." My voice cracks with gentle sobs. Now it's clear I'm crying.

"Leave me alone!" I hear Evie yelling from the background.

"Dad, Evie hit me!" Esther's voice vibrates through my phone, but I desperately need Josh to say something to confirm we're going to get through the damage I've caused.

Knock. Knock.

"Liliana, come out. I have a surprise for you guys. I need to get in there." Nicole opens the door and peeks her head into the bathroom.

"Oh, sorry, I didn't know you were still on the phone." She steps back with a guilty look on her face, and I wonder if she feels bad for seeing me cry.

Josh finally speaks. "I'm sorry, Liliana, I have to go. Evie and Esther are about to kill each other."

I can hear them yelling in that screechy high octave reserved for fighting sisters. My heart deflates when Josh doesn't give me the reassurance I need.

"I'll see you tomorrow," he says. "I want to talk about this more. We have a lot of things to talk about." He ends the call.

I drop my phone into my pocket and push down a choked sob. My shoulders tense. I soften the blow by telling myself he had to deal with the girls. Having an epiphany about how to fix your marriage when you're thousands of miles away from your husband isn't ideal. I'll make things right when I get home. Drying my tears, I dab concealer under my eyes.

As I walk out of the bathroom, Nicole pulls me into a tight hug. "Is everything okay?"

"I hope so," I say honestly. I'm sure Josh tells her more about our relationship than she lets on. I'll have to talk to him about this. I didn't realize until this trip how uncomfortable it makes me. I walk out of the bathroom, and she shuts the door behind her.

"Do you think Nicole's on Ozempic?" Carly whispers when I sit on the bed.

"Probably," Angie says.

I nod, glad to have my focus pulled away from Josh, and relieved Carly and Angie don't seem to notice I was crying.

Carly continues in a low voice. "Don't you think she needs to stop taking it? She's emaciated."

Angie and I lock eyes, and I know we're thinking the same thing. Carly's the last person who should say someone's too thin. She's always restricting and exercising.

"Make sure your eyes are shut." Nicole interrupts our conversation, yelling from inside the bathroom.

"Ugh, Nicole. Come out," Carly says impatiently. "I know you have a surprise, but unless you're hiding Donnie Wahlberg in there, this will be a letdown."

"Yeah, what are you doing in there?" Angie walks to the bathroom door and places her ear against it. She's stunning in bright pink. It's a refreshing change from her typical black and gray.

"I'm coming out."

Angie moves back as Nicole swings open the door. She smiles and looks right at me, like she needs me to reassure her I'm okay. That's friendship. I quickly nod, even though I wanted more from my talk with Josh.

"Ta-da," Nicole says with a grin on her face.

"Um, what am I missing?" Carly shrugs. "You look the same."

"Look again!" Nicole sashays around in a circle as we study every inch of her. I'm still shocked at how tiny she is.

"Oh! I see it!" Carly gasps with excitement. "It's her shoes."

Glancing down, I can't help but laugh. "Are those Steve Madden black platform slides?"

"The MVP of the nineties right here. I couldn't resist ordering a pair." She lifts her left foot a few inches to showcase her nostalgic footwear.

"I can't believe they still make these!" Angie's eyes light up with excitement.

"You guys!" Nicole runs over to the Bluetooth speaker connected to her phone and turns up the Spice Girls song playing in the background. "Yassss! Our Halloween costumes!"

We all sing the chorus of "Wannabe." We're completely off-key when we get to the part about never-ending friendships, all riding the same emotional wave of joy as it reaches its peak.

I close my eyes for a second, and when I open them, I see us, but it's 1997. We're dressed up as the Spice Girls. Carly is Posh Spice, Angie is Scary Spice, Nicole is Ginger Spice, and I'm Baby Spice. Angie's mom is Sporty Spice, even though she didn't join us except for a few pictures before we left for the parties. That Halloween was before we found out she had brain cancer. Everything changed after that.

My head spins with all the love and pain the four of us have shared. Although much of it is heartbreaking, it brought us to this exact moment.

CHAPTER 30

Nicole

Emerald Jewel All-Inclusive Resort
October 4th 🎵 Last Night

"**A**LL RIGHT, LADIES. It's time." Carly grabs her selfie stick off the bed. "Scoot in close. Let's take a pic."

We push our bodies together. I put my hand on my hip, posing the same way I see teenage girls do on TikTok. The flash blinks. Carly puts the stick down and grabs my hand. Angie joins in. Liliana adds her hand to the mix until we're all linked in a circle. Damn, this is insane! The gang's back together!

I catch Liliana's eye again, and she seems fine. Josh probably didn't say anything. If he did, she wouldn't be able to smile and pretend it's okay. Talking to Laura the day we got here made things with Josh feel more official. I'm low-key freaking out.

A sincere expression takes over Carly's face. "I want to be serious for a moment."

I swing my arm forward, and everyone stumbles toward each other, laughing. "I'm too buzzed to be serious."

"No, no, shhh." Carly straightens her posture like she's being evaluated at a country club cotillion class.

We do the same, trying not to laugh.

Carly clears her throat and begins again. "Nicole, Liliana, Angie. We're about to go back in time and see one of our favorite boy bands. Donnie, Danny, Jordan, Jonathan, Joey—you made our hearts race with your upbeat songs and smooth dance moves. Especially you, Jordan!"

"Whoo-hoo!" I shout. "I'd tap that." My body sways.

Angie snickers. "Now that I've seen those boudoir photos, I have no doubt."

"Shhh, shhh, seriously. I'm tipsy, but I'm trying to say something important." Carly leans her head closer inside our little circle, and her eyes connect with ours. "This trip has had its ups and downs. Some fighting, a missing passport, falling in the pool."

"Don't forget about my boss calling every second," Liliana adds.

"And getting robbed of our nineties trivia win. Those bitches cheated!" I stomp my foot on the ground.

Carly smiles. "And, yes, Liliana's monster boss and losing trivia. But I love you guys, and I'm glad that we get to have this one perfect night together."

"To new beginnings with the best of friends." Liliana's getting choked up. *Uh-oh.* That's not her usual M.O. Did Josh drop some hints on their call?

Carly and Angie share a heartfelt look, distracting me, and it makes me smile.

"Enough of the love fest." I snap my fingers. "We out! Let's go to the rooftop restaurant and sit at the bar."

Carrying our champagne glasses, we walk to the main building and take the elevator to the top floor. A sleek bar with a white marble top sits in front of a wall decorated with enormous metal replicas of neon-colored fish. On the opposite side, a spectacular view of the ocean stretches out as far as the eye can see against the blue sky. A gentle breeze blows through the space.

"Will you be having dinner with us this evening?" The restaurant hostess gestures to the dining area to the left of the outdoor bar. "There's a wonderful seafood buffet."

"No, thanks," we all say in unison.

I point to a few open seats at the bar. "Grab those."

Carly walks by a rowdy group of women celebrating a fiftieth birthday.

"Ya'll are pretty in pink." A petite, doe-eyed woman nods approvingly at our coordinating outfits.

"Accurate!" I agree. "A round of shots." I tell the bartender to surprise us.

"Pink shooters for the pink ladies." The bartender drops slim glasses in front of us a few minutes later.

"Oof. That definitely had tequila." My face squishes together as the alcohol burns my throat.

I hear a muffled sound, but then it stops. "Is someone's phone ringing?"

"Oh, shoot, my phone! I meant to leave it in the room." Pulling it out of her pocket, Liliana takes a deep breath. "Maybe it's Josh," she says hopefully. She sighs when she flips her phone over. "It's Amanda." Her shoulders slump.

"Is everything okay with Josh?" I ask, wishing I could pull the words back into my throat. I know too much to ask this question, but Liliana is my best friend and comforting her is a reflex.

"Your boss, again?" Angie leans over, peering at Liliana's screen before Liliana can answer me. "Put Amanda on do not disturb. Or take her out of your phone. Don't let her calls stress you out on our last night."

Liliana glances at us, reminding me of the way Chelsea looks at me to make sure she has the green light before she grabs a pair of my shoes from the closet to play dress-up.

"Do it! Put her on do not disturb!" Angie says.

"I will!" Liliana taps on her phone, drops it back into her pocket, then raises her hands and silently cheers. "I can't wait to tell Josh!"

I get a weird feeling when I hear his name. Afraid I'm about to spiral, I bolt from the outdoor bar into the dining area. Lifeless black fish eyes stare back at me from the seafood buffet. I'm the worst friend ever. I love Liliana. I've always been her loyal friend. Or at least until now. I knew this was going to be complicated, but I didn't realize it would turn into one of those things that makes you question every-thing about yourself.

Searching through my bag, I pull out the tin of mints I filled with edibles. These are super low dose but will take the edge off. I pop one into my mouth. I need to relax.

> **Garrett:** What's a probiotic?

> **Garrett:** Where and what is the quilty wilty?

> **Garrett:** What pharmacy do we use?

Garrett bombards me with texts before I can chew my gummy. Of course he doesn't know what a probiotic is, or that Chelsea uses a special blanket when she's sick, and apparently, he's never picked up a prescription from the pharmacy two blocks from our house. What started as a way for me to recapture what I lost after the pelvic separation has made Garrett helpless.

> **Garrett:** Nicole are you there? I'm not good at
> this stuff!

My fingers fly to my phone.

> **Me:** By stuff do you mean taking care of your
> own children?

> **Garrett:** Not fair! You never let me do anything
> for the kids because you say I'm doing it wrong!

I start to reply, but then my phone pings with another text. Garrett's going nuclear.

> **Garrett:** Seriously Nicole! Remember when you
> finally got out of the wheelchair. You wouldn't
> let me help.

A sharp jolt of electricity radiates through my pelvis. Thinking about that wheelchair brings back the pain I was in after Hank's birth. I reread Garrett's last text.

You wouldn't let me do anything.

Anger, resentment, regret, fear, sadness—the emotions I felt after Hank was born swirl together with the force of hurricane winds.

My fingers fly back to my phone.

> **Nicole:** You're right. I should have let you do more. But at some point you stopped trying. At some point you decided I was going to handle EVERYTHING.

I'll admit writing everything in all caps is aggressive, but can't I have a few nights off from being responsible for other humans? I'm so fucking tired. I watch as three dots appear and disappear. Then I hear the ping.

> **Garrett:** You wouldn't let me help once you got better. When I tried, you always took over. Now you're mad I don't know what to do. This feels like a trap. Or gaslighting. Or whatever people are calling it these days.

I stare at his text. Unbelievable. He's turning this around on me. I'm out! I drop my phone in my bag. Tonight is going to be amazing.

I head back to the bar. Music plays, people are dancing, and the whole vibe is perfect.

"Where'd you go?" Liliana's eyes scrunch together, confused.

"Peeing is a part-time job," I lie, knowing she can relate.

"Hmm, you seem upset." She wraps her arm around my shoulders. "Everything okay?"

Of course, she's the best friend I need right now, even though I'm betraying her. God, I feel awful, but I really need to vent. I've kept my feelings about motherhood bottled up for too long.

"To be honest, I'm completely tapped out from the over-the-top expectations for stay-at-home moms. That, since *mom* is my one job, I have to do it like I'm on steroids. Do you know Hank insists on sandwiches cut in half, while Mack throws a fit if his sandwich isn't cut diagonally? And, for Chelsea, don't even think about serving her a sandwich. Anything but a turkey and cheese roll-up will cause an epic meltdown. Being a mom is so extra these days."

"Wow, that's a lot of granular detail just to make lunch."

"Exactly. My mom just threw a Lunchable and a Capri Sun into my lunch box."

"Oh, yay, you're back!" Angie slides over with Luca by her side, interrupting my conversation with Liliana.

Carly stands behind them, making a disapproving face at Luca. The tunes get louder, and the bar crowd pumps, anticipating NKOTB.

I'm not sure how much time passes, but everything around me gets swirly. The song "Waterfalls" by TLC blares. Luca grooves to the beat, and I jump up and join him. Carly and Angie sing the words next to us as if they're on stage for a sold-out show, and Liliana keeps asking us what song we think New Kids will open with.

Grabbing my hand, Luca spins me, and the crowd around us fans out. A warm breeze blows, and my body hums. It feels like the fun and feisty version of myself is waking up from a long winter sleep. It's the same feeling I had when I took the boudoir pictures. Most moms I know wouldn't be comfortable getting half-naked and unleashing their inner vixen to be captured on film. The experience gave me a surge of power. I've gotta get that feeling back whenever I can.

"The show starts in an hour," Luca whispers in my ear as we continue to dance.

"What? We never ate dinner."

"Oh well." He smirks with his gorgeous, sun-kissed face.

Angie leans close to us, waving her hand toward the beach below. "We should go to the stage. The concert is starting soon."

Liliana chimes in. "We have to beat the crowd. We need to go if we want spots in the front row."

Luca pulls me into his body and circles his arms around my waist as the *Titanic* movie hit "My Heart Will Go On" rings out in the background.

He smells like pine and skunky grass. I'm betting he's high.

"Let us finish dancing to this one song," he tells Liliana. "It was one of my mom's favorites."

We spin and spin, and I am that twenty-year-old badass bitch. There is no Garrett. There are no kids. There is no carpool, meal planning, bath time, or baseball practice. There is nothing to manage. There is no one making demands. There is only me. There is only what I want and what I need.

And that's when it hits me. Maybe I'm too selfish for motherhood. Maybe that's been the problem all along.

But before I can wrap my head around this, Carly's standing next to me, glaring at Luca.

"We have to go." She grabs my hand, trying to pull me away from him.

But, instead of releasing me, Luca hugs me tighter, swaying our bodies to the beat. Frowning, Carly moves closer.

But then Luca takes an unexpected step forward.

Carly stumbles over his foot, losing her balance. Her arms flail. Her body rocks back and forth, and then she lands in a heap on the ground.

CHAPTER 31

Officer Claasen

Now

Emerald Jewel All-Inclusive Resort

October 5th ♫ 6:30 a.m.

OFFICER CLAASEN GIVES a polite nod to a petite lady with firm, sculpted muscles and spiky blond hair. She takes the seat in front of him. Something about her short, wide stature reminds him of a bulldog. He wipes away a bead of sweat forming over his mustache.

Crossing her arms, the petite woman pushes her shoulders back until her posture is perfect. "You should know these women were causing trouble everywhere they went. They *chat and cut* to skip the bathroom line, save beach chairs even though that's against the rules, and shoved through the entire crowd at the concert last night to get to the front."

He pictures the woman's face on the body of the dog she resembles while he waits for her to tell him whatever important information she has. At this point, all the guests know a woman is missing. The entire property is buzzing with rumors. Certainly, this woman has more to tell him about than bad behavior, but she sits staring, as if she's waiting for him to reply or give her a bone.

"That's interesting." He forces himself to act as if what she said wasn't complete nonsense. "But do you know about the missing woman?" He points to the picture, placing his finger above the missing woman's face. They need a break in this case before the resort welcomes the yacht rockers. Detective Ellis is at the end of his rope, yelling about bankrupt hotels and the island's GDP.

The petite woman stares at him. "No, but I thought you should know these women are rule breakers. They pranced around this resort last night in their pink dresses, acting like they were better than the rest of us." Standing, she marches away on her short legs.

As the last guest approaches, Officer Claasen ignores his simmering irritation. A tall, pretty woman sits down and settles into the chair. He's not interested in wasting his time on schoolyard gossip, so he gets right to it. "Did you see anything suspicious involving these women?" He flashes the photo on his phone for the last time.

As the woman leans forward, looking at the photo, her breasts practically fall out of her swimsuit. Officer Claasen can't help but notice the way the perfectly round mounds of flesh sit too high on her body. He's been covering crimes at St. McAna's high-end resorts for long enough to know they're fake.

She leans back again and points to the picture. "This one with the blond hair flipped out on my friend and me last night. We were talking to her after the show when the DJ was playing." She pulls a shawl from her bag and drapes it over her shoulders, covering her deep cleavage.

He scratches some notes down, relieved that he's getting new information. "Can you give me more details?"

"Sure, she stormed off down the beach. Her friends followed. She took a phone call and then walked alone to the stage."

Officer Claasen waits for her to say more, but silence hangs between them. "Was it that young man that upset her?"

"No." She shifts in the chair. "Now that I'm thinking about it, though, I saw that young guy last night."

He wipes another bead of sweat from his face. "Please continue."

"So, my friends and I heard from a bartender that New Kids and NSYNC were hanging out together by the stage. This was long after the concert had ended."

Officer Claasen's body fills with anticipation.

"We walked over to check it out. I was crazy excited. Kinda like my daughter is when I take her to Sephora."

She pauses, like she's waiting for him to laugh, but he doesn't know what she's talking about.

"And…" he says, noticing the woman's high cheekbones and cherry-colored lips.

She glances away for a moment. "Sadly, we didn't run into anyone in the bands, but we saw this woman right here. What's her name?" She points to the picture.

"Angie." He confirms.

"Yes, Angie was talking with the young guy you asked about. What's his name?"

"Luca."

"Yes, Angie and Luca were on the beach behind the stage, talking."

"Did you hear them?"

"No, they were too far away."

"Could you see them?"

The woman nods. "Some of the stage lights were on. It was fairly easy to see."

"Did their body language give any hints about the type of conversation they were having?"

"I mean, two people on the beach in a quiet spot that late at night, we assumed they were a couple."

Officer Claasen is eager to fill in the details. "Were they standing, sitting?"

"They were standing. Their bodies were about a foot apart."

"Were they touching?" he asks. "Can you picture it?"

The woman's eyes scrunch together like they do when she's trying to figure out how to get multiple kids to different after-school activities at the same time. "I'm thinking. I'm not sure how to interpret the image."

"Would it help if we stood? You can arrange us in the same position." Officer Claasen jumps up from his chair.

The woman's tense expression softens. "Sure."

They both stand, and she takes a small step back. "I think there was this much space between them." She waves her hand back and forth in the air. "She had her hand up against him like this." She places her palm in the center of Officer Claasen's chest.

They stand frozen this way for a moment.

"I'm not sure how to read this," Officer Claasen admits. "It could be a friendly move if her palm was resting easily, but it could be defensive if she was trying to push him away." His head spins, wishing he had the deductive reasoning skills of Sherlock Holmes. "What happened after that?"

The woman glances up for a moment. "I'm sorry. I was tipsy. It was late." She removes her palm from his chest.

Officer Claasen's heart pumps. He knows he's close. He needs to make sure this woman isn't leaving anything out. Perhaps this is when the clues come together, revealing what happened to the missing woman. He imagines himself in a tweed suit, holding a pipe like Sherlock, smoke winding its way through his mustache. "Was anyone else around? Was there anyone else who might have heard or seen something?"

"No, not that I saw."

Pulling a pencil from his front shirt pocket, he makes several notes on his case sheet. "Okay, thanks."

"Sure, I wish I had more information, but what I saw probably doesn't matter anyway." The woman shrugs her shoulders, offering a silent apology.

Officer Claasen places his pencil back in his shirt pocket. "Well, that's the thing about investigations. Sometimes the smallest, unimportant detail ends up being the key to everything." From her comment, it's easy for him to deduce that she's never read Sir Arthur Conan Doyle.

The woman looks at him with a puzzled expression. "I guess. But why does this matter?" She glances at the three women in pink, who are staring despondently at the whirl of activity around them. She points to Angie. "She's not even the one who's missing."

CHAPTER 32

Angie

Emerald Jewel All-Inclusive Resort
October 4th 🎵 Last Night

STARE AT CARLY crumpled on the ground next to Nicole and Luca, recalling when I accidentally pushed her in the pool. That was the lowest moment of this trip until now. "Carly!"

She eases herself up, wincing as she stands. Her pink sequin dress twinkles with shards of twilight. Luca moves forward, trying to help her.

"You!" She points at him like he's a villain in a Disney movie. "You tripped me on purpose!" She brushes dust from her knees.

Luca's eyes bulge. "No, it was an accident. I'm sorry."

Although I missed what happened, Luca's apology sounds sincere.

"You're a liar and a thief." Carly's voice booms with anger. "Stay away from me and stay away from my friends!"

I swivel my head back and forth between them. The people at the bar stare with their mouths agape. Anger surges through my veins. I don't have time to react before Luca darts through the crowd, running toward the stairs.

"I can't believe you said that. And in front of all these people!" I stare at Carly, wishing my eyes had laser beams shooting out of them, then rush to catch up with Luca.

He rounds the bottom of the staircase and sprints toward the lobby. I run, but the air is heavy with humidity. It feels like I'm pushing through mud.

As I pass the pool, I hear Carly's voice behind me. "Angie, wait!"

Turning, I see she's running toward me, holding her platform shoes. I'm bursting with rage. This may be when I lose it. When I tell Carly we're sick of her perfect outfits, her perfect body, her perfect macro diet, her perfect daughter, her perfect marriage, and her insistence on fixing every problem the world has ever had. Anyone who has studied statistical noise and randomness knows nothing's perfect. *Master your fashion. Master your life.* What kind of bullshit is that?

"Can we sit and talk for a minute?" She presses her lips together nervously. Before I can answer, she walks to the edge of the pool. She takes a seat, letting her feet dangle in the water.

Although I'm anxious to find Luca, I should give him a few minutes to cool off. Carly ruined his trip to honor his mother. He must be heartbroken. I sit in a chair next to her.

"Fine," I snap. If she wants to talk, she'd better be ready to hear how much I needed her when my mom died. Needed her to hold my hand while I cried.

Then I remember, after the embassy, how she admitted she was grieving, too, and my hard edges soften.

"You're right. He didn't make me fall. I tripped and blamed him. I'm sorry."

Her apology surprises me, and my memories from the past are overshadowed by the situation with Luca. "You need to apologize to him."

Swaying her feet in the pool, she glances at the lobby. "If that's what you want me to do, I will." She pauses for a moment. "But are you sure he didn't take your passport?"

I jump off the chair. "Are you kidding me? Enough already."

She kicks her feet up, splashing water around, and stands. "I know. I shouldn't have asked."

Pulling out my phone. I scroll to the photo Luca texted me earlier when I met him to talk. It's from his ninth birthday party. Carly studies the image of him and his mom standing next to a cake decorated with the logos of several nineties boy bands. A bandana covers his mom's head. Her body's frail.

She takes my phone, inspecting the photo more closely. "He had a boy band birthday party?"

"Yes."

She continues peering at the image, then looks at me questioningly. And although the details are heart-wrenching, I decide to fill her in. "This was after his mom's first round of treatment. He wanted to make her happy."

Carly's eyes flick away from the photo. She inhales deeply. "I'm such an asshole."

"Sometimes you are," I agree. "You don't have to solve every problem. Trust me, I've got a math degree. Some things can't be solved."

"Right," she mumbles. "Why did I think Pizza Hut buffets and hours spent watching *The Secret World of Alex Mack* and *Sabrina the Teenage Witch* would fix things after your mom died?"

Her words make my breath catch.

"I was completely wrong about what you needed. I'm sorry I didn't do better." She shifts back and forth on her feet like she's off balance.

A slow, methodical hum pulses in my ears, recalling our earlier conversation. Carly isn't the only one at fault. "Remember when you said my mom was the linchpin? It made me realize I was scared of causing problems after she died. I was afraid of losing you, Liliana, and Nicole. My mom was the glue. And she was gone."

"Losing us?" Carly's features collapse.

"I know, it makes no sense, but I didn't want to weigh you down with more problems, so instead of telling you I needed to sit in a dark room and sob, I just went along with everything."

"Oh."

"And there's more to it than that. I never told you how hard things were with my dad. I never gave you the chance to help me."

Carly closes her eyes and shakes her head in a way that expresses disappointment with herself. "I finally understood something when I pulled out the infamous yellow prom dress photo to bring on the trip. Your dad mentally checked out. He was barely holding it together, and we didn't even realize."

I feel a wet stream of tears slide down my cheeks. "Yes." My voice is barely a whisper. "He couldn't get off the couch. He couldn't move. He couldn't function. I had to take care of him, the chores, and the never-ending medical bills. When my college forms and tuition were due, I snapped. It was overwhelming. I knew I wouldn't be able to leave my dad for Wash U."

"Seriously?" Carly's voice shakes with emotion. "All of that was happening and none of us knew?"

"It's not your fault," I blurt. "We were kids. You were about to go through a major life transition. Looking back, I wish I had said something. That's all it would have taken to avoid the whole terrible ordeal. I'm sorry. If I had been honest with you, none of it would have happened."

"You don't have to be sorry. I'm glad you told me." Carly reaches for a towel lying on a table.

I continue as she dries her feet and puts her shoes back on. "The pretending was like a boulder barreling down a mountaintop. Eventually, it caught up with me. I couldn't do it anymore."

Carly's long blond hair falls around her shoulders. "Believe me, I know about pretending."

I pause, surprised by her statement, and wait to see if she says more.

"It's just that…it's really hard because…"

She sounds upset. I'm not sure where this is going.

"The thing is," she says, "everything in my life has become an Instagram moment. A fake, curated, filtered image that's far from the truth. It's exhausting."

Her admission is shocking. I remember it seemed like she was about to cry on our way back from the embassy, but despite my tries, she wouldn't open up. Right now, though, it's like we've slipped into a crack in the universe where we can be honest.

"I bet it's hard to live under that kind of pressure. No one's life is perfect."

She looks at me but doesn't say anything.

Swallowing my fear, I bring up what I put our town through. At this moment, it may be the only way to help her realize it's normal to have flaws. I picture myself drifting in the space the universe is providing for our honesty and surrender to its pull.

"I had a breakdown senior year. It traumatized our entire town." Words from one of the kidnapping letters flash through my mind. *Angie has chosen a new life with me. People do not vanish into thin air.* "Everyone saw me screw up. But my life continued." I hear my voice rising with nerves but keep going. "It's okay if your life isn't perfect, Carly. I'm here if you want to talk about it."

She pulls her head back quickly as if she's trying to avoid a bee sting. She's quiet for several moments. It's obvious she's thinking about what to say.

"It's true," she agrees. "Your life kept going. But, to be fair, you escaped to St. Louis to move on. You've spent half your life hiding from your imperfect past."

She's not wrong but hearing it out loud is a lot to take.

"I'm sorry. I shouldn't have said that."

My hurt must be obvious in my expression.

She moves next to me. My mind skips back to the day I packed my car and left for college. The immense pressure in my chest lessened with each passing mile. Carly's right. I chose a new life, where I didn't have to feel guilty about the mistakes I made.

Carly continues. "But I've always wondered why you thought starting over was the only option. If it's okay to make mistakes, if it's okay to be less than perfect, then why didn't you stay?"

She's right. What if I had admitted what I did instead of keeping it buried?

"We miss you, Angie. I miss you. I've never gotten over losing you."

Her words make me feel like I've stumbled off one of those teacup rides that turn you around and around. After years of tension and bickering, she flat-out said she misses me. This is unlike her. She's admitted this hurt, this less-than-perfect relationship we have. An overwhelming sadness hits me like an electrical current. All these years I've avoided my best friends—that time is gone forever. But right now, I face the pain rather than run from it. Reaching my hand out, I grasp Carly's palm.

We swing our hands back and forth, and then Carly embraces me in a tight hug. Our bodies connect for the first time in over ten years, and so do our hearts. We linger for several moments before she pulls away.

A shiver runs down my spine despite the heat. My friends need to know the truth. But Carly and I have just taken a giant step forward. She'd never forgive me.

"Can we talk more about this later? Right now, we need to find Luca."

Carly breathes out slowly. "Yes, of course. I'm glad we've finally left the past behind."

My heart tightens knowing that's not exactly true.

"Okay, let's go find Luca," she says. "You've been right this entire time. He's here to honor his mom. I need to apologize."

Walking into the lobby, we pass by boisterous crowds excited about the concert. We glance from left to right, searching for Luca. I see him tucked away in a corner beyond the gift shop. But he's not alone.

My stomach drops to my toes as I watch the young girl pull him into a supply closet by the check-in desk. Is Carly right about him? Who's this girl that's always hanging around? He hasn't mentioned her.

"What in the world? Did you see that?" Carly's eyes narrow.

"I know." Unease makes my head throb. "That girl is always lurking. They seem secretive. Like they don't want to be seen together."

"Follow me." Carly hurries closer to the closet. She leans against the wall next to the door and pulls me closer.

"What are you doing?" I mouth. "What if they catch us?" My entire body thumps with fear.

But instead of answering, Carly puts a finger in front of her lips, making the sign for *shh*.

I'm terrified of getting caught, but desperate to know what's happening. Is Luca a con artist?

A moment later, we hear muffled voices. I move my ear closer to the door, and Carly does the same.

The girl is speaking. "But tonight's our last chance."

"I know," Luca replies. "But I'm not sure I'm willing to take that chance."

"This is it." The girl sounds angry. "It's now or never."

"I know. I know," Luca agrees. "But the thing is, I don't want to end up in jail."

Carly

Emerald Jewel All-Inclusive Resort
October 4th 🎵 Last Night

#OOTD: Vibrant hot pink, A-line sequin dress with puffed sleeves. Neutral platform sandals with cork heels. Beaded fringe earrings in soft gold. Large gold cuff bracelet. Black canvas Gucci belt bag with large initial motif.

FREEZE WHEN I hear the word *jail*. We hear a soft moan. Angie's eyes widen. The sound triggers an image of Marco cheating with Lilly. Nausea makes me break into a cold sweat. *Can I skip confronting Marco tonight?*

"I have to get out of here!" Grabbing Angie's hand, I pull us through the crowded lobby. We walk past a cluster of women doing a choreographed dance routine, singing "Step by Step."

"Let's find a quiet place to talk. This is scary," Angie says. She looks me straight in the eyes, and I wonder if she's afraid of what Luca said or confused about why I pulled her away so quickly.

I nod and follow her to the beach. I'm still processing everything we said by the pool, but I'm relieved that I understand our past. She finally told me about her dad and why she ran away, rather than keeping it to herself—the same way I admitted I missed her. It occurs to me that sharing our inner worlds is like giving each other a precious gift. A gift that crushes the distance between us.

"You okay?" she asks, probably concerned by my over-the-top reaction to what was going on in the closet. The moment of pleasure we overheard between Luca and the girl in the closet has ignited my fears about my husband cheating.

"It's Marco. Things aren't going well with Marco." *Did I really say that?* My body feels like it's on fire.

Angie grabs my hand tighter. She stays quiet, but her face conveys that she's grateful I've trusted her with the truth. "It's too loud to talk." She looks at the commotion by the stage area.

Glancing to my left, I see the crew doing a sound check while the resort staff sets up a large bar. People are milling about, hoping to get a spot at the front of the pit.

"Over there." I point to the other side of the beach, where it's deserted.

We walk in silence, passing the dilapidated boathouse. She hasn't let go of my hand since I told her. I forgot how calming it is to hold my best friend's hand. We sit on a lounge chair near the gazebo. The wind picks up, causing white-capped waves to crash onto the shore. The sky shimmers purple and pink as the sun dips into the ocean. Neither of us speaks.

I wonder if Marco's cheating again, and my internal temperature skyrockets. I imagine water pouring over my ribs, my veins, and my heart, putting out the flames inside my body. I inhale deeply as I picture the final embers turning black. I don't want to say anything else about my marriage. Not tonight. Not when I can escape into the ultimate distraction before returning home.

Angie squeezes her palm into mine. "What's going on with Marco? Do you want to talk about it?"

"I don't know. I think…I'm not sure I can." My stomach twists.

Can I go against my father's advice and tell her the truth? *Maybe, but only if I take it one step at a time.*

"I think, yes, I want to talk about it, but if I'm honest, not right now. I want to enjoy tonight before my life implodes."

Angie's face pinches after hearing the word *implode*, but she composes herself, trying to respect my wish to discuss Marco later. I'm afraid that if I open up to her now, I'll end up confronting him.

"Like Nicole said, marriage is hard sometimes. We can talk about it whenever you're ready. It means so much that you trust me enough to tell me the hard parts of your life."

Strangely, this moment makes me feel like a weak candle flame that someone can easily blow out, but also like the only thing capable of providing light in complete darkness. It reminds me I can't have connection without vulnerability. And although I'm not ready to tell Angie details about Marco yet, I know I will.

I squeeze her palm. We sit in silence again. She doesn't ask me any more questions, and I know she understands.

"I don't know what to think about Luca." Angie stares at the ocean, and I'm grateful for the topic change. "I mean, things aren't adding up. And jail?" There's genuine fear behind her intense gaze.

My head swirls with the series of events that have led to this moment. Do I think Luca stole the passport? *Yes.* Do I think he would hurt Angie? *No.* I recall what I overheard him say to that girl on the beach this morning while I was hiding behind a palm tree. He didn't want to blow things up further. He seemed to have achieved his goal.

"It's most likely a case of identity theft. He probably wants your personal details. Like your address. Or maybe he's trying to scam the rest of us. He has your passport. The damage is done. What else could he do?"

Angie shrugs. "What did that girl mean when she said it's their last chance? Last chance for what?" She's quiet for a moment. The sound of the churning ocean hangs between us. "I feel victimized." She lets out a sigh.

"I get it. I still can't believe I paid four thousand dollars for fake Eras Tour tickets." *And made a complete fool of myself.*

"Ugh, I know. I'm sorry one of your followers turned out to be a scammer."

"Stupid Instagram. It's the reason for a lot of my problems."

"Then maybe it's time to stop." Angie shifts her body toward mine.

"Maybe it is," I say.

"I'm serious. You should delete your account if it's having a negative impact on your life. Go back to public relations. You'll have no problem finding a job."

"I could," I agree, wondering for the first time how a life focused on strategic goals for a third party may be better than a life where my strategic goal is looking perfect.

White noise from the ocean surrounds us as we sit in silence for a few moments. I kick my feet in the sand, refocusing on Luca.

"I don't think you're in danger. I know that's strange after the way I've been warning you to stay away from him. But I think this is straightforward identity theft." I gently tap my feet together, releasing sand from my shoes. "The good news is that your old passport's canceled, and we're going to the embassy tomorrow to pick up your temporary papers. Then we'll go to the airport, and you'll never see Luca again."

Leaning back in the lounge chair, Angie curls her body into a ball. "But what about his mom, and that picture he showed me?" Her voice trembles, conveying a mix of frustration and disbelief.

"Anyone can pull a photo from the internet and claim it's them." She nods, curling her body tighter.

"And who knows what his story is? Maybe he lives in St. McAna and scams tourists? Maybe he came up with the perfect backstory for this event. Maybe he's been stealing from others this whole time?"

"Right," Angie agrees. "He could be anyone."

"Yes, let's report him to the embassy when we pick up your papers tomorrow morning."

Angie nods.

"When we get home, sign up for one of those identity monitoring sites and lock your credit. Let's keep our distance from him tonight and stick together. The worst of it's over."

WHOOOOSH. POP.

An intense, deafening buzz bangs through the air.

Angie flies off the lounge chair. "What was that?"

My heart hammers in my chest. Turning toward the stage, I point at the band's crew circled around an enormous speaker. "I think the speaker blew." I place my hand over my heart. *Take a deep breath!* I inhale a gulp of air.

Angie clutches her side, laughing. "I need to relax. This thing with Luca has me on edge." The features on her face soften, realizing we're safe. "I will not let him ruin our last night." She straightens up and puts her hands on her hips. "You're right. If he's worried about jail, it's because he stole my passport. Let's find Liliana and Nicole and have a drink before the show."

Getting up from my lounge chair, I swing my arm through hers, savoring the comforting presence of my best friend and the joy of this final night in St. McAna before I have to go home and confront Marco.

CHAPTER 34

Angie

Emerald Jewel All-Inclusive Resort
October 4th ♫ Last Night

"I BET THEY'RE STILL at the rooftop bar. Let's go." Carly pulls our bodies closer.

We stagger through uneven sand, but for the first time in twenty-plus years I feel grounded. I sense my seventeen-year-old self is fading into the background. But I know I need to share my final regret and apologize to my friends if I want her to fully recede into my past.

As we leave the beach, Carly rambles about why Joey McIntyre is the real heartthrob of NKOTB, but my head fills with memories I've tried to forget, recalling the first time I tiptoed out of my house after my mom died. The stars were hidden behind a thick blanket of clouds, making it darker than normal. I took a few hesitant steps, unfamiliar with the way the tree in my front yard cast a long shadow over my mom's cherished flower bed. The fear was exhilarating.

For a few weeks, I took my predawn walks in my neighborhood, glad to replace my grief with fear. The eerie quiet, the dense air, the way terror consumed me when a tree limb would shake before a bird flew away, were a balm to my sadness. But as the episodes continued, I was less afraid.

Determined to feel fear, I began following the main road out of Hamilton Beach, waiting for panic to kick in. As the weeks went on, I kept pushing the limits, walking closer and closer to cars whizzing down the road and trekking through wooded areas, barely able to see.

After a while, though, nothing scared me. I was unafraid, like a child pointing their skis downhill on a snowy mountain for the first time. *What would it take to feel fear and stop suffering?*

It was near the end of the school year when I snapped while walking on the road that led out of Hamilton Beach. I noticed a big rig driving slowly forward. Without thinking, my thumb went out. The driver said he was headed to Sacramento and could drop me off anywhere along the way.

Surprisingly, he wasn't a scary, gruff chain-smoker. He spoke softly, with a Southern drawl. He had a neat haircut, and his face was clean-shaven, though worn like leather. He never cracked a smile. Said he'd get fired if anyone knew he picked up hitchhikers, but he felt a duty to get young girls where they needed to go safely. He slid his eyes to me when he said the word *safely*, and I was unsure if he was being honest or alluding to the fact that I was unsafe. The rush of fear I felt was abnormally soothing.

I hopped out of his truck near the LA airport. He wished me luck and told me never to hitchhike again. Walking into a beat-up motel, a woman who looked to be in her thirties, with smudgy black eyeliner and several face piercings, took my cash without asking for any identification. I collapsed onto the thin, worn bed in my motel room and slept for almost twenty-four hours.

When I woke up, I stared at the cracked ceiling in a daze. Another day passed before I realized that my dad and friends were probably panicking. But I didn't feel guilty. Instead, I felt complete and total relief. There were no eyes staring at me with pity. There was no pressure on me to pretend I was okay. I didn't have to see my dad lying listless on the couch. I didn't have to accept that the world kept going without my mom.

That's when I knew that a life free from this crushing burden was possible. I would start over far away from California. Maybe I'd go to Colorado. A state my mom said was beautiful. I didn't care about the heartbreak of those who loved me. I was selfish. My desperation to escape the charade of my old life outweighed everything. I was lucky when Alice, the pierced woman at the motel, told me she could use some help. Her kid had a fever. After explaining the basics of check-in, she agreed to let me stay for free as long as I continued to help.

I'd been gone for about two weeks, using the name Natalie and helping at the motel desk, when Alice asked if my name was Angie. I tried to stay composed as I shook my head.

"I'm not going to call the cops. Maybe you're her. Maybe you're not. Maybe you have a good reason for running away. But someone is sending letters saying they kidnapped a girl named Angie, and I thought you should know."

Kidnapped?

A wave of icy fear washed over me. Obviously, I wasn't kidnapped. My head spun with confusion.

That night, I sat on the corner of my bed and watched the news. Sure enough, my face was splashed across the screen while a reporter read a harrowing note from the kidnapper claiming I didn't vanish. I was safe and starting a new life with him.

But despite the bizarre circumstances, I didn't want to go home. I didn't want to deal with my dad. I didn't want to keep pretending with my friends. But who was the crazy person claiming to have taken me?

The complexity of the events was shocking. I continued to watch the coverage for several more nights, paralyzed. The only conclusion I could draw was that the "kidnapper" was some deranged person exploiting the initial runaway reports. A hunch that ended up being true.

I felt terrible shame for putting the people that loved me through such a traumatic situation. Part of me wanted to go home and alleviate everyone's fears, but I didn't want to sacrifice this newfound inner peace.

The next day, while I stacked the checkout cards, Alice appeared carrying her fussy toddler on her hip.

"Have you been watching the news about Angie? Her dad's a mess. Her friends too. I hope she gets home."

I averted my eyes from her face.

She slid her child down her leg and let him roam the small office area and leaned closer to me by the desk. "If Angie felt unsafe at home, I get that. I left when I was sixteen. But my mom never cared about finding me. No one cared to find me. This feels different. There are a lot of people who want her to come home."

I knew I should call my dad right then and there. But it felt like a vise was squeezing my body, keeping me from picking up the phone.

Over the next few days, my senior photo appeared on the front page of every newspaper in Southern California. I hated that picture, recalling the ache in my cheeks from the effort of forcing a smile. My only thought when taking the photo was that my mother would never see it.

With my face everywhere, and the police searching for my "kidnapper," Alice kept encouraging me to go home. "These people love you," she said. "They will forgive you."

But what she didn't understand was that I couldn't forgive myself for the way things escalated. With this huge mistake hanging over me, there was no way I could be honest with my dad and friends about why I left. Yes, they hurt me, but they didn't mean to. I, on the other hand, intentionally hurt them by running away and allowing them to think I was kidnapped. How had I let the people that loved me suffer for another few weeks?

It wasn't until the FBI got involved that I knew I had to go back. They would find me, and then everyone would know that I stayed away, even though I knew my dad and friends were terrified.

I called my dad from the motel. "I'm sorry I ran away," I said. "But nobody kidnapped me. I just saw the news on TV. I'm in LA. I'm safe." I hated myself for lying.

He arrived with an army of police and the FBI soon after. I'll never forget the way he pulled me into his arms, crushing me against his large frame. It felt like he was trying to absorb me into his soul so he would never lose me again. A strange sensation flooded my body while he sobbed, and I immediately vomited on his shoes.

The FBI interviewed Alice, a few motel guests, and finally me. I admitted hitchhiking to LA but said it was with a woman to protect the big rig driver. It was easy to convince the detectives I didn't pay attention to the news or papers flashing my photo. I was a depressed teenager who had lost her mother. I'm not sure what Alice said to convince them she didn't realize either, but then again, maybe she didn't need to. After all, she didn't commit a crime.

Four weeks after I disappeared, the whole town greeted the police car bringing me home, showing their love with signs, flowers, and tears, relieved the nightmare was finally over. News trucks and cameras swarmed me as my father walked me back to my house from the driveway.

As I reached the doorstep, a reporter leaped out, blocking my path. "Tell us, Angie, how does it feel knowing your friends and family were terrified they'd never see you again? They believed someone had kidnapped you. They feared you were dead."

My dad, noticing my distress, pushed past the reporter and led me into our house. Shortly after, Carly, Angie, and Liliana came running in. They sobbed uncontrollably.

"I love you," they said with trembling bodies. "Thank God, you're safe," they said in voices shaky with fear and relief.

"I thought some crazy man murdered you. I haven't slept in weeks. I can't believe you're here, standing in front of me, safe." Carly squeezed me tight, her body shaking against mine.

I could feel her unsteady legs and had to keep her from falling over.

I knew I had to give them an explanation. I told them the same story I told the FBI. I omitted how my dad's collapse overwhelmed me. I didn't mention that my friends' support fell short. How could I? They didn't mean to hurt me, but I'd consciously hurt them by running away and staying away.

I never admitted to my dad or my friends that I waited to come home. I never admitted that I had let them suffer for several weeks when I could have told them I was safe. Instead, I told them I called home as soon as I found out about the fake kidnapping. A lie that changed the course of my life.

My friend's hugs, their tears, and their overwhelming relief all made my guilt sink deep into my bones. I couldn't face them anymore.

Seeing them reminded me of what I hadn't admitted. What I didn't understand was that my omission would transform into an invasive weed, pushing me away from everyone I loved.

"Hmm, I don't see Liliana and Nicole." Carly's voice echoes in my ear.

Looking around, I realize I'm not in that grim motel in LA, hugging my dad, but standing in the middle of the rooftop bar on St. McAna Island. But it's like I'm caught between two worlds, and my seventeen-year-old self is standing right beside me.

Carly waves a hand in my face, apparently realizing I'm distracted. "Did you hear me? They're not here. Why are you making a weird face?"

I shrug a few times trying to release myself from the past, but my entire body shivers with the emotions that live trapped in my body from all those years ago.

"Oh, duh, I have my phone. It's finally dry. I'll text them." Carly unzips her belt bag.

I force a smile.

"You okay?" she asks again.

Am I okay? I remind myself of what I decided when Carly and I were leaving the beach. I need to tell my friends and then let it go. Staying in LA when I knew my dad, my friends, and my entire town were terrified was wrong. It's the biggest mistake I've ever made, a decision that haunts me to this day.

"I'm fine." I smile at Carly, hoping deep down that our mended friendship can withstand my confession.

CHAPTER 35

Liliana

Emerald Jewel All-Inclusive Resort
October 4th ♫ Last Night

TURN MY HEAD around, looking for Carly and Angie. Where are they? They've been gone a long time. Nicole and I walked down to the pool bar searching for them, but with no luck. A gust of wind blows, and the palm tree leaves surrounding us make a loud clapping sound.

My head buzzes from the Aperol spritz I just drank trying to calm the whirl of emotion I'm feeling about my life. Can Josh and I salvage our marriage? He still doesn't understand how broken I feel. I'm afraid I might do something crazy that I can't take back. Is this what Britney felt like before she shaved her head?

"Hopefully, Carly's not hurt," I say to Nicole, trying to get out of my head. "That was a nasty fall."

"He didn't trip her." Nicole's head bounces awkwardly like a bobblehead toy on a spring. "He did not. Nope. But who cares! Look what I snagged." She waves Carly's selfie stick around and cackles with laughter. "It's mine now." She takes her phone and lip gloss out of her bag, folds up the selfie stick, and stuffs it inside. Opening the lip gloss, she glides it across her chin, completely missing her lips.

She's drunk and high. Maybe this is why she's having problems with Garrett. She needs to grow up. I wonder if Josh finds her immature, but he's never mentioned anything.

"Yeah, he didn't trip her," I agree.

We both look down when her phone lights up with a text. She paws at her device and smirks after reading her message. "Yes, of course they love driving that mini-Mercedes wagon."

"What?" I'm confused.

She pushes her phone near me and shows me a picture of a child driving the kid's version of a miniature Mercedes G-Wagon inside the Hamilton Beach Mercedes dealership.

"What's that?" I ask, studying the photo.

Nicole lets out another piercing cackle. She's wasted.

She slumps over the bar. "I said, and I was right. I said, if you want to sell these mini-Mercedes kid wagons to bougie parents, you need to do it at the dealership. Duh. So basic."

"What?" I ask again, staring at the photo, noticing it's from her new friend Jessica. As my eyes pull away from the image, I feel a strange sensation. The kid in the photo is blurry, and the photo is from a weird angle, but it looks like Esther.

"Wait, is that...?"

But before I can say more, Nicole grabs her phone and points across the bar. "Those bitches are back." She stumbles off her stool, staggering toward Angie and Carly.

I need to ask Nicole to show me that picture again later. Something odd is going on.

"We were at the rooftop bar looking for you. I sent a text. Did you get it?" Carly waits for me to answer, interrupting my thoughts, then leads us to an empty table. The hotel's signature scent of coconut and vanilla wafts from the candle in front of us.

I shake my head. "I guess we both missed it. What took so long?"

"I'm like the main character in one of those off-beat mom detective books." Carly recounts the details of Luca and the young girl sneaking off into a closet together. "We think it's a case of identity theft and nothing more. We'll report him to the embassy tomorrow."

"Really?" I ask. "You okay, Angie? I know you believed Luca's story."

"I don't know what to believe anymore. I felt like we really connected because of our similar experiences. But maybe it was all a lie."

"That hottie did not take your passport." Nicole snorts as she laughs.

The waitress appears, and we ask for a round of water. We've all had a lot to drink and need to slow down. I'm thankful when Nicole lets the waitress leave without ordering anything else. She's had enough for the night.

"So, the bottom line," Angie says. "Let's stick together and stay away from him."

The waitress returns with our water.

Angie takes a long sip from her glass and then puts it back on the table. "Before we go to the show, I want to say a few things."

Carly grabs her hand. Their affection is surprising after years of tension. Maybe this really is a new beginning for us, but I can't help but wonder what's coming. It's not about Luca, because we already discussed that.

"A lot of crazy things have happened on this trip. And part of the reason is, well…it's that…" Angie can't get her words out.

I worry she's going to call me out because I'm consumed with work. Or maybe she's had it with Nicole acting half her age. Or does she sense something's off with Carly?

"I want to talk about what happened in high school." She fidgets nervously.

My stomach flips in surprise.

Angie nods. "I know. You didn't expect me to say that. But I finally understand that talking about the hardest moments in life with people who care is the only way to move beyond them."

Her statement makes my head pulse. It makes me wonder why I haven't been more open with Josh. To him, I've always been obsessed with my career. I know it's going to take a lot of conversations for him to truly understand about my mom and how deep this goes.

Angie continues. "I hate what I put our town through, but even more, my very best friends. I want to start by helping you understand why I ran away." She clasps and unclasps her hands anxiously. "You know how senior year was. We'd been waiting for it since the day we walked in as freshmen. Everyone was so damn happy all the time. And every few weeks, there'd be some new senior event." Angie's voice breaks with emotion.

My mind wanders to that last year at Hamilton Beach High. Senior prank, spirit week, awards, portraits, sunrise brunch, prom, graduation. Life was an endless stream of events marking the end of our childhood. It's true. While we were riding high on attention and brimming with excitement for college, Angie was suffering.

Guilt makes my stomach churn. "I'm sorry we missed how hopeless you felt."

"You shouldn't be," she says and then explains how her dad fell apart. "And I was scared of losing you. I thought if I pretended everything was okay, it would be. But obviously, I was wrong."

As I listen to her, I think about Josh and how I've ignored my fears about our marriage, hoping everything would magically fix itself. My mom was wrong. To have a healthy, stable, and happy life, we must be honest about our emotions. Even when it's hard.

Nicole runs her finger over the condensation on her water glass. "Man, we were clueless. Carly tried to distract you, Liliana avoided it, and I tried to crack jokes, thinking if you laughed, you were okay." This conversation seems to have sobered her up a bit.

Angie shifts her eyes back to us. "But that was my fault. I should have told you none of that was working and explained what I needed. But I was a kid too."

"What did you need?" I ask.

"Just to sit in a room and cry and then cry some more. And I needed to see *you guys* cry. And I needed us to cry all together." Angie looks at Carly. "It was actually an immense relief yesterday when you told me you cried too. I always wondered why all of you weren't more shaken up."

"Wow," I say. "We were afraid that we'd upset you. We wanted to be your break from the pain, but what you're saying makes so much sense." I look at Angie. "It's time for each of us to stop blaming ourselves. All the anger, all the guilt, all the regret—it turned into a destructive force, and it's the reason we've lost each other."

As Nicole and Carly nod, agreeing with me, all I can think about is how my regrets and Josh's anger have also twisted together into a destructive force.

"No!" Angie raises her voice, startling me. "It's my fault!" The color drains from her face.

I shift in my chair, overcome with the need to clarify that we don't blame her. "It's not your fault some drifter saw a news story about you running away and sent letters to your dad, saying he kidnapped you."

"Exactly this," Nicole says. "There was no way for you to know about the fake kidnapping letters. It's not like we had phones and the internet back then."

Angie sinks into her chair. "It's just... What I wanted to say is that..." Her voice trembles. She inhales deeply. "The truth is, I knew about the letters. I told the police, my dad, and everyone that I called home as soon as I saw the news story about my kidnapping, but that's not true."

None of us moves or breathes or blinks for several moments.

"I knew about the letters for almost two weeks before I called home. I let you worry. I let you suffer. I put you through the worst pain imaginable, and I've never been able to forgive myself."

"Wait. I don't understand." Carly's mouth falls open with shock.

My head spins, thinking about how scared we were. How we stopped living, consumed by Angie's kidnapping. Even now, my body vibrates, remembering the sheer terror we felt.

"Can I get you dolls anything more to drink?" The waitress glides to our table, interrupting the moment.

None of us responds.

"Ladies, do you need anything?"

Carly snaps out of our shared trance and looks at her. "We need a minute."

Although she looks confused, the waitress nods, then walks to another table.

"I made such a terrible mistake. I wish I could take it back. I'm going to go to my room and let you guys enjoy the last night without me." Angie pushes forward to get out of her chair.

Looking at her, I realize I'm not angry. I'm sad. How could we expect her to find joy in anything when her mom had died? How did we miss her dad's breakdown? Why didn't we let her see us cry?

I glance back at Carly, wondering if she's going to be forgiving. It's possible she's going to explode with anger.

Angie drops her face into her hands. When she reemerges, tears stream down her cheeks. "I was scared to come back after I found out about the letters. Scared everyone would be mad at me. And if I'm being honest, it felt freeing that no one in LA knew my mom had died. I didn't have to pretend I was fine."

Carly's lips twitch, and I lean back, bracing for her anger.

"That's it right there," Carly whispers. "You didn't have to pretend. I've always felt like I failed you for not knowing how broken you were. Instead of asking you what you needed, I focused on quick fixes for your heartache and mine. I've always felt responsible. I was your best friend." She glances down, and a sorrowful expression clouds her face.

We sit side by side in silence. Is it possible that Carly, Nicole, and I feel more regret than anger? It seems logical that we should be angry with Angie, but we're not. But it makes sense. Anger is a fleeting response to a threat. It crashes over you and then dissipates. Regret, however, concentrates itself in your soul. It accumulates like a negative force field, growing stronger, denser, and more powerful over time.

"You didn't fail me. I wish I had come home as soon as I found out about the letters. What began as a runaway case turned into something much bigger." Angie lets out a long breath. "The police and FBI went all out. And for what? I was a sad girl who lost her mom and rented a room in LA."

I recall the press conference where the police confirmed Angie returned to Hamilton Beach unharmed. She had hitchhiked to LA. The deranged person who sent fake ransom notes was being questioned.

"I'm so sorry. I hope you can forgive me, but I understand if you can't. I've missed you." Her hands tremble as she rests her arms on the table.

Carly places her hand firmly over Angie's. "I've missed you so, so much. I forgive you, and I hope you can forgive us too."

Nicole nods, looking at Angie. "Of course, we forgive you."

"We miss you too," I add, wondering how this conversation would have gone if Angie had admitted she knew about the letters when she came home. Perhaps we would have felt betrayed. We were young, and our emotions were razor sharp.

"Your mom was an amazing human." Nicole smiles. "She kept me in line."

"Yes, she really was," I agree, knowing she was the only one who knew how much pressure my mom put on me.

"It was easier to concentrate on keeping us all busy rather than process my grief over the loss of a woman who was such a big part of my life. It's amazing how often I think about her," Carly says. "She always saw the best in people. We all loved her."

Angie's facial features rearrange into a tender, open expression.

Carly continues. "We were lucky to get you back safely."

Tears slip from Angie's eyes. "The next year was tough. You all left for college while I stayed home and took the year off." Lifting her hand, she wipes her cheeks. "I got used to being on my own. And when I finally left for Wash U the next year, it was easy to use the move as an excuse to pull away. Still, every five years, I went on our trip, planning to admit what I had done. But after Miraval, I realized that going on these trips was making things worse."

As I look around, I see all of us crying happy tears.

"Wow!" Carly looks at me. "Even Liliana's crying."

"I am," I say, feeling comfortable showing my tears to my best friends. Life is not a boardroom. I place my palm over Angie's and Carly's hands, and Nicole does the same. "We love you. We want you to be part of our lives."

"I get that now."

"Yasss!" Nicole claps her hands together. "Does this mean you're going to visit Hamilton Beach? It's been forever."

Angie's lips turn up with a small smile. "We'll see. I still need to talk to Patton about my past. He doesn't even know I ran away."

"One step at a time," I say, thinking about my phone call with Josh earlier. Admitting to him that my relationship with Amanda is toxic was just the first step in repairing our relationship.

Angie nods. "I'm glad we're finally talking about this, but let the record show, I will not take part in a text chain called High School Besties Squad. Can we change that to something more dignified?" She lets out a small laugh.

"Hey," Nicole's voice has a sarcastic edge, "I'm the one who came up with that."

"Of course, you are." Angie giggles.

Despite the other issues in my life, I am flooded with joy. At last, I'm certain this moment marks our fresh start. Our laughter erupts as the waitress checks in.

"The show's about to start."

"Yes, thanks! Let's go." Carly jumps out of her chair, and we all do the same. "We have to get to the front!"

Nicole leads us through the crowd, shoving people aside. "I'm Donnie's sister. Let me through."

A short woman with blond spiky hair eyes us disapprovingly, but somehow, we make it to the very front. I press my body against the metal railing that separates the crowd from the stage.

When a group of women get distracted by a joint they're passing, Angie squeezes her body next to mine. Nicole moves in close behind us. I swing my head around, looking for Carly. She's a few steps back, reading something on her phone. Her face has an odd expression.

"You okay?" I ask when she catches up.

"Yes, Marco won't stop texting me. I just want to forget about life and enjoy the show."

I get it. *This is awesome! I can't wait to see NKOTB!*

Soon, the stage floods with bright light.

"Here we go!" My heart pushes against my chest. The words *New Kids on the Block* float across a giant screen while a techno beat blares. My eardrums vibrate as hundreds of high-pitched screams pierce the air.

Angie throws her arms around my shoulders, pulling me into a side hug. Carly and Nicole move in closer. At this moment, we are four twelve-year-old girls with unconditional love for each other.

An image of a giant metal door appears on the screen. The number ten flashes, then changes to nine, then eight. The crowd wildly counts down, pulsing with energy. Screams and groans ring out, creating a deafening noise. Everyone roars.

"Three...two...one!"

The image of the door bursts open with a loud, squeaky bang. And then, on stage, less than two feet in front of me, are New Kids on the Block.

"Hangin' Tough" begins, and the crowd explodes. For the next two hours, I completely disconnect from Josh's dissatisfaction, my mom guilt, my job, and my building desperation. For the next two hours, there is only the music, these songs, the nostalgia, and the magic of this exact moment.

CHAPTER 36

Nicole

Emerald Jewel All-Inclusive Resort
October 4th ♫ Last Night

"**Y**OU GOTTA PLAY 'Pretty in Pink,' by the Psychedelic Furs!" I put a ten-dollar bill in the DJ's tip jar and run back to the after party on the sand. Groups of women hop around, stoked by the chance to dance barefoot in the glow of moonlight.

"Nicole, over here." Carly waves at me.

Liliana dances behind her while Angie sings at the top of her lungs. Boy, she dropped a bomb tonight, admitting she knew about the psycho who pretended he kidnapped her. I'm glad she waited to tell us. There would've been a lot more anger if she'd fessed up right away. Especially from Carly, but I'm glad she told us the truth. Honestly, it's a relief to understand why she kept her distance. All this time, I felt like Liliana, Carly, and I were to blame. I feel lighter now that I know we each messed up in our own way. We're definitely in our comeback era.

"That concert was amazing, but this may be even more fun!" Carly spins me in a disco move while "Dancing Queen" plays. "I think I had one too many shots." She puts her arms around Angie and Liliana, pulling them closer. "Dancing Queen" ends and the new wave song about Caroline and her pretty pink clothes begins.

"We all know who this song is for." The DJ points to us and our pink dresses.

We scream wildly, turning round and round. When the song ends, Carly leads us to the beach bar.

"Hey, are you master of mom fashion?" A woman wearing enough makeup to rival a TikTok filter eyes Carly from across the bar. "Hey look." She pulls her friends and walks over. "It's the mom from Insta we follow."

Carly's lips turn up, but it's not quite a smile. "It's me," she stumbles away from them.

Grinning like an awkward preteen, the woman continues. "We all follow you! You have the best outfit advice, and we love your beautiful daughter."

Carly's jaw clenches, and I can't help but wonder what's wrong. She lives for follower validation.

Another woman, wearing an off-the-shoulder MTV T-shirt, leans into Carly. "And oh my gosh, your husband is adorable."

"Fucking Insta!" Carly shouts. Her eyes bug.

I'm grossed out by the way I can see the tiny red veins against her bright-white eyeball, but her weird reaction is what's really freaking me out.

Angie and Liliana freeze, I guess also shocked by Carly's outburst. Her Insta followers seem confused. But before we can wrap our heads around Carly's behavior, she walks right up to the woman in the MTV shirt and keeps talking.

"Let me tell you about Insta. It's all fake. Every single thing about it. I know it looks like I have my shit together with my outfit of the day posts, my gorgeous daughter, counting my fucking macros, and my perfect, adorable husband. But I'm here to tell you it's all bullshit. My favorite item of clothing is from Walmart. My daughter can be a terror. I sneak chocolate all day long, and my fucking husband is having an affair!" She tosses her fresh cocktail onto the ground and storms off.

I stare at the lime twist, half covered in sand. What in the actual fuck is happening?

"Well, that was rude!" The TikTok makeup woman glares at us, waiting for an explanation, but we dash off, following Carly.

Catching up, we circle around her. She breaks down, bawling in our arms. The four of us sit, dropping onto the ground. Cold ocean water creeps around us. The smell of rotten seaweed makes my eyes water. Angie, Liliana, and I swap concerned glances as we let Carly cry it out.

After a bit, she stops. "I'm sorry. I couldn't hold it in anymore. Marco's probably having an affair." She looks at Angie. "That's what I was trying to say on the beach before. But I didn't have the guts to admit it."

Did I hear Carly right? I didn't see that coming. I hug her closer. Angie rubs her back. "Oh, no! I understand."

Liliana takes Carly's right hand in her own. "What happened?"

Carly leans into us, like she needs us to keep her from falling over. "I saw some text messages. But the worst part is…" She remains quiet for a second. "The worst part is I sent Marco and his maybe girlfriend a group text right before the show."

"What?" I ask, confused.

"That's what you were texting Marco about?" Liliana asks.

Carly answers through choked tears. "Something about watching Luca sneak off with that girl. I snapped. I had to know if Marco was cheating." She locks eyes with me, like she's Mack confessing he hasn't brushed his teeth in a week. "I have the woman's number." She buries her face in her hands and lets out a sharp sob. "I sent a text to her and Marco. A group text. I'm so stupid."

Pulling her phone from her belt bag, she flips it around, letting us read the message to Marco and another number.

Carly: I know about the affair.

Marco: Call me right now

Marco: Call me

Marco: I'm calling you

"Oh, oh…whoa. This is…this is…" I stammer, unable to put words together. Carly always has her shit together. This is insane.

A wave rushes in, spraying us with water.

Carly suddenly jumps up, power walking toward the empty stage. Angie, Liliana, and I chase after her.

"I can't talk about it right now," she shouts. "I'm a mess. I'm…"

Her phone rings before she can finish. Her screen illuminates in the darkness with Marco's name.

"I don't want to pick up." She lets it go to voicemail. It rings again. "He's been calling ever since I sent the text." Her voice shakes.

"You don't have to talk to him until you're ready," Angie says.

Carly nods, but her phone rings again. She focuses on Marco's name. "Maybe it will be easier with my best friends here."

"Wait!" Liliana shouts, but she's too late.

Carly clumsily slides her finger across her phone and answers the call.

Here it comes. This is happening.

"Ma sei pazza?!" Marco's voice rings out.

"Shoot, she shouldn't have picked up. We should've told her to wait until tomorrow." Angie moves toward her.

Carly glances back at us with a strange expression. Her features are out of place and exaggerated, like one of Chelsea's preschool drawings.

"Just leave me," she mouths. Rushing to the deserted stage, she turns a corner and disappears out of sight.

"Should we follow her?" Liliana eyes us with worry. Liliana never worries. It gives me the chills.

"I'll go." Angie runs down the beach.

I start to follow, but Liliana puts her hand on my shoulder, stopping me. "Let them be there for each other. It seems important."

"You're right," I agree, thinking about how they've finally made peace.

But as Liliana and I walk side by side in the other direction, all I can picture is how Liliana will react to Josh's news.

"This way." Liliana points, and we push through a crowd, enjoying an over-the-top midnight breakfast buffet.

The smell of bacon grease makes me feel sick. Or is my stomach cramping because Garrett and I are in a fight, on top of the guilt I'm feeling for betraying Liliana? My head pounds as we pass the boathouse and sit in the sand by the gazebo.

"My heart's breaking for Carly." Liliana sounds concerned. "I mean, Josh and I have our problems too. But cheating. How do you come back from that?" Liliana fishes her phone from her pocket and twists it back and forth in her palm. "And this is why it's been hard. This is exactly why. Eight calls from my boss today." She taps the center button, showing me her call log. "I'm going to throw this thing into the ocean." She angrily swings her arm forward.

I wait to hear the splash, but then see her phone still clenched in her hand.

My body bursts with adrenaline, and I jump up from the ground.

"What's wrong?" Liliana tilts her head. Her soft curls fall around her face.

"My stomach is kicking." I lie. "Gotta find a bathroom." I bolt before she can say anything.

Whipping out my phone, my fingers fly to text Josh. No more secrets. It's time to come clean. I look at Liliana as I try and figure out what to text him. She's stumbling into the ocean, waving her phone over her head. As she gets deeper in the water, my guilt swallows me like quicksand. I've got to chill out.

I crack open my tin of gummies and pop two into my mouth. When I glance back at the coastline, I can barely make Liliana out in the darkness. The wind whips and waves surround her. She's too far out. It's not safe. I move toward the ocean to get her back on shore, but then I hear a voice.

"Hey, Nicole!"

I turn my head around and see Luca holding the hand of that gorgeous young girl.

"Where's Angie? I've been looking for her all night." His eyes dart back and forth, and then he gets right in my face.

My pulse speeds up, and I move back. I don't know if it's the crazy events of the last twenty minutes, or if my gut is spot-on. But he's riled up and giving off some sketchy vibes.

"Hey, where are your friends?" the young girl asks.

Suddenly, it's like I'm in a thick fog. All the alcohol and gummies I've taken hit me like a truck. Everything's confusing. I'm out of it.

"Where's your crew?" Luca asks. His words sound long and slow.

"I need to go," I blurt, turning away. I take a step, but then feel his large palm grasp my arm.

"Wait a minute." He shoves his face closer to mine. He reeks of pot. His fingers dig into my arm. "I need to find Angie. It's important, and she's not answering my texts." He pulls me around to face him, and immediately, I'm aware of how strong he is.

"Leave me the fuck alone." I shake myself loose from his grip and haul ass to the lobby, putting as much distance between us as I can. My heart races like crazy. I'm not sure why, but I'm desperate to escape him.

CHAPTER 37

Mr. LaFleur

Now
Emerald Jewel All-Inclusive Resort
October 5th 🎵 7:30 a.m.

MR. LAFLEUR LEADS Detective Ellis, Officer Claasen, and his young security guard, George, down the beach. Holding his shoes in his hand, he contemplates what Detective Ellis expects to find where the missing woman was last seen. Clues remain elusive despite the exhaustive search. A few curious hotel guests mill around even though the St. McAna police have surrounded the small area with a human blockade.

"Let's stop here."

The group assembles in front of construction materials by the boathouse. Lifting his right foot, Detective Ellis shakes sand out of his shoe. A small grin spreads across Mr. LaFleur's face; he knows the grains will continue to irritate the detective for months to come. Three women in pink dresses trail behind.

"We know she went to the gazebo because of the evidence found there. It's possible she fell into the ocean." Detective Ellis's voice sounds grim.

Mr. LaFleur nods, praying the woman fell and wasn't murdered. He knows that an accidental death caused by alcohol will move quickly through the news cycle without too much attention. If the worst has happened, he needs it to blow over fast. He's counting on this promotion. This can't become another true crime story for *Dateline*.

"My focus is on the facts. And right now, the only evidence I see is that a drunk woman was near a body of water in the middle of the night. I need to consider the obvious explanation before I think about others. But I want to question Luca." Detective Ellis stares at Officer Claasen. "Have we located him yet?"

"We walked the property again and questioned people, but no."

Mr. LaFleur refrains from criticizing Officer Claasen's wasted morning questioning guests.

Detective Ellis clears his throat. "I think it's time to call a dive team. It's possible the woman was intoxicated, fell into the ocean, and drowned. Maybe she hit her head." He speaks in a hushed voice, not wanting the women in pink to overhear.

"Oh no, no, no." Mr. LaFleur shifts his bare feet in the sand as if he's trying to balance himself on unstable ground. He can't have a dive team show up, searching for a dead body. Although corporate was happy with the way he kept Emerald Jewel's involvement in the jewelry heist from the headlines, there's no way he can keep the news of a dead American female tourist secret. He envisions the resort's picturesque pool area swarming with camera crews and reporters.

The women in pink move closer, as if sensing Mr. LaFleur's unease.

Tugging on George's sleeve, Mr. LaFleur looks skyward, locking eyes with the tall security guard. "Are you sure you did a thorough search of the grounds?" He gestures with his arms, pointing towards various places on the resort's property. "The kitchen of the outdoor restaurant? The stock area of the bar? The broken closet in the lobby? The stage area? The boathouse?" He knows his rapid, erratic gestures are a clear sign he's unhinged, but losing his promotion means a lifetime of working with whiny, unreasonable, demanding hotel guests.

All of a sudden, the woman with the ripped dress snaps to attention.

And then she's running. She strides past the orange cones and barrier tape surrounding the boathouse and shoves open the door.

"What in the world?" Mr. LaFleur runs behind her, and the entire group enters the boathouse.

"Anyone here?" She shoves aside a stack of wake boards, walks around a small rowboat, and makes her way to the bathroom.

"Miss, we checked the boathouse." George catches up as she reaches the bathroom door.

"But did you open the bathroom door?" The woman pants her words, twisting the door's handle.

"It's stuck." Mr. LaFleur sighs. "It warped shut after the boathouse was flooded by a high tide. That's why it's under construction."

"Break it down!" the woman screams.

Scanning the dilapidated space, she grabs a heavy oar and slams it against the door. It doesn't budge.

She tries again, but the door remains fixed in place.

George grabs an oar and joins her.

"One, two, three." They slam their oars against the warped door in unison, and it pops open.

"Oh, no! Oh my God, no!" The woman throws down her oar and quickly kneels over the body lying on the floor. Her torn dress strap falls over her shoulder.

"Oh my God, Angie, tell us she's breathing!" The woman with wild hair stares at Angie, who gently repositions the body of the woman lying on the floor, so she's flat on her back.

Mr. LaFleur ceases to breathe. "Please," he begs. *Let her be alive.*

Everyone exhales with relief, observing the rhythmic rise and fall of the woman's chest.

"Carly, get a life vest to support her head."

The woman with wild hair does as Angie says. "She's alive!" Carly brushes her wild hair out of her face and hands the life vest to Angie.

Sobs suddenly ring out in the small space. "It's okay, Liliana," Carly says, comforting the woman with streaky black makeup.

"She's alive. Nicole is alive!" Liliana shouts.

Angie's eyes run up and down Nicole's body and then furrow in confusion. "What on earth? Why is she wearing her hot pink lingerie and nothing else?"

"Nicole, Nicole…" Angie strokes Nicole's arm.

"Mmm." Nicole mutters something unintelligible.

"Nicole, we've been scared out of our minds. Are you okay?" Leaning down, Liliana looks at Nicole.

"Mmm…" Nicole mumbles again, but then her eyes pop open. "Oh, shit." She bolts upright. "Oh, shit," she says again, glancing at the people gathered around her. She crosses her hands over her body protectively.

The group stares at Nicole, wide-eyed.

"What happened?" Carly asks. "Why are you wearing the lingerie from your boudoir photos? You look like a Victoria's Secret Angel."

Everyone's jaws hang open, baffled by the thigh-high stockings, hot pink bra, underwear, and feathery garter belt.

Mr. LaFleur rushes away, returning with a dusty emergency kit. Pulling it open, he hands Nicole a large, shiny, plastic blanket made for shock victims. He is both relieved and horrified. She's alive, but he prays that what happened on his property isn't material for a *New York Times* exposé on the stupidity of privileged Americans.

"Ma'am, what happened? Did someone assault you? Does this have anything to do with Luca?" Detective Ellis hovers, while Angie, Carly, and Liliana help Nicole stand.

Her face flushes bright pink, matching her underwear. "I'm fine. This is my fault. This has nothing to do with Luca."

"Oh, thank goodness!" Angie says.

"Ma'am, are you sure?" Detective Ellis probes again.

"Can I have a few minutes with my friends?" Nicole wraps the blanket tightly around her body.

Detective Ellis nods. "Yes, but, after, I'll need to ask you some questions so I can close this case."

At last, the ten-ton weight that's been crushing Mr. LaFleur dissipates. He's dumbfounded knowing George could have prevented all of this if he had kicked open the bathroom door when he checked the boathouse hours ago. But, then again, he didn't try opening the door either. It warped shut months ago. Or so he thought.

The women in pink huddle together in a long, tight embrace.

Pulling away from the group, Nicole speaks. "Get ready to laugh. This story is the GOAT!"

Stunned and silent, Mr. LaFleur leads Detective Ellis, Officer Claasen, and George back toward the hotel lobby, already devising ways to keep corporate in the dark.

CHAPTER 38

Angie

Emerald Jewel All-Inclusive Resort

"THIS STORY BETTER be the GOAT." I give Nicole a stern expression but then can't help but break into a smile. "You know what, for once, I'm fine with you sounding like a sixteen-year-old. Thank God, we found you." My heart beats wildly. It takes several minutes for my adrenaline to dissipate.

"I'm a total idiot, but I'm fine." Nicole steps back from our group hug. "I need to sit down." Walking to the beat-up rowboat, she gets inside and takes a seat.

Liliana, Carly, and I follow, squishing onto a slim wood bench facing her.

"When did you realize I was missing?" Nicole asks.

"We've been looking for you since two o'clock this morning," Liliana says. "I texted everyone to check in before I went to sleep, since we got split up. You never responded."

I picture us banging on Nicole's door last night, but she didn't answer. "We did a lap around the hotel grounds, and that's when we found your clothes. It was terrifying!"

"We all assumed Luca was involved," Carly says.

"I'm so relieved this had nothing to do with him." But I still wonder what happened to him and if he has my passport.

"I saw him last night, but he's not the reason I was stuck in the bathroom." Nicole pushes away the clump of bangs hanging over her eyes, then shifts her gaze down. "I don't know where to start. I just… it's just… Do you ever feel like you're doing life wrong?"

Carly raises her hand like she's a fifth grader who knows the answer to the state capital of Montana. The rowboat wobbles. "Are you kidding?" she continues. "My marriage is on the brink, and I'm sick of pretending I'm perfect. I've definitely taken a wrong turn somewhere."

"I'm shocked about Marco." Nicole's eyes cloud with concern. "What did he say?"

Carly drops her arm. "This isn't about me right now. We can talk about that later. What happened to you last night?"

"No," Nicole says. "This is about all of us. We love you and want to know what happened."

"Are you sure?" Carly glances at Liliana and me.

We both nod, confirming we agree.

"He's furious with me for the group text. He swears he hasn't cheated."

"What made you text him before the show?" Liliana asks.

Carly tries to tame her crazy hair. "At first, I was triggered when we caught Luca and that girl in the closet. But then, I don't know if this will make sense, but it was such a relief when the four of us finally got everything out in the open. All the hurt. All the pain. All the misunderstanding. And at the bottom of it all was love. We deeply love and miss each other. I wanted the same feeling of relief about my marriage. I wanted to know that, at the bottom of it all, was love."

"I get that," Nicole agrees.

"But sending a text to him and the woman, accusing them of cheating…that was a huge mistake. This is exactly why I need to tell my best friends when life is hard. You would have told me not to send that text. But it's impossible to get advice if you don't tell your friends what's really going on."

"Amen!" I say.

Carly gives me a nod. "But let's talk more about Marco later." She turns her attention to Nicole. "What happened to you last night?"

Following Carly's lead, the rest of us let the subject of Marco drop…for now.

Nicole crosses her legs but stays quiet. The air is thick with the odor of musty life vests. It's hard to tell if she doesn't want to over-shadow Carly's problems or if she can't find the words she needs to start. I decide to help.

"You can tell us about last night. It's better to talk about it than to push it down. I learned my lesson the hard way."

Nicole grabs the side of the boat like she's trying to keep herself from going overboard. The emergency blanket slides off her body. She's quiet, and I understand what's happening. It's hard to be honest and vulnerable, even with your best friends.

Pulling up the silver blanket, she wraps it back over her shoulders. "I feel lost. Like my entire existence revolves around taking care of my kids and Garrett. I used to be a confident, independent woman, with a career, cool hobbies, and way more interesting things to talk about than non-GMO school lunches and gentle parenting." Tears well in her eyes, despite her joke. "But that person is gone, and all that's left is this outline of who I used to be."

I squeeze Nicole's hand, and she continues.

"I had big dreams of running an ad empire. But after being stuck in a wheelchair for months, I couldn't do all the things I was dreaming of as a first-time mom—bath time, rocking my baby to sleep, even changing diapers. I thought being a full-time mom was what I wanted."

Liliana leans toward Nicole. "But you made the right decision for who you were at that moment. Don't you remember all the hours we spent talking about whether you wanted to go back to work? You didn't take the decision lightly. And if you went back, you might still feel incomplete, but in a different way. A hollow version of the mom you want to be." Liliana scoots closer to Nicole and puts a reassuring hand on her leg, but Nicole goes stiff. It's strange, but maybe Nicole's feeling overwhelmed.

"But how did you end up in the boathouse bathroom?" Carly interrupts with her question.

Nicole looks at Carly, appearing relieved to move on. "Last night I had a fight with Garrett before the show. The bottom line is that, since becoming a stay-at-home mom, I've been prioritizing Garrett's needs and deprioritizing my own. And I always let him off the hook with the kids. I do everything."

"Then why don't you ask him to help?" I ask.

"I don't know. It started after I recovered from the pelvic separation. I wanted to make up for lost time with Hank, and then it seemed easier to do things myself. It never seems like a big deal in each brief moment."

"It sounds like all these brief moments where you choose Garrett over yourself have made you feel less than, or even resentful. I remember feeling like that when my twins were little." I can easily recall the bitterness I felt toward Patton when I breastfed Ethan and Everett at night while he slept.

Nicole's voice shakes. "But I'm the mom, and *momlife* is different from *dadlife*." She dramatically screws her eyes together. "I know. I know. Me and my slang."

"*Momlife*. Can you define that for me?" Liliana presses her lips together, causing the corners of her mouth to droop.

I wonder if this conversation is triggering her own insecurities.

Nicole sits up straight, and the silver blanket slides onto the rowboat floor. She pushes her shoulders back, like she's the president about to address Congress. Her lacy lingerie barely covers her breasts, and she doesn't seem to notice or care.

"*Momlife* is all the crazy thoughts, feelings, and to-dos that come with being a mom. Things like constantly putting shoes away, stepping on a LEGO and screaming out in pain, eating Cheerios with wine for dinner because I ran out of time to cook dinner for myself. It's trying to get Mack to baseball at the same time Chelsea has soccer. It's making sure Hank has cans for the school food drive. It's scheduling well-checks and haircuts. It's covering all the bases so Garrett can work without ever having to know the ticker tape running in my head with the wants and needs of every person in our family." She exhales for a long moment, then sucks in a breath, as if her explanation has taken all the air in her lungs.

"That's it!" Liliana throws her hands up into the air like she finally understands something she's been struggling to figure out. "The ticker tape. That's what I never realized before. Josh is always scrolling through a mental ticker tape that never stops. I provide project support, but I'm not the lead. I'm not the accountable party. I think I finally understand something Josh has never explained."

"But how did you end up in the boathouse?" Carly asks again. "I'm eagerly anticipating Jennifer Coolidge's arrival to get some answers about our *White Lotus* season."

"Ha!" Nicole laughs. "I took too many gummies last night. I was desperate to relax after all the drama. Then I bumped into Luca. He was acting weird. Like aggressive. It freaked me out. I ran up to my room. And then I was sobbing. I couldn't stop. The dam burst."

"Luca?" My body tenses. "You're sure he had nothing to do with this?"

"Nope, he has nothing to do with this. And honestly, I can't say for sure that he was acting weird. We were both high." She shrugs, and relief washes over me. "I couldn't stop crying, so I grabbed my phone to get out of my head. I started looking at my boudoir pictures. And that's when I got the idea to do my own photo shoot. I wanted to feel fierce. I wanted to feel the way I did when I was twenty-five and my whole life was ahead of me."

"And you happen to have your sexy lingerie with you?" Carly asks, confused.

Nicole's cheeks flush red. She glances up and then makes a soft sigh. "This sounds dumb, but since my boudoir session, I've been wearing lingerie under my clothes. It reminds me, yeah, I'm a mom, but I'm still that badass bitch too."

She forces a laugh, but I can sense her unease.

"Last night, I put on my lingerie and went down to the beach to take pictures. I had Carly's selfie stick. There weren't any people around, so I stripped out of my romper and dropped it in the sand. I walked to the gazebo, took off my shoes, but then I had to pee. I saw the boathouse and figured I could go in there. Next thing you know, I'm locked in the bathroom. And then I must have passed out. I'm sorry that I was M.I.A., that you thought I was dead or something." Her voice trails off.

"But you knew Liliana got locked in this bathroom the first day. Why did you go in there?" I ask my question gently.

Liliana talks before Nicole can answer. "Actually, she was on a call with Laura when all that happened. She didn't know."

Nicole nods, agreeing with Liliana.

"And that's why your shoes were on the gazebo floor as evidence," I blurt out, remembering the fear I felt when the security guard brought us to the gazebo at sunrise to confirm the item left behind was Nicole's.

"Yes." Nicole nods.

"And I guess you didn't bother putting your romper back on to go pee," Liliana adds.

Carly stands and claps her hands together. "That makes sense! It's impossible to get out of a romper when you have to pee. So, you left it on the beach."

"Yes." Nicole jumps up, facing Carly. "I'm here to lay it out for you. Rompers are the devil disguised as carefree-looking clothes in adorable prints."

A second later, we're all gasping for air, consumed by infectious, hysterical laughter. Right at this moment, I realize we are no longer jagged ends that don't fit together. At last, we're back to being a perfect square.

We hear the scrape of the boathouse door opening.

Detective Ellis glances at us with an unsettling expression. "Ladies, I need you to come with me. We've located Luca. He has Angie's passport."

CHAPTER 39

Carly

Emerald Jewel All-Inclusive Resort

N O ONE SAYS a word as we trail the detective past the pool area and into the lobby. So, it turns out Luca is a fraud. I hate this for Angie. I grab her hand, sensing her unease.

As we pass a large mirror in the hotel lobby, I see my knotted, frizzy hair. *If the Metaverse could see me now!* But I don't care. I'm sick of worshipping follower counts and reel views like false idols. When I turn from the mirror, I notice suitcases lining the walls.

"Oh no, with everything going on, we forgot we're leaving later." My eyes scan the women dressed comfortably for travel in casual outfits from Evereve and the latest style of New Balance sneakers. *Great choices for a travel day.*

I walk around a group of women sitting on the floor surrounded by Louis Vuitton Neverfull bags and follow the detective into the meeting room the police have been using as a makeshift headquarters.

Shuffling inside, Luca's sitting across from the redheaded police officer. My body stiffens.

Luca stares at Angie with wide eyes. "Can you tell him what happened at check-in? I think that's why I have your passport." He gestures to the police officer, who turns to Angie. Her face is pale.

"We found your passport with Luca's." He holds up a cheap, light-blue leather passport case with a white airplane embossed on the cover. Opening the case, he pulls out both Angie and Luca's passports.

"I knew it!" I throw my hands into the air, feeling a strange mix of triumph and despair. A part of me hoped I was wrong, and Angie wasn't scammed the same way I was.

Angie glances at Luca, and then they both start laughing. "Oh my God," she says. "I have the same passport case!"

The rest of us stare at them, confused. She continues to giggle.

Luca catches his breath. "We both always buy the Amazon overall pick, and…" But he breaks out in another fit of laughter before he can finish.

Angie places her hand on his shoulder. She's so amused by whatever's going on that tears are rolling down her cheeks. She puts her other hand on the police officer's arm. "When you search Amazon, certain items come up with a box that says *Amazon overall pick*." She gasps with laughter again, barely able to get her words out. "I always buy the items Amazon recommends, and so does Luca." Her eyes light up with genuine delight. "We both came with the same shit-brown tumbler, and we both have the same passport case."

Immediately, I recall Angie showing me the same light-blue case with an airplane on the cover the day she discovered her passport was missing.

Angie continues talking to the police officer. "Did Luca tell you how they started checking us in? Like we were a couple?"

The officer nods.

"We both took out our passports. I explained that Luca and I weren't together. The employee at the desk—she was embarrassed." Angie does that weird laugh-cry thing. She squishes her face together like she's connecting the dots. "Then the champagne came. I took a glass, but then it dropped and shattered on the ground. I got distracted. I must have slipped my passport back into Luca's case by mistake. Then I guess I grabbed my empty passport case when I left to go to my room."

Jumping up from his chair, Luca stands and grabs Angie's hands.

"I didn't know your passport was on top of mine until Officer Friendly insisted I show him mine. I was shocked to find it."

"But why was your closet ransacked?" I ask. *Is Luca a mastermind con artist?*

Angie stops, eyeing Luca. "Hmm, yeah, why was my closet a mess? Do you know?"

"You don't remember?" he asks.

Angie shakes her head.

"When we got back to your room that first night, you said something about getting a pink dress delivered from Amazon. You tore apart your closet looking for it, then ran to the bathroom and threw up."

Angie's hands fly up to her forehead. "Oh, wow. That's right. Now I remember. After you left, I went back into the closet, still searching for the dress. That's when I saw the safe and threw my wallet and passport case inside. I remember everything spilling out. I didn't know my passport was missing until the next day, when my friends came."

Angie pulls Luca in, hugging him. "I'm glad we figured it out." She presses her body against his solid frame.

The tense clench of my jaw relaxes when they embrace. Angie wasn't a victim of a con. What happened to me was an isolated event.

The officer smooths his red mustache. "I've heard some crazy explanations in my time. This is one of the wilder ones, but it seems the whole thing has been a series of missteps and misunderstandings." He pulls Angie and Luca aside for further questioning.

Watching Angie, I think back to her admitting she knew about the kidnapping letters. My emotions are a mix of anger, sadness, and regret. I missed her father's emotional collapse. So, while it was a shock to find out she knew about the letters, a bigger part of me understands why she didn't come home. When our emotions have us in a chokehold, it's hard to think clearly. I can't believe I sent that text message to Marco and Lilly last night.

Liliana, Nicole, and I step away to give Angie, Luca, and the police privacy.

Ten minutes later, Angie walks over and leads us to the lobby. "Let's pack up. Maybe we can still make our flights."

"But there's still one thing I don't understand." Liliana looks at Angie questioningly. "What about the girl and hearing Luca say he didn't want to go to jail?"

Angie stops and motions for us to huddle close. She lowers her voice and fills us in. "Last night, while Carly was on the phone and I was by the stage waiting, I saw Luca. He was alone. He approached me, and I was scared. But then we started talking. I asked him about the girl."

"What? I don't remember you telling the police about this."

"I didn't tell them at first," she confirms. "But then, when I decided I should, I did it privately to protect the girl. She's the daughter of a boy band member we all know and love, and she's been trying to get Luca into bed all weekend. She pulled him into the closet, but Luca refused. She's only seventeen and…well. You know. She's underage."

"No way!" I interrupt, filling in the crucial detail. "And he didn't want to sleep with her because she's underage!" I recall the threat the girl made on the beach. *If you don't stay out of our business, you'll regret it.* She was scared her dad would find out about her and Luca.

"Exactly," Angie confirms. "Luca didn't want to chance it, since she insisted they sneak around, knowing her dad's crazy overprotective."

We all nod with relief now that the bizarre, unexplainable events of this vacation have fallen into place.

"Um, guys…" Liliana gestures around the lobby. Women pile carry-on bags on top of rolling suitcases and clamor to the valet area, hoping to get a good seat on the first round of buses heading to the airport. "We're not packed. I don't think there's any way we're making our flights. And, Angie, even though you have your passport back, you'll need the paperwork from the embassy."

Glancing around, I notice a forgotten pair of flip-flops and a red feather boa lying over a chair. A long line of tired women exits the hotel's open-air lobby, getting onto several luxury buses. Two resort workers are up on a ladder replacing the *Boy Bands at the Beach* banner with one that says, *Sail Away with Yacht Rock.*

Immediately, I feel out of breath, the way I always do when things fall apart. My mind jumps to Marco. When I married him, I was certain he'd never hurt me. As the thought flies through my brain, my heart skips a beat. This perfect world I've built is a house of cards. Inhaling, I gasp for air.

"Carly!" Liliana notices first. She hurries me to a chair right when my eyes lose focus.

"Breathe slowly, in and out." Angie mimics deep breaths until my body settles. Her torn strap slides down her shoulder, and I replay the image of her chasing me on the beach last night, tripping, and tearing her dress.

"We'll get home." Nicole hands me water.

"It's not that," I admit. "It's Marco." They watch while I swallow several sips from the bottle. "He said I misread the texts between him and his colleague. He said they're friends and nothing more." Placing the water down, I recall our conversation last night as I paced the beach.

"Sending a text accusing an affair to Lilly. Sei completamente pazza! What were you thinking?" Marco yelled so loud it felt as if he were standing on the beach next to me.

"How am I the one on the defensive?" I screamed over the sound of crashing waves.

"Because I did not, and am not, having una relazione! You should've talked to me first. Before you sent that text!"

Suddenly, I feel hot, heavy tears slide down my face. Angie wipes them away with her palm.

"Do you want to tell us more about what happened last night when you talked?"

I open my mouth to speak but then snap it shut. It's terrifying to admit what I'm feeling inside. Angie places a hand on my shoulder, while Liliana and Nicole each put a hand on my arm. Warmth flows through each point of contact. I open my mouth again, and this time, the words come out.

"He admitted they talk and text regularly…that they've talked about our marriage. He apologized. But he insists he didn't cheat." I focus on the protective cocoon my friends have formed and let their touch soothe my anxiety. "But something feels irreversible, like there's a level of trust I'll never have again. I told him, at the very least, he's having an emotional affair." My body shakes. Why was it so hard for him to understand my devastation? Even if their relationship wasn't physical, they felt a connection and mixed it with secrecy. Pain is born from betrayal, physical or emotional.

"I agree," Angie says. "He's been giving her his energy and attention. Daily phone calls, texts, emails. That's not friendship. That's crossing a line."

"Exactly," I say, as soul-crushing questions run through my mind. Does he daydream about her? Do they share inside jokes? Does he invest time and effort in their relationship instead of ours? Does he give her parts of himself that he no longer gives to me? The words Marco said last night explode through my brain. "Instagram…looking perfect. You won't admit we're having problems. I've tried everything… even an app…I'm lonely…*sei anche tu*, no?"

I hesitate, questioning whether I have the courage to share this with my friends. My heart beats wildly. "I struggle with letting people see my flaws. The truth is, Marco and I have had problems for a while." I brace myself for a disaster, like my father always warned, but my friends huddle closer, offering comfort.

"But it's time to stop pretending I'm perfect. I have to stop focusing on everyone else's problems and face my own. And right now, it's that Marco may have cheated, even though he swears he didn't."

"Do you believe him?" Angie asks.

"Do I believe him?" I ask out loud as my friends surround me in support. Support I've finally allowed them to provide by being honest. "I think the only thing I believe right now is that nothing, absolutely nothing, is perfect."

Immediately, I'm filled with the impulse to share this truth with the world. "Perfectionism is just insecurity wearing a dress, high heels, and lipstick." Pulling out my phone, I flip it around to capture a photo. "Lean in, guys."

Although confused, my friends scoot closer. Angie leans against me; her ragged dress hangs around her shoulder. Liliana inches closer on the other side, her face a mess of last night's makeup. Nicole shifts next to Angie, her thick bangs plastered to her forehead. And in the center is me, with my frizzy hair.

While it's true, I don't know what's going to happen with my marriage, right now I have faith my life will improve because I've finally admitted I'm an imperfect, messy human. *With big, frizzy hair!*

"Smile...or don't," I say to my friends. "Whatever you're truly feeling in this moment is all that matters."

I snap the photo and post it on my Insta account with the caption *Life is not perfect, but every once in a while, there are moments that are.*

CHAPTER 40

Luca

Emerald Jewel All-Inclusive Resort

LEAVING ANGIE AND the police officer, Luca finally relaxes. That entire situation was legit off the charts. The story is epic. On the upside, he's hoping he can see Brooke one more time before heading home. He takes out his phone.

Luca: I'm still here

Brooke: Thought you left at seven

Luca: Crazy story that involves the police.

Brooke: What???

Luca: Where are you? I'll fill you in

Brooke: With my dad. Meet at our spot?

Luca: OK

His sneakers sink into the sand as he jogs on the beach to the secret spot where he's been meeting Brooke to avoid her dad. He recalls what she said after they kissed for the first time. "You don't know what it's like being the daughter of a boy band star. Girls throw themselves at him. He's seen too much. We have to keep this a secret."

For selfish reasons, Luca wanted to meet her dad and tell him that his band's name was on his birthday cake when he turned nine. He wanted him to know about his mom and why he came to Boy Bands on the Beach. But Brooke said no. She insisted they keep everything on the down-low. He accepted it, considering that she's seventeen and he's twenty-two. But he's been a perfect gentleman, refusing to do anything but kiss and cuddle—restraint that's taken superhuman strength when she's wearing that white bikini.

He approaches their hideout house on the beach, jumps the fence, and then lies in the cabana. He remembers Carly catching them in this very spot. Brooke freaked, telling Carly she'd regret it if she told anyone. He knows the incident only added to the crazy set of circumstances that led police to think he was involved with Nicole's disappearance.

When he looks up, Brooke's walking toward him. Her golden-brown hair rustles in the ocean breeze. She's gorgeous.

"You're still here." Brooke smiles.

He closes his eyes for a second, trying to memorize her face. She lies down in the cabana next to him. Her intoxicating smell reminds him of a juicy peach, ripe for picking.

"I am. We should take advantage of it." He leans in, kissing her. It takes all his willpower to pull away.

"What went down with the police?" She tilts her head, waiting for him to fill her in.

"When I got to the lobby to get on the airport shuttle, a police officer came up to me. He said he needed to ask me some questions. The detective made me show him my passport, and Angie's was in my passport wallet!"

"What?" Brooke's jaw practically falls to the ground. "How?"

He springs off the cabana, unable to control the adrenaline coursing through his body, and explains about the mind meld, matching passport wallets, and what happened at check-in.

"That's insane." Brooke shakes her head.

"Right! But the wildest part is that Nicole was missing last night, and the cops thought I was mixed up in her disappearance."

"Huh?" Brooke looks confused.

"Nicole passed out drunk in that abandoned boathouse. Her friends couldn't find her. The police got involved." Luca sits again.

"That's crazy." Brooke leans into his shoulder, laughing.

"It's not funny. Well, it's kind of funny."

Brooke slides her hand over his. "You'll always regret not sleeping with me." Her sexy lips curve into a slight smile.

"Accurate." He leans in and kisses her again. "But, technically, we slept together. It was sweet, sleeping next to you in this cabana last night."

Brooke smiles. "Well, you can thank my dad for getting extremely high and passing out. I had a chance to escape, and I took it."

Luca's mind wanders to last night. After finally finding Angie so he could say goodbye, he went to his room, packed his duffel, and met Brooke here. They decided it would be cool to sleep in the cabana. It's the reason he wasn't in his hotel room when the police came.

Ping.

Brooke pulls her phone from her pocket. "Shoot, that's my dad. I've got to get back. We're leaving for the airport." She wraps her pinky around Luca's. "What's your plan? Have you booked another flight since you're going to miss yours?"

"Not yet. But I'll get home."

She softly kisses his cheek. "Text me soon. Hopefully, we'll see each other again."

"I hope so." He grabs her hand.

Standing, she faces him and steps back. Their hands fall to their sides. She turns and walks back to the hotel. He lies on the chair and watches as she becomes a small dot.

Staring out at the crystal blue ocean, his mind flashes with snapshots of the weekend. The songs, the music, the shows, Angie and her friends. He knows all his bros think he's crazy for coming here. Maybe. But it was for his mom.

A warm, comforting feeling overwhelms him as he convinces himself she orchestrated the entire thing. It can't be a coincidence that he met Angie. Their stories are so similar.

"Mom." He whispers the word. His voice shakes. "Mom." He says the word again, but this time his voice is steady. "Can you hear me, Mom?"

He continues talking. "You would've been living your best life on this trip. Your boy band crushes have gray hair...or very little hair. And some of them probably use Viagra. But, man, they still got it. Each time they sang, I felt like I was back in the kitchen watching you sing your favorite songs."

He takes out his phone, finds Spotify, and plays his mom's favorite boy band tune. His mind wanders with thoughts. The music is like a supernatural phenomenon. It defies space, time, love, loss, life, and even death. At this moment, he feels his mom's love. He feels her warmth. *He feels her.*

Turning his face up to the sun, the heat penetrates every inch of his body. The music is magic.

CHAPTER 41

Liliana

Emerald Jewel All-Inclusive Resort

"**A**LL RIGHT. DONE!** I got everyone booked for one more night. Can't say I'm upset we're staying while Angie gets her passport figured out." Nicole smiles.

"Great, thank you." I text Josh again as I follow Nicole to the beach.

> **Liliana:** Did you get my message? Everyone is staying another night. It's a long story. I want to talk more about my job and everything as soon as possible.

I stare at my phone, but there's no response. I'm sure he's upset I'm staying another night. I decide to call him, but it goes to voicemail. I text him again.

> **Liliana:** Called you. Call me back. I love you!

I wait a few seconds for him to respond. The silence is deafening. I think about these past few days. How many of Angie's smiles,

Nicole's booty shakes, and Carly's well-intended overreactions did I miss while on the phone with Amanda? How many small moments have I missed with my family? Moments that add up to what really matters. A heavy feeling weighs on me as I settle into my lounge chair.

"Everything cool?" Nicole removes her sunglasses and sits in the chair next to me.

Glancing around, I notice the crowd of yacht rock guests who've been arriving since we decided to stay an extra night. "You, of all people, know Josh is sick of the way I put work first. I'm just hoping it's not too late to prove to him that our family is everything to me." Although I've been feeling uneasy about Josh and Nicole's relationship, I'm desperate for support.

Her eyes shift, and I wonder what's wrong.

"I'm sure it's hard being Josh's sounding board while also being one of my best friends. Sorry if that's put you in an awkward position." Despite my discomfort, I try to be gentle.

Nicole stands and then sits on the edge of my chair. Her rigid posture confirms something's up.

Clearing her throat, she pauses for a second, like she's stalling. "Listen, I need to talk to you about something."

"Okay." A knot tightens in my stomach. *Has Josh told Nicole things I don't want to hear?*

"I've been wanting to get this out…in the open…the entire trip. It's been a struggle. It's been… well, it's been tough." She stumbles over her words as if she's about to confess some terrible truth. "I hate that Josh made us keep it a secret."

"Secret?" I repeat. "What secret? What's going on?" My brain scrambles. Josh and Nicole went out on a date all those years ago.

Suddenly, I'm experiencing a strange out-of-body sensation, like I'm observing myself from a distance.

I watch as Nicole leans toward me. "I have something to tell you. I owe you this." Her cheeks sink in. She looks dull, like someone's shaken off all her glitter.

Are they having an affair? Have I been too consumed by work to notice?

I jump out of my chair before my brain can process what's happening.

I recall the text Nicole's new friend Jessica sent with a photo of a girl who looked like Esther. *Is Jessica really Josh?!*

"Are you sleeping with my husband?!" When the words leave my mouth, my brain shakes with everything I've known but ignored. All the time Josh and Nicole spend together, the way they support and understand each other.

My feet pound the sand, and I'm running to the ocean.

"Wait!" Nicole chases me but can't quite keep up.

I whip my head around, and my curly hair falls from my topknot. I can't shake the image of Nicole wearing the hot pink lingerie. My eyes bulge as she approaches.

"Oh, my God. Are those boudoir photos for *Josh*?" My stomach churns, and I break out in a cold sweat. Has my husband cheated on me with my best friend? Have the two people I trust most in the world betrayed me?

"We're not having an affair!" she screams over the crashing waves.

A woman wearing a baseball cap that says *Here for the Kenny Loggins songs* stares at us. The Bluetooth speaker in her hand blares with the song "Heart to Heart."

"We're not having an affair," Nicole repeats, moving closer. "We want to start an advertising firm." She pauses and kicks her feet at the water's edge. "Those boudoir photos aren't for Josh. They aren't for Garrett either. I needed them for some sort of confidence boost. The photos are for me." Her eyes dart away like she's embarrassed by her admission.

Relief washes over me. They are not having an affair. They want to start a business.

Wait. "You're starting a *business* together?" I repeat, confused.

"Maybe." She pauses and submerges her feet further into the water.

Joining Nicole, I move forward and let the water swallow my ankles. It's cooler than I expect and I shiver. "I don't understand."

"We got the idea when we met this mom at the playground. She was starting a mommy-and-me class to teach toddlers about manners.

It got Josh and me thinking. With our backgrounds in advertising, we knew we could promote her business to stay-at-home moms and dads."

"When was this?" I ask, wondering how long I've been oblivious to my husband's activities.

"A few months ago." The waves swirl away from our feet as the water rolls back out into the ocean. She continues. "We reached out to the mom and offered to market her business pro bono, a kind of trial run."

Nodding, I watch as the next wave rushes forward and submerges our feet.

"Anyway, we blasted her business on social using mom influencers in the area and did some guerrilla campaigns, like setting up a free impromptu class at the playground downtown. Things really took off."

My shoulders stiffen, wondering if by "mom influencers," Nicole means Carly. "Carly also knows?"

"Oh, no, sorry, we didn't bring Carly into it. Josh insisted we keep it under wraps until we decided if we were going to move forward."

"Well, are you? Moving forward?" I ask.

"That's the thing. We've been going back and forth about it. We've run numbers, created a business plan, we've even had a couple of businesses approach us about promoting them, but we haven't pulled the trigger yet."

"Really?" I'm completely surprised. "What businesses?"

"Just a few who noticed how great our promotion for the toddler manners classes went. Laura actually called me the day we got here. She's been hounding Josh and me to promote her real estate business. But we haven't moved forward because it means both you and Garrett will have to share more of the load. It will require both of our families to make changes."

"Right," I say, still trying to wrap my head around it.

"It's just that Josh knows how stressed you are about work. He didn't want to drop this on you until we were certain, since it means he won't be able to handle all the things you're used to him doing for the girls."

I think about what Josh said before I left. *I'm done waiting around for you to find the balance.* It makes more sense now that Nicole's told me this. My head spins. "But why keep it a secret? This is the part I'm having trouble with. Your husband and best friend should not share a secret, ever, under any circumstances." I know I'm glaring at Nicole, but I can't stop myself.

"To be honest, I don't understand either. Garrett knows. But Josh said he didn't want to force you to make changes. He said you needed to make changes for yourself and your family, not because we might start a business."

"Oh." My mind processes her words. Josh wanted me to make the choice to put our family first on my own. He didn't want to force me. "Is Jessica really Josh?"

"Yes, and now that we're talking about it, I realize how messed up it is that I had a secret name for him on my phone. I did that just in case you saw any messages he sent. The photo you saw was for a guerrilla campaign we're considering doing for a toy company that makes those stupid luxury, kid-sized cars. They want to hire us."

I lock eyes with Nicole. "That was Esther in that mini-Mercedes Wagon?"

She nods.

"Having a secret name for my husband on your phone is completely unacceptable." My tone is as cold as the water submerging my feet.

"You're absolutely right. He doesn't know I did that, if that helps." Nicole's face clouds with regret like she's been caught drinking vodka from her Stanley at a Little League game.

"A little," I say, honestly.

"I understand if you're mad. I really messed up."

"I'm angry, yes. But you've always been crazy, so changing Josh's name to Jessica sounds about right." My words surprise me, but they are the truth. Nicole's always been a live wire, but it's one reason I love her.

"Thank you for understanding my crazy." She screws her eyes together to emphasize her point.

"Understanding might be a stretch. It's more of an acceptance."

We both laugh, and a bit of the tension between us eases.

"I don't know if starting this business is the right decision for you and Josh, but developing our business plan woke up that part of me that had big dreams—that part of me that thought I'd rule the world, or at least be the reason people decide which brand of toothpaste to use." Nicole pretends she's brushing her teeth and laughs. "These past few days I've been thinking a lot about Josh's enthusiasm, his encouragement, and his belief that I've still got killer creative instincts. And I have to say, I'm ready to chase a dream I never realized because of the health issues I had after Hank's birth."

Staring out at the horizon, I can't pinpoint what I'm feeling. "This is a lot to think about."

"It really is. But Josh wants to talk everything over with you before we decide."

A large wave swells forward, swallowing our calves. Nicole grabs my arm, and we both move back.

Her green eyes search my face. "I get it if you're angry. Secrets never end well. Never. I should have made Josh tell you."

"It's not just anger. It's more like a mix of anger, surprise, relief, and disappointment that Josh didn't think he could tell me. And the only reason I'm not losing my mind is because I've known you my entire life."

Nicole steps back from the water onto the dry sand.

"But mostly, I think I'm proud and happy for both of you."

"Yay! I knew you'd get it." Nicole hugs me and bounces with excitement.

I wrap my arms around her, and we celebrate for a moment longer.

"This makes total sense," I say as we step back from our embrace. "An advertising firm that specializes in marketing to parents."

Nicole nods. "Exactly!"

Looking at her fills me with a wave of love. "No cap, as you would say, my best friend is the smartest person on the planet."

"Love you so much, Liliana." She gives me another hug.

"I'm going to call Josh." I take a step back. Turning, I walk to my beach bag to get my phone.

"AN AFFAIR?" JOSH peers at me. His eyes blaze with intensity, and I wonder if my computer screen is going to burst into flames in the middle of my hotel room.

"I didn't accuse her. I asked." I squeak out my words, knowing how devastated I would be if Josh thought the same about me.

As he leans back in his chair at our kitchen table, I notice a basket of folded laundry on the island behind him. He stares into his phone's camera. The girls are still at school, and I can hear his breathing quicken in the stillness.

My shoulders tense. "But you and Nicole were sneaking behind my back, creating a business plan, working with a couple of clients. On some level, I must have sensed there was a secret between you."

He nods his head, possibly grasping this kernel of truth.

Gathering courage, I say the next part. The hard part. "And we haven't been having sex. In fact, the night before I left, you blew me off. The call from Amanda didn't help, but you can't deny you were pretending to be asleep."

Josh places his elbows on the table, opens his palms and rests his head on his hands. "To be honest"—he lifts his head—"you always choose work. You're a slave to your job. Your number one priority is Amanda. You choose her over our family every time. And no matter how many times I tell you that things need to change, they never do."

He's right. Of course, he's right. I want to tell him how I left things with Amanda. But he continues before I can say anything.

"The girls need you. And I need you too. But I had to figure out how *not* to need you. And part of not needing you is not needing you physically."

My hands tremble, but I don't hide them.

He presses his fingers together. "I realized, at some point, that part of the reason I pulled away physically was to punish you. To make you feel rejected, the same way I do. It wasn't something I planned, but I know it's true. I'm not proud of it. I just feel so angry. So resentful."

My neck feels like it's on fire. Now I understand why we haven't been having sex.

"It's why I didn't tell you about the business plan. I didn't want to resent you even more for saying I should wait until your work slowed down. And I was still hoping that you would make the choice to put our family first on your own. Without me having to make an ultimatum."

The heat in my neck shoots down my spine and spreads out into my body. I place my hand over my chest and say what's in my heart. "I'm sorry, Josh. I know it's one little word. And one I've said a lot without taking any action to correct what I've done wrong. The word hardly seems big enough to convey all the things I'm feeling right now."

Josh nods but stays quiet.

"I've made a lot of mistakes…a lot of excuses."

"But why now? Why are you finally ready to let work take second place?"

I know I'm on the verge of tears, but I don't care. "It took traveling 3,000 miles to realize I've unconsciously adopted my mom's ambition, thinking it would make me happy, but I'm not happy."

"Oh, your mom." He pauses. "That makes sense." Josh's face relaxes, and his signature casual, inviting smile overtakes his face. The one he used to give me daily. The one I haven't seen in a very long time.

"This time, things will change. I told Amanda that she has to respect my boundaries. I may have quit, or I may get fired. Either way, I'm certain I did the right thing."

"Really?" Josh asks.

"Is that Mommy?" I hear Esther in the background. A second later, her face takes over the screen. "Look, Mommy. Look what I made at school today." She drops her backpack on the kitchen table and pulls out a large white piece of construction paper. She holds it in front of her small body, smiling proudly.

I lean toward my screen and look closer at a paper with her profile outlined in black, titled with the Hebrew words, *Zot Ani*—this is me. Inside she has drawn the things she believes represent her—music notes, a smiley face, the word *Hamilton* with a figure that resembles the artwork from the famous musical, the name of her sleep-away camp, and a stick figure drawing of our family.

"I love it!"

"Esther, let's go." I hear Evie's voice.

"Bye, Mommy. Evie and I are going to the playground." She drops her paper on the table and trots away before I can ask her to have Evie say hello.

Josh picks up the picture and starts to put it back in Esther's backpack.

"Wait, I want to see it again." My finger points at the stick figure drawing of our family. "This right here is everything. Nothing's as important as you and our girls." I feel my eyes well, but I don't fight it.

Josh rubs his fingers over the drawing and then looks at me.

I can feel a steady stream of tears rolling down my cheeks.

"Oh, Liliana, it's okay. It's going to be okay."

I catch my breath between soft sobs. "It's hard for me to cry so openly. It makes me feel weak." My sadness, distress, and regrets pour from my eyes. The pain I've been feeling all along is finally visible—*I'm crying on the outside*. Surprisingly, my body eases. I feel a shift. Not total relief, but a dulling of sharp corners.

"It's not weak, Liliana. It's human. By the way, you know that date with Nicole all those years ago was a case study in incompatibility." Josh smiles.

I let out a small laugh, thankful he is lightening the moment. I've always loved the way he explains their one date. "You've always described it that way. But you've never told me why?"

He moves his face close to his screen, like he's about to tell me a juicy secret. The tension between us diminishes. "Hmmm, let me think for a minute." He taps his free hand on the table. "Here's an example. I tell a story with three key points. She goes on for hours. I value brevity."

"Totally agree. What else."

"Let's see. Here's one. She's nineties rap. I'm Nirvana. Which you saw for yourself at karaoke night."

"That makes sense. Grunge is all about looking like you don't care. Nicole has always loved the flamboyant style of bands like Salt-N-Pepa."

"Yes, that's exactly what I mean." He points at me like I've got all the right answers. "And she's not you. I love you. I'm sorry for everything."

"Me too." My mind flashes back to the night we met. If I could do it over, I'd turn the corner and walk into that karaoke bar to meet Josh every single time.

CHAPTER 42

Nicole

Emerald Jewel All-Inclusive Resort

"**B**ONUS VACATION NIGHT!"

After Angie got her passport papers at the embassy, she and Carly joined Liliana and me for one last day in the sun. I feel a tiny bit guilty that I'm still in St. McAna while my kids are puking, but I'm glad Garrett and I are no longer throwing punches. I think about the conversation we had earlier on the beach when Liliana went to call Josh. I knew I needed to apologize for not responding to the text he sent me before the New Kids show.

"I'm sorry I never got back to you. I hope you found the quilty wilty."

"Hank knew where it was."

I could tell from the tone of Garrett's voice that he was angry.

"Listen, what you wrote in your text last night. It wasn't wrong. I didn't let you help when I got better. That's on me, and I own it." I paused before saying what I'd needed to say all along. "The thing is, I need you to be more involved in the details of raising our kids—like knowing the names of their teachers and doctors. I need you to be one of the team managers rather than a player willing to fill in for whatever position I need at the moment."

"Ha! I love a good sports analogy," he said. His laugh made me believe we could handle this. "And I agree. When you stopped working, I became the breadwinner, and you became the homemaker."

I couldn't breathe as I listened. We had never talked about the basic guidelines that shape our lives.

"But also, my job is stressful, and hard, and pretty thankless. And there's a lot of pressure knowing I have to support our family."

"Totally true," I agreed. "I know your job is a never-ending grind. I appreciate your hard work."

"The thing is, if I'm being honest, you make me feel excluded from the kids' stuff. In fact, when you could finally take care of Hank, it's not just that you never asked for help, you made it clear you didn't want me to. You always told me I was feeding him wrong, burping him wrong, swaddling him wrong. At some point, I stopped trying to help. No one likes being told they're wrong all the time."

"Wow," I said, overwhelmed by his point of view. "I'm sorry I made you feel you didn't know how to be Hank's dad. I'm sorry you feel excluded. I need to work on that."

"And I need to work on getting in the mix with the kids. Send me an email with all their doctors and put their after-school activities on my calendar. I think that will help."

"I can do that," I said.

"It's kind of crazy how we follow these unspoken rules about what moms do and what dads do, without thinking twice."

"Seriously!" I said. "Maybe that's part of the problem. There's not a checklist of tasks for *dadlife* beyond the original concept of being the breadwinner. Everyone expects moms will cook, clean, drive carpool, manage school responsibilities, kiss boo-boos, and on and on and on. And for many, that's on top of working full time. The world has universally accepted the tasks moms are expected to do. But when it comes to dads, there's no clear playbook."

"Dropping in another sports analogy to keep my attention! Nice," Garrett joked.

"Ha!" I laughed, feeling in sync with him, the way I always did when we'd sing Mariah and kill it at karaoke. "That wasn't intentional. But I guess my point is, we need the right language for *dadlife*. It's more than being the breadwinner. The definition needs a rebranding."

"Well, you're obviously the best person to launch a world-changing rebranding campaign. Speaking of that, any news about the ad business? Did Josh finally tell Liliana? It would be good for you. You seem excited about the possibilities."

"I think we're going to take on a couple of clients and see how it goes. But I'll need more help with the kids if we're successful."

"Yes, I understand, and I'm not worried. That powerful, creative, and successful woman is the person I first fell in love with. And although I love the mom version just as much, I'm not sure you do. I always get the sense that you feel like something's missing."

BOOM, I thought, realizing slang, chasing an unrealistic body type, and taking boudoir photos have all been my way of trying to hit an easy button for the emptiness I feel inside. And that Garrett understands this is everything.

He continued. "When you get home, we can figure this out. I'm feeling better, and I hope you are too."

"Yes!"

"Believe me, Nicole, after taking care of three sick kids while you've been away, I have a new appreciation for what you call *momlife*."

As we hung up, I smiled, thinking we were like kids on the playground who just figured out that taking turns on the swing is a million times better than fighting over it.

I hold my drink in my hand and motion for my friends to circle in. Angie, Carly, and Liliana push their small cups toward mine, and they all clash together. "Here's to an extra night of being with my squad! Tonight's going to be straight fire!"

Carly eyes me. "A simple cheers would have been fine." She winks.

"Wait, don't forget about me." Luca raises his arm up and over Angie and taps his glass with ours.

"I can't believe you stayed an extra night with us." Carly pats Luca's muscular shoulder. "But I'm glad you did."

Finally, these two aren't throwing shade. That's a win. I never thought Luca took Angie's passport, and I still can't believe the police thought he killed me. I'm not a boring side character after all. I've got main character energy!

Luca beams back at Carly as the bartender looks at us, confused about why we're rolling with club soda and lime. I take a swig of the tart drink, and my lips pucker.

Liliana swirls the straw in her tiny cup. "Well, it's not a mai tai, but with six a.m. flights tomorrow, this will do."

"But can we survive this yacht rock show sober?" Angie giggles, glancing around at groups of people dressed in seventies chic clothing and captain's hats.

Liliana nods. "Right, when I hear this music, I'm transported to 1989 in the back seat of my dad's clunky, gas-guzzling car while he jammed to the song 'Sailing.'"

"Get hyped!" Luca puts on a captain's hat lying on the bar and struts around.

"You could literally wear a bag of shit on your head and still look good." Angie watches Luca with an amused grin as he takes the hand of a woman with silvery-gray hair and twirls her around to the song about a fine girl named Brandy.

"Facts," I agree. "But there's no way in hell I'm wearing one of those stupid hats."

Liliana laughs.

My entire body relaxes in a way it hasn't this entire vacay. She's genuinely pumped about the advertising business Josh and I hope to launch.

"The show's about to start." Luca gently pulls at my sleeve, and I notice Angie, Liliana, and Carly walking toward the stage.

Catching up to them, we all stop short when we pass the bathroom.

"We should go before it starts." Liliana points to the line. "I mean, I don't have to go right now, but that could change in the next three seconds."

"I'm going to get in the front by the stage. Come find me." Luca pushes through a crowd of people in round sailor hats and disappears.

Liliana, Carly, Angie, and I get in line to wait for the bathroom.

"This has been a crazy trip." Angie tucks a chunk of hair from her neat brown bob behind her ear, then her eyes glisten with tears. "Thank you for standing by me, even though I tried to disappear. I'm lucky to have you as friends."

"And the fact that everyone thought I was straight-up murdered outdoes Angie's kidnapping story. So, she should never be embarrassed about what happened in high school ever again."

"Well said!" Angie laughs.

"I'm the GOAT!" But then I quickly speak again. "Let me rephrase that into something more appropriate for my age. I'm a totally awesome badass bitch."

"You totally are!" Carly hugs me, and Angie and Liliana join in.

"Hey, you want these? I have extras."

As we pull apart, a man in a Hawaiian shirt, aviator sunglasses, and a captain's hat holds a bag toward us.

Angie takes it and peeks inside. "Yes!" She hands each of us a captain's hat.

Carly, Liliana, and I groan when the man walks away.

"Put them on and get over it." Angie places the hat on her head.

"Fine." Liliana grabs one.

We each place a hat on our head and move forward in the line.

After we exit the bathroom stalls, we stand next to each other in front of the mirror.

"The hats are actually lit." Checking my reflection in the mirror, I realize there's something magical about boating attire.

"Yes, they really are." Carly smooths her long blond locks of hair, beaming at her image.

The four of us hook arms and exit the bathroom.

"Anchors away." I glimpse Luca up ahead.

"Let's cruise." Liliana laughs.

"Ahoy mateys!" Carly adds.

We focus on Angie, waiting for her to add one more yacht rock pun to our impromptu game.

She's quiet for a moment. "I'm thinking."

She breaks free from our hooked arms and steps a few feet ahead. A second later, she turns back to us. Her face glows in the moonlight with the purest smile I've seen from her in years.

"Love you a yacht!"

CHAPTER 43

Anonymous Boy Band Star

Emerald Jewel All-Inclusive Resort

WALKING THROUGH THE sand, one of the biggest boy band heartthrobs from the nineties stops and stands a few feet back to the right of the stage. The air pulses with excitement. Nothing in life compares to the energy of hyped fans anticipating live music. His clothes fit in with the yacht rock crew. No one here has any clue that he performed on that stage. *Isn't life fucking amazing?*

The band performing tonight is cool. He saw them in LA a while back. They cover all the yacht rock hits but bring their own spin. They've even written some of their own songs that pay homage to the breezy tunes of the genre.

It would surprise his fans to know that he loves yacht rock. But these tunes were the backdrop of his childhood. Songs like Ambrosia's "You're the Biggest Part of Me" and Little River Band's "Reminiscing" instantly bring him back to summer weekends with his grandpop, picking through garage sale junk in search of small treasures.

Pulling his hat lower on his head, he overflows with a satisfied hum. It's not often that he can disappear into a crowd and enjoy a concert. Sure, being a star has its perks, but sometimes he wonders what his life would be like if his band hadn't shot to fame with the force of a comet flying through space.

Maybe he'd be a teacher like his mom, or work in welding like his dad. Or maybe he would have ended up in jail like his cousin Frankie. Maybe he'd have married a girl from his neighborhood and had kids young. Maybe he'd be a grandparent by now. *Who the hell knows?* But he certainly wouldn't have traveled the world, owned a douchey green Ferrari, and been married and divorced three times. Not that he's complaining. He knows he's lived a charmed life. One that he never dreamed possible.

But the music industry has changed, and things are different than they used to be. He's glad he's not coming up in these crazy times, with streams instead of records and auto-tune instead of harmony. He knows he's old, but he doesn't get it. He likes that his band was fresh-faced and innocent. He likes that they evolved before man-scaping. Today, everything is *in your face*—songs have cuss words and choreography that resembles pornography. Back then, his band only flirted with the possibility of what might happen after the music turned off or the video ended.

Just recently, he read that boy bands consist of an average of 5.25 members, including one bad boy, a few boys next door, and one member with a megawatt smile. The article went on to say that his band was the foundation for everything that's come after. *What a ride. What a ride.*

Truly, though, he's glad to be where he is at this moment. There's no stress about reaching number one on the Billboard charts or waiting for Carson Daly to announce his band's latest song is in the top three on *Total Request Live.*

And although journalists from music magazines like to write stories about how the mighty have fallen, he remains unfazed. His band is not washed-up because they do events like Boy Bands on the Beach. They are still serious musicians. The shows they did here and the others they do around the world are always a total blast. There's nothing like the energy of loyal fans. He and his bros have so much fucking fun on stage. When the lights come up and those first notes play, they're still surprised by the thousands of faces staring back at them. When they come together with their fans and sing their songs, they do what no one thinks possible. They time travel. They journey back to their youth. And that's what makes these shows much more than a washed-up career. The concerts they do are a way to say thank you to their fans for taking the ultimate journey with them. *We're so fucking glad you were part of it.*

A few rows ahead, he spots the four women who were rocking pink last night. He heard they're still here because of a stolen passport or something. When he saw them by the bathroom a few minutes ago, he offered them his extra captain's hats. They're all wearing them. He can tell they're having a blast.

He can't help laughing as he melts into the crowd and gets closer to the stage. His Hawaiian shirt, captain's hat, and sunglasses must be a great disguise. Those women didn't even realize who he was. *Isn't life fucking amazing?*

CHAPTER 44

Carly

Hamilton Beach, California
Two Years Later

#OOTD: Who gives a crap

ANGIE, NICOLE, LILIANA, and I walk to the intersection of Wrightwood and Carlyle. Angie's visited a couple of times since the boy band trip. I love touring our childhood landmarks together. We stop in front of the house where she grew up. The Spanish colonial is unchanged. Smiling, Angie peers through a large window with the shades drawn open and watches the woman inside fluffing couch pillows. Her smile collapses. The woman does kind of look like her mom.

Angie takes a step, but then looks back at us, teary-eyed.

"Oh no." Nicole reaches out, circling her in her arms. "You're crying."

I rush over and hand her a tissue from my belt bag.

"She looked like your mom." Liliana moves closer.

Angie nods. "I need to talk about her. I miss her every day."

"Yes, let's do it." Liliana says.

I zip up my belt bag. "We loved her too."

Angie smiles. "After our trip, when I finally told Patton about my past, it felt like this impenetrable wall I kept between us burst into a million tiny pieces—like it was ignited by a bomb. And all it took was words."

She turns away from the fresh-cut lawn we're standing near and faces us.

"Why don't we grab a slice of pizza and talk?" Angie asks.

Liliana and I nod.

Ten minutes later, we crowd around a red-and-white checkered tablecloth, enjoying the thin-crust pizza we grew up on. *Melty cheese and sauce is one of life's greatest pleasures!* My brain flashes with a quick calculation of the macro breakdown. It's a habit I'm still trying to break as an intuitive eater.

Gazing at Nicole, I notice her body is more muscular and powerful-looking than it was when we were on our boy band trip. She finally told us about using Ozempic. She's dropped the medication and traded it for a gym membership. She looks amazing and ignores the haters who think she took the easy way out. And while I'm still working on my insecurities in a world where almost everyone I know is slimming down, I get that these medicines have helped a lot of people with health and body image issues.

"Angie. Is that you?"

Laura, our former classmate from Hamilton Beach High, walks by carrying a pizza box.

"Oh, my goodness. It's been years." She strides to our table. Her eyes meet Angie's, and her face flashes with a mix of shock and surprise.

I assume her mind is running with memories of the alleged kidnapping. It's an expression Angie seems to get more and more used to as she realizes everyone is happy to learn she's doing well.

"Hi, Laura. Good to see you. I've been visiting, but I'm heading home in a few hours."

Laura places her pizza box on our table and then rifles through her bag. "Here, let me give you my card. In case you decide to move back. I'm the best Realtor around." She slides her card to Angie. "Ask Nicole. I found her an amazing space for her advertising firm."

Nicole barely stifles her eye roll, making it clear she's ready for Laura to move on.

"Well, great seeing you. Gotta run, meeting people to discuss some new ideas for the Hamilton Beach Moms' Facebook page." She picks up her pizza box and leaves.

"The what page?" Angie asks.

"Oh, don't worry about it. It's internet mama drama." Nicole waves her hand in the air like she's trying to swat away an irritating gnat. "What time's your flight?"

Angie glances at her watch. "Four o'clock."

"Sorry, I can't come to the airport." Liliana brushes a strand of curly hair out of her face. "It's been a great few days together, but I have a couple of things I need to do before I leave for that family retreat at my daughters' sleep-away camp tomorrow."

"Wow, you've taken an entire week off?" Angie asks. "How's Amanda dealing with that?"

"Well, as you know, I told her after St. McAna that I'd stay only if she respected my boundaries." Liliana removes the beaded bracelet she's been wearing since our trip. "Esther gave this to me. It's become my talisman, reminding me to be intentional about where I'm getting pushed and pulled, making sure my family comes first." She slips the bracelet back onto her wrist.

"You're a queen!" Nicole shifts her attention to Angie. "Part of the reason she stayed was so Josh and I could get our business off the ground."

"It made sense with our new hire taking over a lot of my responsibilities. The timing was perfect."

"See, total queen!" Nicole repeats. "And now that I'm a lady boss… sorry, but I can't come to the airport either."

"By the way, Nicole," Angie says, "Carly sent me that link to the *Los Angeles Times* last month." Angie pulls out her phone, searches for a minute, then flashes her screen toward us.

Nicole and Josh have gained a lot of attention for their out-of-the-box marketing strategies, like their most recent stunt of handing out samples of the latest must-have organic snack in preschool carpool lines.

Peering forward, we all look at the photo of Nicole presenting at a recent advertising conference about guerrilla marketing.

"That headline is perfect." Angie reads it out loud. "*When it comes to marketing, Mom (and Dad) knows best.*"

Nicole smiles from ear to ear.

"And what you said after they asked about how you juggle being a mom with work." Angie reads the quote out loud. "*Momlife, what's that? Every single person with a child should step up and contribute to the entire ecosystem of responsibilities that defines the one, all-encompassing term parent life.*"

Nicole laughs. "Not to flex, but I'm kind of unstoppable right now. Anyway, we came here to talk about your mom."

Angie sinks into her chair as she puts her phone down on the table. "I'm surprised I cried when we passed my house. I didn't even cry when my dad and I had that great visit here last year."

We all nod in understanding.

"It was my heart playing tricks on me."

Liliana puts down her pizza slice. "I don't think it's tricks. This place is your past, and everything reminds you of your mom."

For the next hour, we share happy memories.

"We're here to support you. What else do you need?" My messy ponytail sways as I take another piece of pizza.

"Need?" Angie asks, wondering out loud what the answer to my question is. "What do I need?" She pauses. "What I need, I've had all along. I need all of you!" She drops some cash on the table. "My treat. Thanks for a great visit."

Nicole hums a tune. Liliana joins in. Angie dances around. Then, we're all belting out the chorus of our favorite Spice Girls song, about what we want, our future, our past, and these friendships that define us.

Pushing out of our chairs, we make our way to the exit.

Angie pulls Nicole and Liliana in for hugs. "Had the best time."

I hold the door open, and we walk outside. After another round of hugs, Angie and I get into my car for the airport.

"Thanks for letting me stay with you."

I pull onto the 101. "Wouldn't have it any other way."

"Things seem to be going well with you and Marco."

"They are," I agree, thinking about how, after the boy band trip, Marco offered to let me see his texts and emails. I recall how uncomfortable I felt reading through them. After looking through everything, it was clear Lilly was the aggressor, always reaching out first and probing about our marriage and when they could hang out. When I got to that text exchange that kicked off my suspicions, I saw she was the one who used the word *date*. Can I go as your date? *Who says that to a married man!?*

It was Angie who helped me take the next step. She was the one who suggested that Marco and I go to counseling. She was the one who suggested I ask him to move out.

"But then everyone will know," I said.

"It will be okay," she promised. "There's no such thing as a fairy tale."

That's when I saw my Instagram for what it was—a modern-day fairy tale presented digitally instead of in a hardbound book with gold binding. That's when I changed the name of my Insta account to *@unfilteredmama* and started to let go of perfection.

"Are you happy?" Angie asks. "Has he gained back your trust?"

"This is strange to say out loud, but I'll never know for certain if things went one step too far with Lilly. I had to either release or reclaim our broken relationship."

My decision to stay with Marco was based on shades of gray—the hazy area between the crisp perfection of black and white—but it feels good to admit this truth to Angie. Vulnerability is a hard choice, but it's the only way for us to feel an authentic connection.

"That makes sense, and I admire everything about your honesty."

"Want to hear our cute anniversary story?" I ask.

"Yes, tell me! How did you celebrate?"

"We cooked a delicious Italian meal together while drinking a bottle of wine."

"That sounds nice."

"It was, but the best part was after dinner. He planned a movie night."

"I love a good movie night, although Patton always falls asleep. And if I'm being honest, I do too. We're close to fifty. Now, it's all about thirty-minute shows."

I laugh, picturing Marco and me dropping onto the couch after eating our delicious meal. He leaned in and kissed me. I sank into his body, and the moment intensified.

Pulling away, his face took on a mischievous grin. "We start the movie. I pick something I know you will love." He grabbed the remote, scrolling until he found Taylor Swift's Eras Tour. "You never got to see the concert. I shouldn't have exploded over the tickets. *Mi dispiace.*"

"Thank you for apologizing." I snuggled into him, ready to start the movie.

"Solo un minute!" He jumped up off the couch. Five minutes later, he walked into our TV room wearing a powder-pink tuxedo. *Perfetto*—for her Lover Era!

"What? You didn't!"

As we started watching, I thought about being at the concert with Bianca, imagining it would have been a perfect moment. But then, I realized, watching it with Marco, despite our messy and complicated relationship, was so much more than perfect. It was real.

"A pink tuxedo! That's hilarious." Angie laughs after hearing me give her a short version of the special moment. She turns up the music from my Spotify best-of-high-school mix. "Oh, I always loved this one." She dances in her seat.

As the chorus plays, we both belt out the words of Wilson Phillips' ultimate girl anthem of the nineties, "Hold On."

"You know, these lyrics are spot-on." She puts her hand over her heart, and I stifle a giggle. *Cheesy!* "Are you laughing at me?" she asks playfully.

"No. No way. The sound is easy breezy, but the lyrics are deep."

"They are!" Angie laughs.

When the final chorus begins, our voices join, belting out the last lines of the song. It feels like Angie and I are back in high school, free from wrinkles and hot flashes, free from laundry and deadlines. Free from husbands and children.

And for the first time, I know without a doubt that we're finally free from our past.

CHAPTER 45

George

The Next Reunion Trip

Happy 50th Birthday!
Emerald Jewel All-Inclusive Resort

G EORGE WATCHES FOUR women get out of the resort's VIP limo. He's been waiting for Angie, Nicole, Liliana, and Carly. It's hard to believe that, after only five years, he's one of the resort's assistant managers. If he's honest, he knows it's partly because Mr. LaFleur, who now lives in Florida, convinced him there was no need to tell corporate they never checked the boathouse bathroom while searching for the missing boy band vacationer. Instead, Mr. LaFleur insisted they say they tried the door repeatedly while the police were investigating Nicole's disappearance. Since then, Mr. LaFleur ensures George receives regular promotions.

"I can't believe we made it. Thanks for sending a limo to pick us up."

"My pleasure," George says.

It's the least he could do. When Angie called a few months ago to let him know they would be returning to celebrate their fiftieth birthdays, she launched into a story about how the Emerald Jewel will forever be the place where she found peace with her past. He wanted to make this trip special.

She smiles as she bends and extends various body parts. "You can't imagine the number of aches and pains you have after sitting in a car for two hours at my age."

"Here I am, George! I bet you missed me!" Bending down, Nicole fixes the laces of her gold platform sneakers. "And no canceled flights this time."

"And hopefully no murder investigations, either." George chuckles.

Nicole gives him a playful pouty face. "It's kind of a letdown that no one's going to suspect I've been murdered on this trip. That last vacation has reached legendary status!"

Liliana pushes the sunglasses she's wearing on top of her curly hair. "I can't believe it's been five years." George watches her inhale the resort's signature scent of vanilla and coconut. "This time I'm buying the ridiculously overpriced diffuser."

"Wonderful to have you back." George speaks in the gentle cadence Mr. LaFleur insisted all staff at the Emerald Jewel use with hotel guests.

Carly rolls her small suitcase over.

"Traveling light," George notes.

"Yes, sir. I'm even planning to wear one of my skirts twice."

An image of these women dressed in bright pink fills his brain. "I do hope you brought something special to wear for the fiftieth birthday celebration."

"Do not say the f-word," Liliana jokes.

"Fifty. How crazy is that?" Looking around the airy space, Carly stares at the groups of women wearing nineties boy band swag.

Angie chimes in. "Seriously, I'm excited about our trip, but how in the world did we get to fifty? George, I'm here to tell you that time moves faster than the speed of light once you hit thirty."

"Angie!"

Hearing the loud voice, she turns her head.

George watches as Luca runs past the suitcases lining the lobby's perimeter. He runs over to Angie, and they give each other a tight hug. A gorgeous woman, two inches taller than Luca, steps next to them. Her silky black hair cascades down her back.

"Clementine, good to see you." Angie embraces the tall, gorgeous woman and then pulls away. "Last time I saw you was at your wedding."

Nicole eyes Clementine in tiny jean shorts and a cropped shirt. "So, this is who Free People makes their clothes for." She speaks under her breath, and although George hears her, he has no idea what she's talking about.

Luca grabs Angie's hand. "It was great having you on our big day." His face lights up.

"There was no way I was going to miss it." Angie digs through her bag for a moment and takes out her phone. "Did I show you guys the pictures from the wedding?" She turns toward her friends.

They laugh in unison. "Are you kidding? We've seen a million photos. It's like we were there."

"George, look at these photos!" Angie invites George to move closer into their little circle, and he's pleased to be included. Mr. LaFleur always said *guests aren't friends.* But George feels different and has kept in touch with many people who have visited the Emerald Jewel.

Carly faces Luca and Clementine. "Congratulations on getting married. I'm happy for you."

"Thank you. It was the best day of my life. And thanks for sending such a fabulous gift." Luca smiles.

"Ha!" Nicole smirks. "I heard she sent monogrammed passport holders."

"I sure did. With initials on the front, there's no chance of a passport mix-up." Carly and Luca laugh. He gives her a quick hug.

"And we're excited you're letting us crash your reunion trip." Clementine's perfect white teeth flash when she speaks. "Luca told me everything about the last time you were here." She shakes her head as if still processing the bizarre story.

"Right!" Luca points to George. "This guy thought I was a murderer!" They both laugh.

"Not to change the subject, but I'm going to change the subject. Where can I fill my tumbler? I need a famous St. McAna Mai Tai." Liliana pulls a large cup from her bag.

Luca leads Clementine toward the elevators. "We need to go up-stairs and get our cups. I brought the shit-brown one for old times' sake. We'll meet you at the lobby bar."

They stride away before George can tell them that the first thing he did as assistant manager was insist the resort upgrade to bigger cups. Corporate made the change after George showed them numerous Tripadvisor reviews with complaints. He impressed the higher-ups with his ability to look for easy ways to improve the resort's reviews by monitoring social media sites. He's now the resort's social media liaison.

"The lobby bar would be happy to whip you up a fresh batch of the hotel's specialty drink." George motions across the way. "Follow me."

The group walks to the bar where George shows off the resort's large cups as he orders his special guests a round of mai tais. They all circle around a high-top table with big servings of the frozen cocktail.

A group of women walks by rolling their suitcases. "Bye, George!"

"Come visit again soon!" George waves.

"I hope they had fun," Carly says.

"Yeah, me too," Liliana agrees.

"I'm sure it was lit," Nicole adds.

"But now we know better!" Angie says. "So, what's new around here, George?"

"I'm glad you asked, Ms. Angie. Check out our fully renovated boathouse, including a new bathroom with a working door!"

They all laugh. George feels almost drunk with happiness. Working with hotel guests is such fun.

"What color dresses are my beautiful ladies wearing to celebrate this year?" George asks.

"This year's color is navy. We all agreed." Carly nods at her friends and then fishes around in her belt bag for something. She pulls a selfie stick out and wiggles it around. "Don't get any funny ideas about using this in the middle of the night, Nicole."

"Haha, I won't. But since you have it out, let's get together for a pic."

"I was going to suggest that." Carly starts to attach her selfie stick to her phone.

"Actually," George says. "Can I take the photo? I'll upload it to our web page's sidebar where I post pictures of our guests enjoying themselves." Another of George's ideas that was a hit with corporate.

"Absolutely." Carly hands George her phone. "Does anyone mind if I also post it on my *@unfilteredmama* on Insta? I haven't posted in months, and we all have that I've-been-up-since-five-in-the-morning-traveling-look to us."

"Sure, why not!" Liliana says.

Nicole and Angie nod.

"Everyone put on your hat."

The group of women scrunch together, and George takes the photo. He hands Carly back her phone.

"Oh, it's cute!" She posts it on Insta and then AirDrops it to George and her friends.

Ping. They all open their phones and look at the picture.

"Love the hashtag you added on Insta." Nicole shapes her hands into a heart.

"I haven't read it yet." Angie swipes at her phone, trying to find the post.

"I used only one hashtag, and I kept it simple." Carly flips her phone so George can read it.

#MomsOnVacation 🖤😁👯👯

"Yes! I'm so excited!" Angie shifts their attention, pointing to the hotel staff removing the Boy Bands at the Beach sign.

Nicole adjusts her hat. "We're full-on anchor head yacht rock fans now."

"Yes, let's go to the beach!" Liliana gathers her things.

"I'll get your bags stored with our bellman." George smiles. "Have fun, ladies. Find me if you need anything."

"Thanks, George!" the women say in unison.

George watches as they walk past the three-piece band in the lobby, tapping on steel drums, playing the famous song about piña coladas.

With their captain's hats on their heads, the women link arms, eagerly anticipating Sail Away with Yacht Rock.

THE END

If you enjoyed *Moms Love Boy Bands*, please leave a review. Reviews boost sales and help others find my book. Paperback readers, please visit Amazon, Goodreads, or your favorite book site and leave your review. You can also help me find new readers by sharing my book on social media and recommending it to your friends. And please email me at jenifer@authorjenifergoldin.com if you'd like to schedule a Zoom book club.

Join Nicole, Liliana, Angie, and Carly for the most epic girls trip ever! Turn it up and sing the tunes from *Moms Love Boy Bands*. 🎤🎶 Let's gooooo!

Search for the Moms Love Boy Bands playlist on Spotify.

I got the idea for *Moms Love Boy Bands* in 2022 after a trip to Jamaica to see Yacht Rock Review. Yes, I've been writing this book for that long! Like in the book, my friends' connecting flight was canceled, so I spent the first night of the trip by myself. Sort of anyway... thanks, Amanda and Annie, for letting me hang out with you until my friends arrived the next day. And Carrie, Kayla, Noelle, and Kate, thanks for the MOST amazing trip stealing away with yacht rock. Everything else in this book is completely made up. Except for the midnight buffets and moonlit dance party in the sand. And maybe a few other things. ☺

So why did I make this book about nineties boy bands? Well, as Nicole would say, OBVI! Is there anything more relatable to mid-life moms than this genre? Also, including nineties pop culture was a blast! So, whether you identify as a nineties boy band fan or a yacht rock anchor head, thanks for reading!

Continue reading about another group of snarky moms from Hamilton Beach in my book Anonymous Mom Posts.

If you've ever taken a screenshot of an unhinged post in a mom group and texted your bestie "OMG you HAVE to read this" then you're going to devour this book.

In the sunny, Botox-boosted bubble of Hamilton Beach, the local moms' social media page is the go-to spot for crowdsourcing advice. Need a last-minute babysitter? A gently used Chanel bag? A bakery that nails dairy-free, gluten-free, and sustainably sourced birthday cakes? This is the place.

But what started as a space for humble brags about overachieving kids and daily updates on the hot dad jogging shirtless through the neighborhood takes a sharp turn when Laura Perry, the page's moderator, launches a new anonymous posting feature. Suddenly, nothing is off-limits. From a mom who suspects her husband is wearing her underwear, to a marriage unraveling over political differences, to a woman quietly contemplating an affair with her high school sweetheart—each anonymous post is a call for advice and connection.

But what Laura hoped would foster support among the moms quickly devolves into a minefield of judgmental comments, snarky replies, and public shaming. Desperate to fix the chaos, she plans an in-person event to help the moms heal. What she doesn't know is that behind the scenes, one mom with a score to settle is watching, waiting, and ready to strike. As rumors fly and the event approaches, can Laura stop one mom's ruthless plan to expose the secrets that will destroy a picture-perfect community?

Anonymous Mom Posts is perfect book club fiction. Grab a glass of wine, put on your most comfortable joggers, and read the book described by bestselling author Rochelle Weinstein as "witty prose with an honest and hilarious depiction of mommy drama and challenges. But there are also lessons here. A fun read you won't want to put down."

CHAPTER 1

Laura Perry

M Y NOSE BRISTLES with irritation at the recent rash of snarky comments on the Hamilton Beach Moms' Facebook page. Is it bringing this community together or tearing it apart? Earlier, a mom posted looking for a company that could provide "unicorns" for her daughter's birthday. The comments were ruthless.

Naturally, I'm a fixer, so I'm hoping the new anonymous posting feature will decrease the cattiness and remind these moms we're here to support each other.

Pulling my SUV in front of the Edge of the Water Hotel, I'm glad my new client, Julie Wu, took my suggestion to stay at the waterfront property. House hunting goes much smoother when my clients are dazzled by the blue of the ocean.

As I inch my car around the hotel's white brick, circular driveway, I notice the building gleams with an iridescent hue. It reminds me of the day I married Troy at this hotel eighteen years ago. My heart thumps in my chest as I consider the ups and downs our family has experienced over the years.

An image of my sixteen-year-old daughter Nora's face flits through my mind. Her best friend moved to Florida last spring, and her other close friend is busy with a serious boyfriend. Nora's having a hard time finding a new place to land.

Julie raps on my passenger door, and my mind shifts away from thoughts of Nora. I roll down the window and give Julie my big, wide, real-estate agent smile. "Hey. So nice to meet you, Julie. Hop in."

She smiles, opens the door to my Volvo, and folds her slender body into the beige leather bucket seat next to mine.

"I'm sorry to meet you in my car," I say as we pull away. "Normally, I'd come inside for coffee, but this first showing is at eight-thirty."

Julie runs her hand through her dark, tight, curly hair. "Not a problem. I'm on East Coast time since we live in DC. I've been up for a few hours."

As Julie talks, I'm struck by her beauty. She's gorgeous, but not in the blond California way. Her skin is creamy white, and her eyes sparkle green, like the gardens I frequented when times were harder. The color grounds me in nature. Instantly a warm, tranquil wave courses through my body.

As we drive along the windy coastal road leading to the upscale neighborhood of Hamilton Beach Estates, I review several points I've made over email. "The schools here are top-rated, so there's no need for private school."

"That's appealing," Julie replies. "Right now, Talia and Van attend private school. They're getting a great education, but everything is so controlled. There's also very little diversity."

I nod my head as I listen. Julie's voice is calm. Her energy is laid back considering she was just hired as the head of legal for the most prominent dot com in the area. Her simple white t-shirt and brightly colored tote bag make me believe she's not flashy or concerned with high-end labels, like many of my clients. I like her already.

"If you're looking for a diverse community, Hamilton Beach is the right place. My daughter, Nora, went through various stages, where she demanded to celebrate Hanukkah, Kwanzaa, and the Chinese New Year." I laugh out loud, but then worry maybe I've offended Julie.

When she chuckles, I'm relieved. "Well, we celebrate just about everything in our house. I'm Jewish, and my husband, Eric, is Asian. It's a real cultural hodgepodge."

"I love that," I say, envious of the varied outlooks that shape Julie's family.

"Eric and I always say the biggest benefit is all the different foods. Traditional Jewish brisket, scallion pancakes, and Asian dumplings.

Oh my god. The dumplings. But we digress. Tell me more about Hamilton Beach."

My mouth waters at the thought of homemade dumplings. I swallow hard and continue. "We have gorgeous beachside neighborhoods, swim and tennis communities, single-family homes, townhouses, apartments, and even a retirement community. Everything in Hamilton Beach is clean and California coastal. Lots of white buildings against a bright blue ocean and sky."

"It looks lovely," Julie says as she glances out the window.

"Oh," I continue, "be sure to join the Hamilton Beach Moms' Facebook page."

"The Hamilton Beach Moms' Facebook page?" Julie cocks her head to the side. "You'll have to excuse me. I'm not a social media person. What's that?"

"Oh!" I reply. "Well, are you on Facebook?"

"Van created an account for me a few years ago. But I hardly use it. I notice, every year on my birthday, I get assaulted with messages from people I haven't seen or spoken to in over ten years."

"Don't you just love that!" I gush with enthusiasm.

"To be honest, I think it's disingenuous. It feels like spam." Julie shrugs.

"I get what you mean," I reply as I pull into the entrance of Hamilton Beach Estates. "But I love connecting with friends, even if our current relationship lacks face-to-face interaction. Plus, the Hamilton Beach Moms' page is a great resource for anything you need—doctors, restaurant recommendations, tutors. The moms in this community are all-knowing. Their collective wisdom rivals Alexa and Google."

Julie looks at me and smiles. "Well, that's interesting. We'll need new doctors. Van will want to continue private coaching for soccer. I want to find a book club."

"Yes! The page can help with all of that." My tone of voice jumps an octave, but it's hard to contain my excitement. "This is exactly why I started the page a few years ago. Why don't you open Facebook on your phone, and I'll direct you to the page? You can leave the group if you find it spammy and annoying."

"I haven't opened Facebook in months, but okay. You sold me."

"Ha! Great. Now let's see if I can sell you this amazing home."

Julie opens her bag and hands me her phone. I pull up the page as I wait behind a car in line at the gatehouse for Hamilton Beach Estates.

"All set. Now you'll be in the know for all things Hamilton Beach." I give Julie her phone and pull up to the guard on duty.

"Hi, yes, I'm Laura Perry from Perry Properties. I'm here to show my client the property for sale on CoCoplum Way. The homeowner should have left my name."

The guard glances at a paper inside the small gatehouse, searching. "Yes, here we go. I'll buzz you in." He looks at Julie and smiles. "Welcome to Hamilton Beach Estates."

CHAPTER 2

Julie Wu

Can anyone recommend a great dermatologist for teenage acne?

My husband and I need a new mattress. Who has one they love?

Where can I find tops for my 10-year-old daughter that cover her stomach? This mama is struggling to find appropriate clothes.

GLANCING THROUGH POSTS on the Hamilton Beach Moms' Facebook page, I get the sense it's harmless enough. Maybe it's time to embrace social media. It could be a way to make friends. I've always envied women with good friends and a strong sense of belonging. I'm still hesitant to be my true self in personal relationships, and this leaves my friendships feeling hollow.

As Laura parks her car on a stately driveway, I marvel at the perfect green grass and curb appeal of the home before me. It's gorgeous—two stories and three times the size of the house we have in DC. It's one hundred percent California vibes, with its red clay roof and white stucco exterior.

"So, this is it. As you can see, the home's style is Mission Revival. A popular style in Southern California. It's five bedrooms, fully renovated, with an open floor plan. The backyard has a pool that faces the ocean. Let's go inside and look."

Glancing at Laura, with her tan complexion, thick blond hair, and athletic build, I want to run away. Moving to California, buying a house on the beach, starting over with friends. It's so much at once.

But my new job at Click Com is the opportunity of a lifetime. And when Eric and I looked through the real estate links Laura sent through email, we fell in love with the idea of living the true California dream.

"Look at that ocean!" Eric said when we clicked through Zillow images for this home. "Perfect balcony views every single day."

"Do you enjoy cooking?" The image of Eric's excited face disappears, and I land back in the gorgeous kitchen where Laura has asked me a question.

"When I have time," I say, picturing myself preparing Rosh Hashanah dinner in this unbelievable space.

"Well, this kitchen has everything you could ever want—a double oven, two dishwashers, a warming drawer, a chef-grade stove and range, a beverage station."

"It's beautiful." I run my hand over the gleaming white countertops, shimmering in the sun.

"The natural light in here is fantastic," Laura says, looking toward the immense glass doors that slide all the way open to create a seamless flow between the inside of the house and the ocean.

Laura leads me outside to get a good look at the pool. It's large and square-shaped, surrounded by a deep indigo tile. I can't help but ooh and ahh at the stunning ocean that sits behind it.

"Oh, and I almost forgot to tell you. The owners planted a vegetable garden on the side of the house. It has tomatoes, bell peppers, garlic, broccoli, and several herbs."

"Talia will love that," I say as I follow Laura to the garden. "She's an environmentalist and wants our family to live an eco-friendly lifestyle."

"Perfect!" Laura says. "Talia will love it here."

I nod in agreement but can't help thinking about what Talia said a few days ago. She admitted she's nervous about making new friends.

"What do you mean?" My heart fluttered. Fitting in has always been a struggle for me. I never want Talia to feel like she doesn't belong.

"Look at me, Mom. I'm not blond, I'm not girly, I don't wear makeup. I'm Jewish and Chinese. I'm afraid I'll be surrounded by blond robots with big fake boobs and perfect teeth."

"Oh, honey," I said. "I get that. I totally do. For God's sake, I grew up in Georgia in the 1980s."

"Yes, Mom, you've told me a million times. You were the only kid in Daisy Springs who was Jewish."

"I've saved the best for last," Laura interjects as I push away my concerns about Talia. "Follow me, so you can see the ocean and get a complete view of the back of the house." Laura slips off her metallic sandals. Following suit, I pull off my flats.

As we step onto the beach, I see a woman about my age jogging along the shore. She's quintessential California. Tall and blond, with a Barbie-doll figure, barely covered by a tiny sports bra and itty-bitty running shorts.

"Isabell!" Laura yells in the woman's direction, waving her hand furiously. "Isabell!"

The woman stops and rolls her eyes, appearing annoyed by the interruption.

"Isabell and I grew up together in Hamilton Beach. We've been friends forever." Laura walks toward her and motions for me to follow. "Hey, Isabell. I was wondering if I would see you running today. I know you never miss a day."

Isabell smiles, but her lips spread out tight. It's obvious the smile is forced.

"Julie Wu, this is Isabell Whitmore. She lives in the house next door." Laura points to the enormous mansion nestled in a private area down the beach. Her house may be *next door*, but it's secluded and set apart on its own.

"Julie and her family are moving here from DC," Laura continues.

"Nice to meet you," Isabell says as she jogs in place. She's clearly more interested in exercising than making conversation with a potential new neighbor. I can tell she's growing impatient by the way her eyes wander down the shoreline.

"I'll let you get back to your run," Laura says as she moves back toward the house.

"Thanks. I need to get this run over with." As Isabell picks up her pace and passes me, her large breasts hardly move. Maybe Talia was right to be concerned about blond robots with fake boobs.

Turning away from the ocean, I cup my hands around the top of my eyes, bringing my dream house into focus.

"It's a gorgeous property." Laura's eyes shine with enthusiasm as she heads back to the house.

Following behind her, I wonder if this piece of coastal perfection will really be my family's new reality. I picture Talia and Van tossing a football on the sand after swimming in the ocean.

Suddenly, my lungs deflate, and my body sags. I am reminded that one child is missing. There should be *three* children frolicking on the beach in this daydream, but there are only two.

Immediately, I'm struck by the thought that Eric and I don't deserve this life. We absolutely don't deserve any of it. I wonder if he's ever tormented by our past? We never talk about it.

A line of sweat forms around my hairline. I must look unwell, because suddenly Laura is fanning me with the glossy brochure that describes the beautiful home before us.

"You look hot. Are you okay?"

Composing myself, I ignore the sharp stabs in my gut. "It must be the heat," I say. "It's warmer here than in DC."

"Do you want me to run inside and get you water?" Laura asks with genuine concern.

"No, that's okay. Just give me a minute to catch my breath. I'll be fine." But the words are a lie.

Follow me at

jenifergoldinwrites

Author Jenifer Goldin

jenifergoldinauthor

Acknowledgments

Jonathan, thank you for your support. You give me the time and space to write without making me feel the least bit guilty. As you know, marriage is a topic I love to explore in my books. Relationships exist in a complicated and layered place that is always changing. It fascinates me. After almost twenty years together, I have learned a few things. 1. Sneezing can be annoying. 2. There's always something to say about college football. 3. Wood floors can turn pink. 4. Eating dinner at five and getting into bed early is a lifestyle, AND I'm here for it. 5. It rains a lot in Puerto Rico. 6. Marriage can be hard, but the good things in life always are. *It takes work and compromise, but our complicated and layered space keeps changing for the better.*

Anna and Micah. Is it just me, or did everything go into fast forward in the last few years? We're constantly on the go with sports, BBYO, and countless school, community, and social events. Somewhere in the middle of all the running around, you both have grown into the most amazing young adults. Time is a thief, and soon it will take you both to college. Yes, you've caught me crying about this, even though it's a few years away! A book titled *How Moms Empty Nest* may be on the horizon. As I wrote in my book *Moms Who Read Romance Novels,* "Motherhood is a constant toggle between feelings of guilt, exhaustion, joy, crankiness, pride, fear, and love. And as terrifying and exhilarating as it is, when I look at my kids, I understand I am the luckiest person in the world to be riding such a tumultuous wave of emotions." I love you both without end. And for anyone wondering where the name of the island for this adventure came from, now you know. Micah + Anna + St. McAna!

To my brother, Andrew, I love our relationship and the unwavering support we provide for each other. Allison and Carrie, how did I end up with the two best sisters-in-law on the planet? Joel, thanks for being my attorney and always offering support. Natanya, thank you for your support. It's kismet! And to my parents and all of my extended family. Thanks for your support and interest in this crazy hobby of mine.

Scenes in this book were also taken from a girls' trip I took to Mexico with Heather, Jodi, and Lauren. What an amazing getaway, and I had tons of inspiration for one particular character!

I also want to take a moment to mention Alexsis, one of my roommates and dear friends during the first few years of the 90s. Memories of you wearing your beret while Hootie and the Blowfish played, before we went out to the bars, will stay with me always. The world lost you too soon.

To my Beta readers. Thank you so much for your time and willingness to read. Stacey Brown, Heather Carlin, Sam Katz, Amy Rosen, Laurie Rubin, Rabbi Dalia Samansky, Lorna Sherwinter, Ivie Sparaco aka Ana Ivies, and Stephanie Tavani. Thank you for your feedback, insightful commentary, and honesty. I appreciate it more than you know!

To my advanced readers. Thank you for your final edits. You are a big piece of this puzzle. I could not do this without you! I'm amazed and overjoyed that after publishing three books I have this many readers I could personally reach out to. I am so grateful for your time and willingness to read the advanced copy of *Moms Love Boy Bands* and am lucky to have people like you on my team! Noelle Abarelli, Heather Abbott Vogel, Heidi Adams, Jaime Aitkens, Melissa Amster, Betsy Arndt, Susan Ballard, Rachel Becker, Marni Bekerman, Kyla Berry, Amy Beyer, Karen Bowen, Cassie Bower, Jenn Boyd, Jennifer Budinger, Rachelle Carmel, Candice Chupashko, Jen Cleveland, Jennifer Collins, Tamara Costanzo, Tammi Creed, Diana Daniele, Hilary Dempsey, Tracy Eskra, Stephanie Feinberg, Alina Feingold, Allison Feldman, Sharon Fisher, Aimee Fogel, Jessica Foster, Caryn Friedman, Kara Friedman, Julie Furney, Lauren Giacalone, Anna Gieryna, Tara

Goldstein, Jennica Graham, Alison Greenberg, Dana Gross, Melanie Grossman, Lisa Guggenheim, Keri Halperin, Mackenzie Hansen, Neda Hanson, Elizabeth Harris, Cari Hernandez, Pam Herstein, Teresa Huff, Kristen Hughes, Nisha Jafari, Adina Judovin, Kathy Kalmon, Laura Karpf, Harper Kincaid, Melissa Kirshner, Erin Lane, Heather Laskos, April Leake, Cynthia Leder, Meredith Lee, Lauren Lemmons, Sara Levine, Rachel Levy Sarfin, Barbara Libbin, Britney Lloyd, Jodi Loar, Natasha McMillan, Katherine Melone, Kerri Merrill, Donisha Miller, Debbie Minsky, Lee Morris, Kimberly Murphree, Rebecca Nathan, Michelle Nicholas, Rachael Novello, Dana Pace, Lauren Potischman, Beverly Ramsey, Michaela Remtulla, Sheila Roche, Sarah Rollins, Elayne Rose, Janiece Sanderson, Jill Sanko, Dawn Scher, Heather Shapiro, Kellee Sheik, Mara Silver, Fay Silverman, Stacy Smith, Chantal Spector, Cheryl Spitalnick, Ilyssa Tabor, Kristina Thornton, Nicole Tornambe, Madeline Vaughn, Moran Videletz, Tammy Walden, Beth Walsh, Judy Wang, Kyla Webber, Liz White, Brooke Wilcox, Lauren Williams, Jennifer Wood, Sarah Zapata, and Joyce Zimmerman

To all my friends who ask about my writing and support me on this journey. There are so many of you. I am so blessed and appreciate and love all of you.

To the Bookstagrammers who have posted and reviewed my books. I love getting glimpses into your life on Insta, and I'm happy to be part of this awesome community of book nerds! And to the readers who post about my books on pages such as Peloton Moms Book Club, Jewish Women Talk About Romance Books, Renee's Reading Club, Great Thoughts Great Readers, and more,…You may not realize it, but whenever I feel like giving up, that's when one of your posts pops up, sharing how much you enjoyed one of my books. Those moments are everything. They're wins for my heart, my soul, and my drive to keep chasing this crazy dream.

To Tiffany Yates Martin. Your approach to editing is outstanding. You challenged me with encouragement and support. I'm so grateful for your guidance in making this book the strongest version of itself.

Thank you to my copy editor, Shannon Cave. This is our fourth time working together. You make the hard part of writing easy. I am thankful to have you as an editor and friend.

Thank you to the team at Miblart for the amazing cover. I had strong feelings about this cover, and I appreciate your willingness to work with me through all the revisions. This cover is incredible!

Thank you to Stephanie Anderson from Alt 19 Creative for the beautiful interior pages. It's also our fourth time working together. I love your creative eye.

Thank you Rochelle B. Weinstein. Your kindness, advice, and support are greatly appreciated. You're always willing to answer a text or call. You truly embody the phrase *real queens fix each other's crowns*. And thank you to Jean Metzler for creating a supportive atmosphere for Jewish authors not only on Facebook but in the world.

And last but certainly not least, thank YOU! You are holding my dream in your hand. My writing is my heart and soul put into words. Thanks for reading.

About the Author

Jenifer Goldin didn't always write contemporary fiction about modern-day moms. After graduating from the University of Florida, she earned a master's degree from Gallaudet University in audiology. She did her fellowship in pediatric cochlear implants and eventually got a job as the lead cochlear implant audiologist at a renowned Children's Hospital. She eventually left clinical work and began a career on the industry side. After spending over a decade in the field, Jenifer gave up her career to be a stay-at-home mom. She didn't realize that trading stylish suits for yoga pants would stir up a well of emotion. Struggling to adapt to her new role as a mom, she sought solace in her lifelong love for writing. She began by opening a box crammed with hand-written notebooks that formed the basis of a book she began in her twenties. She was determined to finish writing the book, and she did. It's no surprise Goldin's topic of choice is motherhood. Her first novel, *Anonymous Mom Posts*, was published in April of 2023. Her follow-up novel, *Moms Who Read Romance Novels*, was released in December 2023. Her books focus on motherhood, friendship, relationships, and self-acceptance, mixed with soul and just a dash of snark. The Miami native now lives in Atlanta, Georgia, with her husband, two children, and her mini-golden doodle.

Follow me at

jenifergoldinwrites Author Jenifer Goldin jenifergoldinauthor